A
MCQUAID BROTHERS
NOVEL

samantha christy

Saint Johns, FL 32259

Copyright © 2023 by Samantha Christy

All rights reserved, including the rights to reproduce this book or any portions thereof in any form whatsoever.

This is a work of fiction. Names, characters, places and incidents are either the product of the author's imagination or are used fictitiously, and any resemblance to actual persons, living or dead, business establishments, events or locales is entirely coincidental.

Cover designed by Coverluv

Cover model photo by WANDER AGUIAR

Cover model – Vinicious F.

A MCQUAID BROTHERS NOVEL

Samantha Christy

# Chapter One

*Hawk*

The doorbell rings.

I ignore it and roll over in bed. Nobody I know is stupid enough to come to my house this early.

Just when I doze off again, the pounding on the front door starts. It mimics the throbbing in my head. I'm no stranger to hangovers, but at least I have the luxury of sleeping them off whenever I need to.

"Hawk!" someone screams loudly enough to reach my bedroom at the back of the house.

Sitting up, I curse the sharp pain behind my eyes. "Someone better have fucking died," I say to no one as I pull on wrinkled sweatpants that lie in a ball next to my bed.

I check the time. 7:09 am. Too goddamn early. And on a Monday. Everyone at work knows not to expect me on Monday mornings. If I decide to go to work on a Monday, it's always in the afternoon. Same with Fridays. As far as I'm concerned, the weekends start on Thursday and don't end until I say they end.

Ambling my way to the front door, I squint (which hurts like a mother) to keep out the morning light streaming through the massive picture windows in my great room. I stop and peek at my newly constructed pool including all the impressive bells and whistles and landscaping that go along with it. I wasn't about to let Quinn Thompson have the best pool in town. My setup puts that pussy-whipped cowboy to shame.

Not that my beef is with Quinn, per se, but his wife is best friends with Tag. And Tag is a Calloway. McQuaids hate all Calloways; therefore I hate Quinn by association.

My fuzzy brain reminds me that my mother is a Calloway, something I've tried to ignore these past dozen or so years. She'll never let me live down the fact that I was the only one of her children who didn't attend her second wedding—to none other than Jonah Calloway, uncle to my archenemies Tag, Jaxon, and Cooper. And I'll never let her forget that by marrying into that derelict family, she effectively cut ties with me.

This town has a proverbial line drawn right down the middle that stems back to a bet made by one of my ancestors and a Calloway. It resulted in our town, that previously bore the name McQuaid Plat, being renamed to Calloway Creek. It's bullshit. We own this town, yet their name appears on a crap ton of it.

If you're a McQuaid, it's incumbent upon you to hate the Calloways. If you're a Cruz, it's more than likely you hate them as well, even though they are technically Calloway descendants in addition to being related to us McQuaids. Conversely, if you're a Montana or an Ashford, all basically cousins to the Calloways, you hate all the McQuaids.

There are some exceptions to this. Namely my rich-as-shit idiotic grandfather, my brainwashed sister, and of course Jonah and my mom, who all try to keep the peace in their own pathetic ways.

The doorbell rings again, this time in quick succession. I complete my walk to the door, still pissed as hell that someone has the balls to wake me. I make a mental note to have a gate installed at the beginning of the driveway.

"Hawk!" a shrill voice shouts from the other side of the door.

I rip the door open. "What the ever-loving fuck could be so goddamn important at the butt-crack of dawn?"

It's Melissa Greer. She visibly deflates when she sees me. I scan her from head to toe. Her hair is unkempt, her makeup scarce, her eyes as puffy as a blowfish. The shirt she's wearing is wrinkled as if it were yesterday's, possibly picked up off the floor before doing a walk of shame.

Melissa Greer doing a walk of shame? Doubtful, but I suppose stranger things have happened. It would explain the hair and the makeup, but not the eyes. Unless maybe she was dumped after a one-nighter. *Oh, shit.* Did Hunter or Hudson one-and-done her and she's come here to chew me out as if I give two shits what my brothers do?

And then there's her knuckles which are red from pounding on my door.

"Christ, Melissa. You look worse than I do and I may have downed an entire bottle of tequila last night. What the hell is it?" I turn away and shuffle into the kitchen, not really caring if she follows or not. Thankfully, I had the good sense to program my coffee maker to come on early. A fresh pot is waiting for me as if it knew I'd be up at this ungodly hour.

I grab a cup from the cabinet, not bothering to offer one to Melissa, who may or may not be behind me.

My answer comes when a kitchen chair scrapes across the hardwood. I don't have to turn around to know she's sitting. I hear her weight crash upon it like it's the only thing keeping her from hitting the floor.

After pouring my cup, I turn and lean against the counter. "If you're here to tell me what a douchebag one of my brothers is, don't bother. There's nothing you could tell me that I haven't already heard. Not to mention I'm not my brothers' keeper and I couldn't care less what they do and don't do with the women they date. Just as they don't care about what I do with mine."

"This isn't about them." She swallows and it looks painful. "It's Shannon."

Inwardly, my eyes roll. Shannon Greer. Melissa's stepsister. Must it always come to her? If Shannon isn't incessantly hounding me herself, she has her impish sister or sickeningly cheerful friends coming after me.

Shannon and I hooked up last year, and ever since then she's been trying to extort money from me. I wanted to take a paternity test and prove the zygote she claims she's carrying isn't mine. Hudson, who's a pregnancy doctor, said it could be done even while she was knocked up. And the fact that she never consented means she good and well knows mine is not the sperm that impregnated her. She's always been after a meal ticket. I knew that. Everyone did. I blame tequila, my overactive cock, and Shannon's salacious rack for my night of weakness.

I sip my coffee, glaring at her over the rim. "If this is some lame attempt to guilt me into giving her—"

"She's dead."

Another sip warms my throat as I digest her words. "What do you mean, she's dead?"

"Just that. She's dead. She died." She shoots me a venomous stare. "Giving birth to *your* child."

I set my cup down with enough force to make her jump, irritated over having been accused of not only being the kid's father, but of somehow having that implication make *me* responsible for killing her. Still, I'm not a complete jerk. I can see she's torn up over this. "Hey, I'm sorry about your sister, or uh, whatever you call her. That sucks."

"Don't you even want to know about the baby?"

Part of me wants this conversation to end right now. Because I have a feeling deep down I know where it's headed. But I haven't had enough caffeine to fully comprehend anything. "I'm guessing it died along with her."

"It didn't."

I pick up my coffee and take a large swallow. "Not sure why that has you pounding on my door."

"Can we stop with the games, Hawk? Shannon is dead. Gone. She was barely twenty-five years old and her life is over. Don't you get that? And we were more than stepsisters. We were best friends. We told each other everything. Yes, she slept around. Yes, she wanted a guy who could take care of her. But that didn't make her a bad person. And I'm one hundred percent sure the baby is yours. She'd have told me if there was a chance it wasn't."

"She refused to take a paternity test. That's all I need to know."

"I wanted her to get the test, too. She thought it was funny making you squirm not knowing the truth for nine months."

"I don't squirm."

She looks me up and down, shaking her head. "Obviously. But there is a baby at the hospital now. Alone. Without a parent. Without anyone."

"Not my problem."

"If you think it's not your problem, then go take the test. They already collected cord blood; all they need is your saliva. A quick mouth swab. Under these circumstances, they said they could expedite the test and you may even have the results tomorrow or the day after."

"Whatever." I nod to the door. "Do you mind? I need to get back to my beauty sleep." I glance down at my bare chest. "All this doesn't just happen magically you know."

She stands. "You're a real asshole, Hawk McQuaid."

"Tell me something I don't know."

Halfway to the door, she stops and turns. "Don't you even want to know how it happened? How she died?"

"You told me how she died. Giving birth."

Her eyes fill with tears that do nothing to me. I get that she's sad and all, but it's an emotion I've never had to feel before. I've never been close enough to anyone to feel it. I suppose if one of my brothers died I'd feel like her. And for a second, when I think about that happening, I can almost empathize with her. Almost.

"I have no idea what Shannon ever saw in you," she says. "Why she would want to be with you let alone have you raise a child with her is beyond my comprehension. You are the most uncaring narcissist I've ever known. Except for maybe those you share blood with. This baby will be lucky if it's not yours."

"Money," I say.

She narrows her brows.

"My trust fund. All those dollar signs. That's all anyone ever sees in me."

"Yeah, well considering there's not much else beneath the surface, I can believe it."

I consider coming back with a snarky remark but restrain myself. She did just lose her sister. "Shut the door after you leave."

Her stare tells me she thinks I'm lower than the flies that feast on dog shit. "Just go to the hospital today, let them swab your cheek. And until then, I'll pray Shannon was lying to us all along. You're not fit to be anyone's father."

"From your lips to God's ears," I say, and take another sip.

"Later, Melissa."

The front door closes. I head back to my bedroom but then realize the caffeine is kicking in and I'll never be able to go back to sleep. I go to my bathroom instead, step into the shower, and let the warm water soothe my aching head.

I realize any other man might be trying to avert a headache that resulted from anxiety over the situation. I have none. The only stress in my life comes from the stupid job I was forced into years ago. I couldn't give a rat's ass about selling cars and running my grandfather's dealerships. Hell, half the time when I'm at work, I'm doing other shit. Surfing the net. Watching YouTube videos. Writing mindless shit. Figuring out ways to increase the wealth I'll inherit nine years, ten months, two weeks, and three days from now.

Getting out of the shower, I only have one thought. Melissa was right. I shouldn't be anyone's father. And the fact that it's just now occurring to me that I didn't ask if the baby is a boy or a girl proves it.

Samantha Christy

# Chapter Two

*Addison*

"My leg fell off again."

Lionel, my physical therapist, stares down at my prosthetic with a frown. He's been my PT since I lost the lower part of my left leg four years ago. I don't see him nearly as much these days as I did back then, but I still need him from time to time. Being an amputee comes with a good deal of pain as the imbalance can lead to lower back problems, shoulder pain, and neck discomfort. Lionel is a god at helping me relieve it. He's the reason I wanted to go into physical therapy in the first place. Something I'm not so sure I want to do anymore.

"Also," I add, "my hip really hurts lately."

He runs a hand over the socket of my prosthesis, down the pylon, and across the foot. "I hear you've been working at Donovan's."

"For a few months now."

He looks at me like I'm five years old. "Addy, I know you don't like to think of yourself as having limitations, but being on your feet all day is going to cause you issues. Walking on a flat foot that doesn't have flexion like your real one is very hard on the hips."

"I know. I know. I just thought…"

He hops up on the patient table next to me and puts an arm around my shoulder. We've become close over the years. He's like another brother to me. "You're not only my favorite patient, you are an inspiration. Do you know how often I talk about you to my other patients when they claim they can't do the exercises I prescribe? I can't refer to you by name because that's against the law, but when others hear about a patient who lost part of her leg and still hikes, swims, works, and goes after all life has to offer, it gives them that extra push they need to overcome their own obstacles."

I laugh. "Like they don't know who you're talking about, Lionel. Name one other person in Calloway Creek who has a prosthetic."

"Okay, you've got me there. My point is, although you can do pretty much anything, there are consequences for you that people with two functioning meat legs don't have. Not to mention, your prosthetic is showing wear and tear. You should think about having it replaced."

"My insurance will only cover one every five years unless it's broken."

He raises an eyebrow. I can read his face like a book.

"Yeah, I've considered it," I say. "But if I break it, I'll have to live with crutches for weeks, maybe even months, while the insurance goes through."

"You've been keeping up with your exercises?"

"I have." I pound a fist on my left thigh. "Hard as a rock."

Lionel warned me early on that atrophy of the remaining part of my leg would occur if I didn't keep up with my exercises. In the beginning, I did them religiously, not wanting to have my left thigh look a lot skinnier than my right one. Back then I thought I already looked freakish enough without that adding to my disfigurement. Then it became a habit, one I've kept to this day, like brushing my teeth.

"Let's take it off and have a look at Eileen," he says.

I still snicker at the name. When I first met Lionel, he suggested naming my stump. He said it was one way to embrace it as being a normal part of me.

I put my left leg up on the table, press the button down by my fake foot to release the suction, and slide my prosthetic off. Then I remove the sock cover and the silicone liner.

Lionel visually inspects my stump and all the areas where the prosthesis tends to rub on me. He shakes his head. He's displeased. "Just how many hours are you working?"

I shrug. He stares me down. "Fine. A lot. Sometimes eight or more. They've been short-staffed. But now that Lissa is back from Europe and Donny has recovered from his surgery, I won't have to work as much."

"I can't believe you're still on your feet, Addy. If you don't slow down, these irritated areas will turn into open sores. When that happens, you'll be on crutches whether or not your prosthetic is broken."

My gaze meets the floor. I refuse to admit defeat.

"Listen," he says. "Even the strongest people need help sometimes. Asking for it is not a sign of weakness."

"Says the guy with two meat legs."

"Addison Calloway, I haven't seen you feel sorry for yourself in over three years. Don't start now."

"I'm not. It's just that…"

"What?"

"There's all this pressure on me. My family—well maybe not Cooper, but the rest of them—they all want me to go to PT school."

"Wasn't that the plan?"

"It was."

"Was? As in past tense? So this job at Donovan's, it's not temporary?"

"I guess I was trying to prove something to everyone. To myself."

"Prove what? That you can carry a tray of beers to a bunch of drunken college students?"

I sigh. "I didn't make the grades, Lionel. I wasn't accepted into any of the grad schools I applied to. But it's not only that. I'm not sure I want to do what you do anymore. At first you were this amazing mentor who helped save me. If it weren't for you, I might be some shrinking violet hiding myself away and believing I wasn't worthy of anything. I thought I wanted to be a physical therapist. I took four years of classes. Graduated in April."

"I know. I was at your party."

"I'm not sure I would have even gone to college if it weren't for you. Well, and the 'cripple' scholarship I got."

He doesn't scold me for using the word. He knows I'm kidding. *Kind of.*

"Okay, so you changed your mind. You shouldn't feel guilty about that. Lots of people go to college for things they never end up doing."

"That's the thing, though. I'm not sure what I want to do. That's why I got the job at Donovan's. I needed to do something until I figured it out. I didn't want to be a drain on my parents any more than I already was. They've spent so much time and money on this," I glance at my prosthetic on the table, "and they've never once made me feel guilty about it even though it was all my fault. So I guess I needed to prove that even though I'll never be a physical therapist, I can damn well be the best waitress this town ever saw."

"There you go, overachieving again."

"Ha! If I was an overachiever, I'd be earning my DPT from NYU."

"There are other things you can do with a degree in exercise science, you know. You could even get a job working with other amputees. You could be an orthotic assistant."

"But I want to stay in Calloway Creek. There isn't a prosthetic center here."

"So commute to the city."

I shake my head. "I don't know. I'm not sure what path I want to take, but I know one thing. I want to work with kids."

"Kids?"

I nod. "Over the past year, my brothers have all become fathers in one way or another and it's made me realize that I want to work with kids. I love being around them. The way they smell. How they laugh. Everything. Besides, adults can be a pain in the ass."

He chuckles. "That they can."

Lionel turns my silicone sleeve inside out and hands it to me. I put it to the end of Eileen and expertly roll it on without trapping any air bubbles. And while it will always take a minute or two to fully get my leg secured, I'm as quick as one can be at it. I hop off the table and put weight on my prosthesis until it clicks in.

"My professional advice is to cut back on your hours. Give your leg a rest. I know how stubborn you can be, Addy, but I don't want to see you back here being treated for all the shit that goes along with having to be on crutches. And that's where you're headed if you keep pushing yourself. The last I checked, you can't waitress that way, so think hard before taking another long shift."

I put more weight on my left leg and feel it rubbing. I know he's right. He's always right when it comes to my leg. I roll my eyes and reluctantly agree. "Fine."

"That's my girl," he tells me as he wraps me in a hug before I leave.

"I appreciate you working me in so early on a Monday. I'll bet you're regretting giving me your cell phone number right about now."

He smiles. "Never. I'm here whenever you need me. Now go home, put your foot up, and binge watch some mindless Netflix series."

I'll do what he says, but only for a few hours. Because I'm due at work by eleven.

~ ~ ~

News in Calloway Creek travels fast. Everyone who comes into the pub is talking about it. Serenity, Cooper's girlfriend, is pretty broken up over Shannon's passing. They were close once, having been on the cheer squad together. "I just can't believe it," she says with red-rimmed eyes. "How does someone just die during childbirth in this day and age? Haven't there been advances over the past twenty-five years?"

The moment she says it, it dawns on me why she seems especially distraught. Ren's own mother died while giving birth to *her*. "Oh, gosh," I say, walking over. "I totally forgot. This must be really hard for you."

"Hard for *me*? What about the little baby who was basically just orphaned? People are delusional if they think Hawk McQuaid will step up and take responsibility."

Cooper puts an arm around her. "Rumor has it he went to the hospital for a paternity test. He's insisted all along that he's not the father."

"You don't think he is?" I ask.

"Who knows. But with his track record, it wouldn't surprise me if he was. You sleep with that many women, shit's bound to happen."

Ren and Cooper share a look. They've been through a lot over the past few months. And the five-year-old boy playing dominoes in the restaurant office is a big part of that.

"Hey," I say. "Now that you're both here, I wanted to talk to you."

"What's up?" Ren asks.

"I had to go see Lionel this morning."

"Her physical therapist," Cooper explains to Ren.

She looks concerned. Serenity and I were close as teens. She was practically a permanent figure around my house, being Chaz's high school girlfriend, and then his fiancée. But that was before my idiotic brother had to go off and die on that mountain, leaving his twin, Cooper, and the rest of us in so much shock that I got stupid drunk and totaled my parents' car, losing my leg in the process.

Serenity lived in Alaska for the last four years but recently returned. We've bonded again over these past few months and it's like having my sister back.

"Is everything okay?" she asks.

"I'm fine." I tap my prosthetic against a barstool. "It's this damn thing. Lionel says I'm on my feet too much and it's taking a toll."

Ren looks horrified. She immediately pulls out a chair and tries to make me sit. I wave her off. "It's okay. I'm not quitting or anything. But I will have to work shorter shifts. It's that or end up on crutches, which will make it impossible to do the job."

"You need a better prosthetic," Cooper says. "Don't they make fancy new bionic ones?"

"It wouldn't matter if I paid a hundred grand for the Lamborghini of legs, wearing any prosthesis too much will always cause friction and chafing."

Serenity's hand lands on my arm. "Why didn't you say anything?"

Cooper laughs. "And have her admit defeat? Do you know nothing about my little sister?"

"Shush," she scolds. "This isn't a laughing matter. Addy, you can work as many short shifts as you need. Summer is almost over and things will slow down a bit until the holidays. Plus, I have a dozen resumés back in the office if we need to hire someone quickly. I don't want you to give it another thought."

"I'm sorry. I really thought I could do it."

"You're the best waitress we've ever had," Ren whispers. "A fact I'll deny if you repeat it to any of the other servers. But if you need to quit, we'll understand. Just know you'll have a job here for as much and as long as you need it."

"I'm not quitting," I say. "But for the next week or so I think I should probably stick to shifts that are four hours or less. If that's okay."

"Whatever you need," Cooper says. "Right now, though, I'd love it if you could go help Cody write some words. He's determined to master his new name before he starts kindergarten."

I tilt my head and death-stare him. "I know what you're doing. I also know you promised me you'd never treat me like a cripple."

"Who's treating you like a cripple? I was just in the back helping him myself. I'm an employee, too. So what's the difference if it's you back there instead of me? Besides, Cody loves spending time with you. And you're always saying how much you like working with kids. So go work with one."

"The man has a point," Ren says.

I open my mouth to argue, but my leg starts throbbing, reminding me why we're having this talk in the first place. Plus, I might also be hearing Lionel's voice in my head telling me accepting help doesn't make me any less of a person.

Before I say anything, a guy at table seven gets my attention. "What happened to your leg?" he asks.

It's not an uncommon question from strangers who think they have the right to know my business. This one looks like he might be a freshman at Calloway Creek University. Every year around this time, we see a new batch of students moving into the dorms. And every year around this time, I get inappropriate questions from ill-mannered strangers.

I take a menu over and drop it on the table, smiling. "Welcome to Donovan's." I put my foot up on the chair next to him and tap on my prosthetic. "It's hollow," I say. "I got tired of paying for beer at sporting events. This baby holds at least three or four." I nod to the menus. "I'll grab you some water while you look this over."

"I'll take the table," Cooper says as I head to the bar. "And your two others. You—go to the office. Help my kid impress his teacher."

"Mind if I make a call first? I'm dying to get details on the baby who may or may not be Hawk's. I'd like to talk to Holland. She's close to all her brothers and might know more about the situation."

"Go ahead. I wouldn't mind knowing myself. I can't wait to rub it in that asshole's face if he turns out to be the kid's father. Seems just a few months ago he was trash-talking me for the exact same thing."

"Give it a rest, Coop. You all need to look at Holland and me and see that the McQuaids and the Calloways can be friends."

"Friends? With those twatbags? Never. I mean, yeah, Holland is okay, but the others—fat chance."

I curl my lips at him and pull out my phone as I head into the back, calling my friend once I'm out of range of any nosy customers.

"Girl, I need the scoop," I say. Then I lean against the wall, listening intently to every word she says.

# Chapter Three

*Hawk*

Hudson opens the fridge in my outdoor kitchen and comes away with three beers. When he hands one to Hunter, he raises a brow, scolding him. He turns his eyes to the large television hanging in the corner over the fireplace that's tuned to the Yankees/Nighthawks game and asks our middle brother, "How much did you bet on this game?"

Hunter opens his beer. "Two thousand on the Nighthawks money line."

Hud exhales noisily through pursed lips. Our little brother has never understood why Hunter likes to bet on sports. I get it. I bet on the occasional game myself. But Hunter has made it his full-time job. He's good at it, too. Which is why Hudson shouldn't have a stick up his ass about it. Hunter makes money. He doesn't win every bet. Not by a longshot. But enough that he's always in the black. Hell, if I could make a profit, I'd do it too. But I've probably lost about five grand this year alone. My goal is to grow my bank account, not piss it away over a baseball game. Or football, basketball, soccer, and whatever the hell else he bets on.

I give a low whistle because Hunter has upped his game. He usually keeps his individual bets lower than a thousand. If I had to guess, though, I'd say he bets ten-to-twenty grand in any given week, depending on the sport and time of year. "What are the odds?" I ask.

"Plus 125."

"That means he'll win twenty-five hundred if the Nighthawks pull it off," I explain to Hudson like he's a five-year-old.

He tosses me an eat-shit-and-die glance. "Just because I don't like to bet doesn't mean I'm an idiot."

"You bet on the over/under?" I ask Hunter.

He nods. "$1100 on the over, for a total of eight."

"Odds on that?"

"Minus 110."

I lean toward Hudson. "That means—"

"I know what it means, fuckwad. He'll win a grand if the total runs scored in the game are over eight."

I have to admit, I'm slightly impressed Hudson knows that. "Well, look at that," I say. "Guess you're good for something other than fingering pussies all day."

He shakes his head. "Jesus."

Hunter spits out beer as he and I laugh. "Hey, if you didn't want us to make jokes about your profession, you should have become a brain surgeon, not a lady doctor."

Hunter turns to me. "You got anything on the game?"

"Hell no. The last time I bet on the Nighthawks, Marco Rivington got hit in the head by a line drive and ended up with a concussion. I think I'm a jinx. Since I quit betting on the Hawks, he's gotten five home runs, three of them grand slams."

"If he keeps it up, he may just overtake the title of GOAT."

I lean toward Hudson. "That means Greatest of All Time."

He responds with his middle finger.

"I'll bet he breaks Sawyer Mills' homerun record by the time he's twenty-five," I say.

Hunter eyes me from over his beer. "You really have a boner for Rivington, don't you?"

"He's fucking good."

He picks up his phone.

I laugh. "You're betting on him right now, aren't you?"

Hudson breathes an angry sigh in the background as Hunter taps away on his screen.

The phone goes back into Hunter's pocket.

"Well?" I ask.

"$300 on Rivington to hit a homerun at a plus 200." He takes a sip then points the neck of his beer bottle at me. "You owe me if I lose."

"I don't owe you shit, brother. Your bet, your loss."

Hudson, clearly upset by Hunter's gambling habit, goes for another beer. "Not on call tonight?" I ask.

"If I were on call, I wouldn't have had the first one."

"Such the little rule follower."

"Unlike some people, I'm not a gambler. And I'm sure as hell not going to risk pissing away a shit ton of school and a top residency just to get drunk with you two jagoffs."

"Well, la-de-fuckin'-da," Hunter says, earning him a punch in the arm.

Hudson turns to me, "Speaking of my job."

With the way he's looking at me, I know exactly where this conversation is headed, and I'd rather take it up the ass with a cactus. "We've moved on from that. We're watching the game now."

"You're the one who brought it up. And, seriously, are we not going to talk about the elephant in the room?"

"Nope."

Suddenly, Hunter is more focused on me than the baseball game. Both my brothers are staring me down.

"I wasn't there," Hudson says, "but I heard all about it. Peterman's partner, Lyle Richards, was on call when she went into labor. I'm telling you it was a mess. He said it was the worst placental abruption he'd ever seen. She never had a chance."

"When do you get the results of the paternity test?" Hunter asks.

"Any minute." I hold up my phone. "When they swabbed my cheek, they said they would have the lab expedite it and email me."

"Aren't you freaking out?" Hunter asks. "Just a little? You could have a kid."

"Do I look worried? She slept around. You of all people should know that, Hunt."

"Yeah, but I have to say with the sheer number of women you've been with, I'd bet the money line on you being the dad."

"Goddamn traitor." I get up and fetch another beer.

"Say she is yours," Hudson says.

Hunter's brows touch his hairline. "She?"

"She's not," I say.

Hudson moves to sit on the table in front of me. He gets in my face. "Say for argument's sake she is. What would you do?"

I do not want to talk about this. But my little brother is not bound to let me enjoy a second of this game if I don't get it over with. I take a long drink, downing half my beer. "For argument's sake, what are my options?"

"Other than the obvious one that has you raising her,"—I hear Hunter spew beer behind me—"you could give her up for adoption, or even name someone as guardian. A family member maybe."

I raise a mocking brow. "You offering?"

"Me? Shit no. I bring *other* people's babies into the world, not my own. I was talking about Mom or one of Shannon's relatives."

"So I could just give the kid to anyone I wanted?"

"It's not that easy. If it's a blood relative, then yes, you can name them guardian. If it's a directed adoption, like say Shannon's stepsister wanted to raise her, she'd have to apply and go through a home study and all that in order to get approved."

I watch Stryker Taylor of the Nighthawks pitch three consecutive strikes while thinking about shit I don't want to be thinking about. "The kid isn't going to be mine," I say. "But hypothetically, if I were ever to be in a situation like that, I wouldn't want the kid anywhere near me. He'd probably come after my money at some point or another. Maybe they could find someone in another country to adopt him."

"*Her*," Hudson says.

"Yeah, whatever."

"You know it would kill Mom to know she had a grandchild out there without being able to see her."

"You think I give a shit about how *she* would feel about it?"

"Cut her a break, Hawk. She's still our mother. What she did, she did to Dad, not us. And you of all people know what an asshole Dad can be given that you work with him."

"Are we done with this conversation now? The kid isn't mine."

"How can you be so sure?" Hunter says.

"Because I know, okay?"

Hudson moves back to his chair. "You can't just wish it into being true, brother. I've seen women get pregnant even when they were on the pill and their partner wore a condom. Shit happens."

"It doesn't happen to me."

As Rivington scores a homerun and Hunter jumps off the couch in celebration, my phone pings with an email from the lab. And my goddamn stomach flips over as I open it.

# Chapter Four

*Addison*

Lissa is behind the bar and I've never seen her happier. She recently returned from two months in Europe with my cousin, Lucas Montana. He asked her to go with him after they'd only been dating a short time. Unfortunately, it's hard for me to get too excited for her. This is his MO. He falls fast and hard and then crushes hearts. He's left two women at the altar already. The *actual* altar. That's not hyperbole. He literally didn't show up at the weddings. A third engagement he broke off two weeks before the wedding. All this and he isn't even thirty years old.

"You seem chipper today."

"Lucas said he loved me last night."

"Oh, wow. Congratulations."

What I really want to say is that I love my cousin, but she should run. Run *now*.

"I know what you're thinking." She pours two beers for table three and sets them on the counter for me. "It's different this time. He was younger then. He didn't know what love was."

"I'm sure it is. And I'm happy for you."

I deliver the drinks, drop a check at another table, and take orders for the rowdy group of college students in the corner.

Serenity comes out front carrying a bag of limes from the local grocery store. Someone forgot to include them on the last order. *Someone* is my brother, Cooper. He's still learning the ropes around here as he's co-managing Donovan's with Serenity and her father, Donny.

"I heard a rumor when I was at Truman's Grocery," Ren says from behind the bar.

I step closer. "Lot of those around this town. Be careful which ones you believe."

"I hear that. But this one might actually be true. I ran into Ava Criss who heard from Regan Lucas who heard from Sarah Morton—"

"Who's Sarah Morton?"

"A nurse at the hospital. She moved here a few months ago. Anyway, keep up. Sarah overheard some people talking about lab results." She looks around to see if anyone is listening. She lowers her voice. "Hawk McQuaid's lab results."

My eyebrows shoot up. "And?"

"Seems the eldest McQuaid just became a daddy."

I cover my mouth, trying not to laugh. Because, come on, this is funny. "Oh my gosh. But, wait, doesn't that violate some law, Sarah telling Regan?"

"It does. We should make a mental note to never trust Sarah with any personal information."

I pull out my phone and text Holland. When we spoke last night, she didn't know anything more than Hawk had gone to take a paternity test.

Me: Hey, Auntie Hol.

Hol: OMG. Can you believe it? I think I'm the only one who's excited. I mean, you have like a zillion nieces and a nephew. I honestly never thought any of my brothers would have kids. Wait. How did you know? He only found out a few hours ago. I didn't think he told anyone. The only reason I know is that I came over to Hawk's house to borrow his toolbox.

Me: You know how it goes around here. Someone spilled the beans at the hospital. The news is spreading like wildfire. How is he? What's he doing?

Hol: Drinking heavily. Are you at work?

Me: Yes.

Hol: I'll be there in ten.

I put down my phone. "It's true," I tell Ren. "His sister just confirmed it."

She tries not to smile. "Cooper will be so pleased."

"I have the feeling he won't be the only one who will think Hawk just got served a heaping dish of well-deserved karma."

I take care of my tables, wanting to have a little time to get more details when Holland arrives.

Over the next half hour, I hear Hawk's name tossed around at least four times—and not by Ren or me. Apparently Regan is not the only person Nurse Sarah bestowed this little golden nugget upon.

When Holland is late, and I can't stand it anymore, I text her again.

**Me: Hol, I'm dying here. Actually, the entire pub is. NEED DEETS!**

No response. *Hmm.* That's unusual for Holland.

I distract myself by closing out a few tables. It's almost nine thirty now, and we're down to two couples outside on the patio and a small group of college kids in the corner booth.

"Take off," Serenity says, glancing at my leg. "I'll close out your last table."

"I'm fine. It was only a four-hour shift."

"Addy, your brother would kill me if I let you work one minute over. If you want to wait for Hawk's sister, fine, but sit your butt on a barstool."

I look at my phone to see if she texted me. "I'm not sure she's coming."

The second the words exit my mouth, the front door opens.

Ignoring Serenity's order to sit down, I race over to Holland. "What took you so long? I expected you an hour ago." Her face is long and sad. She no longer seems as excited as she was when we were texting. "Hol? What's wrong?"

Ren walks over with two glasses of water. "Take the booth over there," she says, leading us to the private table. She sets down the waters and we sit. "Need anything stronger?"

We both shake our heads, and she leaves.

Holland takes a large drink. "He's not keeping the baby."

"What does that mean exactly? Like he's going to let family raise it?"

"Her," she says. "It's a girl. I have a niece."

I put a hand on top of one of hers. "You've seen her?"

She looks down sadly. "No. He won't even go to the hospital. He doesn't want to see her and he claims we can't either without his consent."

My jaw goes slack. "He won't *see* her?"

"He says he's going to file a petition to terminate parental rights and put her up for adoption. Preferably as far away from New York as possible."

"But… Can't you take her? Or your mom? I'll help. It's a baby. She just lost her mother. And now she's being abandoned?" I can physically feel my heart breaking.

"He says he'll do everything in his power to keep us from getting her." She wipes away a fallen tear. "I'll never get to meet her. I won't even be able to see a picture of her. In eighteen years, I could pass her on the street or sit next to her in a restaurant and never know we're blood relatives."

"Maybe he'll change his mind."

"Have you never met my brother?"

"I know. But you said he was drinking. People aren't rational when they drink." I touch my leg absentmindedly. "They make stupid decisions. In the morning when he's sober he could see things differently."

"He said he's calling the family lawyer first thing in the morning to make sure everything happens quickly."

"Oh, Hol. I'm so sorry."

"I just don't understand, Addy. There are so many people who would take her. I know I'm only twenty-two, but I could do it. I'd be a good mom, don't you think?"

"You'd be a great mom. As long as you don't bring all your dates home." I wink.

She offers a sad smile. "I'd change. I'd quit sleeping around. For her. I'd do it and be a responsible mom. A perfect mother. Why is he being so stubborn about it?"

"Did your mom offer to raise the baby too?"

She nods. "It pissed Hawk off something awful when I called her and told her the whole story. He keeps her out of every loop. Never tells her anything."

"Like I said, a good night's sleep can work wonders."

"I honestly think it would take a miracle to change his mind. The baby is going to be released from the hospital tomorrow. Do you know where she'll go? I looked it up. To some foster home decided on by social services. And she'll stay there, or maybe even get bounced around between multiple ones, until the paperwork is finalized and she can be adopted."

I stand and hold out my hand. "Come on. We're having a good old-fashioned sleepover at my house."

"At John and Libby's?"

"Thanks for pointing out the fact that I still live at home, but not all of us have trust funds we can draw from to live in fancy apartments. It'll be fun. We'll get a bottle of wine and reminisce about high school. When you didn't have to worry about having nieces you'd never see again, and I could kick anyone's ass at soccer."

"Addison, you could *still* kick my ass at soccer." She scoots out of the booth. "And a sleepover sounds exactly like what I need. But on the wine? I'm thinking we'll need two bottles."

I laugh. "As long as no one's driving, we can even get three."

We lock elbows and walk out the front door.

# Chapter Five

## *Hawk*

"Get up, boy!"

I pull a pillow over my head to muffle the dream.

Seconds later, sheets are ripped off my body, the stern, rough voice returning. "I. Said. Get. Up."

Okay, so not a dream. My eyes open despite the pounding behind them. My grandfather is standing next to my bed. Arms crossed. Back straight. Looking decades younger than his eighty-five years. But the thing that strikes me the most about him is how goddamn pissed he looks.

"Hey, Pappy," I say as if I don't know he's here to pound my skull into the ground.

At least I have the good sense to remember to call him by his preferred nickname. Most grandparents let their grandkids choose whatever name comes to them naturally. Not our grandfather. He decided for all of us. Forced the name on us. Corrected us every time we tried calling him something else. Dad said it stemmed from his hatred for his own grandfather. Still, I'm thirty goddamn years old, not three. I should be able to call him whatever the hell I want.

But we all learned early on that Tucker McQuaid wasn't a man you argued with. That song—*Bad Bad Leroy Brown*—it was a well-known fact that it played on a reel in people's heads when he was around. At least it used to be. Before he went soft after Grandmother died. Now people hear another version of the song: *Bad Bad Leroy Brown, richest man in the whole damn town.*

He doesn't move a muscle when I roll to the other side of the bed and pull on my pants. He's a warrior, ready for a fight. A wolf hunting his prey.

I cross the room and get a shirt off the chair. Then I head into the hallway. "Coffee?" I ask without turning around.

He follows me out without saying a word. I pull two cups from the cabinet, pour us each one, and get cream from the fridge, having been taught long ago exactly how much he likes in his. I amble over and set both mugs on my kitchen table. I sit. Anxiety crawls up my spine. He's here to punish me and we both know it. Chew me out for being an irresponsible person. For tarnishing the McQuaid name. For giving this town something to gossip about, laugh over, and speculate.

He pulls something out of his pocket. A blood pressure cuff attached to a small automatic machine. He sets it in front of me. "I took it before I got here. If I have to, I'll take it again before I leave. For every tick it gets above 130 you owe me a thousand dollars. Got it?"

What choice do I have? I nod.

"I asked you a question, boy."

"Yes. I understand."

He sits, leans back in the chair and waits a painfully long time to take a sip of the hot coffee. Each second seems like an hour. Each minute, an eternity.

The last time I saw him like this was when he and Hudson fought when Hud was eighteen. He'd been accepted to several colleges, knowing even then he wanted to be a doctor. My grandfather wanted him to go to an Ivy League school. Hudson wasn't so keen on it. Tucker said no grandson of his was going to get his medical degree from Walmart. Hud pushed back to the point that he actually renounced his place in the McQuaid family and went on his own, refusing to take a penny from his trust. He worked odd jobs to earn money. Took out student loans. It was years before the two of them made peace.

The silence is its own form of torture. And the longer he waits to speak, the more I feel like a frightened boy waiting to get paddled. I know it's coming—I just don't know how much it's going to hurt.

Finally, he takes a deep breath, blows it out, and speaks. "There is a baby girl lying in a bassinet three miles from here. She has no one. Only the nurses to comfort her."

"I—"

"You'll let me speak, boy. I believe I've earned the right."

I hold my tongue, burning it with large gulps of coffee.

"For years I've let you boys get away with too many things. Things I thought I couldn't speak out against considering my own sordid past. But there comes a time in every man's life when he has to figure out how he's going to be remembered. For me, it was your grandmother's death. That was my wake-up call. And the guilt I carry around with me is a heavy burden I'll have to bear until the day I die. Your father is older and set in his ways, like I was. He'll have to find his own path outside of my guidance.

"You and your brothers are another story. You have so much life ahead of you. But you're all stubborn. Not to mention arrogant and entitled. A recipe for a lonely miserable life. Take it from someone who lived one. It's amazing how you can be surrounded by a harem of beautiful women, all wanting a piece of you, but still feel like an isolated man on a desert island." He pauses to drink. "She's beautiful. She has her great-grandmother's nose."

He shifts gears so fast I have to wrap my mind around what he said. "Wait, you saw her? How? I thought there are rules."

"You're naïve if you believe I don't know everything. There isn't a move you could make. A debt you could incur. A bond you could sell, without me finding out about it. If you don't know that by now, you're not as smart as I gave you credit for. Someone like me, with my history, my portfolio, my connections, is able to do anything. If I wanted a meeting with the Pope, I'd get one. Understand?"

"Say what you came to say, Pappy."

"Don't disrespect me, boy."

I scrub a hand across my jaw. "Yes, sir."

"You will step up and raise your daughter."

I know I'm about to lose fifty grand or so, but I can't help it. My chair almost falls over when I stand abruptly, moving away from him as if he could slay me with just his brooding stare. I lean against the counter, saying the only word I can say. "No."

He chews the inside of his cheek. Contemplating. Plotting.

"You know I control your trust fund. It's not yours until you turn forty. Until then, I have every right to change it, rescind it, or direct it to any other person. There are even explicit rules in the case of my death. You don't deserve the money. It's not yours. It's a gift from me. It's money I worked hard for over the years, taking my father's car dealerships from the brink of bankruptcy into a billion-dollar business and making him the richest man this side of New York City. I earned my inheritance. What have you done to deserve yours?"

A sick feeling comes over me. I think I know where he's going with this. But... *fuck.*

He waves his hand around. "You will raise your daughter, or all of this will be a thing of the past. No trust fund. No monthly allowances. Not even a job you barely show up for. Sure, you could find employment as a car salesman somewhere. But if you think that would even come close to supporting the lifestyle you've become accustomed to, just ask your youngest brother."

I digest his words, barely believing he has this kind of control over me. "You're going to cut me off if I don't take the kid?"

He walks to the back doors, the large glass French doors that overlook my impressive backyard. Again, he takes an excruciatingly long time to put together his thoughts. The entire time, I'm plotting how I can get out of it. I know he's right about the trust. My brothers and I took it to a lawyer six years ago. It's fully revocable and ironclad. What he says is right. He can rescind it and walk away without giving me a dime.

I wonder if my brothers would support me. They'd have plenty of money. Then again, my grandfather would have thought of that. He'd probably forbid it and then they'd have to choose between me and their money.

"I don't want to have to strong-arm you into anything. I like to think my bullying days are behind me, Hawk. But this is a life we're talking about. I've talked to Heather about this."

"You talked to Mom?"

"As you're well aware, she's offered to raise the child. She also told me that you forbade it. That, not only do you not want the baby, but you don't want anyone you know to raise her. Well, that simply won't do. Your mother will fight you on this. She's told me as much. You'll both hire lawyers. It'll be drawn out for months, maybe longer, and the whole time that precious girl will be living in a stranger's home while you battle it out. People will take sides. They'll take *her* side, boy. You'll be alienated from the town you grew up in. And rightly so. And when it's all said and done, you'll be a villain. Either way it works out, you will be. So I suggest cutting through all that bullshit because we all know it can't end well."

"You want me to give the kid to my mother? Live in the same town knowing I have spawn out there who will someday come after me and my money?"

"I don't want you giving her to Heather. I told you; I want you to raise her."

"Pappy, I can't."

"You can and you will. And I'm willing to wager your trust fund on it."

My spine stiffens and my full attention is on his last words. "Meaning?"

"Meaning if you refuse to take the girl, I'll redistribute your trust fund elsewhere, most likely to the child."

My jaw drops. "You—"

"But," he says forcefully and with full command. "If you take her, just for a year, I'll not only release the funds to you at that time, I'll double them."

For a moment, a wheel spins in my head. A wheel with dollar signs on it. A lot of fucking dollar signs. I walk to the couch, sink down onto a cushion and cross my ankles on the coffee table. "And after the year?"

"I'm willing to bet that after the year, you'll love that child so much you'll thank God you wagered your trust fund for her."

"You're betting me that I'll fall in love with the kid?" I laugh. "We'd better call Hunter and ask him what the odds are. I guarantee they aren't in your favor, Pappy. And what happens after my time's up and I win? I keep her a year and then what, give her away to an orphanage? You'd be okay with that?"

"No, I wouldn't. But it's a risk I'm willing to take. And I don't make bets I can't win."

"Neither do I."

"Do we have a deal then?"

"One year. That's all. Then I get full control over the money—which you'll double."

"Yes. There will, of course, be conditions to our bet," he says.

"Such as?"

His thumb and forefinger work his lips as he stares outside. "I'll get back to you with my conditions by noon today."

I check the time. It's 9:30 a.m. Guess I won't be going to work today either. "I'll be on the edge of my seat."

His biting stare tells me he doesn't appreciate my sarcastic remark. But he ignores it, taking his coffee cup to the sink to rinse it; something he never would have done years ago. He'd have left it on the table for a servant to pick up and wash. That Rose Gianogi must have him whipped. I still can't believe my grandfather has a girlfriend. One he's living with. And who actually makes him happy. Apparently pigs do fly.

He leaves and I get myself more caffeine. And for the first time today, I smile. I smile because I can do this. Easily in fact. I'll hire nannies. I won't have to do a thing or lift a finger. I won't even have to see the kid if I don't want to. I'll put her and the nanny upstairs in the east wing—far away from my bedroom, where I won't hear the incessant baby noises and can't smell the little creature's bodily fluids. It's totally doable.

The worst thing that could happen is people will call me *daddy*. Hell, they can call me Suzie Sunshine if it means doubling my trust fund. I glance around the great room of my seven-thousand-square-foot home knowing that a year from now I'll be able to afford something three times this size.

~ ~ ~

On my way out of my home gym, I stroll down the upstairs hallway. Yes, this will be perfect. There are two spare bedrooms up here, along with a shared bath and a wet bar around the corner. There's another spare room across the hall from my gym which could be for a second nanny. I might need two for around-the-clock care. Yes, it's all coming together now. One of them could go downstairs and cook meals and take them up to the other. I'd never have to see them or the kid. There's even a back stairway from the kitchen to the east wing.

Pulling out my phone, I do a quick search for the going rate for nannies. Having two will put somewhat of a strain on my monthly allowance, but it'll all be worth it in the end.

I hear myself evil-laughing in my head because of how easy this will be. Tucker McQuaid thinks he can bribe me into falling for a kid, but he'd better think again.

I shower, put on jeans and my *F*ck you, I'm hilarious* T-shirt I usually reserve for special occasions that most often involve drinking with my brothers, and go to my office across the hall from my first-floor bedroom.

Sitting at my computer, I open a file I've been working on, but immediately close it, not feeling inspired today. I check my email. Nothing new there. Nobody I know uses email these days. Maybe Mom and a few of my older relatives.

There's a reply from Kory, our office manager at McQuaid Chevrolet, where my office is located. It's the closest dealership to my house. The next closest is the Nissan dealership on the outskirts of town. The other ten are further out, some of them hours away. My job, along with my father's, is to manage all of them. But they pretty much manage themselves. Dad is the GM of McQuaid Motor Corporation. I'm the 'associate' GM, whatever the hell that means. What I think it means is that I can sit in my office (or not) and do whatever the hell I want. I'm not even sure why I work there anymore. Being the oldest son, it was expected of me. But the truth is, I despise it. I spent three years in sales, two in financing, even one in service, before they made me a manager. I should quit. Maybe I will next year. The $100,000 salary they pay me on top of my trust allowance won't be needed then.

While my grandfather is still the owner, he's removed himself from most of the day-to-day operations. Though he still has his goddamn finger on the pulse of everything. I don't know how such an old man can keep track of twelve car dealerships, his fat portfolio of investments, and every fucking in and out of the lives of his only son, four grandkids, and everyone else in this town.

A new email appears in my inbox. Speak of the devil.

I open and read it, confirming that my grandfather is, in fact, the devil with what he's demanding with his 'conditions.' I can feel my face turning a deeper shade of red with every line I read.

I'm only allowed one nanny.

I must take or accompany the child to every doctor visit.

I must change one diaper every day (I shake my head at the ridiculousness of this one even though I know goddamn well that somehow he would find out if I didn't do it).

I must learn how to bottle feed the baby and do so at least three times per week.

I must go shopping once a month with the child for the purpose of buying it new clothes and other shit.

I must take the child on a walk, to the park, to a playground, or to a playgroup (as if) one time every week.

I must take at least one week-long out-of-town vacation with the child, on which the nanny is allowed.

It's the last one that is the worst condition. In addition to the week-long vacation, I'd be required to take bi-monthly weekends away from Calloway Creek, half of them without the help of a nanny. Just me and the kid.

He must have communication with the nanny along with access to the house (like he doesn't already) to make sure the conditions are being met.

The final paragraph states that no one is to know about the doubling of the money or the time frame of our agreement. He concedes that people will presume he threatened to disinherit me, but I'm to keep the rest to myself. No one else can know the fine print. Not even my brothers.

*What. The. Fuck.*

I throw my laptop across the room. I can't do it. Not even for all the damn zeros in the world.

My phone rings. It's him. I ignore it. I throw it as well, but it doesn't even have the decency to break.

He's got me by the balls. And we both know it.

# Chapter Six

*Addison*

Everyone who knows me knows I hate to say the words *I can't*. Which is why I loathe the fact that I'm driving Mom's car to go to Goodwin's Diner barely a mile away. But I know Lionel would have choice words to say if he knew I was pushing myself before all my friction sores have healed. Working fewer hours the past three days has helped, but I still have a ways to go. Defeat is something I don't like to admit, but I fear working full-time at Donovan's might actually be something I can't do. At least not with this old jalopy of a leg.

Right after I turn onto McQuaid Circle, someone darts out in front of me and I slam on the breaks, my heart in my throat and blood pounding through my ears. When I open my eyes, Hawk McQuaid is staring at me through the windshield, his palms on the hood of the car, his shirtless chest glistening with sweat. For a second, I almost forget I could have just killed him. Because…
*oh my*.

His body is sculpted with hard, lean muscle, a rippling six-pack that men envy and women covet. His angular jaw is exquisite perfection with a dash of roguish wildness, giving him a magnetism that can't be explained with words.

When I snap out of it and realize this jerk almost made me commit unintentional vehicular manslaughter, I put the car in park and storm out. "What in the hell are you doing running out in front of a moving car, you stupid imbecile?"

I expect him to quip back at me with some snarky remark in usual Hawk fashion. But he doesn't.

He wipes sweat off his brow. "Fuck, yeah, sorry."

His dark hair is sweaty and matted. His icy blue eyes are so bright and lustrous, they almost glow even in daylight. His brows are full and, right this second, they slash and dip down, crinkling the skin between his eyes. His heavily stubbled face screams of masculinity and dominance. And it occurs to me that all his amazing features are wasted on a man who doesn't deserve to be so devilishly handsome.

When he doesn't move, I ask, "You okay?"

He rakes a hand through his hair as my eyes focus on the long scar down the center of his chest. I'm not sure why it pleases me to see his otherwise perfect body flawed in some way, but it does.

"Hawk?"

He huffs out a breath. "Yeah, fine. Soooo goddamn peachy."

I move to get in the car, but still think something is off. I dare not risk relinquishing my position as town sweetheart, so, even though this man is my brothers' enemy, I motion to the passenger seat. "Get in. I'll drive you home."

"I can walk," he says. "I'm not crippled."

The second the words leave his mouth I can tell he regrets them. Guilt softens his hard features as he looks down at my leg.

I'm wearing sleeve art over my prosthetic right now—a pretty mosaic-like pattern that's in contrast with my dark blue skirt—but nothing can totally camouflage my prosthetic unless I wear pants and sneakers.

"Fine," he says, walking to the passenger side. "But no talking."

I slide back behind the wheel. "Whatever."

Hawk's house is a few miles away. He lives in one of the new, upscale neighborhoods over by the university.

After minutes of awkward silence, I ask, "Can we not talk *at all* or just about the one thing you don't want to talk about?"

He stares out the window. "The one thing." He spares a glance at me. "I'm serious, Calloway. Not a word."

"Okay." Part of me is wondering why I'm bothering to help a man who is abandoning his own flesh and blood. Maybe I did only offer him a ride so I could try to convince him otherwise, but I'd be foolish to think anyone could tell this man what to do. Let alone a Calloway. "So, nice day for a run. How many miles did you go?"

"About ten."

My eyes widen. "That's a lot for a hot August day. Do you usually run that far?"

"No. It's probably why I wasn't thinking straight. I got dehydrated or something."

I try not to smile. The man is punishing himself. Maybe he has a conscience after all.

When I look over, he's staring at my legs. "Is it hard to drive?"

"I drive with my right leg, Hawk."

"Oh, right."

"I can still drive a stick, though you may not want me to drive your Porsche because sometimes my foot slips off the clutch. And

I can't really tell how much pressure I'm putting on it so I tend to stall them out a lot. But if I had to, like if it was life or death, I could do it. I learned how to drive on a stick. It's kind of like riding a bike, which by the way I can also do." I realize I'm rambling. I ramble when I'm nervous. Why am I nervous?

"Good to know."

I turn onto the street of his neighborhood. The houses here could eat Mom and Dad's house as a snack and have room for more. Long driveways, some with ornate privacy gates. Immaculate yards as big as football fields. A golf course that occasionally peeks through the trees.

It's interesting that Hawk chooses to live on a golf course he and his brothers were banned from several years ago. People still talk about how they stole golf carts, got drunk, and tore up some of the greens and fairways, getting them permanently banned from the country club owned by the Montanas. I'm sure they only did it because of the name: Calloway Creek Country Club. They sure do hate it that more of the town is named after my family than theirs. The irony of it being that his family founded the town and has more money than the other 20,000-plus people combined, well, except for the Montanas. And maybe the Ashfords. But definitely more, a lot more, than the Calloways.

He points. "I'm that one."

"I know where you live."

"You do?"

"Everyone knows everything in this town, don't you know that?"

He shakes his head. "An unfortunate fact, I suppose."

Before I can ask him to clarify his statement, I'm pulling up to his house. Although I know it's his, I've never been this close to it before. It's huge. Is he trying to prove something by living here? Surely one man doesn't need all this space.

He gets out, shuts the door, and nods. Then he turns and walks away.

"You're welcome!" I shout, but he doesn't turn around.

~ ~ ~

"Why are you so late?" Holland asks when I finally make it to Goodwin's.

"Funny story. I almost killed your brother."

She looks amused. "Which one? On any given day there are a dozen women who might say the same thing."

Mia laughs along with us.

"It was Hawk. I practically hit him with my car. He was out jogging and wasn't paying attention when he ran right out in front of me."

"Sounds like a man with a lot on his mind," Mia says.

"I wouldn't know. He forbade me from bringing up his situation."

Holland spits a mouthful of Diet Coke on the table. "He *forbade* you?" she asks, using a napkin to clean her mess.

"What's going on with that?" Mia says. "He's giving the baby up for adoption, right?"

Holland shrugs. "Mom said my grandfather was working on a solution."

"A solution? Like to allow you or your mom to raise her?" I ask.

"Honestly, I have no idea. But knowing Tucker McQuaid, he'll get his way."

"Can you imagine your brother trying to raise a baby?" Mia asks. "It would make a good comedy show for sure."

"You mean a good *reality* show," I say.

Mia giggles. "I can see it now: The Billionaire and His Bastard Baby."

We all laugh, then Holland adds, "We're not billionaires you know. Well, maybe Pappy is. Nobody really knows how much money he has and won't until he's dead."

"I don't get how you turned out so normal," I say. "You know, sleeping on silken sheets on top of mattresses stuffed with hundred-dollar bills and all."

She rolls her eyes. "Shut up. Plus you know I didn't have all that living with Jonah and my mom. Even though she got a lot in the divorce, she's never chosen a lavish lifestyle."

"Seriously," I say. "What do you think will happen with Hawk?"

Her gaze meets the floor. "Honestly, I think he'll lawyer up and then Pappy or Mom will lawyer up too and it will be a battle to the end." Hands cover her face in frustration. "This may end up dividing our family. And I can't imagine having to choose between a brother I love dearly, and his child."

I put a hand on her shoulder. "I hope it doesn't come to that."

Mia comforts her, too. "We're here for you, Hol."

"Thanks. You guys are the best."

"It'll all work out," I say, although I'm not really sure I mean it. "You'll see."

She smiles sadly. Then we order.

# Chapter Seven

*Hawk*

After my second shower of the day, I find myself brooding over the email, once again examining my grandfather's conditions.

He texted me a little while ago. Said he's on his way over. *Oh, goody.* I glance around my house—my bachelor pad—wondering just how much it's going to change. Is this the last time I'll have any peace and quiet for the next year? Will it smell like baby shit? Will there be toys and bottles and kid crap all over? Will I be able to circumvent his conditions?

At least when he arrives this time, he doesn't break into my house, he knocks. And when I answer the door, he's not alone. My mother is with him. She smiles and kisses me on the cheek. Reluctantly, I let her. Mostly because I know Pappy would have something to say about it if I disrespected her in front of him.

"Mom? What are you doing here?"

My grandfather chuckles. "I know a lot of things, boy, but the one thing I don't know is how to raise kids."

"Yet you expect *me* to do it," I say, my words laced with disdain toward the man who has so much power over me.

He turns to Mom. "Heather? Would you mind if Hawk and I have a word in private? We'll join you outside in a minute."

Obediently, she turns and walks out. He's not even her father. He's her father-in-law. Or rather her *ex*-father-in-law. I don't get it. She divorced my dad, *his son*, yet they've remained friends. Hell, my grandfather didn't even take sides during the divorce.

He clears his throat forcefully before speaking. "Are we on the same page about this?"

"Do I have a choice?"

"There's always a choice, Hawk."

"Right."

"So you agree."

"Like I said, I don't have a choice."

He pins me with his stare. "You're going to have to do better than that."

I blink and huff out a large breath before I say under duress, "I agree."

"As I stated in the email, no one is to know about the details of our agreement or you'll forfeit everything."

I shake my head. "Agreement. Is that what you call it?"

"Gentlemen's bet then. Call it what you will, grandson, but my conditions remain the same. Heather has been told I persuaded you to take the child under threat of disinheritance. That's the extent of what you can reveal to anyone. Not a word of the time limit I set nor the money I promised if you succeed."

"I got it. I can read."

"Boy, with that mouth, if we were both a decade younger, I'd have you over my knee. Now,"—he pulls an envelope out of his pocket and opens the pages—"sign here."

"What's this? You want me to sign a contract?"

"This is an emergency petition for guardianship of the baby. I know a judge who can push this through today so you can take the child by this evening."

*"Today?"*

"Otherwise she'll be placed in a temporary home."

"Why do I have to be awarded guardianship if I've already taken the paternity test?"

"The court will need to formally acknowledge paternity before your name can be put on the birth certificate. That will take time. Being granted guardianship assures you can have custody right away." He nods to the papers, refusing to ask me again.

I take them like a dutiful grandson, scribble my name, and hand them back.

"We'll drop these off on our way."

"To the hospital?"

"To go shopping. That, my boy, is why your mother is here."

"Can't I just order everything?"

"Not everything. Come, let's not keep Heather waiting."

I lock up the house and follow him to the driveway. Mom is standing next to a new high-end Cadillac Escalade. I should know. I signed the order to have two of them transported to the car lot last week.

"Whose car is this?" I ask.

"Yours," Pappy says. "You can't drive an infant around in the front seat of your Porsche."

"I'm not getting rid of my car."

He looks over my shoulder at my four-car garage. "Nobody said you had to. Now, shall we?" He hands me the keys.

Mom gives my grandfather the front seat even though he offered it to her. I'd like to say he's gone soft in his old age, but the bet I just agreed to says otherwise.

"Where to?"

"Target," Mom says.

"Target?" I eye her in the rearview.

"Best place to get all the stuff we need."

"Courthouse first," Pappy says. "Then shopping."

I drive down the street of my neighborhood, not at all liking the feel of being behind the wheel of a massive SUV. The Porsche handles much better. I feel like I'm driving a damn dump truck.

"For the record," Mom says from the back, "I'm not exactly pleased you had to be strong-armed into taking responsibility for your own child. But after what you've said the past few days, I'm afraid Tucker is right, and this may be the only way."

"So you get I'm doing this under duress."

"Hawk, I promise you that little angel will grow on you. It may be awkward and uncomfortable at first, but you'll fall in love with her. I'm sure of it."

"Whatever."

What else can I say? She can't know the truth. No one can.

"I took the liberty of ordering baby furniture," she says. "It will be delivered before nightfall. And someone will be by later this week to paint the room."

"Then why do we have to go shopping?"

"Babies need more than furniture, Hawk. They need clothes, formula, toys, ointments, diapers, wipes, and so much more. Not to mention the car seat you'll need to bring her home from the hospital. I don't think we need to worry about baby-proofing the house right now. We'll save that for when she starts crawling. By then, you'll be a pro at this whole father thing."

*No Small* **BET**

*Father.*

*Fuck.*

I tune Mom out as she rambles on and on about what we'll need to get, how she'll help me, and how much I'm going to love being a dad. As if.

She and Pappy talk the whole way. Me—I do anything I can to keep from hearing the depressing shit they're discussing. I try and figure out how much money I'm going to average per day from the doubling of my trust fund. I do the math in my head. It works out to just under fifty-five grand per day. Hell to the yes. *Cha-ching.* I promise myself to play the sound in my head every time I think of the little human.

~ ~ ~

Five hours later, after stopping at the courthouse, buying out the whole damn baby section at Target, grabbing an early dinner at Lloyd's Restaurant (where a courier hand-delivered my guardianship papers), we're pulling up at the hospital.

I glance at the huge pile of totally unnecessary crap in the back of the SUV, not quite believing what's about to happen.

"Well, come on, now," Pappy says. "Best not keep your daughter waiting."

He waits for my reaction. It's like he's daring me to challenge him. But I know better. I'll curse him out later, after he's gone. For now, I swallow everything he says like a shit sandwich.

*Cha-ching.*

"Forgetting something?" Mom asks when I walk toward the entrance.

I give her a blank stare.

"The car seat, Hawk. They won't let you leave unless she's in one."

Rolling my eyes, I open the back door and pull on the seat mom installed right in the middle of the Target parking lot. I tug on it, but it doesn't come out.

Mom opens the other back door and steps up on the running board. "Push this right here to release it from the base. If necessary, you can use the seat without the base, but it's more secure this way. And the stroller we got, the seat will snap right on top of it. Oh, how baby gear has changed since you were born. When you were little, I'd stick you in a swing or a front carrier to sooth you. Now they have sleep sacks, vibrating cradles, video monitors. You're lucky to have all these new conveniences to help you."

I hook the car seat over my forearm. "Lucky. Yeah, that's me."

Her hand lands on my shoulder. "It's going to be okay. You'll have a lot of people to help when you need it."

"Speaking of that, how long will it take to get a nanny?"

"No need to worry," my grandfather says. "One will be waiting at the house when we arrive."

"You hired one?"

"I did indeed."

*A spy.* He hired a goddamn spy to make sure I follow all his rules. This day just keeps getting better.

Up on the second floor I have to show my guardianship papers to a guy in a suit before they let us through a set of double security doors. Then a woman in pink scrubs introduces herself and leads us down the hall to a private room.

"Wait here," she says, leaving the door open.

I've already forgotten her name. My mind is too preoccupied hearing babies cry. The shrills echo off the sterile hallway walls.

I set the car seat down and sink into a chair in the corner while my mother practically bounces up and down.

Within minutes, the nurse returns pushing a rolling crib thing. "Here's your little girl," she says. "She's been a delight. She's strong. A wonderful eater."

I look out the window as my mother gushes over the baby. How in the hell am I going to do this?

"Hawk!"

Pappy's harsh word has me turning.

"Come meet your daughter."

I shuffle over slowly, reluctantly looking at the doll-like person in the crib. She's wearing a beanie covered in pink and blue stripes and is wrapped in a hospital blanket. Mom lifts the hat revealing a full head of fine, dark hair. She makes a comment about her nose—a nose that could resemble *anyone's*, not just mine. She's a lot smaller than I thought she'd be. She looks like she could break, especially if *I* try to hold her.

"Isn't she the most precious thing you've ever seen?" Mom cries. Literally cries. Tears are streaming down her cheeks. She's happy as shit and I'm dying inside.

"Physical contact is very important at this age," the nurse says. "Offering your baby skin-to-skin contact will help keep her calm and allow the two of you to bond. Sucking on her own hands will also bring her comfort."

"I'm assuming the nanny knows all this?" I ask my grandfather.

"She's very well trained, I assure you."

I don't care if she went to the Charles Manson School of Nannies as long as she does her job and keeps the kid out of my hair.

"Have you picked a name?" the nurse asks.

"Uh... no."

I hadn't even given it a thought. I have to name her?

"That's okay," she says. "Until your acknowledgement of paternity comes through, her paperwork can be filed as Baby Girl Greer."

Part of me wants to argue this fact. Her mother is dead. If the kid gets any name at all, it should probably be mine. But I don't say anything. Because in the end, it won't really matter what name she has.

"There is no fee to add a child's given name as long as you submit it within sixty days of birth. The surname, however, if you wish to change that, must be done by way of legal forms. I'm not sure what it costs so perhaps the earlier you decide, the better. It'll save you money."

The urge to spout off who I am and what I can afford is strong. But this situation is so fucked up, all I can muster is, "Fine."

"I'll leave you alone to change her and get her situated in the car seat. We'll send you home with a starter pack of diapers, wipes, formula, and a few other necessities."

I nod blindly, still in a raging river of disbelief. I have to take her home.

As she leaves, my mother pulls something out of her purse and holds it up. It's a piece of clothing she bought earlier. It's pink with clowns on it. I decide I hate clowns.

"A fitting outfit to go home in, don't you think? Come on, I'll help you change her."

"Me?"

"You have to learn this sooner or later."

I step back, but the sheer force of my grandfather's stare has me capitulating, and I let my mother show me how to put the outfit on. She wakes up when we're changing her. Arms and legs go everywhere. It's a lot harder than it seemed it would be to get all her limbs in the clothes. Thank goodness Mom does most of it.

Mom picks her up and hands her to me. I swallow and shake my head.

"Hawk, hold her. Just support her head. You won't drop her, I promise."

She puts her into my stiff arms. I suppose other men might see this as some kind of honor. Me—all I see when I look into her tiny blue eyes is a burden.

*One year* I repeat over and over in my head. *Cha-ching.*

Samantha Christy

# Chapter Eight

*Addison*

I'm proud of myself. That's not always easy for me to say, but I've been taking it easy the past week and Lionel's pleased that my hip is doing better and many of my points of irritation don't look so angry.

As I wait for the elevator after my checkup, I hear a woman's voice around the corner. She's giving some poor schmuck a piece of her mind and she sounds mad as hell. Curiosity has me taking a few steps over to see who she's chewing out. I'm not the least bit surprised when I see that Hawk McQuaid is the target of her boisterous tirade.

She's pushing a stroller and he's trailing behind, looking down at his phone.

"I've had it, Mr. McQuaid," she says, lowering her voice when she sees they have an audience, but still talking loud enough for me to hear. "No amount of money should persuade any sane person to work under these conditions. I quit."

Finally, she has his attention. He slips the phone in his pocket. "You quit?"

Her head snaps from side to side angrily. "I forgot you're hard of hearing. I know this because of how you ignore your child every time she cries. Maybe you'll understand *this*," she says, then does something with her hands. I recognize the movements as ASL. I took some classes back in high school, and also with the Deaf school around the corner from McQuaid Circle, there are often people close by having conversations using sign language. She points to herself. Then she puts two fingers inside of a mostly closed fist and pulls them out up toward her chin.

I can't help but be amused by this woman, who must be north of sixty, putting Hawk in his place.

"You can't quit. I have to go to work."

"Mr. McQuaid, you and I both know you only go to work to avoid being home with her." She takes the diaper bag off her shoulder and drops it to the floor. Then she crouches down. "I'm going to miss you, Baby Girl." She kisses her fingers and presses them to the infant's forehead. Then she turns and heads right toward me and the elevator.

"Mrs. Dodd," he says, looking stunned.

She doesn't turn.

"Mrs. Dodd!"

She doesn't even flinch. "You know," she says to me, "I haven't gotten many steps in today, I think I'll take the stairs." She walks over to the stairway door and turns back to Hawk, who's standing there like he's in shock. "I'll come by tonight to pick up my things." Then she's gone, the heavy metal door closing behind her.

I contemplate taking the stairs, too. It's only three flights. But I promised Lionel I'd keep taking it easy.

When the elevator finally arrives, I get in and hold the doors. When Hawk doesn't move, I ask, "Are you coming?"

He tears his gaze from the stairway door, picks up the bag she discarded and awkwardly pushes the stroller in next to me.

"I thought Holland said Ms. Jamison was your nanny."

"She was."

I cover my laugh because this just got so much more amusing. "This one was your *second*? In one week?"

He doesn't respond. Probably because his daughter is now awake and crying. Hard.

The elevator stops with a jerk. I grab the bar behind me and look at Hawk. He hasn't even noticed that we've stopped. He seems more irritated by the baby.

"Hawk?" I say loudly.

"What?"

"We're not moving."

He looks at me with slashed brows, then he steps to the elevator controls. He hits the button for the first floor. The elevator doesn't move. He hits the other buttons, but nothing happens. He leans against the wall and rubs his temples. "Just my luck to get stuck in an elevator with a screaming kid."

"Shouldn't I be the one saying that?" I huff. "After all, she is *your* baby."

The baby screams louder as if to make a point.

Hawk just keeps pressing buttons.

"Are you planning on doing anything about this?" I ask.

"What is it you think I'm doing?"

"Not the elevator." I look at the red-faced baby strapped into the car seat on top of the stroller. "Her."

"I suppose she'll stop eventually," he says. "She usually does."

59

My jaw drops. "Yeah, when one of your nannies is around to take care of her. When was the last time she was fed or changed?"

He shrugs and pounds on the elevator doors. "Hey! We're stuck in here!"

I raise a brow. "You're not claustrophobic, are you?"

"Only when I'm stuck in a tin can that's louder than a monster truck rally."

The baby's cries are loud. They bounce off the metal walls. "Well, if you aren't going to do anything, do you mind if I try?"

"Have at it," he says without a care. I get the feeling he'd let anyone handle his child if it meant he didn't have to.

I pick her up and cradle her. She's so tiny. It wasn't so long ago when my nieces, Aurora and Ashley, were this small. Fortunately, I've learned a few techniques from being around them. I turn her so her front is along my forearm and I'm holding her like a football. I bounce her gently while patting her back. She instantly stops crying.

"What the hell are you doing?" he asks when he turns and sees me holding her this way.

"Sometimes babies get tummy aches. This seems to soothe them."

He studies me. "How do you know this shit?"

"Jaxon's kids," I say. "I babysit often."

He doesn't necessarily look impressed, just grateful that the noise has abated.

"How long do you think we'll be stuck here?" I ask.

"Hell if I know. Not even the emergency alarm is working."

"I hope you have formula and diapers, just in case."

He shrugs.

"You don't know what you have with you?"

"Mrs. Dodd took care of all that."

Clearly. For a moment I wonder why he's even doing this—raising a child. But then I remember what Holland said about their grandfather forcing him to or he'd get cut off. I guess money is truly all he cares about.

"What's her name?" I ask, still bouncing.

"She doesn't have one."

"You're kidding." I think back to last week. I'm pretty sure she was born on Monday. "Isn't she like nine days old?"

"I guess it's something like that."

"You guess? You don't know?" I shake my head in disgust.

"Yeah, okay, I suppose she's nine days old."

"And you've had her at home for a week. Yet you still haven't named her? What do you call her?"

"I don't call her anything."

"What do your nannies call her?"

"Baby Girl."

"Seriously?"

"It's not that big a deal. I'll come up with something eventually."

"I assume you were at her pediatrician's office," I say. "Is she doing okay?"

"Checkup. She's fine."

I trace her tiny fingers with my thumb. "I'd say she's more than fine. She's perfect." I lean down and smell her head. Her soft tuft of dark hair smells heavenly. I love the scent of baby shampoo. If they made it into a fragrance plug-in, I'd buy it for sure.

A sound echoes from above.

"Shh," Hawk says, straining to hear.

"Everyone okay down there?" a man yells.

"Yeah!" Hawk shouts. "Do you mind telling me how long you plan on keeping me locked in this goddamn box?"

"I'll have it operational soon," his muffled shout assures us. "Sorry. I was doing maintenance and cut the wrong wires. Whole system went down. I'll have it back up shortly."

"Derelict blue-collar workers," Hawk mumbles.

I scold him with my stare. "Do people really let you get away with remarks like that?"

He raises his arms and waves them around. "I don't see any other people around, so yeah."

"My dad is a blue-collar worker, Hawk." I step forward and hold out Baby Girl. "You take her for a bit."

"No. Just put her down."

"Take her, Hawk," I demand.

Reluctantly, he does, holding her so awkwardly it's like he's never done it before.

"You've... held her, right?"

"Once or twice." He stares at the wall and mumbles, "Only when I have to."

"Once or twice? Oh, my god, you've had her for a week. You can't be serious."

The baby starts crying again. I'm not surprised. He's holding her like she's a bag of poison.

"You need to move when you hold her. Bouncing is best. The repetitive movement calms them."

He bends his knees and bounces up and down sharply. It's almost comical.

"Not like that. You'll give her whiplash." I take her from him and demonstrate. "Like this. Fluid motions. Nothing too jarring." When she calms, I strap her back in the car seat but she immediately squirms. "Has she taken to a pacifier yet?"

The blank look on his face tells me he hasn't the slightest idea. I rummage through the diaper bag and find one. I push it against her lips. "Sometimes you have to hold it for them when they're this little." She starts sucking and it soothes her. "See?"

"You're hired," he says.

"What?" I'm sure I didn't hear him correctly.

"You be my nanny."

"Me?" I stiffen. "Are you crazy?"

Baby Girl loses the pacifier and starts crying. I lean over and push it back in place.

"I pay well. Very well."

I'm about to argue, when Lionel's voice in my head stops me. It tells me two things. One: I wouldn't have to be on my feet all day; and two: I'd be working with kids. Or *a* kid. A newborn. An adorable, tiny, precious little girl who has an asshole for a father. Am I really considering this?

"Come on, Calloway, you have to help me. I'm in a real bind here. You asked if I had formula. The truth is I don't even know the last time she ate. I'm not the person who should be taking her home just to hire another geriatric nanny who seems to think *I'm* the child in the family."

I contemplate confirming the last part of his statement out loud, but instead go with something a little less antagonistic. "I don't think it's a good idea."

"I'll double whatever you make at Donovan's."

"I make more than you think." I thumb to my fake leg. "You'd be amazed at the amount of pity tips I get with this thing," I joke.

For a moment, he stares. Then his eyes meet mine. "I forgot for a second."

*He forgot?* Him forgetting would mean that he actually thinks about me not having a leg. Which would be most unusual. McQuaids don't think about Calloways—unless it's to come up with disparaging remarks about our appearance, ancestry, or menial labor jobs.

I laugh. "Yeah, sometimes I do too, especially in the middle of the night when I'm not wearing it."

"You... take it off?"

He doesn't know much about prosthetics. Not many people do. They assume you can just wear them twenty-four seven and go about your life like they can. They don't realize that every physical thing amputees do requires more effort than an able-bodied person with two meat legs.

"Yes, Hawk. I take it off."

"I'll triple your salary. Addy, please."

*Addy.* He called me Addy. I'm not sure he's ever referred to me as anything but *Calloway*. And for a split-second, I almost think I like it.

I calculate what I'd be making if his offer is truly legit. It makes it hard to turn down. "If I do this, it'll be on a trial basis. One week. And I won't leave Donny, Cooper and Ren short-staffed, so I won't be able—"

"So take her with you. I'm sure they won't mind. Aren't they running a preschool in the back office anyway?"

"Very funny." The elevator jumps a bit and starts its descent. My hand flies to my chest. "Thank God."

We reach the ground floor and the doors open. A man standing outside the doors apologizes profusely, even after Hawk directs a few choice words at him.

Hawk picks up the diaper bag and shoves it at me. "Thanks, Calloway." He exits the elevator.

"Wait, you mean *now*? You want me to start right this second?"

"What did you think I meant? You saw Mrs. Dodd leave. I have to get to work. The code to my front door is 6969."

I huff in exasperation. "How original."

Before I can think twice about it, Hawk takes off down the hallway without even sparing a glance at his daughter. "Okay, yeah, I guess I'll... see you later." I look down at the baby. "Looks like it's just you and me, Baby Girl." I shake my head. "And the first thing on the agenda will be to make a list of baby names we can show to your deadbeat father."

I push the stroller to Mom's car and open the back door. I detach Baby Girl's car seat from the stroller, put her in the back and thread the seat belt through the grooves on the side of the car seat. I pull it tight and then make sure her straps are secure. "Don't worry," I tell her. "I know this must be scary for you. You don't know me. You barely got to know your other nannies. I'm sorry you pulled the short straw when it comes to fathers."

I close the door and stash the stroller in the trunk.

Five minutes later, I pull up behind Donovan's. I have a shift today. It's questionable whether or not I'll be able to do it. I put her car seat back on the stroller and walk through the door to the pub. Serenity smiles, skipping over. "Which one of your nieces do you have there?"

It doesn't take a rocket scientist to know Ren loves kids. She dotes over every baby she sees. And she's incredible with my nephew, Cody. I know it won't be long before she has baby fever. But I also know she and Cooper are still getting used to their new situation.

"Neither," I say.

She looks down at the baby and back at me. "Babysitting on the side?"

"Maybe not on the side anymore. But I'm not sure yet. This is Hawk's baby."

"As in McQuaid?"

I chuckle. "Do you know of any other Hawks?"

"Why are you babysitting Hawk McQuaid's baby?"

"I may have just become his nanny."

"His *what?*"

Cooper comes over from the bar, having no doubt heard our conversation. "Yeah, his what?"

I tell them about the elevator and his nanny quitting and me comforting the baby.

"In what world does a Calloway work for a McQuaid?" Cooper asks. "You can't do it. I won't allow it."

I cross my arms over my chest. "Oh, you won't allow it."

"Come on, Addy. Really? Why would you want to do this?"

"I'm not sure I do. It all happened so fast. And like I said, I only agreed to a trial run."

"It makes sense," Serenity says, trying to calm down my brooding brother. "She shouldn't be on her feet as much as working here requires, and everyone knows how amazing she is with kids."

"But—"

"But nothing," Ren says, cutting him off. "She said it might be temporary. Don't get your panties in a twist just yet. He's already blown through two nannies. There's a reason for that. He's a terrible boss. This job could be over as quickly as it started."

"Maybe," I say. "Maybe not. He's paying me triple what I make here."

"For how many hours?" Ren asks.

I shrug. "We haven't exactly talked details yet."

Cooper shakes his head. "He's not father material, Addy. He wants you to raise his kid. He won't lift a finger and we both know it. Rumor has it he only took the baby because Tucker threatened to disinherit him if he bailed. You want to be a mother? To a baby who isn't yours, or worse, a McQuaid?"

"Might I remind you who else wasn't father material," I say, giving him a hard stare.

His arms go up in surrender. "Fine. But don't come complaining to me when you hate your 'job'." I don't miss how he air quotes the word.

"I just feel guilty about today," I say to them both. "I doubt I can work."

"I'll cover your tables," Ren says. "And you're not back on the schedule until Saturday. That will give you three days to decide if you want to do this."

"Thanks. Any advice?"

"Yeah," Cooper answers. "Run away before he tries to make you his servant girl." His body stiffens. "Jesus, Addy, you'll be at his house. I swear if that fucker lays a finger on you."

"I'm his nanny, Coop, not his concubine. Settle down."

"Does *he* know that?"

"He will."

He cracks a knuckle. "Because *I'll* tell him."

"You'll do no such thing. I'm not a helpless girl."

Five-year-old Cody comes out front. He sees me and rushes over to give me a hug. "Is this Aurora, or is it Ashley?" he asks.

"Neither, this is"—I suddenly remember she doesn't have a name—"uh, this is Baby Girl."

Ren gives me crazy eyes. "Baby Girl?"

"She doesn't have a name yet."

Cooper laughs, hands on his knees. "Oh, that's rich. What a stand-up father he's turning out to be."

"I'm going to make a list of possible names today," I say. "It'll be fun."

A group of women strolls through the door.

"We'd better get back to it," Ren says. "Enjoy your days off, Addison."

"Bye, little man," I say to Cody. "See you Saturday for our sleepover at Grandma and Grandpa's."

He claps. "Yes!"

Ten minutes later, I'm pulling into Hawk's driveway, my mother's Nissan Altima a far cry from the high-end vehicles parked in the other driveways in this neighborhood. I get BG out of the back and stare at her. *Yeah, BG.* I like the shorter name. It just takes too much effort the other way. I gather her things and push her to the front door, rolling my eyes as I enter the door code.

I get the stroller through the door and stand in awe. It's practically a castle. The curved stairway in the foyer towers over a grand piano that has probably never been touched by its owner. The entry gives way to a huge great room that itself is amazing, but pales in comparison to the view outside the massive picture windows. A pool! A vision of me sunning by the pool sipping lemonade has me smiling from ear to ear. "You have a swimming pool, BG! This gig might not be so bad after all."

She starts fussing.

"How long has it been since you've eaten?" As I lean down to unstrap her and pick her up out of the car seat I inhale a rank odor. "Okay, diaper change first, then we'll scrounge you up a bottle. Now, where's your bedroom?"

I stand in the great room and look around, figuring I'll need to start somewhere. I spot a hallway. "Let's see where this goes."

The first room I come to is an office. My first thought is what does Hawk do that requires him to work from home? He sells cars. Or he manages the people who do. Back to this room later. The next room is obviously Hawk's bedroom. Large. Sprawling. Humongous bed. And a manly smell. When I realize I'm inhaling the scent, I quickly back out of the room. "Tell anyone I did that, and I'll deny it," I say to BG.

Back in the great room, I go in the other direction to find a kitchen fit for a king, a large breakfast nook at the far end with a bar-height table and six chairs. A second stairway is off to one side. Walking through a butler's pantry, I find a dining room with a table that looks like it's from Game of Thrones. I count the chairs. Twelve.

Down another hallway is a small, unfurnished room, another bathroom, a laundry room bigger than my bedroom at my parents' house, and a mudroom that leads to his garage. I peek inside. His Porsche is there. I wonder what he's driving. I look at BG. "I suppose he had to get something that would accommodate a baby."

On the way back to the kitchen, I find another door. I try it, but it won't open. There's a button to the right labeled 'CALL.' Out of curiosity, I push it and then startle when the button lights up and a mechanical sound echoes through the hallway. For a moment, I wonder if I did something I shouldn't have. Ten seconds later the button goes dark again, and I hear a 'click.' I try the door again. This time it opens. My jaw drops. "An elevator? He has an elevator?"

I've been in nice houses before. Allie's parents have a huge house. But I've never been in one with an elevator. It's so over the top.

I know Holland's dad's house is gigantic as well. But I've never been there. Her parents divorced when she was little, and she went to live with her mom while her brothers stayed with her dad. It almost makes sense, if you think about it, why we're friends. She practically grew up a Calloway, alongside her Calloway stepbrothers, her Calloway stepdad, and her Calloway half-sister. It kind of amazes me how close she stayed with Hawk, Hunter, and Hudson when they didn't live in the same household. I get the idea they felt the need to protect her. As if she were being indoctrinated somehow.

Figuring the last thing I need today is to get stuck inside another elevator, I close the door and go back through the kitchen to the second stairway. "Up we go," I say, now bouncing her to keep her calm as she seems to be growing more ornery.

Immediately at the top of the stairs there are two more bedrooms. One is a nursery, so I don't pay much attention to the other. "Bingo."

No way did Hawk decorate this. The walls are painted a pale pink with the occasional white puffy cloud near the ceiling. A circular white crib is centered in the room on a round rug, also pink, with a colorful mobile hanging over it. In one corner is a changing table stocked with every baby necessity imaginable. I open the top drawer of the dresser next to it to find dozens of name brand baby clothes I only know from Instagram posts from celebrities I follow.

Another corner of the room is filled with stuffed animals, books, toys, and a plush rocking chair that looks so insanely comfortable I just know I will spend hours in it.

"First thing's first," I say, putting her carefully on the changing table. "Let's get you out of this yucky diaper."

It's a good thing I've had so much experience with my nieces. BG's tiny arms and legs flail every which way as I struggle to wipe her messy yellow poop. At least it's not as watery as Aurora's and Ashley's, who are both nursing. I guess formula equals more solid poops.

"Better now?" I ask, doing up the last snap of her adorable strawberry covered outfit. "I'm guessing Mrs. Dodd picked out your cute clothes, not your father."

I laugh. Because even saying the word father when speaking of Hawk McQuaid is weird. And wrong on so many levels.

Thirty minutes later, BG has been fed, burped, and is sleeping in a portable bassinet I brought down from the nursery. Despite an infant living in the house, one wouldn't even know a baby was here by looking around the main level. The only telltale sign when I arrived was a lone bottle drying next to the sink. And if I had to guess, Mrs. Dodd just didn't have enough time to dry it and put it away before they had to get BG to her appointment. Every can of formula is tucked away in a cabinet. All diapers, clothing and pacifiers are kept in the baby's room.

Hawk has a baby, but it's as if he's in total denial.

I decide to call Holland. "You'll never guess what I'm doing right now." I snap a picture of a sleeping BG and text the picture to her.

"Addy, what are you doing with my niece?"

"I think I might have accepted a job as her new nanny."

She squeals. "Oh my gosh. No way. I'm shopping with mom in the city. We're doing a whole mother-daughter day with dinner and all. Otherwise I'd come over. I have to know how this happened."

I hear traffic in the background. "I'll give you the details later. You sound busy."

"Do not let my brother boss you around."

"He is kind of my boss, Hol."

"You know what I mean. Don't take any shit from him."

"I won't. Love you."

"Love you too."

I contemplate calling everyone else, but it's kind of nice to just sit here and have peace and quiet. Life has been so busy lately. Between school, graduation, Tag's wedding, Jaxon's babies, the whole Serenity/Cooper thing, work, and now this, I haven't had much time to breathe.

Tomorrow I plan to bring my bikini and chill by the pool when BG naps. Today, however, I'm grateful I had my Kindle in Mom's car, because the baby is out like a light.

The front door closing wakes me. I must have dozed off while reading. I glance at BG who's still sleeping, and then at the clock, noting it's been hours. I get the feeling she's a good sleeper. Apparently, so am I when surrounded by soft as sin leather. I hop off the couch, expecting Hawk to walk in as it's almost seven o'clock. I'm surprised when Ms. Dodd enters the room.

"Hello," I say.

She studies me. "You're the young lady from this morning. Are you a friend of Mr. McQuaid's?"

"Not exactly. I guess I'm his new nanny." I hold out my hand. "I'm Addison."

She chortles. "Well, good luck to you, Addison. He's a drill sergeant. Actually, that's not a fair comparison. I worked for a drill sergeant a decade ago and he was very kind." She looks in the bassinet and smiles at BG. "She seems content."

"She's slept most of the day."

"She's one of the easiest newborns I've cared for. Shame I can't stand the man who claims to be her father but wants nothing to do with her." She motions to the stairs. "I'll just get my things and be on my way. If you don't mind, I'll use the main stairs."

"Why would I mind?"

"Because Mr. McQuaid doesn't want the help using the grand staircase."

My mouth goes slack. "The help?"

She nods. "I told you, he's an awful excuse for a man."

"Well, this might be temporary," I say. "I told him it was just a trial. So, what did you leave here that you needed to pick up?"

"My things. Clothes, books, personal items." She narrows her brows. "You do know you're expected to live here, don't you?"

My jaw drops for the second time in ten seconds. "Uh… no. I didn't know that."

"Good thing it's only temporary then. Well, I'll go fetch my things."

Two hours later, I'm beyond pissed. I hold BG in my lap and stare at the clock. When it turns nine and he's still not home, my resolve breaks and I text Holland to get her brother's phone number. Before I can call and give him a piece of my mind, the door opens.

I put the baby in the vibrating seat I brought down. In fact, just to spite him, I brought down a lot of things over the course of the past few hours. If he thinks I'm going to live here and stay upstairs not to be seen or heard because it might inconvenience him, he'd better think again.

He sees my expression. "What?"

"Ten hours," I say, arms crossed in a warrior stance. "Are you kidding me, Hawk. And news flash to me—you expect me to *live* here?"

# Chapter Nine

*Hawk*

"Why wouldn't I expect you to live here? That's what nannies do."

"Not all nannies are live-ins. Not most, in fact."

"How would you know?"

"My friend Sophie is a nanny. She watches Amber and Quinn's daughter, Josie. She has her own apartment."

"Well good for her. But that's not this job."

"Listen up, Hawk. You're running out of options here. You've lost two nannies in one week."

"It's not my problem the kid is so high maintenance."

"Are you kidding? BG is the best baby I've ever seen. She barely even fusses. Sleeps all the time."

"Beegee?"

"Yeah. *BG*. Like the letters. Short for Baby Girl."

My eyes roll.

"Don't even get me started on her not having a name."

"You're being irrational."

She huffs in exasperation, hair swirling around her shoulders at the sharp movements of her head. When she stills, her long locks frame her face in a pool of glossy silk. "You truly know nothing about women *or* babies."

"As I was born without a vagina, I'd have to say you're right."

"The nannies quit because of the inhospitable environment, Hawk. They quit because of *you*. And believe me, word gets around. You'll be hard pressed to find anyone who will work for you after that."

"Money talks."

"Maybe that's true, but at best you'll have a revolving door of nannies. That can't be good for BG. She needs stability. Familiar faces. And she needs her father."

"She'll have the best money can buy, that's good enough."

"It's not good enough. It's not nearly good enough. And I'm pretty sure buying childcare for your baby so you don't have to deal with her is not what your grandfather intended when he coerced you into this."

I raise a brow. I know Addy is friends with Holland, but I wasn't aware my family was blabbing about my little arrangement.

"Oh, come on. Did you really think no one in Calloway Creek would find out that the only reason you're keeping her is so you don't lose your inheritance? We all know."

"It doesn't change anything."

"I don't personally know Tucker very well—he's come into the pub with Rose from time to time—but I'm fairly sure he wouldn't be okay with you locking your baby and nanny away upstairs like unwanted houseguests."

"You going to rat me out?"

"I don't know. Are you going to keep me locked away in your attic?"

I pace the room while I consider what she's suggesting. Although I hate to admit it, she may be right. My options are limited here. "What are you saying? You want free roam of the house? That's a little bold, don't you think?"

"If you expect me to live here, I have conditions."

"Don't you all."

She laughs. "So I was right about Tucker."

I stand tall. "So let's negotiate. And don't forget my background in car sales. I know how to make a hell of a deal, Calloway."

She sits and rubs her left thigh. It makes me wonder, not for the first time—or even the fiftieth—what it's like having a fake leg. "First off," she says, "I'm not your servant. I'm *hers*. And I know a lot more about babies than you do. She's your daughter, but you have to let me do what's best for her."

"Meaning?"

"Meaning when to feed her, how to handle crying, things like that. And meaning you can't complain every time you hear her cry. She's a baby. That's the only way they can tell you they need something."

"Yeah, sure. Whatever."

"I'm not a housekeeper. If you don't already have one, hire one."

"Suzanna comes twice a week."

"I get to hire a babysitter on your dime when I need time off. I'm not working twenty-four-seven."

"I'm only allowed one nanny."

"Allowed?" Her nose crinkles and damn it if something doesn't stir inside me. Her hazel eyes bore into me, asking for an answer. But at this point, I'm not sure I remember the question. Ever since she gave me a ride home last week, she's been stuck in my head. And I need a Calloway stuck in my head like I need a shotgun up my ass.

"Huh?"

"You said you're only allowed one nanny. What does that mean?"

I turn away so I don't have to look down into the pouty, pink, fuckable lips that belong to the sister of my enemy. "Like I said, Tucker has conditions."

"If I'm going to work here, you have to learn to communicate, Hawk."

"I suppose you're going to find out anyway once he knows I've hired you. He said I can't have more than one nanny. And I have to do things for the baby like change a diaper sometimes and feed her. Go on doctor visits and"—I roll my eyes—"vacations and stuff."

I can tell she's holding back a laugh. "You have to take vacations with BG? I'd love to see *that*."

"You'll get to as you'll be joining me on some."

"Some?" her full eyebrows lift.

"I have to go alone sometimes. No nanny."

Her shoulders bounce up and down. "And he's going to know all this *how?*"

"My grandfather has his ways. He'll be asking you to report to him I'm sure."

"Which is why you aren't going to banish me upstairs." She nods to the baby. "Or her."

"Fine. You can use the main level."

"And the pool. And the theater room—once you show me how to work things."

"What the hell, Addy? Why don't I just sign the whole damn house over to you?"

"Oh, I'm not done yet."

I sit opposite her, lean back, and hook an ankle over my knee, awaiting her demands and somehow knowing I'm going to cave to all of them.

"If I'm living here, I get to have friends over sometimes. Not parties, just friends."

"If by friends you mean my sister, fine."

"And Mia, Allie, Sophie, Serenity, and whomever else I want."

My instinct is to argue. Some of those are from the enemy camp. But I guess I walked into that one, inviting a Calloway here in the first place. "I put my foot down at your brothers. Or Jonah. Or any of Allie's family."

"I can live with that. But you can't keep me from seeing them. And if BG is with me, she'll see them too."

"Next?"

She rubs the tip of her nose as if it's a nervous habit; her narrow, perfectly straight nose with a slight tilt at the end. I inwardly scold myself for noticing all the details of her face.

"You're going to pay me more," she demands confidently.

"I already tripled what you were making at Donovan's."

"That was before I knew you expected me to live here."

I stand, cross the room, grab a notepad and pen from a drawer, and hand it to her. "Great. Let's negotiate then."

A sly smile cracks her face. She likes this game. And I'm afraid to say I might too. She thinks on it, her slender fingers tapping against her full lips as she stares at me. *Fuck*. I turn away and look at the kid so my half-chub will wane.

She tears a page from the notepad and slides it across the coffee table. I look at it, keeping any emotion off my face. This is a game I know how to play well. I mark through her number and write a smaller one underneath. She lifts a corner of the page and peeks at the number. Her poker face isn't as good as mine. If I had to guess, her heart is pumping at the thought of what I'm willing to deposit into her bank account. Still, she clamps her lips into a tight, thin line, writes another number and slides it back.

My interest, not to mention my curiosity, grows as we go back and forth several more times. Then I write down a lowball number that is completely insulting.

It has the intended effect and she sneers at me in disgust. "I know why the other nannies quit, and I won't let you treat me the same way. I should charge a premium just because I have to put up with *you*."

"You've got it all wrong, doll. I'm the added bonus."

When her eyes fill with fury, my pleasure needle goes off the scale.

"Doll? You really must think you're God's gift, don't you?"

I shrug a cocky shoulder. "You must admit, He outdid himself."

She tosses me an appalling stare. "Your level of conceit knows no bounds."

I nod to the slip of paper. "Are we doing this or what?"

She taps the pen to her lips in thought, then she jots something down and pushes her offer across the table. I'm amused to see she's gone in the opposite direction, raising it to a higher number than her original one. I've got to hand it to her, she might only have one leg, but she's got more balls than a lot of men I know.

"You play hard ball," I say.

Her expressive, luminous eyes become cool and cynical as she watches me. "What's it going to be, McQuaid?"

The determination in her eyes just makes her sexier. *Sexy?* Since when have I ever thought about Addison Calloway as sexy?

The number she wrote won't break the bank. A few thousand dollars more over the course of a year won't hurt my bottom line, but I get the idea it will very much help hers. "Deal."

Surprise crosses her face. No—elation. She tries to control her giddiness but doesn't do a very good job. "Really?"

"Yeah, really."

She crosses her arms. "I have one last condition."

"Sorry. We've already cut a deal."

She glares at me.

"What?" I huff.

"I'm not sleeping with you."

If anything was in my mouth, it would be spewed all over the table between us. "Jesus, Addy. Are you kidding me? I have no intention of fucking a Calloway, unless fucking a Calloway means screwing over your brothers somehow."

"As long as that's clear."

"I have one more condition, too."

"Why do I get the idea I'm not going to like any of your conditions?"

I pull the Cadillac key fob out of my pocket and hold it out to her. "You have to use the SUV when you're on the clock, which, as we just discussed, is pretty much all the time."

Her eyes go wide. "I, uh… I don't think you want me driving a hundred-thousand-dollar car, Hawk."

"I don't want your mom's POS in my driveway, and the car seat thing is already in the Escalade." When she glares at me like I'm pond scum, I add, "Your mom *will* need her car at some point."

"Still." She stares at the key fob, not taking it.

"It's not rocket science, Calloway." I drop it in her lap. "It's a car. And I hate driving it. I miss the Porsche. Go give it a whirl right now. You need to pick up your things anyway."

She shakes her head. "I have my mom's car. I'll drive it home and have her bring me back."

I glance at the baby. "And leave me here with her? No."

"She's sleeping. I'll be gone less than an hour."

"You're sure she won't wake up?"

"No, Hawk. I'm not sure. If she does, hold her. Put her on your lap while you watch TV. It's not rocket science."

"Go. Just make it quick."

A wicked glean lights her eyes. "Just for that, I'm adding ten minutes to the time I'm gone."

"Oh my God, would you just go."

I think I see her smile on the way out, but I can't be sure. I'm too focused on her leg.

# Chapter Ten

*Addison*

"You've had a long day," Mom says when I walk in the house. "I thought you weren't working full shifts for a while."

"I wasn't at Donovan's."

I head back to my room and pull a suitcase out of my closet.

"Going somewhere?" Mom asks, leaning in the doorway.

"I'm moving out. For a while anyway."

"Oh? This is news. Are you going to live with Holland?"

"She's not the McQuaid I'm moving in with." I close my eyes and wait for it.

"Addison Genevieve Calloway, what have you done?"

I stop packing and sit on my bed. "Don't get mad. I accepted an offer to become a nanny for Hawk's baby. It's a live-in job."

Her mouth opens, then shuts, then opens again. "Forget for a minute that he's a McQuaid, but on what planet are you a nanny? You've just earned your—"

"College degree. I know, Mom. You guys never stop reminding me. Listen, an opportunity presented itself. The money is outrageously good. Look at it this way; I won't have to take out any student loans if I decide to get my PhD."

"*If?*"

"Yes, Mom. *If.* Did you miss the parenting class that told you if you try and badger your kids into doing something, they'll most likely do the opposite?"

She sighs and sits next to me. "I just worry about you sometimes."

"Well, don't. I can take care of myself. And this job won't have me on my feet all day like Donovan's did. He has an amazing pool. I'll be getting paid to work on my tan."

"Babies are a lot of work. You'll be lucky to have an hour to yourself."

"I already had four hours to myself today. She's a very easy baby. Even if she weren't, I'd still be doing it."

"Do your brothers know? They must not. I'm pretty sure we'd hear World War Three starting if they did."

"Cooper knows. He wasn't pleased. Other than threatening to kill Hawk if he looked at me the wrong way, he seemed marginally okay with it. But he doesn't know about the live-in part."

"They'll find out."

"I know."

"You should tell them before they hear through the grapevine."

"I don't have time right now. Maybe tomorrow."

"Make sure you lock your bedroom door at night. And take your mace. I don't trust a man who would give up a child only to keep her on the threat of losing his inheritance."

"Can you believe he hasn't even given her a name?"

She looks appalled. "What does he call her?"

"He doesn't call her anything. He doesn't even acknowledge her. I call her BG, short for Baby Girl. I've already started compiling a list of names. Nobody should have to be without one."

"I'm sure you'll be very convincing."

I chuckle. "Like Hawk would listen to me. Hey, can you give me a ride back? He's insisting I drive his fancy Cadillac SUV, but I had to return your car first."

She looks at me in a way only a mother can, making me feel four years old again. "Are you sure you want to do this, Addison?" I can't tell if she's disappointed or just giving me a nudge to think it over, but after spending even a little bit of time with BG, I know I have to do this.

"I'm sure. She has no one, Mom. She's alone in this world with nobody to love her. No mother. Certainly no father. And she doesn't even have a name. I'm doing it for her, not him."

"Well, that's the most convincing argument I've heard. I can hardly fault you for that." She takes my hand. "Just be careful. It may be hard to walk away from BG if things don't work out. You're bound to fall in love with her. Babies tend to make you do that."

"I'm sure I will. I may have already. I'll bring her over on Saturday so you can meet her. I promised Cody we'd have a sleepover and I'm not sure I can hire a sitter by then."

Her eyebrows shoot up. "He's letting the nanny hire a babysitter?"

"It was one of my conditions."

A smile curves her lips. "My daughter is smart."

"And don't worry about the lock or the mace, if he tries anything I'll beat him senseless with my leg. I don't think he will, though. Another one of my conditions was that I won't be sleeping with him."

She tenses. "As if that even needs to be spelled out as a condition of employment."

"It normally wouldn't, but this is Hawk McQuaid."

"Take the mace anyway. I need to know you're safe. So he's paying you a lot, huh?"

I tell her just how much. She's as stunned as I was.

She snorts and says, "That family has more money than they know what to do with."

Her eyes get glassy, and I put my hand on her arm. "Hey, what's wrong? I'll be okay. I promise."

"I just realized we're going to be empty nesters."

"It was bound to happen. I am twenty-two."

She brushes a hair away from my eyes like she used to when I was little. "I know. I just love having my children around. Someday you'll understand."

"But now you have four grandchildren to keep you busy."

Her smile returns. "I do." She squeezes my hand. "And that's enough for now."

I laugh. "Kids are the last thing on my mind. Plus you kind of have to have a boyfriend or husband to have them, neither of which I have or foresee having in the near future."

"That's because you don't put yourself out there. Look at Holland. I see her out with men frequently."

"No offense to her, but she's kind of slutty. I'm fairly sure you'd rather me stay a virgin than be like her."

She swallows. Apparently I've surprised her for the second time tonight. "You're still a virgin?"

"I know, it's pretty pathetic isn't it?"

"It's not pathetic at all. It's an amazing gift to your future husband."

"Uh, Mom, I'm not waiting until I'm married. I just haven't met the right guy yet."

"I understand that, sweetie. But if you've waited this long, I'm willing to bet whoever you choose as your first will be the man you end up marrying."

"I don't know about that. But I guess stranger things have happened in this family."

"Just don't rush it because of your age."

"Hadn't planned on it."

"That's my girl."

An hour later, having dragged my feet long enough to make him squirm, I'm packed and we're on our way back to Hawk and BG. Mom pulls into his driveway where I see a familiar car, albeit not Hawk's. He called in reinforcements. I roll my eyes. Of course he did.

Mom is crying again.

"For Pete's sake, I'm only five minutes away. We'll see each other all the time."

I get out and as I remove my suitcases from the trunk, I realize how optimistic I was packing two of them plus a shoulder bag. Based on the sheer number of nannies before me, I'll be lucky to last a week without stabbing Hawk with a butter knife.

But BG needs me. I've only known her for a day. Even so, I feel a kinship with her. We're alike, she and I. She may not be missing a leg, but she's missing so much more. And I plan on being there to love her when no one else will.

"Addison?" Mom shouts, calling me back when I'm pulling my suitcases up the walk.

"Yeah?"

"Just make sure the baby is the only one you fall in love with."

# Chapter Eleven

*Hawk*

I hear voices, but I'm too engrossed in what I'm doing to care. Then there's a knock on my office door. I quickly shut the lid on my laptop. "Yeah?"

The door opens and Addy appears, brooding as she leans against the door jam. "You called your mother? Seriously, Hawk, you need to learn how to take care of BG."

"Would you quit calling her that?"

"What would you have me call her? *Kid? Baby? Hey, you?*" She pulls a slip of paper out of her pocket. "That reminds me, I started a list."

"Of ways to annoy me?" I glance at my laptop thinking I have better things to do than sit here and argue with Addison Calloway.

"Funny, but no." She comes closer. "Of baby names."

When she hands them to me, I get a whiff of her shampoo. Or body wash. Or laundry detergent. Vanilla I think. Maybe papaya. I scan the list in an attempt to turn off my olfactory nerve.

The page is full of what I'm sure she thinks are cute baby names. Rachel, Sienna, Hannah, Carlie…

I crumple it up and toss it in the trash.

Mom comes up behind her, carrying the baby. Addy holds out her hands. "Let me take her, Aunt Heather."

*Aunt.* That's right. Sometimes I forget I'm related to the Calloways. To Addy. That my mother is her aunt by marriage. And that we're cousins. Third cousins, but still.

I recall the stiffy I had earlier and surmise that's some jacked up shit right there.

"I guess if you have everything under control, you don't need me anymore," Mom says.

"You're welcome here anytime," Addy tells her, as if over the last few hours she's become the lady of the house.

Mom kisses the baby. "See you soon, I hope, little nugget." She turns to me. "And you too, son."

I lift my chin.

She leaves.

As soon as we hear the front door shut, Addy lays into me. "You drag your mother over here at ten o'clock at night, make her take BG while you hide back here and surf the internet or whatever, then you don't even thank her?"

"I thanked her."

"No, you didn't. You lifted your chin."

"Same difference."

"It's not the same, Hawk. God, you are so obtuse."

The baby fusses. Addy crosses the room and deposits her in my arms.

"What do you think you're doing?"

"She needs to be changed before bed."

I stand and hold the baby out to her. "In case you forgot, the insanely high number you wrote on that slip of paper earlier means that *you're* the one who will change her and put her to bed."

"Huh-uh. Your mom gave me more details about your grandfather's conditions. One of which is that you must change one diaper every day. I've been here all day and you haven't changed one."

"Maybe I did it this morning."

She bends at the waist, laughing. "Hawk, everyone in Calloway Creek knows what a Grinch you are in the morning. Or should I say even more of one than usual. I've heard the people you work with never schedule meetings before noon for that very reason. If you changed BG's diaper this morning then I'm the queen of England."

A muscle spasms in my clenched jaw knowing she'll probably report back to my grandfather if I don't do it. "Fine. Take her up and I'll be there in a second."

"Are your legs broken? Take her yourself."

My gaze falls to her false leg.

She raises a brow. "What? I can't joke about it?" She turns and walks away, then tosses me a look over her shoulder. "Are you coming?"

I follow her to the foyer, not the kitchen. She takes the main stairs. Halfway up, she stops when she realizes I'm not behind her. She sees me staring at the staircase and her hands land on her hips. "If you even try to tell me I can't use the main stairs I will walk out the front door right now, leaving you up the creek without a paddle. I'm not a servant. I'm not *the help*. I'm BG's nanny."

"I see you talked to Mrs. Dodd."

"Yes. She's a very nice woman who didn't deserve to be treated that way."

She continues on her way to the top, turns, and stares at me from the balcony above. "Oh my god, you've never carried her up the stairs before, have you?"

"Maybe I should take the elevator."

"Hawk, there are a lot of things you need to learn to do with her, and of all of them, walking up the stairs is a rather minor one. Just hold her close with one hand and leave the other free in case you stumble and need to catch yourself."

"Hold her with *one* hand?"

After giving me a frustrated eye roll, she swiftly comes down the stairs. It occurs to me just how swiftly considering her… situation. That leg must have a lot of mobility. Then suddenly, she grabs the railing, catching herself before she tumbles down, and sinks to her butt. I stiffen, the urge to fly up there and help her is strong, but my hands are decidedly full.

Her shoulders bounce up and down. I think she's crying, but when she raises her head, I see it's the opposite. She's laughing. "My leg came off."

"It came *off?*" I ask. The concern in my voice is completely foreign to my ears.

She's wearing pants, so it's hard to see what's going on underneath. Still giggling a little, she stands up with all of her weight on her right leg, leans over, does something to her left leg, then bounces on it until I hear a clicking noise. Then she continues down the stairs like nothing happened.

She sees the look on my face and says, "It's no big deal. It happens. Especially with this old clunker."

"Old?"

"It's my original. Insurance only covers a new one every five years. Now, put her up against your shoulder, holding her to you with the palm of your hand. Like this."

She helps me situate the baby. The heat of her touch burns through me. At our closeness, I realize the depth of her beauty. It's not an obvious beauty like Holland's, more of a sweet beauty to which I'm inexplicably drawn. And this girl—this *woman*—she's all curves and attitude in one small, sensual package.

*Jesus… quit it.* My brothers would roast my balls on a spit if they knew what thoughts were racing through my head over a Calloway right now.

"I got it," I say, shrugging her away.

Then I climb the stairs, gripping the banister with my free hand like my life hangs in the balance. Because although I hate the predicament I'm in, I'm not about to be responsible for anything happening to the kid.

Back in the baby's room, I set her on the changing table and start to back away.

"Whoa, whoa!" Addy says. "You can't leave a baby alone on a changing table. Not even for a second."

"It's not like she can do anything."

"You'd be amazed how far she can move when she's squirming. You have to have a hand on her at all times."

"I thought you were going to take off her clothes."

"No, *you're* going to take off her clothes."

"He said I had to change a diaper, not dress and undress her."

"You're seriously trying to get out of it on a technicality?" When I don't move, she steps forward. "Fine. I'll do it. But only because I'm tired. I get the idea we may be here all night if you attempt it. Next time, you're doing the entire change."

I don't argue the point. But I will tomorrow.

She removes the clothes that have a million snaps. Then she watches as I take off the diaper. I breathe a small sigh of relief that it's not full of gooey baby shit.

"You're putting it on backwards," she says. "The tape part comes from underneath."

I turn it around, finding it difficult to hold little flailing legs in one hand. A muffled giggle comes from behind me.

"It's not that fucking easy," I say, irritated that I'm paying her out the ass yet I'm the one stuck doing this.

"With your big hands, you'd think it would be."

Finally, what seems like an eternity later, I have the diaper secured. "There," I say. "My job is done. See you tomorrow."

I wait for her to put a hand on the baby before backing away. I make it to the door when she calls me back. "Hey, speaking of technicalities, I think I have a way around the babysitter thing."

"What babysitter thing?"

"My condition of being able to hire a sitter to give me time off. Your mention of the changing clothes issue got me thinking about semantics. A babysitter isn't technically a nanny. And I'd be willing to bet there's a difference if it went before a judge. But even if Tucker has a problem with it, you're paying me enough that I'll pay the sitter myself."

"Great. It's settled then."

I leave. Addy starts talking to the baby and I stop in the hallway to listen.

"Don't you worry," she says. "I promise to find you a good sitter who will love you as much as I do. Now let's get you your nighttime bottle. Are you going to be a good little sleeper tonight? I'll tell you a secret, I'm right across the hall. Don't feel bad if you wake me up. That's why I'm here. Unlike some people in this house, I think you're amazing. Don't ever let anyone tell you you aren't. Got it? Squeeze my finger if you understand."

Addy giggles. My cock twitches. I go downstairs and take a cold shower.

# Chapter Twelve

*Addison*

"Not so loud," I tell Holland when she turns the volume of the music up. I bring the baby monitor closer. "I need to be able to hear her."

"It's a video monitor. You can see her."

"Not with my eyes closed I can't. I'm trying to be a responsible nanny here."

She turns it down and scissors her long, slender, tanned legs in the air before turning over onto her stomach to sun her back. "I'm not ready for summer to be over."

"Because?" I sip lemonade.

"Don't you remember I promised my mother I'd get a real job? She thinks sitting around watching my bank account grow from my monthly allowances is turning my brain to mush."

"You did get a degree in fashion," I say.

"Only because I love clothes. Not because I ever thought I'd work in the industry. And you know I only got a degree because Pappy made me."

I laugh. "Your grandfather sure is demanding. But I guess I have to agree that going to school was a better use of your time than watching reruns of *Project Runway* all day every day."

When I hear BG fussing, I sit up and grab my silicone liner, roll it over my stump, put on my sock and then click my leg into place. Then I pull on my bathing suit cover-up.

"Dang, you're quick," Holland says. "It takes me longer than that to put on my strappy heels."

Holland is one of the few people outside of my immediate family who've seen Eileen. It's not that I'm embarrassed. In fact, I've come to view my stump as almost a badge of honor, a reminder that I'm a survivor—a survivor of a stupid accident of my own doing, yes. But a survivor nonetheless—I looked death in the face and said fuck you. Okay, maybe not directly in the face, but I did see a bright light. And that had to have been death.

But even though I've made peace with it, it makes a lot of people uncomfortable. My brothers tell me I shouldn't give a flying fig how it makes people feel. But I do.

It's strange. People are fascinated by my prosthetic, but I learned early on that once they see the actual stump, they become frightened. I think it makes the loss seem more real to them. Like the prosthesis is a part of me, an actual leg, while I'm wearing it, but once detached from my body, somehow it makes *them* vulnerable. Like if it happened to me it could happen to them. And people don't like to think bad things can happen to them.

Hol follows me to the nursery and skips ahead of me, reaching in the crib and scooping up her niece. "Couldn't you just eat her up?" she asks.

"I know, right? How could anyone not fall in love with her?"

"You're talking about Hawk."

I nod.

"It's okay, BG," she says. "There are plenty others of us who love you."

"Don't let Hawk hear you call her BG. He hates it."

"Screw him. If he doesn't have the good sense to give her a name, he very well can't expect us not to."

"He shot down my list. I'm about to make another."

"He needs a baby name book."

I laugh. "Have you ever seen your brother pick up a book? Not counting school that is."

"I guess not. He's always hated reading. While I have every Harry Potter book ever written on my bookshelves, he claims anything worth reading will be made into a movie so why bother."

"That is so not true. And movies hardly ever do justice to books."

She hands the baby over. "I have to run."

"Big date?"

"Ha! No, not tonight. I have a hair appointment."

"Want to come to John and Libby's for a sleepover on Saturday? I promised Cody."

"Can't. I *do* have a big date that night."

"With who?"

"Some guy I met on Tinder."

I scold her with a hard stare. "Holland. Again?"

"Don't *Holland* me. I've got condoms, mace, and bucketloads of common sense. I'm a big girl, Addy. Besides, look at what happened to your brother when he went on a blind date. Lightning could strike. You never know." She plants a kiss on BG's cheek, then mine. "See ya."

I lean down and tell BG, "I worry about her sometimes." She follows my lips when I speak. "You think I'm just jealous? I've considered that. She is the most gorgeous girl in Calloway Creek.

Supermodel gorgeous. I hope you get her long legs. With those legs and your father's amazing blue eyes, you'll be a heartbreaker for sure." I set her on the changing table. "Come on, let's get you ready. Then we'll do some baking while we make another list for your deadbeat dad."

~ ~ ~

While lounging on the couch in the great room, I stare at BG as the swing gently sways her back and forth. "What's your name?" I ask. I chew on the pen and contemplate. "Katherine? Hmm, I don't know. Abigail? No, they'd call you Abby and that's too similar to mine." I glance around wondering if I'll be around long enough for it to matter.

I jot down a few more names, the last one trailing off when my pen runs out of ink. I shake it, but nothing.

I eye my leg, perched against the couch. I think one of the worst things about being an amputee—or should I say one of the most inconvenient things—is when I need to get up quickly. It's why I learned early on that if I'm going to sit and take the leg off, I need to have certain things: my phone, the remote for the TV, a drink and a snack. You have to think ahead because it's just not that easy to hop up, fetch a new pen, and go about your business.

When I was first getting used to my leg and took it off even more than I do now, I'd often forget to have food handy. And since I wasn't as efficient putting it on, I found it was more trouble than it was worth. But that had its consequences. I started losing weight simply because I was too lazy to get up and go to the kitchen. And losing weight is not good for someone like me who has a prosthetic specifically engineered to fit my body to a T. Even five to ten pounds can cause issues. My leg didn't fit properly for weeks until I put the weight back on. And needing to gain weight quickly, I turned to cookies, cakes, and pastries, discovering a newfound love of baking that has stuck with me to this day.

I think of another name. Eager to add it to the list, I slip on my leg and go in search of a pen. I sift through some drawers in the kitchen, coming up empty. I go to the laundry room and look there, but nothing. "Who doesn't have pens lying around?"

Not wanting to go all the way upstairs and get one from my purse, I come up with another idea. He must have some in his office. BG is happily watching the mobile over her swing, so I head for Hawk's wing. I've gotten to know the house pretty well over the past few days, but this area is the one place I don't frequent. Hawk didn't say it was specifically off limits when he reluctantly agreed I could have the run of the house, but it seemed implied that it was.

"If you didn't want me in here, you should have had more pens in your house."

Feeling justified, I cross the room and go to the large wooden desk. And when I say large, I mean presidential. Why does a man who sells cars need such a ginormous desk? The sleek, closed laptop sitting on top of it gets swallowed by the enormity of the surface beneath it. The chair behind the desk is just as pretentious as the desk itself, but it looks so comfortable I can't help but sit in it. I sink down into the buttery leather wondering what he does when he's in here. Avoid me and BG probably. This is where he is when he's at home. I'm not even sure the man has eaten one meal in this house. In fact, I had to take BG to the market the other day when I realized if I didn't, I'd have to survive on coffee, condiments, and baby formula.

A half dozen framed pictures of him and his siblings in various stages of their lives line one of the walls. It's not lost on me that there are no pictures of his parents. He has a tenuous relationship at best with Heather. I'm not sure how he gets along with his dad, but he must, considering they work together.

On the wall opposite the photos, there is a large, framed print of a quote. It reads: *If there is a book you want to read, but it hasn't been written yet, then you must write it.* ~ *Toni Morrison*

I find it most peculiar that a man who hates reading has a quote about it on his wall. Then again, like BG's room, it's possible someone other than Hawk did the decorating.

Below the quote is a fancy bar cart, smaller than the bar in his great room, but stocked just as fully. A bookshelf is on the back wall behind the desk. What's surprising is that there are actual books on it. Novels even. John Grisham, Tom Clancy, and David Baldacci to name a few. I roll the chair over and pick one up surmising he must secretly be into spy thrillers. Not really my cup of tea.

Remembering why I'm in here in the first place, I swivel back around and try to open the center desk drawer. I can't though, because it's locked. I cock my head to the side and study it. Who locks the pencil drawer? Admittedly, this drawer could hold a lot more than pencils in a desk this size. And I can't help but wonder what's inside. Drugs? Porn? Wads of cash?

Curiosity wants me picking the lock. Human decency has me respecting his privacy.

I tug on the other drawers. They open. And even though I find what I'm looking for in the top right drawer, I can't help myself when I peek in the others. Apparently my human decency doesn't extend to unlocked spaces.

The usual things you might expect are here. Charging cables, business cards, sticky notes and rubber bands. When I come across a pack of condoms (who needs condoms in their home office?), I find myself leaning back in the cushy chair fantasizing about him rolling one on.

Flushed, and absolutely mortified that I'm thinking of Hawk that way, I slam the drawer. He's not even close to being someone I should daydream about. He's grumpy, selfish and ornery. Not to mention he's a playboy.

*And fit... athletic... gorgeous.* With a broad chest, angular jaw, and a smile—albeit rare—that makes you want to follow him anywhere. All in all, an amazing specimen of masculinity.

Then I remind myself that perfect package is all camouflage for a man with the disposition of a rattlesnake ready to strike. I grab the pen, shaking the dangerous thoughts from my head, and go back out to the great room to finish the list.

The doorbell startles me on the way, as if I've been caught snooping. I peek at BG to make sure she's content before going to answer it.

What I see through the peephole is comical. My three brothers are standing outside. And they're on the warpath, all puffed up and tall and ready for confrontation.

I open the front door. "You can save your breath, guys."

"What the fuck are you doing, Addy?" Tag asks.

As my oldest brother, Tag always seems to get the first word. And that word is usually a four-letter one. He's the same age as Hawk, maybe that's why the two of them seem to have the biggest rivalry.

I check the time, noting it's after six, but still too early for Hawk to make an appearance, so I step aside and hold the door. "You can come in, but just for a minute. And only if you promise not to yell. The baby is sleeping."

They storm past me, military style, and I try not to laugh.

When we reach the great room, they turn and stare, a firing squad ready to zero in on their target.

"You didn't tell me the whole story," Cooper says.

"I'm a grown woman. I don't have to."

"Christ, Addy," Jaxon adds, "You're *living* here?"

"That's what nannies do."

"And you're a nanny, why?" Tag asks. "And for *him* of all people?"

"Not that I have to explain myself to you doofuses, but working at the pub and being on my feet all day was taking a toll on my leg. And then I ran into Hawk, who'd been left in the lurch by his nanny. He offered me a lot of money. I could hardly refuse."

Tag huffs. "No amount of money is worth being a servant to that asshole."

BG makes a noise and Jaxon is the first to acknowledge her. He walks over, squatting down to get a closer look at her. "Dang. She's gorgeous. Good thing. She'll need every advantage to overcome being the spawn of the devil."

"Where do you sleep?" Cooper asks.

"Upstairs, across from the nursery."

"Where does *he* sleep?"

I point to the hallway. "Down there."

Tag shakes his head, looking like he's about to explode.

"I know what you're thinking and it's not like that. I'm a Calloway. He hates me just like he hates you. He's not going to try anything."

"If he does—"

"He won't. But just so you know, if he did, I'd kick him in the balls with my prosthetic."

"What the fuck are they doing here?" Hawk's voice booms across the room. "And why does my house smell like the Pillsbury Dough Boy puked all over it?"

"She's our sister," Tag says. "What the fuck are *you* doing inviting her here?"

My brothers stand between Hawk and me. I expect fists to fly at any second, so I quickly work my way between them. "Calm down." I turn to Hawk. "They came to check on me. And now that they know everything is good, they'll be leaving." I stare down my three brooding brothers. When they don't move, I add, "Now."

Tag slinks his way around me and closes the gap between him and Hawk. "If you lay a goddamn finger on her I will have your pea-sized balls on a platter. Got it?"

Hawk takes a step forward. I squeeze between them and push him away. When my hand connects with his chest, his muscles flex then relax. And for one long, vibrant moment we stare at each other.

Then he looks back at Tag, scowling furiously. "You threatening me in my own house, Calloway?"

"As a matter of fact, I am. You gonna do anything about it?"

Jaxon and Cooper stand behind Tag, the three of them spitting fireballs with their eyes.

"Nobody is going to do anything about anything," I say. "Guys, you said your peace. And while I appreciate your concern, I'm not going anywhere. That little girl needs me. Hawk is not going to touch me. Are you, Hawk?"

He steps back. "No. Hell no."

*Okay, so maybe he said that a little too emphatically.*

"See? We're all good here," I say. "You're free to leave."

"Free to get the hell out is more like it," Hawk adds, motioning for the door.

Five seconds go by, then ten, the four of them staring at each other. It's like a showdown in the Old West, waiting to see who will draw their gun first.

I clear my throat loudly.

Jaxon is the first to break his stare. He taps Tag on the shoulder. "Come on, let's go."

I follow the three of them as they make their way to the door. "I'm not your little sister anymore. I can take care of myself."

"You'll always be our little sister, Addy," Cooper says. "There will never be a time when we won't be looking out for you."

"I get that. But you need to let me find my own way. I honestly don't know if I'll be doing this for a week or a year, but whatever I decide, it'll be *my* decision."

Jaxon looks behind me. "Promise me you'll be careful. I don't trust him. And neither should you."

"I promise."

With a final warning glower back toward Hawk, my three protectors leave, albeit reluctantly.

When I return to the main room, I belatedly realize it smells like pizza. I walk into the kitchen to find Hawk standing over a box on the counter. His faded, snug jeans fit him all too well, complimenting the shirt sleeves rolled to his elbows revealing strong forearms.

"They won't step foot through that door again," he says, arms crossed. "You broke a rule. I don't like it when rules get broken." He puts four slices on a plate and grabs a beer from the fridge. "The rest is yours if you want it." He piles the cookies I made earlier on top of his pizza and takes his plate down the hall. Before he goes to his office, he turns, and the look he gives me is the polar opposite of the expression on his face when he told my brothers he wouldn't lay a finger on me. It's more like the look he gave me when I touched his chest. Like his eyes are filled with a sizzling awareness. Awareness of what, I can't be sure.

When he's gone, it occurs to me that he doesn't eat here. At least he hasn't in the past three days. And he hasn't come home before eight or nine o'clock either. As I get a slice from the box, I stare down the hallway wondering if Hawk McQuaid just bought me dinner.

# Chapter Thirteen

*Hawk*

Dad stands in the doorway to my office. "You're here early. And on a Friday."

I don't look up from my computer. "I like the peace and quiet."

He chuckles. "Kids are loud. I know, I raised four of them."

"Raised is a pretty strong word, don't you think?"

"Next time, wear ear plugs. You'll get more sleep and won't be such a shit. What the hell is so important on your computer that you can't even look at your father when he's talking to you?" He crosses the room toward my desk.

I turn off the monitor. "Nothing."

"How's the kid?" he asks, taking the seat across from me.

"Still alive. Very very alive."

"Heard you hired that Calloway girl to take care of her."

"Addison. Yeah."

"How's that working out?"

"Fine."

*With the exception of all her rules and demands. And smells and bounces and... Shit, I'm doing it again.*

Leaning back, a devious smile curls his lips. He laces his fingers behind his head. "I remember nannies. Went through quite a few of them myself. Those were the good ol' days. Make sure she earns her keep, son."

As I study him, flashbacks of when I was eight race through my head. Janice Portman was my favorite nanny. I can't remember how many we'd had before her. My memories of most of them just mesh together. But Janice was different. Hudson couldn't annunciate his 'J's so Janice became Nini and it stuck. All of us, even Mom, called her that. She was so excited when Holland was born. And she was very patient with Hudson, Hunter, and me when we all demanded turns at holding our new baby sister.

It was a complete shock when Janice quit. Mom was away running in some charity half marathon that Dad didn't bother to attend, not even to cheer on his wife. The three of us boys were getting ready for a summer picnic—one of our favorite things—when Janice came out of the kitchen, crying. Dad trailed behind her yelling, "We're not done here." She handed the baby over to him and replied, "Oh, yes we are." Then she kissed the three of us on the head, mumbling apologies, and walked out the front door. We never saw her again.

We were rambunctious boys. I always thought that's why the nannies left. And I specifically remember Dad telling us as much. But now, as I sit here and look at him, I realize *he's* the reason.

"Jesus, Dad. You slept with our nannies?"

"Not all of them." He shrugs. "They were just so young and... available."

"You're a real asshole, you know that? We all suspected you cheated on Mom, but right under her nose?"

Boisterous laughter echoes through my office. "The apple doesn't fall too far from the tree, son. Word has it you're on your third nanny."

"Yeah, well I guess I'm an asshole too, but for different reasons."

He gets up and nods to my desk. "Best get back to work. Those quarterly reports don't write themselves."

I don't bother telling him I stopped doing those years ago. I've tasked Kory, our office manager, with the job. In fact, I delegate most of my duties to other people. Sure, I attend meetings and place orders and go over the numbers. Occasionally I even meet with suppliers and customers. I'm good at keeping up appearances. But I'm even better at looking busy.

As I watch Dad's backside turn the corner into the hallway, I realize how much like him I really am. For years, I've blamed Mom for breaking up the family. I stuck my head in the sand when it came to Robert McQuaid. He's my dad, after all. He was supposed to be my hero. My role model. When all he turned out to be was a bad example.

A half hour passes before anyone else realizes I'm here. A sultry voice from the doorway gets my attention. "Good morning, Hawk. You're here bright and early."

It's our service manager, Kate. Our *hot* and very feminine service manager. We've gone out a few times. Well, *out* is a stretch. We had a drink at Donovan's once when we were both sitting at the bar. And we've had sex. In here, as a matter of fact. On this very desk. She'd like more. I say leave well enough alone. She's like Shannon Greer 2.0. Only older and with smaller tits. She's looking for a meal ticket. I'm pretty sure she's even slept with my father. Then again, there aren't many women in this town north of thirty who haven't. Many of them just want to be the one on the arm of the heir to Tucker McQuaid's fortune. Little do they know my father won't get all of it. The dealerships will be his. The rest of my grandfather's wealth will pass to me and my siblings—I think of my predicament—*well, maybe.*

My predicament. I'd gone a whole half hour without thinking of it. But for the first time, I find I'm not counting dollar signs in my head when I think about what's at my house. Instead, I wonder if Addison is laying out by the pool, sunning herself. Or in the kitchen making my house smell like chocolate and cinnamon like it did last night. And for a moment, I wonder why I'm here instead of there. But when I remember *why* Addy is there, the moment passes.

Kate clears her throat. "Hawk?"

I nod. "Hey."

"I asked why you're here so early."

"Because there is a baby at my house that won't shut up."

"I almost forgot you're a dad."

"Can you not call me that?"

She steps forward. "I'll call you whatever you want."

"Kate, I'm busy here. Was there something you needed?"

Her eyes fall to my desk. Yeah, she's thinking about the time I was pile-driving her from behind as her tits flapped against the cherrywood. Or maybe the time she sat on my desk, lifted her skirt and I got her off with my tongue.

"I, uh… no, I guess not."

My phone pings with a text. When I see who it's from, I swear to God my pants get tight.

**Addison: Michelle?**

Confused by her text, I get up from my desk and go to the door, gesturing for Kate to leave before I shut it. Kate walks out, shoulders hanging.

Michelle? What's she talking about? I rack my brain to think of a Michelle I might have 'dated'.

**Me: Michelle who?**

**Addison: Melanie, Meena, Mikayla, Melina?**

I laugh for a second. Then I realize what she's doing and my amusement fades. She's probably at the house going through a book of names.

**Me: No, no, and no.**

**Addison: An 'M' name would sound good with McQuaid.**

**Me: They all sound stupid.**

I stop short of saying it doesn't matter what goes well with my last name as she won't have it for long.

**Addison: BG needs a name, Hawk.**

**Me: Bye, Addy. Work calls.**

She doesn't text back, but I can almost feel her rolling her eyes at me. She tends to do that a lot. And damn if parts of my anatomy don't like it.

I try not to admit to myself that, for a second, I liked the fact that she was texting me. I liked it until I knew why. But she wasn't texting Hawk, the man. She was texting her boss. I try not to admit another truth: I'm disappointed.

For the rest of the day, I throw myself into work. Only it's not the work I should be doing as a paid employee of McQuaid Motor Corp.

# Chapter Fourteen

*Addison*

Hairs on the back of my neck prickle as I stuff clothes into an overnight bag. I turn to find Hawk staring at me from the doorway. Interesting. I didn't think he came to the east upstairs wing unless forced by one of his grandfather's 'conditions.'

He must have been in the gym. He's wearing shorts, and his T-shirt sticks to his muscular frame. When he lifts a corner of it to wipe his forehead, I catch myself staring.

"Where do you think you're going?" he asks.

I told him days ago that I had promised Cooper's son a sleepover. The man listens to no one. Unless you're a McQuaid. Or maybe an ESPN announcer.

So I mess with him. "I quit. Or did you have one too many whiskeys last night to remember?"

His face turns ashen. "When did you… are you kidding… uh, seriously?"

"No, Hawk, not seriously. I'm going to my parents' house. Sleepover with Cody. I told you about it a few days ago."

He leans against the doorway and tosses a glance into BG's room. "What about her?"

I decide to play with him a little more. "What about her? *You're* BG's dad. A night of bonding will do you good."

The look on his face is so worth it. He's a deer in headlights; shocked to the core with no idea what to do or how to do it.

I muffle a laugh. "I'm kidding. I'll take her with me."

"Or you could do it here."

"Ha! Cooper's son come here for a sleepover? Believe me, Cooper would rather he go to Hannibal Lecter's house. Anyway, you're always complaining about Zoey's baby noises and smells. This will give you a reprieve."

One of his eyebrows shoots up. "Zoey?"

"I'm trying out baby names."

He shakes his head. "No."

"Hawk, she's almost two weeks old. She needs a name. What kind of butthead father won't name his child?"

"Did you just call me a butthead? What are you, six?"

"Sorry, would you prefer *asshole?*" I whisper the last word.

"It's not like she can hear you. Even if she could, she's an infant, what does it matter?"

"It matters. Babies pick up on more than you realize. Words, inflections, faces. You really should spend more time with her to imprint your face in her memory. You don't want to be a stranger to her."

He stretches his long arms up to grip the top of the door frame and his shirt rides up, revealing a sliver of skin along his lower abs that causes my breath to hitch. I try to keep my eyes locked on his face but they drift over his body anyway. His tight, sculpted, muscular body. Through all of his arrogance and entitlement there is a brooding sexuality that swirls around him.

*Look away, Addy.*

The cocky smile spreading across his face lets me know the undressing of him with my eyes didn't go unnoticed. "See something you like?"

I stuff my sleep shirt into the bag, determined not to let him get to me. I put the bag over my shoulder and head for the door, but he doesn't move. "Do you mind? I have to pack for Lila."

"I know what you're doing, and it isn't going to work."

"What? Trying to get you to pick a name? You can't call her Baby Girl forever. It's not right. Now will you please move aside?"

He shifts, but only slightly, and I have to squeeze around him. I can smell him as I move by. He's all man sweat with a hint of cologne. A scent that should definitely not be causing this visceral reaction to our close proximity.

I spare a glance back at him when I enter BG's room.

His narcissistic smirk reveals he knows exactly what I was thinking. "Cat got your tongue?"

"So, um… what are you going to do with your night of freedom?"

It's a stupid question to ask. He does anything he wants whenever he wants to. But I had to say *something, anything,* to get my mind off his abs. His manly smell. His striking eyes.

He shrugs. "Thought I might go out."

"With Hunter and Hudson?"

"No. They're busy."

"Oh?" I don't pry and he doesn't elaborate. And I realize I don't like what that means—that he's probably going out with a woman. *And I care because?* I turn away.

"Hey, little girl," I say, taking her from her crib. "Are you hungry?" I turn to Hawk. "If my calculations are correct, you haven't fed her in three days. Can you go make her a bottle while I pack her things?"

"And, what? You'll report back to my grandfather if I don't?"

"I'm a rule follower, Hawk. If you wanted a rogue nanny, you should have hired someone else."

"He didn't say I had to *make* the bottle, only that I had to feed it to her."

"You really do get hung up on semantics, don't you?"

"You always have to read the fine print, Addison. Details are important."

"Okay, well here's a detail: go make her a bottle or she'll get fussy. She gets pretty vocal when she's hungry. And you'll have to listen to her cry, because I'm not making it."

He crosses his arms over his chest. "I'm *paying* you to make it."

I stop filling the diaper bag and stare him down. BG starts crying. I do nothing.

He turns and stomps down the hallway. "Fuck," he says, leaving the word echoing off the walls.

Five minutes later, I drop two shoulder bags at the bottom of the kitchen stairs and chuckle. Hawk is standing at the sink, three dirty bottles on their sides signifying failed attempts at mixing the formula. He's pouring spring water from a refrigerated bottle into a baby bottle with powdered formula in it.

I step forward. "Have you never made her a bottle before?"

"I told you, he said *feed* three times a week, not *prepare*."

"Here." I hold BG out to him.

He takes her but holds her awkwardly. It's hard to believe she's been living here for over a week, and he still doesn't know how to hold her.

I push the bottle aside and get a fresh one. "First of all, you can use tap water. It's actually good for them because it's fluoridated." I turn on the faucet and let the water warm. "You also don't want it cold. But if it's too hot it will burn her mouth." I put my wrist under the sink. "Test it like this. If your wrist can tolerate it, it's a good temperature." I set the bottle under and fill it up to three ounces. "Water first, so you can tell how much you're putting in. Then measure the powder based on that. She's eating somewhere between two and three ounces a feeding." I add the powder and shake the bottle. "Easy." I eye the mess he made all over the counter and try not to laugh. "You can clean that up after we're gone."

"Can we get this over with?" He sits stiffly on a kitchen chair, balances BG on his legs and holds out his hand for the bottle.

"You should cradle her in your arm and keep her at an angle as you feed her." I help him get her situated, once again noticing his scent as I do. "There. Now when she's halfway through the bottle, you need to burp her."

"Why not just wait until she's done? I mean I could drink this in one swallow."

"Sure. Go ahead and wait. You'll end up with spit-up all over your shirt though."

He slips the nipple into her mouth. BG fights it at first because of how awkwardly he does it. "Why are there so many goddamn rules?"

I walk over and pick up the bags. "I'm going to put these in the car."

"You can't just leave me here."

I momentarily wonder if his statement was born from fear or anger. Regardless of which, he has to figure this out sooner or later. "I'll be gone for thirty seconds."

"What if she vomits or something?"

"Oh my God, Hawk. Man up and learn how to be with your daughter."

His eyes snap to mine. "I'll show you how I can man up."

Butterflies dance through me at all the ways I imagine he could do that.

I toss him a smirk and head to the garage.

~ ~ ~

"He doesn't even know how to feed or burp his own baby?" Mom asks in horror.

"Mom, he doesn't know how to do *anything*. And he doesn't want to know."

"So he really is just doing it for the money."

"Looks like it."

She sweeps her hand over BG's little tuft of hair. "You poor precious girl."

"Can I hold her?" Cody asks, snuggling up next to me.

"Sure. But she's very fragile, like a piece of glass." I put her in his lap and support her head. She stares up at him and he's totally enamored. "I think she likes you."

"She's so little. Like one of Gigi's dolls."

"You were this little too, Cody. It's hard to imagine because you're such a big boy now."

He smiles proudly. "Is she your baby now, Aunt Addy?"

"No. Remember, we talked about this? I'm her nanny, like Sophie is to Josie."

"But you're always with her. Where's her mom and dad?"

"Well, her mom died and her dad… well, he works a lot."

Mom huffs in the background.

Cody stares down at BG. "Her mom is with *my* mom in heaven?"

"I guess she is, little man."

He leans down and kisses her forehead. "It's okay, baby. Daddies are the best."

My heart hurts for BG, because, no, not all daddies are.

I take her back from him and say, "What are we going to play first? Xbox? Candyland?"

"Poker," he says.

Mom and I share a look. "How do you know about poker?" I ask.

"Dad and Uncle Tag and Uncle Jaxon and Uncle Quinn were playing last night. I got to watch but they wouldn't let me play."

I love how Cody calls Quinn his uncle even though he's not. He's married to Tag's best friend, Amber. But everyone in his sphere is just one big family. He's one lucky kid.

Darn—now I feel bad for BG again. She has just as many uncles as Cody, yet not one of them has stopped by the house since I've been there. Not even the one who delivers babies for a living.

"Cody, we're not playing poker. Not for about ten years." I look at BG. "And you, I'm going to love you enough for five daddies and uncles."

~ ~ ~

Three hours and a hundred and twenty-five kid games later, Cody is crashed in Cooper's old bedroom. I feed BG and set her in the port-a-crib Mom keeps here for all her grandbabies.

"You're pretty good at this," Mom says when I join her in the kitchen for coffee.

"I love kids."

"Don't get too attached to her, sweetie."

"It might be a little late for that."

"How's it going, living in that mansion of his?"

"We hardly see each other. I get the idea he likes it that way."

A thin eyebrow raises. "You say that like it displeases you."

I shake my head. "It's just weird. How can he not see what a gift she is? And he's missing out. I know she doesn't do much yet, but her little noises are incredible. And the way she grabs onto my fingers. She needs me, Mom."

"I suppose she does. Even if she *is* a McQuaid."

I scold her with a tilt of my head. "Et tu?"

"I didn't mean it that way," she says. "I have nothing against them personally. But they do have reputations. Reputations that have me wary about you living under one of their roofs."

My phone rings.

It's Hawk. Only it's a picture of Hugh Heffner. I don't have a picture of Hawk, so his profile pic on my phone is of the only other playboy-mansion-owning douchenozzle I could think of.

My heart beats faster than it should when I answer. "Checking up on BG?" I ask. "Admit it, you can't go a night without worrying about her."

"Ms. Calloway?" a strange voice asks.

"Yes."

"This is Sheriff Niles."

Now my heart is thundering, but for a very different reason. Is Hawk hurt? Is he in trouble? "Has something happened, Sheriff?"

"If you mean me coming upon Mr. McQuaid and his friend stumbling along the side of the road, then yes, something has happened."

"But he's okay?"

"Physically, I'd say he is. Mentally, not so much. But he's in a predicament. See, I'm not on duty. I've got three girls in the back of my car—my daughter and two friends who I picked up from the bowling alley—so I can't offer them a ride, not that I'd have it in my heart to do it anyway. And technically, since I didn't catch either of them behind the wheel, I can't arrest anyone for drunk driving. Especially since he claims they weren't drinking until they pulled over and downed a bottle of tequila. Then there's the fact that I don't intend on spending my Saturday night under a mound of DUI paperwork."

"Why are you calling me exactly? Surely he has family that can deal with it."

"Tried some. They either didn't pick up or were in the city. When I threatened to call his grandfather if he couldn't find anyone to get him, he said I should call you. So there you have it."

"You want *me* to come get him?" I ask, confused.

"Just give me the goddamn phone, Niles," I hear in the background.

"You're in no position to argue, Hawk," Sheriff Niles says. Then I hear, "Fine, take it. Make it quick. I don't have all night."

"Addisssssooooon," Hawk slurs.

"Are you kidding me?"

"Come oooooon. It's no big deal. Tucker would have my ass in a sling. And I'm payin' you a shit ton, so get in the tank I let you drive and come n get me."

"I should let you rot on the side of the road, Hawk. Maybe Tucker should know the kind of father you're turning out to be."

"I ain't no father," he slurs.

"Ma'am." It's the sheriff again. "Are you willing and able to come get them?"

"Where?"

He gives me their location as I slip shoes on. "I'll be there in fifteen minutes."

"You're a nicer person than he deserves."

"Don't I know it."

I hang up and explain things to Mom. "Leave the baby here," she says. "Go deal with that. We'll be fine."

"Thank you." I hug Mom and storm out the door.

The entire way, I stew over the fact that I have to pick up a drunk Hawk and his buddy. I'm sure they were lying to the sheriff. Nobody pulls over on the side of the road to get drunk. I get the idea that Sheriff Niles just didn't want to have to deal with Tucker even if it may be what's best for Hawk.

I pull up behind the police car. Hawk is in the headlights, leaning against the back of his Porsche. There are so many words I want to say to him, but not within earshot of three teenage girls. I pin him with my stare. Then his 'buddy' comes out of the woods, wiping vomit from *her* mouth.

He was on a date. And I realize my heart is more fragile than I'd like it to be under the circumstances.

# Chapter Fifteen

*Hawk*

"Who are *you*?" Addy asks my companion with a snarky glare.

"This is Brynn," I tell her. "Her family just moved here. Her dad works for me."

The two women appraise each other. "Are you even old enough to drink?" Addy asks.

"She is," Niles says as his glance shifts to the kids in his car. "Or I'd be hauling his ass in for contributing to the delinquency of a minor. It would be my pleasure to bring him in on something I can prove."

Great. Another girl dad trying to make a point.

Brynn's eyes are trained on Addy's leg that's being illuminated by the Sheriff's headlights. "Oh, my God. What happened to your leg?"

I can almost see Addy sift through her list of comebacks and I wonder which one will spew from her pouty lips. "My dog ate it. What happened to *yours?*" she quips snidely as she looks at Brynn's long, slender, perfect lower limbs.

"Get them home," Niles says. "He can come by the station for his keys tomorrow."

Without another word, Addy goes back to the Caddy and sits behind the wheel, waiting. Brynn follows me to the car and takes the back seat.

Addy tosses her a look over her shoulder. "If you throw up in this car, I'm going to make you clean it."

"No worries. I just puked. I should be good," she says, as if this is a regular occurrence. She leans forward and taps Addy's shoulder. "Aren't you kind of young to have a baby?"

She must have noticed the base of the car seat.

"I don't have a baby." Addy looks at me. "*He* does."

"You have a baby? Are you like… married?"

I guffaw. "Hardly."

"Listen, I love this little get to know each other moment," Addy says, "but mind telling me where to drop her?" She gives me a punishing stare. "And if you say your house, I'm letting you out right here and you can call your grandfather."

I cackle. "Well played, Calloway."

"I'm not *playing* anything," she says. *Liar.* "I'm just not going to be responsible for two drunks when one of them seems barely older than your own daughter."

I rattle off Brynn's address. Addison and I are both silent on the drive. I take it I'm going to hear an earful as soon as my date is out of the car.

"How is it possible you have no one else to call?" she yells once we're alone.

"Everyone was busy."

"As in your brothers?"

"Yeah."

She shakes her head sharply back and forth. "You really have no friends, do you?"

"I tried Nolan."

"Nolan Montgomery? As in the guy who works for you selling cars. He's not a friend, Hawk. He's an employee. You're pretty pathetic, you know that?"

"I have friends."

"Name one you aren't related to."

"Are you saying cousins can't be friends?"

*"We're* cousins," she reminds me. A fact my cock seems to forget every time I look at her.

"Third cousins. That doesn't mean shit. Do you know we might not even share any more genes than random strangers?" It's true. I looked it up yesterday. But I'm not telling *her* that.

"What does that have to do with anything?"

"I'm just saying cousins can be friends just like any other randos can be."

"Either way," she says, "this is the last time I do this. What the hell were you thinking?" She taps her left leg. "How insensitive can you be calling *me* to pick up your drunk ass after you'd been behind the wheel?"

*Ah, shit.* It hits me like a ton of bricks, sobering me up quicker than ice water to the face.

She grips the steering wheel so hard her knuckles pale. "I have one more condition. If I find out that you drive drunk, I'm quitting. And good luck finding my replacement after midnight." She spares a look at me. "I'm serious, Hawk. It may be my only rule that I won't bend on."

My mind pages through her other rules, wondering which of those she'll bend. Or hell, maybe even break.

"So I'm not supposed to drink as long as you work for me? Fat chance, Calloway."

"I didn't say that. I said you can't drink and drive. And don't try to feed me a line about you not doing it tonight. Even Sheriff Niles knows you were bullshitting. He just didn't want to deal with it and he had an out."

"I can drive fine after three or four drinks, been doing it my whole life."

"One," she says.

"That's a little extreme, don't you think?" I pull out my phone. "I'm one hundred and eighty pounds. According to Google, I can drink three-point-five drinks in an hour and still be under the legal limit."

"You're feeding me a load of crap, Hawk. There are so many variables when it comes to alcohol's impact on the body. Different people can absorb it at different rates and mixed drinks can have a wide range of alcohol in them."

"What are you, an encyclopedia? I'm a big guy with lots of muscle if you haven't noticed."

She appraises my arm like it's a piece of mouth-watering candy. "Fine. Two."

I can't believe I'm negotiating with a Calloway over how many drinks I'm allowed to have.

"And who exactly is going to be the drink police?" I ask.

"Are you saying I can't trust you to be honest?"

"Depends on who you're asking. Your brothers or the Montanas don't seem to think so."

"Don't forget the Ashfords. Do we have a deal?"

"What am I supposed to do if I have more than two drinks and nobody is around to give me a ride?"

"Uber."

"There are exactly two Uber drivers in this town, Addy."

"Then walk."

"What if it's too far?"

Fingers trace her brow then pinch the bridge of her nose. She's frustrated with me. And damn it turns me on.

"You'll pick me up, won't you? After all, with the amount of money I'm paying you, you can be my chauffeur from time to time."

We pull into my driveway. She shuts off the engine and stares blankly at the house. "You promise never to get behind the wheel if you've had more than two?"

"I promise."

"Then, yes, I'll fetch you if you've exhausted all other avenues. But rest assured, I'm not a chauffeur. I'm only doing it so you don't end up like me. Or worse."

I swallow the guilt over having driven after drinking too much. Guilt over all the times I've done it in the past.

I get out of the car but she doesn't. "Coming?" I ask.

She rolls down the passenger window. "Did you not notice that your daughter isn't in the car? Olivia is still at my mom's, you blind moron."

"Olivia?" I mock a finger down my throat.

She gets out of the car and stomps over. "Listen you inconsiderate beast, let's settle this right now. You're naming her." She pulls out her phone and rattles off names. "Emelia, Sky, Taylor, Summer, Everly—"

"This is ridiculous. You can't make me pick a name right this second."

"Well, it looks like I am."

This petite woman, who I could pick up effortlessly and carry all the way to... *don't go there*... well, somewhere, is going to win this battle. I know it in my soul.

"This would have been so much easier if she were a boy."

"Hawk Jr?" she asks with lifted brow.

"Hell no. I'd name him after my favorite baseball player." I work my upper lip with my thumb and forefinger. "Wait a second. Why the hell not?"

"What?" she asks, seeing my devious expression.

"Hey, you're the one who's insisting I give her a name. Who says I can't name her after my favorite baseball player?"

"What's his name?"

"Marco Rivington."

She rolls her eyes. "You can't name a girl Marco."

"I can name her whatever the hell I want."

"Marco isn't even a girl's name."

"Okay then, Rivington."

"Rivington," she says flatly. "You want to name your daughter Rivington? No, Hawk, you can't do that."

"Why not? It's my choice. And I made it."

"That's the most ridiculous thing I've ever heard. Rivington McQuaid? It sounds like the name of an ostentatious stockbroker. She's a girl. She needs a feminine name."

I head for the door, turning around to shrug. "It's done. I'll file the paperwork on Monday."

"You're drunk. Go sleep it off. I'll be back tomorrow with BG. We'll discuss it more then."

"No need. I've made up my mind."

She stomps back to the Caddy, gets in, stares me down, then backs out.

I'm left gazing after her, wondering why her being mad at me makes my cock so goddamn hard.

# Chapter Sixteen

*Addison*

The past week has been… unusual around here. Hawk isn't spending as much time at work, but when he's here, he's still not really here, he's in his office. What the heck does he do in there? What if he watches porn all day long? I stiffen as I look at a sleeping BG. What if he watches *child* porn?

To my knowledge, since the night I picked him up almost a week ago he hasn't filed for the name change. I'm relieved because a part of me thought he wasn't kidding. I've continued to leave notes with baby names around the house. Notes that inevitably end up in the trash.

And Hawk has continued to bring home dinner every night, although he eats in his office and I eat in the kitchen. Alone.

Standing in the doorway of his office, I eye the closed laptop wondering what I'm going to find when I open it. But I have to know. It's my job to keep BG safe. But what if it's something illegal? Something that will make me want to quit my job?

I'm torn. Because although I can't believe I'm thinking this—I love my job. BG. This house. The pool. Even the Scrooge that lives here can be entertaining at times. And I'm not sure I want to find any evidence that will change things.

But the need to know why he shuts the lid to the laptop every time I'm near is more powerful than the violation of his privacy. So I cross the room and sit in the large, leather office chair that I've only sat in one other time. My heart races. What if he catches me? Then I remember he has a security system that beeps three times when an outer door is opened. If he were to come home, that would give me enough time to race out of here.

I try to convince myself I'm doing the right thing when I open the laptop. The screen illuminates. A sigh escapes me. Needless to say it requires a password.

Looking around the desk, I try to deduce where I might find a password if he'd written it down. I look under the laptop and the desk lamp but come up empty. I scrounge through a few drawers. Nothing. It's probably in the locked drawer. I tug on it, knowing it won't open, but to my surprise—it does.

My heart pounds as I slide it toward me, revealing the contents. But then confusion overtakes me. It's just a bunch of papers bound by large clips. Work stuff maybe. Financial information from McQuaid Motor Corporation perhaps. I pick one bundle of papers up to look for a password underneath, but I stop when I see the words on the front page.

### Book three – untitled
### By Hawk McQuaid

*No Small* BET

I look at the other piles of bound papers.

**Book one – untitled**
**Book two – untitled**

My jaw all but hits the desk. He writes books? I glance at the Toni Morrison quote on the wall. I look back at the manuscripts. Hawk McQuaid—the man who, according to his sister, made it through school reading internet synopses and Cliffs Notes—writes books. *Three* of them.

The urge to flip through the pages is strong. He keeps the desk locked for a reason. He doesn't want anyone to know this. He's a secret writer. I run my hand across the top of one of the manuscripts. Oh my gosh, I can't not read them. I *have* to do it.

I open the one labeled book one. I read the first paragraph.

**It was a dark and stormy night. Jensen McKnight drove his sleek black car down the winding curves of Italy's most famous road. He was a force to be reckoned with. A man unlike other men. A master of both money and women.**

**On his tail was his nemesis, the man who lived only to take him down.**

I read on, and by the time I reach page three, I have a hard time not cringing. This is bad. It's full of idioms, hyperbole, and downright horrible imagery. It's like James Bond meets Spy Kids— an adolescent attempt at thriller fiction.

I pick up the second manuscript thinking surely it has to get better. Nobody's first attempt at a novel can be good, right? Number two *must* be an improvement. I'm wrong. I have so much secondhand embarrassment I have to put this one down as well. I dare to peek at the third, paging through the mid-section just to find that the writing grates on me like fingernails on a blackboard. It only takes a few paragraphs to know this book shouldn't only be locked away so no human eyes can fall on it, it should be burned.

My phone rings, making me jump as if I've been caught with my hand in the proverbial cookie jar. I slam the drawer shut when I see Hugh Heffner's photo on my screen.

"Hello?" I say, quickly looking around the office. He doesn't have a camera in here, does he?

"I need a middle name."

"Hawk, what are you talking about?"

"I'm filing the paperwork, you know, for the kid's name."

"You're not seriously going to name her Rivington, are you?"

"I told you I was. Listen, I'm holding up the line and I know you have a thousand names on your list."

"I do, so use one of them as her first name, why don't you?"

"We've gone over this. It's been settled. Addy, just give me a goddamn name."

"You want *me* to pick her middle name?"

"I really don't care what it is, so yes."

"Okay then. Heather."

"I'm not naming her after my mother."

"You're the one who said you didn't care."

He huffs. "Pick something else. The line is getting long and people are staring."

I page through my list of names knowing she needs a really great middle name to make up for the first name. I rattle off a few pretty ones.

"That's all the same shit you said before. Give me a new one."

"I don't have a new one. And you're putting me on the spot here."

I hear a woman snap at him in irritation for holding up the line.

"Addy, I need one now. Screw it—what's your middle name?"

"Mine? Genevieve. But that's not any better than Rivington. How about—"

"Spell Genevieve."

"Hawk, no."

"Fine, I'll look it up."

The phone goes dead. I stare at it, hoping he's kidding about using my middle name, but somehow knowing he's not.

BG cries in the other room. Or should I say Rivington does. I shake my head on my way to her. I pick her up and cradle her snugly. "Well, Rivington Genevieve McQuaid, you may have set the record for the most unique name ever given to a baby girl." I kiss her little brow. "And I'll let you in on a secret. It's a good thing your dad is rich, because he'd never make a dime with those pathetic excuses for novels."

As I make her a bottle I realize I never got into his laptop. But I think I left the lid open.

When feeding time is over, I head back to Hawk's office. I go to close the laptop knowing whatever is on there is probably just another failed attempt at being the next John Grisham.

Then, out of pure morbid curiosity, I sit, staring at the password screen. I take a chance and type a code. 6969. The Windows desktop appears. Wow—I didn't expect that.

I crane my neck and listen for BG. *Damn it, not BG—Rivington.* After almost two weeks it may take some time to get used to her new name.

Like his office in general, his Windows desktop is very organized. There are only a few folders on it. One of them is labeled 'Book.' How original.

I open it and then open the file labeled *'book draft.'*

Jensen McKnight was a man to be reckoned with. Not only was he a master with money, but he'd never met a woman who hadn't volunteered to be his subordinate. They'd all puddled at his feet, every one of them wanting to be the next heiress to the McKnight fortune. All of them falling short of the image he'd held in his fantasies for most of the three decades he'd been alive.

He'd traveled the world. Visited every continent. Risked life and limb. His life was full. Rich. Content. But something was missing. Something money couldn't buy. Until the day she walked into his building, time stopping along with the mechanical controls of the elevator. He was trapped with Adelaide Montgomery, daughter of the infamous Rory Montgomery, king of the Italian mobsters. And little did he know, the next twenty minutes would change the course of his life.

> "Don't worry, Adelaide" he told her, stepping on the handrail to push open the emergency exit above.
>
> Her demure hazel eyes bore into him through thick lush lashes. The corners of her full pouty lips curved up into a grin. "Call me Addy," she said, before pulling a gun from underneath her skirt.

Before my brain can even register what I just read, three beeps sound and my pulse pounds in my ears. I quickly exit out of the file and close the lid to the laptop. I hastily look around, making sure there is no trace of my utter transgression before I run out into the other room.

I turn the corner so fast, my leg comes off and I fall onto the hardwood with a loud thud.

Hawk comes racing around the corner, dropping take out containers on the nearest table. "Jesus, you okay?"

He reaches for me, but I wave him off, determined to keep up the charade that I never need help from anyone. "I'm good."

I'm very adept at getting up off the floor using only one leg. I've had a lot of practice over the years. It tends to surprise people when I do it. When I'm up, I bend over, pick up my leg, and hop over to the couch, my pant leg flopping with every step. I shove my prosthetic up the empty side of my pants, put it in place and lean my weight onto it until it clicks.

I turn to see him staring. I shrug. "I told you, it happens."

"Your right leg must be crazy strong, Addy. I've never seen anyone get up off the floor using only one leg without any support."

"Yeah, well, you adapt. Oh, wow, what's that smell?"

"General Tso's chicken."

I'm amused. Last week when he dumped some other low-grade Chinese food in the kitchen, I'd mentioned what my favorite was before he dished himself Lo Mein and hurried back to his office. I didn't think he ever paid any attention to things I say. And now, suddenly, he has me naming his kid, he's bringing my favorite dishes home and—it hits me—he's writing a book with *me* in it?

He picks up the takeout bags, takes them to the kitchen and plates himself some food. As always, he takes a beer from the fridge. This time, however, he turns. "Want one?"

Stunned, I cross the kitchen floor and open a cabinet. "I prefer wine with Chinese."

He puts his beer back. "Make it two," he says, then gets a pricey bottle of Sauvignon Blanc from the wine fridge, pulls out a chair, and sits at the kitchen table.

"Uh, okay." I take two wine glasses to the table. Then I dish out my food.

Joining him at the table is strange. It feels almost like a date, but it's the farthest thing from it. He's my boss. I'm the nanny. Or *the help*, as he would say.

After a few minutes, I break the awkward silence between us. "Did you really change her name to Rivington?"

He washes his food down with a gulp of hundred-dollar-a-bottle wine as if it's water. "Yup."

"And her middle name?"

"Gene—whatever, like we talked about."

"You mean like *you* talked about. Poor Rivi."

"That's not her name, Addy."

"Addy's not *my* name, Hawk. You really think with a name like Rivington, nobody would shorten it?"

His eyebrows slam together in a scowl. "Her name is Rivington. Not Rivi. Not Riv."

"You can't dictate what I call her. And when she's older, she'll have her preference as well. Until then, you pretentious fool, I'll call her whatever the hell I please. I can't believe you did that to her. As if she doesn't already have enough to overcome with a father like you."

I take my wine glass and my plate and leave the kitchen.

# Chapter Seventeen

*Hawk*

I follow her into the great room, where she's hovering protectively over the sleeping baby.

"Don't be like that," I say. "It's just a name." *And it won't matter in eleven and a half months anyway.*

She sets her plate down. "Just a name? Hawk, it's something she'll have to live with for the rest of her life."

*No it's not.*

"It's original."

"It's not a girl's name."

"Why do you care anyway?"

"Because someone has to look out for her. Ordinarily that someone would be a parent. In this case, though, the only person who seems to care about Rivi is me."

"That's not true. My mom and Holland seem to like her. And her name is Rivington."

She looks at me in disgust. "You are infuriating."

"You wouldn't be the first woman to say that."

"Do you really not feel anything for her?"

Addison pins me with her stare. Her hazel eyes singe the skin on my face. I make notes in my head. I take in every nuance of her expression. Every wrinkle of her brow. I want to remember exactly how she looks so I can accurately write it down later.

"Look at her," she says. "She's gorgeous."

*She is*, I want to say. But it wouldn't be the kid I was referring to. Why is she so beautiful when she's angry? Why is it that every bone in my body is urging me forward, not to throw her down on the couch and drive into her, but, amazingly enough, to kiss her. Just a kiss. On those full, pink, pouty lips that send electricity through my veins every time angry words spew from them.

"What kind of man can't even stand to look at his own child?" She turns and tries to walk away, but I grasp her elbow.

"We were having a meal together. Let's finish it." I nod to the right. "In the dining room?"

She looks at me like I'm a crazy man. Maybe I am. We've never even had a meal together and now I'm inviting her into the dining room? Hell, I've lived here for two years and *I've* never eaten there.

Rivington wakes and squirms around. Addy picks her up and then gets her plate off the table. "You bring the wine," she says, walking away.

Dinner for three is not exactly what I meant, but I find myself following her anyway. She stands next to the table, presumably waiting to see what seat I'm going to take. I set her glass down next to mine at the end of the table then sit at the head of it. She walks to the other end, a good twelve feet away, puts down her plate, retrieves her wine glass and then sits opposite me, holding the baby with one hand and picking up chopsticks with the other. I can't help being fascinated at how she can eat while holding an infant.

She takes a drink and holds out her glass. "Would you mind?"

I stand, go to the kitchen, and fetch the bottle. When I return, I refill both our glasses, then move my things from the head of the table to the seat closest to hers. She lifts a brow but doesn't say a word. I know what she's thinking though, that she's the one at the head of the table now. I wonder if somehow she believes that gives her all the power.

It doesn't. But damn, I've never wanted anyone at my table more.

"It's just dinner," I say, knowing the words carry as much bullshit as a half-ton cow.

A smile curves her lips. She tries to hide it behind a bite of food. "You should have your brothers over to meet her. Surely they want to get to know their niece."

"They aren't into babies."

"Yet Hudson delivers them for a living."

"He claims that's the best birth control there is, watching babies come out of orifices nothing that big should be coming out of."

She sets her chopsticks down, brooding. "Men. You think God made vaginas just for your pleasure, don't you?"

"They are quite pleasurable."

"And fascinating." She looks at Rivington. "What other body part can stretch to accommodate something as large as a baby and then shrink down to be tight enough to enjoy sex?"

*Vagina. Tight. Sex. Pleasure.* Every word that comes out of her mouth makes me want to sweep the food off the table, hoist her up onto it, and kiss the ever-loving shit out of her. If it weren't for the kid in her arms, I just might.

I stuff my face with an egg roll.

"You should invite them tomorrow," she says. "I'll be gone anyway."

"Gone?"

"Don't worry. I hired a sitter." Her eyes roll. "You'll like her. She's young and pretty. But I swear, if you try anything I'll have you arrested."

I couldn't care less who she hired. I'm more interested in where she's going. "You have plans with my sister?"

"Nope." She expertly balances rice on her chopsticks and shovels it into her mouth.

"Mia? Allie? That other nanny?"

"Not them either."

It's a date. She's going on a goddamn date. I refuse to ask with whom. I won't give her the satisfaction. I finish the rest of the food on my plate and drain my glass of wine.

Addy holds the baby out to me. "She needs to be changed, and I'd like to enjoy the rest of my dinner."

"I'm not done either. I was about to get more."

"We all have to make exceptions and sacrifices when it comes to raising kids."

"Actually, I don't. That's why I have you."

"Okay, if you'd prefer to change her diaper at three in the morning, be my guest." She settles Rivington back in her lap. "And if my calculations are correct, you also need to take her on a walk by tomorrow night. You wouldn't want Tucker to find out you're shirking your duties, would you?"

I know what game she's playing here. She wants the upper hand. She's not going to get it. The baby starts squirming and crying. Addy keeps eating. How she can do it with only the one hand is beyond me. Then again, she's done a lot with just one leg.

I come to a crossroads when Rivington decides to grace us with her loud, incessant shrills that don't seem to faze Addison. Do I go into the kitchen and finish my dinner in relative peace, or do what she wants?

I push my plate away. "God damn it, fine." I stand up and motion for her to give me the baby. Addy cracks a smile. "You don't have to look so smug about it, I'm still the one calling the shots here." I walk away with the kid, shaking my head, knowing that's anything but true. My grandfather is the one calling the shots. And maybe the tenacious brunette eating General Tso's chicken.

Taking the stairs while holding a baby has become a little easier. I've done it several times now. On the way up, a god-awful noise comes from Rivington's diaper. "Aw, shit. You just took a major crap, didn't you?"

In the nursery, something dawns on me. This is the first time I've done this without anyone hovering over me. Suddenly, I get nervous. What if I drop the kid? What if she rolls off the table? What if I snap her little legs like twigs stuffing them back into her clothes? *Shit.*

I try to remember how Addy does it. Then again, she's an expert. I'm just winging it here. I grab five diapers and pull twenty wipes out of the container and put them next to the changing table. I lay her down and unsnap her clothes. When I lift up her behind, however, I see gooey shit all up her back. Just my fucking luck, her diaper leaked.

"You planned it this way. You and Addy. I swear somehow she knew this would happen. She calls *me* infuriating? *She's* the one who's infuriating."

I undress her, ball up the diaper and the clothes and throw the entire bundle away in the diaper container. I try to use the wipes, but the mess is too big and they're just smearing shit everywhere. I pull a thin baby blanket off the shelf and use that instead. Yeah, that got it. I hold a hand across the naked baby and wrap up all the wipes inside the blanket and throw that away, too.

Finally, after two attempts, I get her into a fresh diaper. If I didn't know better, I'd say the kid was smirking at me. "Don't look at me like that. I'm no good at this. It's not my job. How does she make it look so freaking effortless? I have stinky shit all over my hands after thirty seconds with you. She smells like fruit and roses without even trying. I'm sweating like a pig after changing a seven-pound baby. She always looks perfectly put together. What the hell is it with her? And now I'm going crazy, talking to a damn baby. No way am I eating more food now. It would all smell like baby shit."

I pick her up, grab the first outfit I reach in the drawer, and march downstairs, depositing the kid and the clothes into Addy's lap.

"I have to take a shower."

Addy laughs. "If you shower every time you change her, you'll turn into a fish. Just wash your hands, Hawk."

"There isn't enough hand soap to get this smell off me."

I'm almost out of the room when she says, "You're right. I much prefer the smell of fruit and roses."

I turn around and she nods to the baby monitor in the corner. She was listening the whole time. *See—infuriating.*

"I'll be in my office after."

"What a shock. Goodnight, Hawk."

I flick my wrist. "Yeah."

My shower is quick. The whole time, ideas race through my head. Ideas I can't wait to get down on paper. It's been this way for weeks now. It's like this inexorable, potent, infuriating woman has lit some kind of fire under me. And the knowledge that I could never have her is just fanning the flames.

# Chapter Eighteen

*Addison*

"How do you like working at the winery?" I ask my very tall, incredibly muscular date as dinner arrives.

"The Montanas are great," Drake says. "I used to work in Napa Valley. But there was a lot of competition. And the cost of living in California was through the roof."

"I'll bet living in Calloway Creek is a lot different."

"I don't live here. I live in the city."

"Oh, Allie didn't tell me that."

"Well, what *did* she tell you about me?"

"Just that you moved here a few weeks ago to work at the winery. That you were single. That maybe she would have asked you out, but since her dad frowns upon her dating winery workers, she thought she'd set us up."

"Do you go on a lot of blind dates?" he asks.

"No."

"Because of your leg?"

I cock my head. "No, Drake. Not because of my leg."

"Allie didn't tell me about it."

"Why would she?"

He shrugs. "Maybe because some guys would have a problem with it."

He gets the waitress's attention and motions for another round of drinks. I get the feeling this may be a long night. Or possibly a very short one.

"Do you?" I ask. "Have a problem with it?"

"Nah. It's cool. If you weren't wearing a skirt, I'd never even have noticed it."

Our drinks are served. He downs his quickly. I stare at his empty glass knowing at this rate he won't be driving me home. Which kind of stinks because it's raining outside and I'm not too keen on walking the two miles back to Hawk's house.

*Hawk's house.* All through dinner, I can't help but wish I was back there. In his office. Reading the manuscript on his laptop. Why did Adelaide pull the gun? How will they get out of the elevator? What's going to happen between them?

Did he write it because of me? Or is it a coincidence? Adelaide I might be able to wrap my head around. But Addy? And then the elevator? No way. When did he start writing this one? After I became his nanny?

"Sweet house you live in," Drake says. "What does your dad do?"

"He's a plumber. That wasn't my dad's house. I'm a live-in nanny."

"Must be kind of hard chasing after kids all day what with"—his gaze shifts to my leg—"well, you know."

"It's not."

As our dishes are cleared, I pull out my phone and type out a text under the table.

**Me:** What a winner you set me up with. Thanks a ton.

**Allie:** Oh, no. I thought you two would hit it off. He's always nice when I see him at the winery. Want me to call you with some emergency?

**Me:** Not just yet. But maybe.

**Allie:** Say the word and I'll do it.

Drake orders a third round of drinks, making his a double, and then a fourth, despite the fact that I'm still sipping my second glass of wine. Then he asks for the check. "So, what do you want to do now?"

"Something that doesn't involve driving after all the drinks we've had."

"Don't worry your pretty little head. I can hold my liquor. What floats your boat? Movie? Bowling? Dancing?" His gaze falls to my leg again. "Maybe a movie is the best option."

"We could play soccer or go hiking if it weren't raining so hard."

"You can do things like that?"

"I can do a lot of things."

He waggles a brow, obviously thinking I was referring to something else. I rub my palms down my thighs wishing I was anywhere but here. Maybe I *should* have Allie fake some emergency.

The check comes. He stares at it. "So, do we split it down the middle? I'm not sure what you East Coast girls expect, and I don't want to offend you."

I want to tell him that no, we should not split it, because one: he ordered the most expensive steak on the menu while I had a chicken Caesar salad. And two: he ordered twice as many drinks as I wanted without even asking me if I wanted them. Instead of pointing all that out, I put my debit card on the table. "Sure, that's fine."

"Hey, look at that," he says, on our way out. "It stopped raining. Looks like we can play soccer after all."

He winks and I think maybe I've been judging him too harshly. After all, Allie didn't tell him about me being an amputee. He was probably more than a little surprised. And I shouldn't be upset by the fact that most people who don't know me don't think I can do things that people with two meat legs can do. I decide to give him the benefit of the doubt.

"I think a movie would be nice," I say. "The new Tom Cruise movie is playing at the duplex down the street. We can walk."

"Do you, uh... need help?"

"Drake, listen. I have a fake leg. But I can walk. I can even run. I can climb stairs and drive and kick a ball. And I can sure as heck walk two blocks to the movie theater. So if there are any other questions you have about my abilities, let's just get them out of the way right now."

He chuckles. "You're feisty. I like it."

On the way down the sidewalk, a delivery truck turns the corner, one of the wheels catching a pothole full of water, which splashes all over the left side of my body.

"Oh, no!" I race over to a bench and sit. I assess my leg. It's drenched. Right down to the sock covering my silicone liner.

"What's wrong?" he asks.

"My prosthetic can't get wet. Can you go back inside the restaurant and ask for a bunch of napkins or paper towels?"

"Yeah, sure."

This is all I need. Water will break down the material causing more wear and tear on the leg than already exists. I can't afford to have anything go wrong with it.

As Drake heads back to the restaurant, I take off my prosthesis, set it next to me, and remove the soaked-through sock. I roll off the liner to make sure water didn't seep underneath. I'm wringing out the top part of the sock when Drake steps back in front of me. He's holding a handful of paper towels but doesn't give them to me. He's too busy staring at Eileen. Mouth-open staring. In disgust. Like he's witnessing a freak show.

I swallow, fighting tears that burn my throat. "Do you mind?" I ask, holding out my hand.

He hands over the paper towels. "I, uh, didn't think it would look so… weird."

"Is that what women say when they see your tiny pencil dick?"

"Low blow, Addison." He watches as I dry off my prosthetic. "Yeah, so, listen, maybe a movie isn't such a good idea after all."

"You think?"

He thumbs to the parking lot. "I can drive you home."

"You have got to be kidding me. Are you the stupidest jerk alive? I lost my leg in a drunk driving accident, Drake. And *you're* drunk."

"Suit yourself. Take care, Addison."

He leaves. Actually leaves me sitting alone on the bench and walks away. I get out my phone and call the police. "So there's a guy driving a blue Chevy Tahoe down McQuaid Circle. He's swerving all over the road like he's drunk."

I finish drying my leg and wring out my stump sock once more before I put everything back on. I contemplate calling someone to give me a ride. But I don't. I don't because I wouldn't want anyone to see me like this. Embarrassed and broken and humiliated. He was utterly disgusted. The expression on his face was exactly how I thought everyone would look at me right after my accident. Then, with the support of my friends, family, and Lionel, I started to believe people didn't really think I was a freak of nature. I almost had myself convinced.

Drake's Tahoe whizzes by. I salute him with my middle finger. But he doesn't see it. He isn't looking at me. A minute later, I feel marginally vindicated when I see blue and red lights flash at the far end of the street.

I walk the two miles back to Hawk's house promising myself I'll never let anyone set me up again.

~ ~ ~

"Thanks, Cindy." I hand the nineteen-year-old daughter of Mom's friend enough cash to cover the five hours I hired her for even though it's only been two.

Her eyes go wide. "Anytime, Addison. Hey, are you okay?"

I wipe a finger under my eye hoping it catches any smeared mascara. "Fine. It was raining."

"Is her name really Rivington? I thought you might have been pulling my leg or something."

"It is." I hear boisterous laughter dancing all the way up from the back porch. "They didn't bother you, did they?"

"No. Rivington and I pretty much stayed here in her room."

"You don't have to do that."

"I didn't want to get in the way."

I laugh. "I get it. Well, I hope you'll be up for doing this again sometime."

"I'd like that."

"Can you let yourself out?" I nod to the crib. "I just want to check on her."

"Sure. Bye, Addison."

"Call me Addy."

"K." She smiles on her way out.

I lean down and smell Rivi's head. It's like crack cocaine. I can never get enough. I touch her soft hair and may even let out a sigh when her little lips pucker and move in a suckling motion.

"You may have all your limbs," I whisper, "but somehow I'm not sure that's going to make your life any easier."

I take the back stairs and go right for the bottle of wine I keep in the fridge. There isn't much left, a few sips at best. Not nearly enough to forget about Dickhead Drake. How could Allie have been so wrong?

Peeking around the corner to see Hawk and his brothers engrossed in a baseball game on the patio, I slink through the great room over to the bar cart. There are all kinds of bottles lined up on top of the long, sleek marble countertop. Whiskey, vodka, rum, tequila. I'm not a big drinker, so the labels don't mean a whole lot to me, but there is a bottle of Don Julio. It's something I remember Hawk and his brothers ordering when they came to Donovan's. I remove the top and hold it under my nose. Even the smell of it burns. Still, I pull a shot glass from the cabinet below and pour a small amount. Then, I pinch my nose—because I remember Allie telling me if you do it, you won't taste the alcohol as much—and swallow.

I start coughing. Allie was wrong. *Mama Mia, that was strong.*

Next, I pick a bottle of Grey Goose. Mainly because I like the way the bottle looks, but also because you can't go wrong with vodka. It pretty much mixes with anything. Except I'm not mixing. I'm doing shots. By myself. Pathetic.

I down the shot noting it wasn't as harsh as the tequila. And a little sweet. I cock my head and study the pretty bottle. "Hmm. Not too bad."

"At five hundred dollars a bottle, it better not be."

I spin around to see an amused Hawk standing behind me. How long has he been there? I look down at the bottle, feeling guilty. "I'm sorry. I didn't know it was that expensive. I shouldn't have had any." I take the shot glass and head for the kitchen.

"Addy." He follows. "It's okay. You're welcome to it. I just didn't realize you liked that stuff."

"I don't." I open the refrigerator, get a bottle of water, and wash the alcohol taste from my mouth.

He comes closer, nostrils flaring. He takes in my eyes, that are likely puffy, and my clothes, that I should have changed right when I got home. "What happened and whose ass do I have to kick?"

"Nothing happened."

"Bullshit. You're soaking wet, you've been crying, and you just downed several shots of high-end liquor. I'd say that's the very definition of something happening."

He crosses his arms reminding me of my dad and how he used to confront me when I came home past curfew.

When the events of tonight come rushing back, I almost cry again.

"Shit," he says, closing the distance between us. His arm goes around my shoulder and for a moment I'm unsure if it's the heat from his touch or the alcohol that's burning through me.

He walks me to the kitchen table. "Sit. I'll be right back."

Taking deep breaths in his absence, I vow not to let the tears fall. Especially in front of him. I'm sure he already thinks of me as a vulnerable girl—maybe even a charity case based on what he's paying me. Nope, I will not cry. I chug my water.

"Here." The bottle of Grey Goose is placed in front of me along with two shot glasses. He pours two shots and holds his up. "To shitty dates."

I don't pick mine up. "What do you know about shitty dates?"

"Addison, every goddamn date I go on is shitty."

I narrow my brows. "Every one? How is that even possible?"

"It's true. They all want one thing."

Without realizing it, my gaze falls to his crotch. When I catch myself, my cheeks flame.

He laughs heartily. It's the most genuine laugh I've ever heard come from him. And it makes my insides all warm and gooey. Then again, that might be the alcohol.

"Money, Calloway. They all want my money. But I'm amused you think my cock has such a large following."

That has me picking up the tiny glass and gulping down the vodka. Even though it's smoother than the tequila, it still burns on the way down.

"Tell me about your date."

"It's not a big deal."

He stares me down, a mixture of interest and compassion filling his eyes. It makes him seem almost… human.

"He ordered the most expensive thing on the menu and then asked to split the check with me."

"Sounds like a douchebag."

"He made assumptions of what I could and couldn't do because of my leg. And, hey, I get that most people do, so I wasn't going to hold it against him."

"But…?"

"We were walking to the movie theater and a truck went through a puddle and soaked me."

He nods, eyeing my skirt that's still wet. "Damn, that *was* a shitty date."

"That wasn't even the worst part."

He traces the rim of his shot glass with his finger, his jaw tensing. "Tell me."

"I had to take my prosthetic off. All of it. It was wet. I had to wring out the sock and make sure water didn't get in the liner. When he saw my stump he…"

"He what? What did he do?"

I close my eyes. "He looked at me like I was a freak. Then he left."

"Are you fucking kidding me?"

I shake my head, vowing not to cry in front of him.

His finger comes under my chin, lifting my head until I'm looking at him. "You are not a freak." The firm, steady grip of his large palm stills my restless hands on the table.

Instead of agreeing, I pull away and pour myself another shot. I drink it, then get up and go for the stairs. "I'm going to bed. And you should get back to your brothers."

"Addy?"

I turn.

"Anyone who would think that of you isn't worth wasting one goddamn tear over."

"Yeah, I know."

It's a lie. I *don't* know. How many people out there think the way Drake does? How many think it but never say it? Maybe I've been kidding myself this entire time believing that somewhere out there are men who would want a woman that isn't a whole woman.

That they wouldn't be disgusted when my stump touches them under the covers. Or when they see me naked.

I know I'm being ridiculous. Drake wasn't the first person to have such a reaction to my leg. And he certainly won't be the last. I thought I had thick skin. A stronger spine. I guess I was wrong.

I make it all the way to the top of the stairs and around the corner before more tears fall.

Suddenly, strong arms wrap around me. Hawk is pulling me toward him, looking down on me almost like I'm a goddess and not the freak Drake thought I was. He wipes the wetness from under my eyes. And when he cups the sides of my face with his hands, his icy-blue eyes spear me with a gaze so strikingly possessive it could carve a woman to pieces. I'm melting into his arms as if I belong there. As if it's somewhere I've always wanted to be. Somewhere safe. I ignore the faint voice in the back of my head that tells me it's not. It couldn't possibly be.

"Holy shit you're gorgeous," he says, right before his lips crash down on mine.

My head is swirling. With his words. With the alcohol. With the feel of his tongue sweeping into my mouth. Blood rushes through my ears, pounding with every heartbeat. The heat of his hands on my face, my neck, the small of my back, is toxic in the best of ways. I'm held tightly against him as his lips continue to press against mine. I'm a willing participant in what I can only describe as a fantasy. He's forbidden. The enemy. Dark and dangerous. But maybe that's why I crave him the way I do. Because he's someone I can't have.

He tenses as if realizing what he's done. What we're doing.

When he pulls away, I want to protest. But I don't. I won't give him the satisfaction.

His hands rake through his hair as he paces down the hall and back, finally pausing at the top of the steps, looking as guilty as I've ever seen a man. "I shouldn't have done that." He stops halfway down the stairs but doesn't look back. "Please don't quit."

When he's gone, a million thoughts bombard me all at once. My butt slides against the wall until it meets the floor. Only a few thoughts remain front and center. Because two things just happened that have never happened before.

Hawk McQuaid kissed the shit out of me.

And he said please.

# Chapter Nineteen

*Hawk*

I'm up earlier than normal, but I lay in bed, listening. Is she still here? Did she pack her things and leave in the middle of the night? She should have. She should have run far and fast. Addison Calloway needs someone like me like she needs another limb to go missing.

What was I thinking kissing her?

For the first time, I wish there was one of those baby monitors in my bedroom. That way I could hear what's going on upstairs.

I pull on sweats and pad my way to the kitchen. When I see the back of her head, a relieved breath gushes out of me. And I'm... *happy?* I almost laugh. Happiness is not a word I'd use to describe myself.

Coffee is percolating. I pour myself a cup in the silent room. Leaning against the counter, I watch.

She must know I'm here. I'm making noise. But she doesn't move. Doesn't turn.

Rivington appears on her shoulder. Addy pats her back gently. My insides are being torn in fifty different directions. I barely slept at all last night. I couldn't stop thinking about her. Her lips. The soft curve of her neck. Her tears.

I wanted to rip a hole in the gut of the man who made her cry. I wanted to carry her to my bed and show her how a real man treats a woman.

*A real man.* Is that what I am? I use women. Or rather, I let them use me.

A real man would take responsibility for his kid. A real man might value people over money.

I'm about as far from a real man as you can get.

Convinced she's going to ignore me from here on out, I take my coffee and go out on the patio. It's not often I'm up early enough to see the sun come up. It's strange. But at the same time, oddly beautiful.

The door opens behind me. I don't turn around. I choose not to start my day with her looking at me like the jackass I am.

In my periphery, I see her walk to the couch, sit, put her feet up, and sip her coffee.

Neither one of us speaks.

The silence is deafening.

"I'm not going to quit," she says, finally.

I nod. "Good."

"But, what *was* that?"

"That?" I ask, like I don't know exactly what she's referring to.

"Were you drunk?"

I take a drink of coffee. "Were *you?*"

"Obviously. Did you not see the four shots I took? And that was after the two glasses of wine I had at the restaurant."

Regret works its way up my spine. I can't even look at her. If I do, I'll see those incredible eyes that make me want to do unthinkable things to her, those pouty lips that make my dick stand at attention. She's my nanny. The sister of my enemy. I shouldn't think of her as anything else, no matter how much my brain tries to take me there.

"You should quit," I say, walking to the door.

"Why?"

I put my hand on the knob and pause. Then I tell as much of a truth as I've ever told. "Because if you don't, I can't guarantee it won't happen again."

I refill my cup, go to my office, and lift the lid of my laptop.

~ ~ ~

A knock on my office door has me grumbling. I was on a roll. I've never written so much in one sitting. Words have been flowing out of me all morning. When I don't say anything, the door opens. My grandfather glares. I shut the laptop.

"How's your new nanny working out?" he asks.

"As good as can be expected. But I'm sure you know that already."

"She's still here, so that's something."

"I guess."

He crosses the room and hands me a slip of paper. "Your itinerary for next weekend."

"Come again?"

"It's time you take that daughter of yours on her first trip."

"That's ridiculous. She's not even old enough to know where she is."

"Even so. It's part of the agreement." He takes the seat across from me, leans in, and taps a finger on the itinerary. "You'll go to Martha's Vineyard. I've rented you a beachfront house in West Tisbury. You'll fly out Thursday night and back Sunday afternoon."

"You want me to fly with a baby?"

"The tickets are for two with a lap infant. Take Addison."

Last night's kiss flashes through my head. "Uh, no."

"Suit yourself then and go it alone."

*Fuck.*

"If I refuse?"

"You won't."

I turn the itinerary upside down on the desk then nod to my laptop. "Do you mind? I have work."

"Your father tells me you've been working from home more frequently. In my day, you had to sell cars and have meetings in person. I'm not so sure I like all this technology mumbo jumbo."

"Yup. Sure does make it easy."

He stands and stares. "Unless there are other things keeping you from going to the office. Little eight-pound things perhaps?"

"Pappy, I know you think you're going to win this bet. You aren't. I'm keeping up my end, but both of us know why."

He works his upper lip with a finger. "Hmm. Guess we'll see. Now that pretty little thing out there offered to make me lunch, so excuse me while I go take a meal with a beautiful lady. And the nanny's not half bad either." He chuckles at his joke.

Thirty minutes later, I can't take it anymore. Pappy and Addison have been laughing almost nonstop. I go out into the great room and listen.

"Next time, you must bring Rose," Addy says. "I know she loves kids."

"If I knew how hospitable you were going to be, I'd have brought her with me today. But hospitality is not something I expect when I come to this house."

"He can be brusque."

Pappy laughs. "If that's your way of telling me my grandson is a jackass, you don't have to sugarcoat it. I'm well aware. And I'm sorry to say the apple hasn't fallen too far from the family tree. I was just like him once."

"But you changed."

"Took a lotta years. And if I wish anything for my grandchildren it's that they find happiness at a far younger age than I did."

"Is that why you're making him raise Rivi? You think somehow it will make him happy?"

"Rivi? Is that what you call her? I like it. It suits her. It's a spunky nickname. And somehow I get the feeling she's got spunk, just like you do. But to answer your question, sometimes you have to take risks to get what you want, young lady."

"Risk? How is forcing him to raise her risky? Are you afraid for her?"

"Let's just say not in the way you might think. I suppose I'm more afraid for him. I know what it's like to be surrounded by people yet still be lonely."

"And you think if someone forced your hand at a young age, you'd have turned out differently?"

"That's a tricky question. You see, if things had turned out differently for me, I wouldn't be with Rose. That woman is the light of my life. I think maybe all the things in my life happened for a reason."

I just know Addy is looking down at her prosthetic wondering if his statement is true. It's not. Things don't happen because of some predetermined fate. Things happen because of dumb luck. I lean against the wall. Or sheer stupidity.

"Well, I mustn't keep Rose waiting. Thank you for lunch and the pleasant conversation. What a delight it must be for Hawk to have you around."

I swear I'd give my left nut to see her face right now.

"Don't let that grandson of mine rub off on you too much. You're good for him. You're good for *her*." I hear chair legs scrape the floor. "And good luck next weekend. I dare say all three of you are going to need it."

"What's next weekend?" she asks.

"I'll let Hawk tell you." He chuckles. He's enjoying this. Me being his goddamn puppet. Him pulling all the strings. It makes me all the more determined not to let him win.

And just to prove a point, I collect my keys and head out the door to go to work.

# Chapter Twenty

*Addison*

We've tiptoed around each other all week. And he's definitely not happy about having to go out of town today. I searched up the house Tucker rented. Well, house is a bit of an overstatement, it's more like a cottage. A far cry from the sprawling mansion Hawk is accustomed to.

I'm not sure how I feel about being in such close proximity for three entire days. Especially when he's done nothing but ignore me and hide away in his office. It's even worse than before. Maybe he doesn't trust himself around me. He obviously regrets the kiss. Not to mention he's probably dreading this weekend more than a root canal.

I drop a second suitcase by the garage door. Hawk eyes it. "We're not leaving for a month, just three days."

Pointing to the larger one, I explain, "Babies require a lot of stuff. You never know what she might need."

"She eats, sleeps, and shits. There's not much to it."

"Says the man who hasn't lifted a finger to take care of her. There's a lot more to Rivi than that."

He huffs his annoyance, but at least he no longer corrects me when I use her nickname. In fact, he hasn't picked a fight with me at all this week. Strange for a guy who seems to thrive on confrontation.

I strap Rivi into her car seat. "I guess we'd better get going so we don't miss the flight."

"What a shame that would be."

Sitting in the back of the SUV with Rivington, I mentally go over everything in my head, hoping I haven't forgotten to pack anything. I've never been to Martha's Vineyard before.

A few times, I catch Hawk looking at me in the rearview mirror. His eyes don't give much away, however. Is he wondering how he's going to survive the weekend with a woman he's trying to avoid and a baby he doesn't seem to want?

At the White Plains airport, we pull right up to the departure area and Hawk hands off his keys. Who knew they had valet parking?

When we approach the security checkpoint, Hawk looks down at my leg.

"Don't worry," I say. "They won't make me take it off. But they will have to touch it and wand me."

"I wasn't worried," he says.

When they pull me aside, Hawk looks irritated. He glances at the people looking my way then stands next to me, like he's trying to block the view of curious onlookers. Maybe he's embarrassed that I've been singled out.

"What the hell are you looking at?" he spews at a group of teens who slow down and turn their heads to stare as they pass us. "Move the fuck along."

"It's not a big deal," I tell him as the female officer checks out my leg. "And who knows what I might be hiding in here?"

The lady scolds me with her eyes.

"Kidding," I say, but I can tell she's not amused.

"What happened to your leg?" a boy asks as we walk away from the security checkpoint.

I set Rivi back in her stroller and lean down and knock on my prosthetic. "I wanted to be a pirate."

His eyes go wide.

I lift a devious brow. "You should see me when I'm wearing my peg leg."

"I'm so sorry," the boy's mother says, rushing over to fetch him. She drags him away, yelling at him not to be mean to crippled people.

Hawk shakes his head. "Well this is getting off to a great start."

An hour later, when I'm sitting in an airplane seat larger than Dad's Barcalounger, I find myself almost looking forward to the weekend.

I lean over. "I've never been in first class before."

"Yeah? Well I've never flown in steerage. Just try and keep her quiet. People can't stand it when babies cry on planes."

"You mean *you* can't stand it."

"Oh my gosh, your baby is gorgeous," a flight attendant gushes. "How old is she?"

When Hawk doesn't answer, I say, "Almost four weeks."

"She's got her daddy's eyes and her mother's nose."

"Uh, she's not—"

"I'll have a whiskey," Hawk says. "And my *wife* will have a club soda." He lowers his voice. "She can't hold her liquor, and she's already nursing a horrible hangover. She almost got the kid drunk last night, because, you know." He fake grabs his chest like he has breasts. "So she really needs to lay off the sauce."

My jaw goes slack. I haven't had a drop of alcohol since last weekend. Two can play at this game. "We mustn't forget *you're* the one who spiked my drinks," I say. I put a hand next to my mouth as if telling a secret to the flight attendant. "With his offensive body odor, it's the only way I'll let him touch me."

The flight attendant takes a step back. Her eyes ping-pong between us.

Hawk smirks. "I'm not about to be the only one in our house who showers, babe. Honestly, since this one arrived, have you even brushed your teeth?"

I huff in his face, giving him a large dose of coffee breath. "You know, I just can't remember. Here, *babe.*" I set Rivi on his lap. "You take her while I catch up on my sleep. You'll wake me when we land?"

He stares me down. Will he break character? He settles Rivi into his arms and looks back at the flight attendant. "Better make it two whiskeys." When the woman leaves, he turns to me. "Well played," he says, trying to hand his daughter back to me.

"Can you hold her for a minute?" I pick up my purse and sift through it. "I know her ear plugs are in here somewhere."

"Can you hurry? She's starting to squirm."

"She'll squirm a lot more if I don't find the ear plugs. Babies can't make their ears pop like we can. I ordered special plugs that will regulate the pressure for her."

"They make shit like that?"

"Yes, Hawk, they make shit like that. They make a lot of shit that's useful for infants if you cared enough to research it. What are you going to do if I ever get sick and you have to care for her for more than ten minutes?"

He shrugs. "That's what Mom and Holland are for."

"You really want her to grow up thinking her dad doesn't care about her?"

He looks past me and out the window, not bothering to answer. I find the plugs and take Rivi back, having a pacifier handy in case she needs that, too. Luckily the flight isn't much more than an hour. By noon, I'll be laying on the beach. My head falls back against the headrest. "Oh, no."

Hawk's eyebrows go up in question.

"My bikini." I close my eyes. "I was so intent on making sure I had everything for Rivi that I completely forgot to pack it."

"You think this is a vacation?"

"Well, yes."

"It's not. It's a test. Tucker is making sure I'm following his rules. I plan to buy myself a very large bottle of Tequila and sleep my way until Sunday."

"Suit yourself. But I plan on enjoying it. The beach. The sunrise. How can anyone take things like that for granted?"

The flight attendant drops off our drinks, giving us the side-eye as she quickly retreats.

Hawk pours one of the miniature whiskey bottles into a glass and downs it, licking his lips. "Just like this."

Rivington is a model passenger for the entire flight. I think she likes the noise and vibration. I'm not sure why, but I wish she would scream her head off just to annoy the grump in the seat next to me. It would serve him right.

The second we took off, he put in his earbuds. He hasn't said a word since. I wonder if this is how the entire weekend will go. What am I thinking? Clearly this is how the weekend will go.

Two hours later, we're in a rental car driving to the cottage. When he pulls in the driveway, he checks his phone. "This can't be the right address."

"It is. I googled it."

"Why in the hell would Tucker rent this shithole?"

"It's actually quite charming. I did a virtual tour. Wait until you see the back porch. They claim the wooden swing is the best place on the island to watch the sun rise."

He turns off the car. "Let's get this over with."

"Rivi needs a change. You'll get the bags?"

At the front door, I input the door code. 4865. "How perfectly normal," I mutter.

"What's that?"

"Oh, nothing. Just that it's obvious an adolescent didn't program this keypad."

He hauls our luggage inside. I take Rivi and the diaper bag into the living room, taking a moment to admire the view before changing her. The deck seems almost as large as the house. And beyond it, cattails line a sandy pathway to the beach. I'm excited just looking at it.

"There's only one goddamn bathroom," Hawk says.

"I think you can slum it for three days."

"The bedrooms are small."

"It could be worse," I say. "There could have been only one of those as well."

For a moment, we make eye contact. Something passes between us. I'm just trying to figure out if it's disappointment or relief.

After changing Rivi, I tour the cottage, noting a crib has been set up in the larger of the two bedrooms. I'll bet Hawk is chaffed over that. The kitchen is small, but well-stocked. His grandfather did a great job making sure we had lots of food options. I eye the two bottles of tequila on the counter that we stopped for on the way. *Two.* I guess he wasn't kidding about how he planned to spend the weekend.

"What do you think, Rivi?" I ask when I walk onto the deck. "This is paradise if I've ever seen it." I get out my phone and take a selfie.

I glance through my most recent pictures. Almost all of them are photos of Rivi. Or Rivi and me. With that gorgeous face, it's hard not to record every moment of her life.

"I can't wait until you're smiling," I tell her. "You're going to be a heartbreaker, aren't you? Can I tell you a secret? You don't have to be like your Aunt Holland to get a man. I love her to death, but sometimes I worry she's going to end up pregnant or with an STD. Don't ever let a guy pressure you. There is nothing wrong with waiting until you meet the right one. Take it from someone who's still waiting. Got it?"

I laugh. She's not even looking at me, she's watching a cattail blow in the breeze.

A deck board creaks and I turn to see Hawk leaning against the side railing looking pensive. I mentally palm my face. Did he hear me? "I, uh… I'm going to feed her and put her down for a nap." I walk past him without looking up, feeling completely mortified.

Then again, he's not laughing or making snide comments like I'd expect had he heard me. I breathe a small sigh of relief.

After Rivi's bottle, I sing her a song until she falls asleep. Then I quietly unpack our things. When I come across my undergarments, I run my hand over the black boy shorts underwear. Then I pick through the others until I find my black bra. I glance out the window, looking up and down the beach.

There are very few people. A family a few houses down. A guy walking his dog. It's pretty isolated.

I undress and slip on the two black pieces, look at myself in the mirror, and conclude it just might be able to pass for a bathing suit. In the hall closet, I find a beach towel. I grab my phone and the baby monitor and head outside.

Hawk is sitting on the swinging bench, slumped over like he wants to be anywhere but here, and he's sipping what I can only imagine is tequila. I drop the baby monitor in his lap.

"Where are you going?" he asks, clearly annoyed that I would have the gall to do what I did.

"Beach."

Finally, he looks up from his glass. His shoulders square as his predatory eyes give me a once over. He focuses on my bra, tracing the lacy outline with his stare. Then his gaze drops to my stomach, his eyes stopping when he sees my belly button piercing. The heat of his eyes burns into me. They go lower, practically caressing my body until they land on my boy shorts. I've never been so offended yet turned on at the same time. I'm not sure if I should call him out on his blatant ogling or high-five myself.

"Wearing *that?* No."

"Don't be such a prude, Hawk. Nobody is out there. Even if they were, you can't tell me what to do."

He sips his drink. "Whatever." He holds out the monitor. "But take this."

"The signal won't reach."

"Then take her."

"She's sleeping."

"So she can sleep on the beach."

"And get a sunburn? Hawk, I'll be fifty feet away. Besides, navigating the sand with my leg will be hard enough without holding Rivi. I wouldn't want to drop her." I throw the towel over my shoulder. "She'll probably sleep for an hour. I'll be back around then. Or better yet, if she wakes, take her for a walk."

As I make my way down the sandy path through the dunes, it belatedly dawns on me that all the while when he was looking at me, he never once looked at my leg. The urge to glance behind me is strong—I'd love to know if he's watching me—but I don't. I'm trying to make sure I don't fall flat on my face and make a fool of myself.

Somehow, though, I know he *is* watching. I can *feel* his eyes on me. And I'm not sure I like how much I enjoy it.

Later, when I spare a glance back at the cottage, I see him still on the deck. Only he's not looking at me, he's typing on his laptop. He's completely preoccupied with what he's doing, as if nothing else exists. It makes me wonder just what he's writing. Is he writing about Jensen and Adelaide? Did she shoot him? How did they escape the elevator? Did they kiss, and if so, was it as good as the one we had Saturday night? The one I haven't stopped thinking about.

He said it might happen again. Then he avoided me like the plague. I turn away and gaze over the ocean, trying to put the mercurial man out of my thoughts, but having a damn hard time doing it.

~ ~ ~

With Rivi down for her evening nap, I take a glass of wine (courtesy of Tucker McQuaid) out on the deck and sit on the swing. It's chilly outside, being that it's September and the sun has gone down. I pull my cardigan around my shoulders and stare out across the water thinking this has to be the most peaceful place in the world.

The sliders open. Hawk appears. For a second, I think he might sit next to me.

"Going for a walk," he says instead.

"Have fun."

He cocks his head at my statement as if having fun is something he doesn't know how to do. It dawns on me that he might not. I've only been living in the man's house for a few weeks so I can't be sure, but I've never seen him genuinely happy. The man rarely even smiles. What a miserable existence.

He walks down the sandy path and out of view. I glance around the deck. There are fairy lights hanging from a pergola overhead. One might even say it's romantic. *Me*—I might say that—if I were here with anyone other than Grumpy Grumperson.

With my foot, I give myself a push and swing gently back and forth. My mind wanders as I sip the wine. Where is he going? And why? The moon isn't even out yet. It's dark. What if he can't find his way back? Did he take his phone?

Different scenarios play out in my head. Him calling me for help. Him leaving, never to return to the life he doesn't want. Him walking back up the path, taking me into his arms and kissing me stupid.

I cast the thoughts from my head, not needing to feed my inappropriate fantasies about my boss who is the last man I should be fantasizing about.

Then I have another thought—one about him being buried in his laptop all day. What was he writing?

I take a gulp of wine, stand, glance down the beach (even though I can't see beyond the dunes), and head into the cottage. It doesn't take me long to find what I'm looking for. He left his laptop sitting on the coffee table. It's closed, but it's there. Calling to me. And if he didn't want me looking at it he should have put it in the bedroom.

I open the lid, keeping one eye on the sliders, and enter the code. Scanning his desktop folders, I click on the one labeled *'Book.'* Inside it, I don't see the file *'book draft'* like before. I do, however, see one titled *'Forbidden Fruit.'*

My pulse races as I click on the folder and open the file. I have no idea how long he'll be gone. I'll need to read quickly. I pick up where I left off last time and become engrossed in his writing. This book is nothing like what I read of the other three locked away in his drawer. This is... good. *Really good*. I'd almost go so far as to say it's a romance, not a thriller. A romantic suspense novel perhaps. And Jensen and Adelaide are the perfect example of enemies to lovers. The sexual tension between the two is off the charts, and I'm only on page three. Adelaide is some sort of operative who's been sent to get information on Jensen. They clearly have the hots for each other. She's hesitant to report back to her superiors. He's trying not to fall for her.

I check the time, knowing I'm pushing my luck. I should wait until we go home and he's away at work. Then, just before I close the file, I spot the word *cock* and my heart stops. Because when I read the word, I hear *him* saying it in my head. And in my head, he's whispering it in my ear. His voice is rough and sexy and sweet all at the same time. As I read what Jensen is doing to Adelaide with his cock, I feel my insides turning into mushy goo. Because suddenly, I want to be Adelaide. I want him to throw me against the wall, rip off my clothes and make me come as hard as she did. I want him to claim me like I'm a harlot in heat, not a lily-white virgin.

A noise from outside has me quickly closing the file and shutting the laptop. I lie on the couch and pretend to be sleeping.

I hear the door open. Footsteps become louder as he approaches me. They stop. Silence. Hairs on my neck prickle. Is he looking at me? Can he tell I'm breathing heavily? Not just from almost being caught, but from the words I read that are still swirling in my head. I try to remain perfectly still and control my unsteady breaths.

I startle when fingers brush against my forehead, sweeping a chunk of hair away. I stretch, eyes closed, as if waking. Footsteps take him away. I open my eyes. He's gone. And so is the laptop.

~ ~ ~

*A bright light appears. Too bright to look into, yet I can all the same. There's a person there. Is it God? Brighter now, I'm being pulled in. I want to go and not go. It's the worst kind of torture, being torn apart by a decision that doesn't seem under my control. When I can't stand it any longer, I scream.*

Arms come around me. "Addy."

The light is gone. Darkness surrounds me. I'm at the cottage. And Hawk is… *sitting on my bed?*

"Oh my gosh," I say, realizing what just happened. "Rivi?"

"Sleeping. You okay?"

I nod, but I'm not sure he can see it. Only the dim light of the moon filters into the room. It's enough, however, that I can tell he's shirtless. It does nothing to calm my breathing.

His hand is on my shoulder. "You're shaking."

"Bad dream."

He blows out a long breath. "I have those sometimes."

"You do?" His chest is inches from my face. In a bold move, I reach out and touch his scar. "Because of this?"

He flinches when I touch it, but he doesn't move. "Yes."

"What happened?"

"I had a sternotomy due to an aortic aneurysm."

I chuckle. "That's a lot of words I don't know."

"I was in a minor car accident when I was thirteen. I was cleared medically. Nobody knew my aortic wall had gotten bruised. I was fine for a while but then suddenly had difficulty breathing and I passed out. The next thing I knew I was waking up in the hospital and had this massive scar down my chest. I was lucky. A lot of people die from ruptured aneurysms."

"Amber's dad saved you, didn't he?"

"He did."

"Which is why you don't totally hate her even though she sides with us Calloways."

"I guess. And just for the record, I don't hate *all* the Calloways."

I realize my hand is still on his chest. But I don't move it. It feels nice there. Surprisingly, he doesn't seem to mind it much either. I wonder if it's light enough in here for him to read my eyes. Because if he could, he'd know I was looking at him the way Jensen was looking at Adelaide.

"I showed you mine, now you show me yours."

My hand falls away and I stiffen. "You want to see Eileen?"

"Who's Eileen?"

"My stump."

"You named it? And why Eileen?"

I wait to see if he gets it. He laughs incredulously when he does.

"You can't be serious," he says, his tone both shocked and playful.

"Well, I do lean quite a bit when I'm not wearing my prosthetic."

"Addison, I've never met a person who is so blasé about something so life altering."

"It's better than wallowing in self-pity, wouldn't you agree?"

"You may not pity yourself, but you do have nightmares. I want to see what causes them. This isn't the first time. I've heard you before."

This is news. I know I have nightmares. Some are about the lights. Some are about waking up without my leg. Others are about dying. I remember Jaxon telling me once that you can't die in your dreams or else you really die. It's not true. I die in my dreams. Frequently. But I had no idea Hawk could hear me in his massive house. Maybe through the baby monitor in Rivi's room across the hall.

"I was dreaming about bright lights."

"Lights?"

"They're coming right at me. The therapist I saw after my accident said many people who lost a lot of blood like I did have near death experiences. I guess that's what it was. But, I don't know, sometimes it seems more like... headlights."

A hand scrubs across his face. "Jesus."

"Maybe," I joke. "Or maybe it's God. I can't really say."

He doesn't laugh. Maybe he had a near death experience too.

The silence grows between us. Neither of us moves. For a minute I feel like we're bonding over our scars. I swallow as his warm breath skims the hairs on my arm. I think he's looking at me, but the moonlight is behind him. His eyes are dark pools. Pools I want to dive into no matter how dangerous they may be. He's off limits to me. I'm forbidden to him. But none of that matters. My body tingles at our closeness and I've never wanted to be kissed as much as I do right now. Because I know what his lips feel like. I've had a taste. He's the crack cocaine I want to the bottom of my soul. Even though I know it could destroy me.

"So, you're not going to introduce me to Eileen?" he asks.

He has no idea the moment he just ruined. I pull the covers tightly over me. "I think it's your morbid curiosity."

"How bad can it be?"

I turn away. "I... don't want to."

Drake's reaction floods my memories. I couldn't stand it if Hawk looked at me the way Drake did. With disgust. I know I shouldn't care about how he looks at me. How he thinks about me. But I do. And all I can do is think about him. If I'm being honest, I haven't stopped thinking about him all week.

His hand cradles my chin and urges my face back in his direction. "I'm not that guy, Addy. I might be an asshole, but I wouldn't sink to that level."

"Even so…"

"Don't show me then. I don't care what's under the covers." I can feel his eyes trace the outline of my curves beneath the blanket. "Well, maybe I do." His thumb brushes against my neck. "*Fuck.*" He springs off the bed.

"What's the matter?"

"You." He backs away. "You're what's the matter. You should run far. Because I'm not sure how much longer I can keep my hands off you."

I want to tell him he doesn't have to. That he can have me right here, right now. That my heart is pounding so hard *I'm* the one who might need a sternotomy.

Sound comes from across the room. Rivi is waking for her two o'clock feeding. I sit up, ready to put on my leg and fetch her. He crosses the room and flips on the light in the hallway. "I've got this."

"Are you sure?" I ask, stunned.

"Go back to sleep, Addy."

When he turns to walk to the crib, I catch his silhouette. His erection is all but poking out of his sleep pants. He does nothing to hide it. Or perhaps he thinks I can't see it. He reaches down for her. "Come on, Riv."

*Riv?*

I watch him cradle her as he leaves the room, wondering how it's possible that this is the same man I arrived here with earlier. The coldhearted grump who's been my boss for weeks. The callous tyrant who not only hates Calloways, but kids too.

And as I listen to him mumble to her as he fixes a bottle, I wonder how it's possible that he's the man I think I just fell in love with.

# Chapter Twenty-one

*Hawk*

I top off my coffee and gaze out the window. Not at the sunrise. At *her* watching it. Her hair is held haphazardly in a bun with strands coming out every which way. I'm sure she hasn't bothered with makeup yet, it's too early. She doesn't need it anyway. Her eyes are closed, her chin tilted up as her face catches the first rays of light. She looks more at peace than anyone I've ever seen.

But she's not at peace. Her nightmares prove it.

And she sees headlights. Fucking headlights. I turn away feeling as guilty as I deserve.

When her phone rings, she answers immediately. "What's up, Tag? You're up early."

"What the hell are you doing in Martha's Vineyard?" Tag's voice thunders through the speaker.

I stand next to the window and peek out. I shouldn't listen, but I do anyway.

Her body stiffens. "I, uh... how did you know? Are you tracking me?" She taps around on her phone. "I'm too old for that. I turned it off."

"Turn it back on," he demands.

"Quit treating me like I'm a child."

"You didn't answer the question, Addison."

She's silent.

"Damn it, you're there with *him*, aren't you?"

"As Rivi's nanny, yes."

"But he's there too."

"Yes."

"Why would you go there? Why would *he*? Doesn't he hate his kid?"

I strain to hear if she's going to tell him about my agreement with Pappy. Has she already? She's close with her brothers. Maybe even closer than we are with Holland. I wonder just how much they know about my situation.

"Calm down, Tag. It's just a weekend getaway. And he doesn't hate her. He's just not used to her yet."

She's defending me. I lean against the wall, a satisfied grin stretching across my face.

"Damn it, Addy. Are you sleeping with him?"

Now *my* body stiffens. I'm on full alert waiting to hear what she'll say. "That would be none of your business now, would it?"

I almost laugh out loud. I'd give anything to be a fly on the wall in that dickwad's house right now. He fires off a string of expletives, causing Addy to take him off speaker and walk to the other side of the porch. I can no longer hear what she's saying, but I can read her body language. The body language that tells me she's on my side, not his. She's a Calloway, yet she's defending a McQuaid. The South Pole has just become Polar North.

I was so busy not wanting to come here that I didn't think of all the ramifications this weekend would have. I suspect I may have a lot of shit to clean up when we get back in town. I won't be surprised if Tag and his brothers are waiting at the airport with reinforcements ready to hang me up by my ball sack.

But that's a problem for another day. Right now, I'm still stunned that the gorgeous woman on the porch would even dare to defy her brothers. And a woman is exactly what she is. Somehow over the past weeks she's gone from being the little brown-nosing Calloway sister to... *Addy*.

She turns around and almost catches me watching her before I hastily get out of view and round the corner to the kitchen.

She'll come in for breakfast soon. It's always the same thing: scrambled eggs on toast. I open the refrigerator and stare. How hard could it be?

Fifteen minutes later, the kitchen is a mess, but at least I think I've made something edible.

Giggles come from behind me. I briefly close my eyes at the sound. If I could only hear that on a constant reel. I turn nonchalantly. She doesn't need to know that a short time ago I was studying her like she's part of my portfolio. "Hey."

Her lips turn up. "Hey yourself." She's wearing a sleep T-shirt that falls just below her thighs, the large throw blanket from the couch wrapped around her. One side of the blanket falls open and I see words on her shirt. I stride over. When I move the other side of the blanket, her breath catches. Does she think I'm going to kiss her?

We had a moment last night. Not to mention the one we had last week. Is she expecting more? Does she want it?

*Do I?* My hand brushes against her breast. She looks up into my eyes. *Of course I fucking do.*

She's Tag's sister, I remind myself.

"Your shirt," I say, clearing my throat. "I wanted to read it." Then I laugh when I do. It reads: *Some assembly required.*

Addison is like a coin. On one side, she's a bright and cheery person who doesn't seem to have a care in the world. On the other, though, there's a vulnerability she works hard to hide. But I see it.

"You made breakfast?" Her brows narrow. "What gives? And why are you so happy? You're never happy in the morning. Or… *ever.*" She eyes my coffee mug. "Irish coffee?"

I back away. "Sit." I pull out a plate, shovel food onto it, then place it in front of her. "I hope they aren't too runny."

She picks up her fork. "Thank you. This is very nice of you."

"Don't thank me yet. You haven't tasted them."

"I was taught to never complain when someone else cooks."

For a moment, I wonder what it was like growing up in a house without money. A house where maybe you weren't even sure if there was going to be enough food on the table.

"They're good," she says.

I hope she's not just saying it. I can't even describe the feeling inside me that was utterly paralyzing when she pressed her hand to my chest last night. For some reason, I want to please this woman. In every way possible. Even though nothing can come of it. Addy is light and I'm shrouded by darkness. She sees only the good in people. Somehow, she even sees good in me. But I know she wouldn't be looking at me the way she is if she knew everything there was to know about me. Women like her—honorable women—don't end up with guys like me.

"You aren't eating?"

I lift my mug. "This is my breakfast."

She pauses mid-bite. "You made eggs just for me?"

"Thought you might be tired after last night."

"I... just... wow."

"It's not a proposal, Calloway. It's just eggs."

She smiles. "Are there more?"

I fetch the pan and deposit the rest onto her plate. "I've never seen such a small person put away so much food."

"I need more calories than you'd think, especially given part of me is missing. But that's exactly why I need them. Being an amputee means the rest of my body has to work harder."

"You call yourself an amputee?"

"Amputee isn't a bad word, Hawk. It's who I am. I'm a woman, a sister, a daughter, and an amputee."

I smirk. "And a nanny."

The giggle returns. My cock likes it.

"Yes, and a nanny. Speaking of which, thank you for feeding her last night."

I shrug. "I was due. And I didn't need you reporting back to my grandfather that I'm shirking my duties."

"What's with the two of you? Why does he have all these rules you have to follow? I get that he's trying to make you bond with Rivi, but do you think he'd seriously disinherit you if you didn't change diapers?"

"If you're asking that, you don't know Tucker McQuaid very well."

"He seemed nice when we talked last week."

"That's because you aren't related to him."

"Or maybe it's because I'm actually nice to him."

Rivington cries in the front bedroom. "That's my queue to leave," I say, collecting my laptop. "I'll be outside."

On the back porch, I sit on the swing, set down my coffee on the side table, open the lid to my laptop, and read what I wrote last night. I wrote a lot. Five chapters. Words were flowing out of me faster than I could type them. I never did go back to bed—thus the five cups of coffee.

As I read, I hear Addy talking to Rivington. Then I hear her singing to her. Then I start thinking about that short sleep shirt she's wearing and what she looked like yesterday on the beach in her bra and underwear. Before I even realize it, my fingers fly across the keys of the laptop, writing all the emotions I imagine normal people have. Emotions I feel when I look at her. Hell, when I *think* of her.

I write all the things I'd like to do to her. And how she'd feel when I'd do them. I write about the subtle nuances of her face when she looks at me. The sexy body language she doesn't even know she exudes. The sound of her throaty mewls when I would make her come.

I've got a full-on boner tenting my sweatpants. I set aside my laptop and sneak into the house, ready to do something about it in the shower. But I run right into Addy on my way. Her eyes go straight to my crotch. With a red face, she turns away.

"I, uh… sorry," she mutters, rushing into her bedroom and shutting the door.

In the shower, I stroke myself the way Adelaide stroked Jensen. I think about the shirt again. The quasi-bikini. The kiss. Addison Calloway is without a doubt the sexiest woman I've ever met. Which is strange because I've never thought about moms as being sexy.

Wait… she's not a mom. *I'm* a dad. I start going soft as reality strikes. Somewhere along the line I stopped thinking about Rivington as mine and more as hers. She's the one raising her. For all intents and purposes, Riv *is* hers. Except she's not.

And I wonder what Addy will do when the year is up and Rivington goes away. But I don't have to wonder for long, because I know what she'll do. She'll hate me. Just like everyone else will.

*Fuck.*

I sink down and sit on the edge of the tub knowing I've gotten myself into quite a situation.

# Chapter Twenty-two

*Addison*

Something changed the other day when he made breakfast. He was different. But then as quickly as it came, it went. After I saw his erection and ran away, he went back to being his old self. Locked away in the tiny bedroom tapping on his laptop or walking the beach alone.

I thought we had a connection. A breakthrough of sorts. But the temperamental man sitting in first class to my right with earbuds in is anything but the valiant guy who rescued me from my dream and made breakfast.

Rivi fusses more on this flight. When she starts crying, Hawk looks irritated. He glances around to see if others are too. Unlike the last flight, he's not playful. He barely even looks at me or Rivi. Finally, he turns up the volume on his music and reclines his seat, acting just like the asshole everyone thinks he is.

Once I get Rivi calmed down, I stare at his profile. His strong jaw, chiseled to godlike perfection. His long lashes that surely are the envy of every woman alive. His unruly hair that my fingers yearn to rake through.

Here's the thing though: he acts like an asshole, but I'm not really sure he *is* one. Maybe it's one and the same, but I get the idea he acts the way he does because he's putting up a front. Hiding from his true self maybe.

I close my eyes and think of the single kiss we shared. I can almost hear his voice. *"You should quit. Because if you don't, I can't guarantee it won't happen again."*

There were fleeting moments on the trip when I thought it *would* happen again. Like when he came into my room after my nightmare. Or when he made me breakfast. And I find myself utterly disappointed that it didn't. Despite the fact that my brothers would kill me; regardless of it being the worst idea on the planet; aside from the reality that nothing could ever come from it—I want him. I want him so badly I can feel it in every bone in my body. Every cell of my being.

I gaze out the window wondering how I can be in love with a douchebag.

~ ~ ~

Back at home (it's not lost on me that I call it *home* now), I unpack Rivi's stuff, feed her and get her settled in her electric baby rocker that has more Bluetooth settings than the Cadillac. I watch her sway lightly back and forth, wondering why Hawk bothers to buy only the best, most expensive baby stuff for a kid he doesn't seem to want very much.

Then again, like I told Tag on the phone, I believe he just hasn't found that connection with her. He's a bachelor to his core. Everything about being a father goes against the man he's grown up to be. Maybe when Rivi smiles at him his icy heart will thaw. Or when he hears her giggle, which I already know will be the best sound in the whole world.

He's fighting it. But in the end, I believe Rivi will win him over.

Is he fighting something else? I glance around the empty room knowing he's probably back in his office. Is that why he's been ignoring me the past few days?

Refusing to sit around and brood about it, I make plans to meet Holland at Donovan's for dinner and then go up to my room to get ready.

~ ~ ~

The minute I push the stroller through the front door of Donovan's Pub, Holland dances over and unstraps Rivi. "Oh my gosh. She's gotten so big. I can't believe how fast she's growing."

"She is," I say proudly. "And she's so much more aware. I swear she looks at me when I walk in a room. Sometimes I think she's excited to see me."

"I'm not surprised." She snuggles Rivi into her arms as we head to our table. She sits and looks up at me. "She probably thinks you're her mother."

"She's four weeks old," I say. "She doesn't think anything."

"You're not going to quit, are you?"

"What makes you think that?"

She shrugs. "The way you sounded on the phone earlier. You didn't seem very happy. Did something happen over the weekend? Was Hawk horrible to you?"

"Of course not."

Gino comes over to take our order. Holland is eyeing me the entire time.

"That didn't sound very convincing," she says when Gino leaves. "Oh hell, did he try something? He did, didn't he? I'm going to kill him. Doesn't he know he's going to ruin the best thing that ever happened to this little girl?"

"Stop it, Hol. He didn't try anything. He *definitely* didn't try anything."

She stares. It's like she's trying to see into my very soul. I take a sip of water, feeling claustrophobic under her perusal.

Gino approaches. "Not now," Holland says, holding up a palm. She turns back to me. "You stupid girl. You went and fell for my brother, didn't you?"

I drink a gulp of water in silence.

She sighs. "Oh my god, you did. Addy, no. What are you thinking?"

I glance around to make sure nobody is listening, least of all my brother, Cooper, who just came out from the kitchen. "I'm not exactly sure you're the one I should be talking about this with. You're not only my best friend, you're his sister."

"Which makes me the best person to be talking about this with. It's just a crush, isn't it? The good girl falling for the bad boy and all that?"

"Yeah, I'm sure that's what it is."

Cooper comes over. I try to decide which is the better of two evils: Holland giving me the third degree about my feelings for Hawk, or Cooper yelling at me for going away for the weekend with him.

"Addy," Cooper bites. "A word?"

I roll my eyes and get up, following him to the end of the bar where he corners me. "You can save your lectures, Coop. I went over all this with Tag."

"I know, we talked. We had to convince each other not to get on a plane and haul your ass home."

"I'm a big girl. I can take care of myself."

"Not around that asshole you can't."

"Cooper, give it a rest."

Serenity walks by. "Yeah, Cooper, leave the poor girl alone. Table three needs menus."

"We're not done here," he says, eyeing me protectively.

When I go back to my table, Holland is uncharacteristically quiet. She's staring at Rivi who's now asleep in her stroller. Finally she looks up. "You haven't acted on it yet, have you?"

I shake my head, not eager to tell her about the kiss we shared, because I'm still not sure it meant anything—to him anyway.

"Good. Because you know what kind of guy he is. I love my brother to death but he's not exactly boyfriend material. It would end badly, and then my niece would lose her most favorite person in the whole world."

Like a freight train barreling through my brain, I realize just how right she is. Hawk and I could never have a relationship. I'm a fool to believe for a second he would treat me any differently than all his other conquests. It's true, there have been moments of... *something*... between us. But I'm sure it's only because I'm the proverbial forbidden fruit. It *would* end badly. And then where would Rivi be? She'd be without the only person she's ever bonded with, and I'd be nothing more than another notch in his belt. No, falling for him is a bad idea. *Epically* bad.

I rub my temples because I know it's too late. I've already fallen. It's not like I can just turn off my feelings.

"Jordan Westerbrook," Holland says out of left field.

I cock my head.

She motions to the booth in the corner where Jordan is nursing a beer. "You should ask him out."

Jordan moved to town right after my accident. He and I had some classes together at CCU before he transferred to a university in Scotland. I wasn't aware he was back. He's tall and slender with long blonde hair and a sleeve of geometric tattoos that arguably makes him seem much edgier than his teddy bear personality. He looks over and catches us staring. I wave awkwardly, but only because I'm awkward, not because I'm interested. "Hmm, maybe," I say, just to please Holland.

"Okay great." Then before I realize what's happening, she calls over to him. "Jordan! Come eat with us."

My eyes go wide. "Holland!"

"Shush. It'll be fine."

Jordan picks up his drink and comes over. "Hey, Addison." He sets down his drink and hugs me. "Long time no see." He looks in the stroller then at me and Holland. "Which one of you had a baby?"

"Neither," I say. "This is Holland's niece, Rivington. I'm her nanny."

Jordan tries to hold back a laugh. "I heard Hawk had a kid. Rivington?"

"My brother is a sadist. We just call her Rivi," Holland says. "Funny that we saw you. Addy and I were just talking about you."

I kick her under the table as Jordan settles into a chair.

He smiles brightly. "Is that so?"

"She was wondering how you were doing since you left for Scotland. Why don't you tell her?"

Holland flashes me a wicked smile then tends to Rivi as Jordan tells me all about his time overseas.

The front door opens and Hol's three brothers walk in. They stroll to the bar like they own the place. "Uh, hello?" Holland says loudly.

The trio turns and comes to greet their sister. Hudson kisses her on top of the head. "Hey, Hol."

"Want to join us?" she asks. "We could pull up a few chairs. You remember Jordan Westerbook."

The men greet each other. Then Hawk's younger brothers look at him to see what he wants to do. He motions to the bar. "We just came to watch the baseball game. We wouldn't be good company. But I'll call you tomorrow, eh, Hol?"

"Whatever. Go watch your stupid game."

They leave, never having acknowledged me or Rivi. Or should I say *he* didn't acknowledge us. At least I got a head tilt from Hudson and a chin lift from Hunter. Hudson may have even spared a glance at the baby, which is more than I can say for the other two.

"See?" Holland leans over and whispers out of Jordan's earshot. "When a baseball game trumps having dinner with his sister and child, you know that's a red flag."

*Not to mention he didn't acknowledge my existence.*

As Gino deposits our food on the table, I tell my inner self that Holland is spot on. Not only are there a multitude of red flags where Hawk is concerned, there are neon-flashing stop lights. I try my best not to look over at him during dinner. It's like trying not to look at a traffic accident, especially when he tosses erratic glances my way. I'm thankful Jordan is here to distract me.

Holland stops eating and blows out a breath. "You'll never guess who just walked in."

Rivi fusses so I pick her up, put her to my shoulder, and bounce in the chair. "Who?"

"Kylie."

No other explanation is necessary. Kylie Hendrix was our friend way back when. Until she stole my first boyfriend, Luke Kelly, right out from under me in eighth grade. Luke and I had been dating for two months. I was in love and practically planning our wedding. He was my first kiss, even though there wasn't much tongue to it. I was walking on air.

Then, rumor has it, Kylie 'accidentally' came out of her room naked when Luke was over at her house studying with her stepbrother Kurt. And then Luke 'accidentally' felt her up when Kurt's girlfriend came over and they got drunk and played Spin the Bottle.

I was devastated. Especially when the whole school found out what had happened. Instead of Kylie being labeled a slut, *I* was the one being called a prude because my boyfriend had to 'get it' elsewhere. I was thirteen.

Kylie tried to steal Holland, too, but Hol sided with me. We've hated Kylie ever since. She's the only person in Calloway Creek I'm not nice to. Thankfully, we don't cross paths much because she lives on the other side of town with her on-again-off-again-girlfriend, Macie. Oh, yeah… and she's bisexual—a fact she loves to flaunt as if she's the only bi person in this sleepy town.

"Hey, girlfriends," she sings as she passes our table, like we're long-lost BFFs.

Holland huffs. "Eat shit and die, Kylie."

Kylie laughs and saunters to the bar.

"We hate her," Holland explains to Jordan. "Kylie is a back-stabbing bitch to the nth degree."

"Okay," he says, raising his beer. "To hating back-stabbing bitches." He winks at me.

"What's she doing here?" I ask. "I worked here for months and never saw her set foot inside this pub."

"Looks like she's getting take-out."

"At least she'll be gone quickly."

Holland's lips form a thin line. "Maybe not so much. Don't look now, but she just took a barstool next to Hawk. And she's flirting with him."

I whip my head around.

"I said *don't* look," Holland scolds as I watch Kylie throw her head back in a throaty laugh.

But now I can't turn away. Because her hand is resting on Hawk's arm. They look comfortable with each other. Oh god. I close my eyes and swallow, vowing not to look again. "Please don't tell me they've, you know…"

Holland's eyes spew fire as she watches Kylie and her brother. "Okay, I won't tell you."

I hate to admit even to myself that my heart just sank into the pit of my stomach.

Hol's hand captures one of mine. "It's for the best, you know, her coming in. It only reinforces what a playboy he is."

"What am I missing here?" Jordan asks.

Ignoring him, I stand and deposit Rivi on Holland's lap. "Bathroom," I say.

I head to the hallway that leads to the back. Before I get all the way there, I turn and look over at the bar. It's a mistake of epic proportions. Because Hawk's eyes are boring into me. For a moment we stare at each other. I can't read him at all. Is he *mad at me?* And if so, why? Or is that heat in his eyes? Maybe he wants me as badly as I want him. Maybe he's upset with himself for not kissing me again. Maybe he's fantasizing about it right now. Maybe he's going to push Kylie's hand off him, follow me to the bathroom, hoist me up onto the counter, and do things to me that he only does in my dreams.

He breaks our stare, diverting his eyes from mine over to Jordan's. He whispers something to Kylie. Then they get up and walk out together, his hand guiding her on the small of her back.

And then… my heart implodes.

# Chapter Twenty-three

*Hawk*

"Oh my god, I love your Porsche," Kylie says.

"I know. You said that the last time we hooked up."

I glance at the pub in my rearview mirror as we pull away, knowing I'd rather be back there fighting with the tenacious virgin amputee than fucking the attractive able-bodied woman sitting next to me. But I had to get out of there. I couldn't stand watching it anymore; Addy flirting with Jordan What's-his-name.

Maybe this was the right call. I need to get Addison Genevieve Calloway out of my head. And I can't think of a better way to do it than with the self-proclaimed sluttiest bi-sexual in town.

I turn into my neighborhood, then onto my street, then into my driveway, the whole way wondering how many women I'll have to sleep with to make me stop thinking of Addy in my bed. My shower. My hot tub. She's everywhere in the house. Earlier today, I couldn't walk from my room to the goddamn kitchen without imagining all the places I could have her.

Kylie claps. "If your house is anything like your car, I know I'm in for a real treat."

She goes for the passenger door handle, but I stop her. I can't do this here. "I changed my mind. We can't go here. I forgot I'm… having it fumigated."

I back out and drive away. "What's your address?"

"We can't go there either. Macie is home. In fact, she's probably wondering where her dinner is. We should probably move this along."

I pull into a bank parking lot, drive around back and turn off the car. "Let's move it along then."

She glances around the dark, empty lot. "Here?"

"Are we doing this or not?"

To the depths of my soul, I'm not sure I've ever wanted to hear the word *not* more than I do right now. But I started this thing. And I've never been one not to finish.

She unbuttons her top and pushes it aside. Normally seeing Kylie Hendrix's tits would have my cock swelling in my pants. Hell, seeing *any* tits would. But not today. I surmise I'm tired from the weekend and all the sleep I didn't get because of the writing.

*The writing.* Suddenly, my head is in my book and I'm thinking of what Adelaide would do if Jensen were about to bang another woman in his car. She'd rip open the door, drag Jensen away by his cock and fuck him so hard he'd forget his name.

A hand travels up my thigh and cups my junk through my jeans. For a moment I revel in it because I'm Jensen and she's Adelaide.

"Hawk?"

The voice jolts me. It's not the smooth, seductive, demure voice that sounds like honey. Kylie's is husky, low, and curt. And she reeks of cigarettes.

I remove her hand.

"Something wrong?"

"I forgot I needed to be somewhere."

She leans back. "At eight o'clock on a Sunday? And who gets their house fumigated on a weekend? What's going on here? You having second thoughts?"

I start the car.

"Are you *seeing* someone?" she asks, clutching her chest in a mock state of shock.

"No."

"You don't sound very convincing."

"I'm not seeing anyone."

I catch her appraising me out of the corner of my eye. "It's Addison Calloway, isn't it?"

I almost run the car into a curb. "What the hell would make you say that?"

"I heard she's your nanny. Which means she's most likely living in the house you didn't want to take me into. And then there was all the staring and brooding between the two of you at Donovan's."

"I wasn't staring at her. And I sure as shit wasn't brooding."

She laughs. "Yeah, okay. But you know you could do way better than that one-legged freak, don't you?"

I pull up behind the pub, lean over and open her door. "You're such a fucking bitch, Kylie."

"Maybe. But I'm a bitch you like to fuck. Until today apparently." She buttons up her shirt and gets out. "Call me when this… *whatever* you have with the cripple passes. Because it will pass. You're Hawk McQuaid, if you've forgotten. You don't do relationships."

The door closes and I'm left staring at the pub. I look around the parking lot and spy the Caddy. She's still here. *With him?*

I turn the car around, pull onto the street, and run the Porsche as fast as I can along the stretch of road that leads out of the town bearing *her* name. Let Sheriff Niles catch me. I don't give a shit. I run it up well over 120, hoping this will do the trick when Kylie couldn't. I drive as fast as I can for as far as I can. Then I pull over, put it in park, and bang a fist on the steering wheel as I spew out every cuss word I can think of.

~ ~ ~

The Caddy is in the garage when I pull in. I enter the mud room and toss my keys on the table. The house is quiet given the late hour. Momentarily, I wonder if Addy would dare to bring a man here. Before I get much further on that scenario in my head, I walk through the dark great room and go to the bar to pour myself a double. I lean against the counter and take a sip. Over the rim of the glass, a shadow catches my eye. Someone is on the couch.

Not someone. Addy. Her back is to me. And she's completely silent.

I flip on the light. "What are you doing here?"

"What are *you* doing here?" she quips without turning. "Shouldn't you be on your *date*?"

"It wasn't a date."

She snorts a curt laugh. "Of course not. Hawk McQuaid doesn't date."

My insides warm. And not from the bourbon. She's jealous. I walk around the couch and take the seat opposite her. "What about you? You were getting awfully cozy with that Jordan jagoff."

Finally, she looks at me. Her face is makeup-free. Dark shadows fill her usual happy gaze. She's wearing that ridiculous *'Some assembly required'* shirt along with a pair of sweatpants. She hasn't been with Jordan. She's been waiting here. For me.

"I wasn't getting cozy with anyone. Jordan and I are friends."

"That's not what it looked like from the bar."

"Well, you should be one to talk the way you were flirting with Kylie."

"Jealous much?"

I sound like a complete hypocrite because if anyone is jealous here, it's me. Then I realize this may be the first time in my life I've ever felt this way.

"You think I'm jealous?" she asks, seemingly horrified.

"If the shoe fits."

She scoots off the couch and stands. "I'm not jealous. It's just… Kylie Hendrix? She's a backstabbing tramp."

"But if I'd hooked up with someone else, *that* would have been fine?"

"I…" Her eyes close for a second. "You're so infuriating." She walks to the kitchen, and I follow.

She pulls a water bottle from the fridge, yelling at me the whole time about what a horrible person Kylie is. It's comical almost, watching her get so worked up over it. She can't even open her bottle properly. I put down my drink, go over and take the bottle from her, break the seal, and return it. "Calm down, Addy."

"Don't tell me to calm down. *You* calm down."

"I'm not the one in a tizzy," I say, finding it hard not to smile at the temper smoldering in her eyes.

She huffs at the ceiling, clearly frustrated. "Your sister is right. Jordan is right. *Everyone* is right."

"What are you talking about? Jordan was right about what exactly?"

"About you being a douchebag." She gulps water.

"Jordan doesn't even know me."

"Maybe not, but your reputation precedes you."

My jaw twitches in anger. "You and Jordan were talking about me?"

"Your name might have come up."

I take another swig of my drink. "Did you leave with him?"

"Yes, Hawk, I left with him," she deadpans. "In fact Holland and I brought him back here and had a threesome. It may have fucked up your kid a little, seeing an orgy right here in the kitchen, but I figure having you as a father, she's already destined to be fucked up so what's a little more going to hurt?"

She cursed. I don't think I've ever heard her curse before. And she did it twice. Why that turns me on is beyond my reasoning. Everything this woman does turns me on. She looks about as put together as a stray mutt at a dog show right now, yet all I can think about is lifting her onto the counter, standing between her legs, and kissing the word *fuck* right out of her mouth. Instead, I do the opposite. I fan the flames. "The only one who's going to have an orgy in this house is me."

"You're a real jerk, you know that?"

My lips curve into a sinister half-smile. "As a matter of fact, I do."

"And for your information, I'm going out with Jordan Friday night."

"No you're not."

"He's got two tickets to the Reckless Alibi concert in the city."

"You're lying."

"Google it." I do as I listen to her ramble, "He got the tickets from Sophie who nannies for Amber and Quinn who are friends with Maddox McBride whose best friend is Reece Mancini who's married to the drummer for Reckless Alibi."

My search tells me that Reckless Alibi is in fact playing on Friday in the city. And her story was way too elaborate to be made up.

I down the rest of my drink and leave the room. "Goddamn it," I say, thinking I'm out of earshot.

"You stub your toe?" she asks, trailing behind.

I turn. "No, Addy. I didn't stub my fucking toe. And I didn't have sex with Kylie. At least not tonight. Didn't you notice she came back to pick up her food fifteen minutes after we walked out? Or maybe you were too busy fawning over Jordan."

Unnamable emotions play out on her face. "You… didn't have sex with her?"

"No, Addison. I didn't. I wanted to. I needed to do something to get you out of my goddamn head. I thought if I slept with her"—I run my hands through my hair—"forget it."

She looks stunned. Then her face softens. "I'm not really going to a concert with Jordan."

Relief rolls through me like a tsunami hitting the shore. "She smelled like cigarettes." I lean against the wall. "All I could think of was you. Looking at you. Kissing you. Fighting with you. I mean, Jesus, why is fighting with you better than having sex with anyone else?"

She closes the distance between us, the intensity of her gaze sucking the air out of my lungs. Before my brain can catch up with what's happening, she's in my arms, kissing me. Her lips are just like I remember. Soft. Plump. Amazing. Our mouths brush together softly, delicately, like butterfly wings. I inhale her breath. I feel the warmth of her skin. I taste a hint of her strawberry lip balm. Her lips are intoxicating, filling the hunger of my emptiness with passion.

I thrust my tongue into her mouth, demanding more. And she gives it to me, opening like a flower in the sun. She hungrily pushes back, ignoring the sharp bristles of my short, manicured beard as her mouth devours mine in a way I've never been kissed before.

There's a fierce awakening inside me as I experience an ignition of every sensation imaginable. The flame turns into a full-on blow torch when I touch her breast over her top. My hand settles onto it, cupping it as if it was made to be held by only *my* hand. The throaty sound that escapes her only heightens my desire.

Her hands run a path up and down my back, leaving a trail of want and anticipation. I can only imagine what they'll feel like on my bare skin. I've had a taste before, when she touched my chest at the cottage. When she might as well have reached in and wound her fingers around my goddamn heart. Because that's exactly where she is.

And it's precisely where she shouldn't be.

I pull away. Her dreamy hazel eyes peer up at me with a million questions I don't have answers for.

"You shouldn't have done that," I say, peeling her hands off me.

"Why not?"

I start down the hallway to my bedroom, pausing momentarily to respond with as much truth as I've ever spoken. "Because I'll hurt you."

# Chapter Twenty-four

## *Addison*

For two weeks he's walked on eggshells around me. Maybe he's afraid I'll quit. Neither of us has mentioned the second kiss. Or his proclamation afterward. Or the fact that we stare at each other way more than is appropriate for any intellectual beings.

Like right now. He's staring from the couch on the back porch as I feed Rivi in the great room. He doesn't think I see him. I do. The light from his laptop screen is illuminating his face. But even if I didn't see him watching me, I swear I'd be able to *feel* him doing it. And every time he looks at me, it's just like the way he was looking at me that night. Right after he said he'd hurt me. With a rebellious expression and dark thunderous eyes that contradicted his threat to stay away. The man is clearly torn with indecision.

I try to focus on the baby, but I can't help being self-conscious. Do I have a double chin looking down at Rivi? Has the bun on top of my head fallen too far to one side? Does he have any idea what his incessant glaring does to me? And if so, does mine do the same thing to him?

It's torture living in the same house with someone you're so attractive to but can't have.

*Why can't you?* my brain asks, not for the first time.

*Because he'll hurt you,* my conscience replies.

I put Rivi on my shoulder and illicit a burp. Hawk closes his laptop and comes inside. He holds out his hands. "I'll change her."

For weeks now, I haven't had to coerce him into meeting the obligations set by his grandfather. Without me asking, he's fed and changed diapers exactly as directed. That doesn't mean he's warming up to her necessarily. I hoped after Martha's Vineyard, with the way he took control of her in the middle of the night, that he'd turned a corner. But he's more like a robot performing a programmed task. He does what he's supposed to do then returns her to me immediately.

"Ah, man!" I hear through the baby monitor. "Are you kidding me, Riv?"

My heart melts when he calls her that. Even though I know it doesn't mean anything.

"How can someone so small produce something so fucking disgusting?"

I laugh.

"Addison!" he yells through the monitor. "Help!"

I should pretend I don't hear him. Let him figure it out on his own. He's cleaned her poops plenty of times before.

"Shit," I hear. "Shit, shit, shit. Hold still. Oh, Christ, I just got some on my face. Addy!"

Deciding he's had enough torture, I make my way upstairs, albeit slowly, and stand in the doorway. He's so busy trying to hold her with one hand and wipe her mess with the other, he doesn't even notice me. I giggle silently because he's managed to make an even bigger mess. It's comical watching him. His lips are pinched closed like he's trying to prevent any poop from getting into his mouth. And he's making funny sounds. He loses hold of her leg, and her foot smears the feces. "Shit, shit, shit," he repeats comically. I'm about to step forward to help when I glance at Rivi and see it.

My heart stops. She's smiling.

"Oh my god!"

"I know," Hawk says. "How the hell am I supposed to clean all this up? It's on my face, Addy. *My face!* Get it off."

"Not that," I say, striding over. "Hawk, she smiled."

"What?"

"She smiled. At *you.*"

He stops and looks at her. But the smile is gone. "That's ridiculous. Why would she smile at me?"

"Because you looked funny with your face all scrunched up and then there were the noises you were making. I guess it made her happy. Do it again."

He turns and glares at me. "I have shit on my face. I'm not going to stand here and try to make her smile."

"You are such a baby." I grab a wipe and carefully clean his cheek. "And I can't believe she smiled at you first. That is unfair on so many levels." I tickle Rivi's cheek. "Hey, sweetie. Can you do it again?" I try to imitate what Hawk was doing a moment ago, but it doesn't work. I step back. "So unfair."

He jerks his head sharply in my direction. "Are you going to help or what?"

I get four wipes out of the dispenser and hold them out.

He takes them. "Gee, thanks."

Finally getting her out of her dirty, soiled onesie, he holds it out to me, pinching it carefully between his thumb and index finger. I roll my eyes and take it from him, then hand him a fresh sleep outfit.

"Where are you going?" he asks as I walk away.

I hold up the poop-stained clothes. "To soak it."

"Just throw it out."

"I'm not going to throw out a perfectly good onesie. You must've paid thirty dollars for this."

"Who cares? I don't want her wearing it again after it's been covered in shit."

"I guess we need to throw *you* out in the trash too then, considering you were covered in her shit as well."

"Very funny."

Thunder crackles outside.

He glances out Rivi's window. "Damn. I was hoping to get out of here before the storm hit."

"Going somewhere?"

"To Hudson's to watch a game."

I roll the onsie up in itself and put it on the dresser. "Go. I'll finish up here. She needs a bath anyway. You know, one of these days, you'll have to give her one yourself."

"No I won't. That wasn't part of the deal."

"You're never going to give your daughter a bath?"

"Not if I don't have to."

I shake my head. Comments like that have me wondering just what I see in him.

He walks out of the room then pokes his head back in. "Hey, thanks."

"No problem."

His mouth curves indulgently into a blatantly sexy yet roguish smile that hints toward mystery. He looks dashing, handsome, and deadly.

*That.* That's what I see in him.

He disappears. "Bye, Addy."

~ ~ ~

I put down my book and try to fall asleep, but it's hard with the wind whipping the trees right outside my window. Flashes of lightning illuminate the room and a loud clap of thunder shakes the house. I listen to the baby monitor hoping Rivi doesn't wake up.

The storm is right on top of us. Thunder crackles in quick succession. I love a good storm, but this one is quickly turning severe. As soon as the thought crosses my mind, my phone goes off with a piercing alarm alerting me to a tornado warning.

My heart drops thinking back to when I was little and a young girl from school was killed when a tree fell on their house as a tornado ripped through their backyard. With no time to think, I grab my phone and hop across the hall. I throw a few things into a diaper bag and get Rivi out of her crib. Then I half crawl and half walk on my knees to the top of the stairs. I peer down thinking maybe I could scoot down on my butt. No, not with Rivi. It's too dangerous. Lightning strikes, followed by another loud boom of thunder. I make my way to the elevator, get us inside, close the outer door and then the inner gate, and push the button for the ground floor.

I look around as it descends thinking this may be the safest place in the house. No windows. Reinforced walls. And it's as middle of the house as you can get. I decide we'll stay inside it until the storm passes.

The elevator jerks to a stop and the lights go out. I'm shrouded by blackness. It's the most darkness I've felt since my accident. I begin to panic. Rivi fusses and I realize I'm squeezing her too hard.

"It's okay, Rivi." I take deep breaths and close my eyes to trick myself out of feeling claustrophobic. It's not working. Then my eyes fly open. "My phone!" I dig around blindly in the diaper bag where I stashed it. I touch it and the wake screen faintly illuminates the elevator. After turning on the flashlight, I sit back with a relieved breath. "See, we're going to be just fine."

I get a blanket out of the bag and lay Rivi on it. Then I try to open the door. It won't budge. I know from experience that the door won't open unless the elevator is fully on the landing of floor one or two. We aren't completely down yet. But we must be close.

"It's fine," I tell her. "We were going to wait out the tornado warning in here anyway."

But then my mind goes crazy with all the things that could go wrong. I try the gate on the inside of the door again. I hit all the buttons on the small elevator control pad, including an ALARM button that doesn't do a thing. Oddly enough, there is a phone in here. But I already have a phone. I pick it up and scroll through my favorites until Hugh Heffner's picture appears. I tap on it.

Hawk answers on the first ring. "Addy?"

"We lost power."

"Here too."

"And there's a tornado warning."

"I heard. But there's not an actual tornado, and the warning expires in like twenty minutes. I'm sure it'll be fine."

"Maybe so, but I'm kind of stuck."

"Stuck where?"

"The elevator."

"Jesus, really? Shit, where's Riv?"

It takes a second to process his question because part of me is still in full-on freakout mode. But when I do, I'm elated he even asked about her. It might be the first time he's bothered to care.

"With me. I thought it would be the safest place, but then we lost power, and I can't open the door. I'm not sure it's down all the way. Is there some kind of emergency release or something?"

"I don't know. I don't ever use it. I'm sure the power will be back on soon."

"Says the guy safe and secure on the ground floor."

He laughs. "Addy, it's fine. And it probably is the safest place to be."

"Not if there's a fire. What if lightning hits the house and a fire starts?" My stomach rolls. "We'd be trapped. Oh my god. There's no way out. Hawk, you have to get us out."

"Okay, okay. I'm on my way. I'll be there in twenty minutes."

"A lot of good you'll do since you don't even know anything about the elevator. I should have called 911. And twenty minutes? That might as well be an eternity."

Sounds are muffled. He's having a conversation with someone else.

"Hawk?"

"I'm here. Hunter is calling the fire department. He'll give them the door code. I'm leaving now. Just sit tight, okay? I'll see you soon."

"Wait! You're hanging up?"

"Uh... no. I guess not."

I have to remind myself to breathe. I peek at Rivi, thankful one of us is oblivious. Then I glance down at my phone and see the red battery indicator in the corner. It's been days since I charged it. "Oh, no. My phone is at two percent."

"Don't worry, it'll last until someone gets there."

"I doubt it with the flashlight on."

"Turn it off then."

"Are you kidding me? It would be a tomb in here."

"Addy, you sleep in the dark. What's the difference?"

"I don't."

"You sleep with the lights on?"

There's no time to be embarrassed, so I tell him. "A nightlight. The darkness makes me claustrophobic, like I'm back in the car after the accident. It was so black. The moon wasn't out. And I was trapped. I passed out and then the lights, and—"

"Addison, calm down. Breathe. I'm here. Keep the light on, the fire department is on the way. You're going to be okay."

"Just don't hang up. Please."

"I won't."

"What if my phone dies?"

"If your phone dies, I'll call you on the landline in the elevator."

"But it'll be pitch black."

"I'll talk you through it."

"But—"

"Addy, stop. Quit thinking the worst will happen."

"But the worst *can* happen. I know it all too well. Because it happened to me. Bad things happen. Even to good people." I feel myself on the brink of hyperventilation.

"The worst did *not* happen to you. You're alive. You survived. Now breathe with me. Come on, you can do this."

He's huffing and puffing into the phone. *Is he stressing out?*

I breathe in and out. "Are you on your way?"

"Yes."

"You probably shouldn't be driving."

"I shouldn't. That's why I'm running."

"You're running all the way from Hudson's? In the storm?"

"I had more than two drinks. Hunter and Hudson were drinking too. And I did make a promise."

"Yeah, you did."

"Hey, look at that. You sound a little better now."

"You probably think I'm an idiot being scared of the dark."

"You're not an idiot. And I'd be freaked out too in a dark elevator without power."

"I doubt it. But thanks."

I listen to his heavy breathing. It's actually quite soothing.

"I hear something," I say, straining to listen through the door.

"Addison? It's Patrick Kelsey from CCFD. Are you okay in there?"

"If you would call a woman going berserk in a broken-down elevator with an infant okay, then yeah, I'm totally fine."

He laughs. "We'll have you out in no time. Move to the far wall. We're going to pry the door open."

I pick up Rivi and scoot to the far corner. "Okay." I turn my attention back to the phone. "Hawk, they're here."

"I heard. I'll be there in a few, okay?"

"Will you stay on with me? I know I'm being stupid. It just helps to have someone in here with me, you know?"

"Yeah, I'll stay on."

There's banging outside the door. Then light filters in as the door comes off the hinges and flashlights illuminate the elevator. "Oh, thank God."

"Just sit tight," Patrick says. "We have to force the gate as well since it won't open unless it's seated into the release."

I watch them get out more tools.

"I'm sorry," I say into the phone. "It looks like you might have some repairs to make after this."

"Don't worry about that."

A loud noise has the gate latch snapping off. It opens and I breathe a huge sigh of relief. Patrick takes Rivi and hands her off to another firefighter. Then he looks at my leg—or lack thereof. He swiftly picks me up and carries me out into the great room.

Hawk comes bursting through the front door. Someone hands him a flashlight and he strides over just as Patrick deposits me on the couch. He shines the light onto my stump. I'm well aware it's fully visible as all I'm wearing is my sleep T-shirt. I can't see his eyes, but I can only imagine what he's thinking.

"Oh my God," he mumbles.

The other firefighter puts Rivington into my arms. "She's no worse for wear, ma'am."

"Thank goodness."

They pack up their gear and leave, giving Hawk recommendations on who to call to repair the broken elevator doors as he escorts them to the entrance.

I'm still on the couch, holding the baby when Hawk comes back in the room. He doesn't sit. I use what's left of my battery to shine a light on him. He's soaking wet.

"I can't believe you ran all the way home in the rain."

"I can't believe you got yourself, Rivington, and a diaper bag into the elevator without your leg."

"You pick up a thing or two when you're an amputee and have to do things quickly."

"How'd you do it?"

"Getting to her room was easy. I hop pretty well. Carrying her and the bag to the elevator was a bit more difficult. I may have scraped up my knees." I look down at a sleeping Rivi. "But it was worth it."

"Let me see," he says, moving closer.

I reach for the throw blanket to cover up Eileen. "That's okay."

"I've already seen your, uh…"

"Stump." I say. "It's called a stump."

"Yeah, okay. I've seen it. You don't have to cover up."

"Fine." I shine the light on my knees, trying to keep my eyes off his face.

"I don't mean to stare," he says. "I just didn't think it would be so—"

I close my eyes. "Weird? Ugly? Freakish?"

"I was going to say cute."

I open my eyes and cackle. "You're full of horse crap, McQuaid."

"No, really. I didn't think it would be so smooth looking. You must have had a great surgeon, Calloway."

"I did. Just ask my parents. They're still paying off the hospital bill. Which reminds me, I should take over those payments now that I'm so gainfully employed."

He cracks his neck left then right. Then he reaches for Rivi. "Let me take her up."

"Thanks. Mind bringing my prosthetic down?"

He doesn't reply. A few minutes later, he comes back downstairs.

I eye his empty hands. "Forget something?"

"No." He walks over and hands me a flashlight. Then he sweeps me into his arms.

Our faces are inches apart. The wetness from his clothes soaks my T-shirt. My heart pounds so hard I'm sure he can hear it through my chest wall.

I can smell whiskey on his breath. I'm not a fan of the taste, but somehow I've come to crave the smell. And right now, I want to taste it. I want to taste him. I want him to carry me to my bed and climb on top of me. I want him to kiss my lips, my neck, my body. Every inch of it. I want to feel his hardness. I want him to push it inside me. I want to hand this man my virginity. And I want to take everything he's willing to give, for as long as he's willing to give it.

I shine the light on the stairs so he can see where he's going, the whole time wondering if he's looking at me. And if he is, what is he thinking? He could have just as easily gotten my leg. He *wanted* to carry me.

My body is shaking hard by the time we reach my bedroom. Surely he can feel it. He stops right outside and puts me down at the door, his eyes raking over my T-shirt that's now almost translucent over my right breast where it was pressing against his wet clothes. He swallows. "I'm sure you can take it from here. I need a shower."

Disappointment stabs me like a dagger to the chest. I avert the flashlight, not wanting him to see how devastated I am. Not wanting him to see how much I crave him. How much I want him. Maybe even how much I need him. I hop a step over and put my hand on the door. "Yeah, sure." Then I shut it.

# Chapter Twenty-five

*Hawk*

She slams the door in my face. As well she should. I was ogling her wet shirt like an adolescent in a porn shop. I lean against the wall in the darkness. Damn I want her. My dick dances against the fly of my pants.

"Fuck it."

I turn the doorknob. She's sitting on her bed, naked but for her panties, her silhouette visible in the hue of the flashlight. She gasps and grabs her shirt to cover up.

"Leave it." I stride over and push her back onto the bed. The flashlight crashes to the floor leaving the room dark with the exception of a round ray of light on the nearby wall. I climb on top of her. "I'm going to kiss you. I'm going to kiss you and more. If you don't want me to, say so now. I'll leave and this never happened. But you have to say it."

I'm close enough to feel her breath on my lips and the rise and fall of her chest. She doesn't speak. Still, I hesitate, waiting for a sign. I get it when her hands grasp the back of my head and pull me toward her.

Our lips collide in a hungry kiss. This one doesn't start soft and innocent like the others we shared. It's feral and needy and, holy mother of God, so incredibly hot. I revel in it, forgetting that the woman underneath me is practically naked. But the tiny brain in my cock doesn't fail to remind me. He's tired of only seeing the inside of my fist. He wants the inside of *her* fist. The inside of *her*.

Then I remember she's a virgin. A better man would pull away. Addison Calloway should not lose her virginity to a guy like me. But I'm not a better man, so I work my tongue down her jaw, around the cords of her neck, across her clavicles, and down to her luscious breasts. She arches into me when I take a nipple into my mouth. Making a sexy little sound when I flick it with my tongue, she grabs onto my head when I gently rake my teeth over it.

Holy shit, if this is what she does when I suck her tits, I can only imagine what it would be like if my tongue was on her clit. Just thinking about it makes my cock even stiffer. It's throbbing painfully, begging for escape. If she were any other woman, I'd be naked and shoving my dick in her hand, mouth, or other orifices. But she's not any other woman. She's not even close.

My shirt gets untucked. Then her hands are on my back, blazing a trail up, down, and around like she can't get enough. She works my shirt up and over my head, and I smile when a disappointed sigh comes out of her when my mouth momentarily leaves her breast.

My mouth works one stiff nipple. My fingers work the other. She's writhing and moaning, her sultry sounds driving me to the brink of insanity. I let my fingers wander slowly down her abs knowing if she doesn't stop me soon, I won't be able to help myself. I need this woman like I need food and water. Like I need blood flowing through my veins. Like I need air.

Because that's what she is. She's air. And somehow, over the course of the last month, she's become what I need to breathe. To truly live.

I stop when I reach the hem of her panties, just long enough to gauge her reaction. If she doesn't give me permission to touch her, I might actually die. Right here, right now.

When she slides her panties down her legs I feel like I've won the fucking Powerball. Because the odds of me being with her are about as unlikely. Yet here I am, kissing her, touching her. And still it's not enough. I need more. And deep down in a place I never go, I'm sure I'm not talking about physically.

I run a hand over her scant, manicured pubic hair wondering how many men have done this before me. Just because she's a virgin doesn't mean she's never been touched. And for the first time, I become possessive over a woman, wanting to hunt down and skin alive anyone who beat me here.

"Christ," I say, when my fingers find her soaking wet. I slip one easily inside her, working it in and out slowly. Her walls are tight, and it turns me on even more. A moan escapes me. I can't hold it in anymore. "God, Addy. You feel incredible."

I wonder if my words will scare her back into reality. Will she come to her senses and stop me? Will she push me off and run away? Slap me, punch me, accuse me of terrible things? She should. She should do all of that and more.

Instead, she pushes herself down onto my finger. So I add another.

"Hawk," she says breathily. It makes me want to pound on my chest and howl. She said my name. She wants this. She wants me. *Me*, not some freckly-faced banker who drives a Volvo. Not an uptight computer engineer who takes her out for wine and cheese night. *Me*. How is it possible when the banker and engineer would be so much better for her?

"Can I... touch you?" she asks hesitantly.

I process the most amazing four words I think I've ever heard. I lean in close to her ear. "Sweetheart, you can do anything you want."

I replay my words in my head. *Sweetheart?* Where in the hell did that come from? But the thought immediately dissipates when her fingers dip under my waistband and graze the tip of my cock. With the speed and agility of a gazelle, my pants are on the floor before she has a chance to change her mind.

When she touches my dick, sensations I've never felt zing through me. I've been touched hundreds of times before. Never like this. With hands so delicate, touching me as if I could break. Most women don't realize that men don't want to be tugged on like a dog's pull toy. They launch in there and pump on it as if their lives depend on it, when it's much better to start out gently, holding loosely and allowing their hand to glide easily up and down, varying the pressure. Her soft strokes and tactile caresses drive me wild.

Then she surprises the hell out of me. She moves my hand aside, runs her fingers through her wetness, coating them with her juices before her hand returns to my cock.

*Holy shit.*

Strike another one up for the lily-white virgin. How the hell does she know lube can take an otherwise ordinary hand job and turn it into a mind-blowing event?

And this mind-blowing event is about to have me blowing my wad, which is something I do *not* want to do. Not yet. Maybe not at all.

I can almost hear my brothers cackling in my head and calling me a pussy-whipped dingleberry.

I pull away before reaching the point of no return.

"Was I doing it wrong?" she asks.

"Believe me. There wasn't a goddamn thing wrong with what you were doing." I lean down and kiss her stomach, then my lips find her belly button ring and I toy with it like I want to toy with her clit. I pause. "I just wasn't done with my turn yet."

A few fingers back inside her have her breathing heavily again. As my mouth goes lower, her thighs tighten. Am I pushing my luck here?

"Relax, sweetheart."

I can feel the moment it happens. The tension leaves. Her thighs fall open. And without a moment's hesitation, I dive in. When my tongue touches her clit, she claws at my head, her fingers threading through my thick hair. I work her tiny nub back and forth, round and round, up and over. She squirms, sighs, and mewls. I work myself lower, my cock rubbing and humping against her right leg as I feast on her.

"Ah… oh… ah… Hawk…God…"

Her staccato of incoherent words has me ready to combust. I can feel it building inside me like a freight train barreling downhill. I'm going to explode any second and she's not even touching me.

Her thighs tighten, a sure sign she's ready to get off right along with me. I twist my fingers inside her, hoping to find the spot that will push her over the edge. When I do, she falls apart spectacularly underneath me, bucking into me, shouting to the heavens as she rides my fingers and tongue.

Three more thrusts against her and I grunt loudly, burying my face into her soft stomach as I come all over her bed.

Her body is still shuddering as I crawl up next to her. "Dang, Addy."

"I..."—she blows out a deep breath—"Wow."

I smile triumphantly.

When I lie next to her, she turns on her side. "Don't you want to...?"

"Already did. And no matter how goddamn sexy I think you are, my limp cock is not getting up anytime soon." I pull her tightly against me. "You might not want to roll over."

"Oh, okay." I can practically *hear* her head spinning. "Does that normally happen?"

I laugh. "No, that doesn't normally happen. Especially not to me. Now I have a question for you."

She rises on an elbow, waiting.

"Have you done that before? You are a virgin, aren't you?"

I wish I could see her face, but all I can see is the outline of her. "So you *did* hear me talking to Rivi that time."

"I did. Sorry."

"I suppose there's no point in denying it now."

"So...?"

"In high school I went to third base with Anthony Silverman."

Suddenly, I'm jealous of a pimply-faced adolescent. "Define third base."

"You must know the bases of sex."

"Yeah, but I think it's changed over the years. I'm not sure anyone knows where oral fits in."

I'm dying to know if she's blushing right now.

She giggles. "Right. No, we did the other third base."

"So I'm the first to go there?"

"Yes."

More desire to pound on my chest.

Her head settles onto the pillow. "Are you going to be the first to do *other* things?"

*Hell to the fucking yes,* I want to shout, but don't. Because I need to see where the dust settles first. "Why don't we take it one step at a time, or should I say base?"

She pulls the blanket over her. "Okay."

I snuggle into the crevice of her neck, not quite knowing what to do next. My usual MO is to hightail it out. Leave as quickly as possible so I don't give the wrong impression. But now, I'm... *snuggling?* "What the hell are you doing to me, Addy?"

"I don't know, but I'm kind of hoping it's the same thing you're doing to me."

Alarms go off in my head. Warning bells. Nuclear fucking sirens. I ignore them and fiddle with her belly button ring. "We shouldn't be doing this."

"Probably not."

"But I'm not sure I can stop."

"Me either."

"Good." I kiss her cheek. "Now get some sleep. I know you'll have to be up in a few hours to feed her." I pull on my damp skivvies, gather the rest of my clothes, and head for the door. "Goodnight, Addy."

"Night."

"I'd stay, but..."

"It's okay, Hawk. I know you're not the kind of guy who stays and I'm okay with that."

I want to tell her she shouldn't be. That she should demand better. That she, if anyone, deserves it. But I already know I'll be knocking on her door tomorrow and every other night that she'll let me, despite the fact that I know how it will end—with her hating me.

    I leave without a word, only stopping for a drink and a change of clothes on my way to the office. Because I know I'm about to finish the book. And it's going to have a very different ending than we are.

# Chapter Twenty-six

*Addison*

Holding a hungry Rivi, I'm on my way into the kitchen when I see him standing and staring into the refrigerator. Not wanting things to be awkward this early in the morning, I spin around to head into the other room. Only my prosthesis doesn't seem to understand the command my brain gave the rest of my body, and it falls off.

I grip the wall and balance myself. "A little help?" I ask Hawk over my shoulder.

He rushes over, takes Rivi, and puts her in the Peg Perego reclining highchair—the one made in Italy—while I reattach my leg. Then I busy myself making her a bottle.

He leans against the counter as I feed Rivi. "We should get you a new leg."

My eyebrows lift. "*We?*"

"I meant me, I'll get you a new leg."

"No."

"You can't keep walking around on a leg that continuously falls off."

"It doesn't happen that much. And I only have eleven months to wait for a new one."

"That's too long. You need one now."

I shake my head. "I'm not letting you buy me a leg. Do you know how expensive they are?"

"I didn't ask, and I don't care."

Is this about last night, I wonder. "You don't owe me anything."

"That's not why I want to do it."

"Why then?"

"I suppose to do something nice."

I can't help it when the edges of my mouth turn up. "Careful. You might ruin your reputation."

He laughs. He never laughs. I love his laugh.

"Seriously," he says. "I want to."

"You pay me way too much already and you know it."

"You're really not going to let me do it?"

"I'm really not."

He cocks his head and stares.

"What?" I ask.

"You're the only person who hasn't taken a handout from me. And you're probably the most deserving of one."

"Being an amputee doesn't make me a martyr, Hawk."

"No it doesn't. Besides, you have to die to be one of those."

"Aren't you... literal." I want so badly to say something about his writing. I've come close to revealing that I know about his books so many times. But I keep my mouth shut. Mostly because I want him to continue doing it so I can keep sneaking in and reading it.

He pulls an egg carton from the fridge. "Breakfast?"

"If you're offering."

I burp Rivi, watching him scurry around and cook for me. His tight-fitting T-shirt hugs his rippled chest and broad back. His sweats cling to the globes of his ass. When he turns, I can see the outline of his penis. It makes me think of last night when that very penis was in my hands. Actually I haven't stopped thinking about it. I spent the better part of the night wondering what was going to happen this morning.

He places scrambled eggs, toast, and coffee (just how I like it with one splash of milk) in front of me and sits across the table with his mug. I settle Rivi in her seat.

If I didn't know any better, I'd think we've done this a thousand times before. It all seems so normal. Maybe even habitual. For a moment, it even feels like we're a family. I can almost hear him calling me sweetheart. Nobody has ever called me that.

He drinks his coffee in silence, and the whole time I'm wondering what he's thinking.

"We don't have to talk about it, you know," I say, when the awkwardness gets to me.

"That's good. Because I've never done this before."

"Done what?"

"Had breakfast with a woman. After."

Part of me wants to high five someone. Another part, the sensible part, knows it's only happening because I live here.

"Oh, well, it's no big deal."

"Good. Because it's not like anything has changed."

*Aaaaand* this is where my heart shrivels down to a third of its normal size. "Right. Nothing's changed."

He gets up, refills his mug, and heads out of the kitchen.

"Addy?" I hear, then he reappears.

"Mmm?"

"Are you on the pill?"

I cock a brow. "Why would I be?"

"I guess you wouldn't. But maybe you should. I could hook you up with Hudson."

I snort air. "Hawk, believe me, I don't need *two* McQuaid's down in all my business. I'll take care of it."

For the second time this morning, laughter dances out of him. And even though he claims nothing has changed, something has. *He's* changed.

~ ~ ~

Although Rivi is too young for playdates, we meet up with Sophie and Josie at the park. Maybe because *I* need a playdate.

I watch Josie navigate the three steps up to the toddler slide. "She's getting so big."

"It's amazing watching them grow. Just wait until Rivi says her first words and takes her first steps."

"Do you feel like a mom sometimes?"

"Ha! Not even close," she says, chuckling. "And anyone who says being a nanny is the same thing as being a mom is clearly mistaken. There's no comparison. For one, I go home at the end of the day, barring the occasional overnight. I'm not the one who reads her to sleep every night. Or who has to worry about who she's going to date or where she'll go to college. And if I need a sick day, I take it. Mothers don't get sick days. And they never stop thinking about their kids and wondering if something they're doing is screwing them up."

"Oh." I gaze down at Rivi who's sleeping in her stroller.

*No Small* BET

"Wait. Do *you* feel like a mom?"

"Having never been one, I can't be sure. But, Sophie, I *am* the one who puts her to sleep every night and wakes up for two o'clock feedings. I'm the one—maybe the *only* one—who worries about her future, and who she's going to date and where she'll go to college and when she should start solid food, and what kind of baby food she should eat, and will it upset her little tummy. And I wonder every day if there's something I could be doing better to give her the best chance at happiness."

Her arm comes around my shoulders. "Wow. I knew you were doing the live-in thing, but I guess I didn't know how intense it was. You really think Hawk doesn't worry about her future?"

"I don't know. He doesn't seem to have thoughts or emotions about much of anything."

"Sounds like a pitiful existence. Maybe you should ask for more time off."

"That's the thing. I don't *want* time off. I love being with Rivi. She's so easy. Much easier than my nieces Aurora and Ashley, who were both colicky at this age. She's just perfect."

"Addison." Sophie leans away and studies my face. "Do you *want* to be her mother?"

"Of course not." Thoughts race through my head. "But what if Hawk gets into a relationship one day and that woman becomes Rivi's mom? And what if she decides she doesn't want a live-in nanny who's around all the time? Or maybe not a nanny at all. And then what happens to me, I just leave? I never see them again?"

"Them?" she asks. She blows out a long sigh. "Oh, Addy, have you gone and fallen for the dad? Girl, rule number one: don't fall for the father."

"I'm fairly sure that only applies to married fathers."

"It doesn't. Believe me. I have more than one nanny friend who fell for the single dad. Guys are attracted to nannies because they know they're supposed to be off limits. It's exciting for them. Dangerous. Forbidden. But once the nannies are no longer the nannies, the lure isn't so strong. It rarely works out and then you're left without the guy *and* the kid. My advice, fall for one or the other. Never both." She puts a hand on mine. "But I see I might be too late for that. Hawk McQuaid? Really?"

"Trust me when I tell you that was never my intention. But what's the old saying, you can't control who you fall in love with?"

"Love? You're in *love* with him?"

I swallow. "Please don't say anything. Especially to Amber. She's friends with Tag, and if this got back to one of my brothers, they'd handcuff me, haul me out of there, and hide me away until I was forty. Holland thinks it's just a crush. I was hoping she was right. But after Martha's Vineyard and then last night—"

"Addy!" she yelps with the scolding tone of a tried-and-true mother. "Did you sleep with him?"

"No. But I would have. If he hadn't, um, peaked early."

Giggles flow out of her. "Oh this is precious. Hawk McQuaid: king of one-nighters, breaker of hearts *and* vaginas, couldn't hold his load?"

"Shhh," I chide, glancing around to make sure no one is listening.

"You do realize you're asking me to keep one of the best secrets in Calloway Creek. *So* not fair."

"I'm sorry. But I had to get it off my chest. And speaking of things that aren't fair, this little one smiled yesterday. At *him*. Not at the person who's raising her. At the man who barely lifts a finger to do anything for her."

"And this is the guy you fell for?"

I cover my face in shame. "I know. It's ridiculous, isn't it?"

"Good girl falls for bad boy. It's a classic." She stands and calls to Josie. "Come on, Jojo, we have to go meet Mommy for lunch." She turns. "It was nice seeing you, Addison. Let's not wait so long to do it again. And peek-a-boo might work."

I look at her with an odd stare.

"For getting her to smile. Try peek-a-boo. Especially with funny noises."

"See, a real nanny would know that. I'm just a glorified babysitter."

"Don't sell yourself short. From what you've told me, it seems to me you're way more than just a nanny. Bye, Addy."

I pick a squirming Rivi up out of her stroller. "I'm going to get you to smile today if it's the last thing I do." I make a silly face. "Yes I am." I blow raspberries. "Yes I am." I waggle my tongue. I scrunch up my nose and shake my head back and forth. But still nothing. Not a hint of a smile.

I swing my legs up onto the bench and perch her against them. Then I cover my face. "Peek-a-boo!" I sing as I quickly move my hands.

Nothing.

I do it ten more times.

"What do I need to do? Why did you smile at him and not me?" I make more ridiculous faces and then give up, utterly frustrated as I place her back in the stroller. "Shit, shit, shit."

She smiles.

My jaw drops. I say the curse trifecta again, knowing what a bad nanny that makes me. She smiles a second time.

"Oh you poor baby. You sure are your father's daughter, aren't you?" I tickle her chin. "We're going to keep that little fact to ourselves and get you to smile some other way."

I stop by Donovan's for takeout on our way home. When Serenity brings my order to the bar, she fawns over Rivi. "She's growing more adorable every time I see her."

"You're going to have a baby with my brother, aren't you?"

"Getting a little ahead of ourselves aren't we?"

I stare her down.

"Fine. Yes, probably. And definitely more than one."

"I thought so. When do you think he's going to man up and propose?"

"We've only been dating a few months, Addy."

"Yeah, but when you know, you know, right?"

She ties up my takeout bag and pauses, looking at me with curious eyes. "Oh boy."

"What is it? Did you forget to put something in my order?"

"I've seen the way you look at him," she says.

"Him?"

"Don't play dumb." She leans against the bar. "I'm the queen of knowing what it's like to want someone you shouldn't."

I glance around. "Am I wearing a neon sign or something?" I let my head slump into my hands. "Am I really that obvious?"

"I think you're just that in love."

"And apparently everyone in town knows this but him."

"He probably knows more than you think he does."

"Not a chance. He'd run the other way for sure."

"Maybe he feels the same about you."

I muffle my laughter. "Come on, Ren. You and I both know the man isn't capable of relationships. Let alone with a Calloway. This town is divided enough without that drama."

"Who cares what the town thinks? The only thing that matters is what you and he think."

"He's not thinking anything. Except that maybe he has an easy lay under his roof." I wring my hands together nervously. "Which he doesn't. We haven't gone there yet."

Her eyebrows shoot up. "You're not going down that easy, are you? The Addy I know is tougher than that. The Addy I know is nobody's doormat. The Addy I know is strong, independent, and capable, and doesn't need a man to validate her existence."

"No, I don't need him." I sigh. "The problem is with how much I *want* him."

"Yes, well, that would be a dilemma considering your close proximity to each other. If you don't think he feels the same way, you may need to lower your expectations and decide what you're willing to put up with. Say you sleep with him and it's all fun and games, but then he sleeps with someone else, because, well, he's Hawk McQuaid. What would happen then?" She touches Rivi's foot. "What happens to her? All I'm saying is you have more than yourself to think about here. It's a delicate balance, deciding how much to listen to your heart versus your head."

"What did *you* listen to?"

"Me?" She chuckles. "I'm a terrible example. I threw all caution to the wind."

I pick up the bag and tuck it under the stroller thinking *and yet now you have everything*. "See you soon, Serenity. Tell Cooper and Cody I said hello."

She shakes her head, wanting to say more, but knowing she's said enough.

On the way to the car, my phone pings with an email. I get Rivi settled into her car seat and check the message. It's from the hospital billing department. I called this morning to have future bills sent to me and not my parents. But there must be some mistake. This email claims I have a zero balance.

At home, I put Rivi down for a nap and call the number on the message. "This is Addison Calloway."

I explain to the nice man on the other end of the phone that an error was made.

"There's been no error, ma'am. The entire balance was paid off a few hours ago. It's what prompted the email to be sent. It's customary to give confirmation when accounts have been settled."

"But I didn't pay it. I just called to change the email and billing address."

"It looks like the payment came from an account at your new address."

My head falls back against the couch cushion. My blood boils. I'm about to yell at the innocent man on the phone when I stop myself. He's not the one I'm mad at. "Okay, thank you."

"Have a nice day, ma'am."

"Not likely, but thanks."

I put my lunch in the fridge, too pissed off to eat. The nerve. I just told him at breakfast that I didn't want his money for a prosthetic, so he goes and does this? I'm physically shaking. I need to calm down.

I go to my room, change into my workout clothes, grab the baby monitor, and head to the gym. Then I put on my favorite playlist and try to exercise the infuriating, exasperating, irritating, provoking, insanely gorgeous man out of my head.

# Chapter Twenty-seven

*Hawk*

I glance around at the walls of the office that seems smaller somehow. Pictures of my grandfather with founders, CEOs, and presidents of most of the world's car manufacturers are proudly displayed. He's smiling in every one of them. He looked genuinely happy to be doing what he was doing. I suppose he felt some sort of purpose. It's a feeling that's been foreign to me until very recently. I've gone through the motions of coming to work day after day, putting on a good front that maybe this was what I was meant to do—manage the family business. Carry the torch—but the more I do it, the more the walls close in on me. I feel like an imposter.

This is not where I'm destined to be.

Then again, what *is* my destiny? I'm not sure I fit in anywhere. In less than eleven months, I'll have more money than I'll know what to do with. Maybe I don't need to fit in anywhere. On the other hand, what am I going to do, sit around and write fairy tales all the time? That's not a life. That's a pitiful existence, hiding from reality and living in a dream. And I know for a fact, after Addy is gone—and she *will* be gone—I won't be writing anymore. She's my muse. My inspiration. She makes getting up in the morning not so lonely and going home to a big empty house not so pathetic.

I hear a commotion in the break room down the hall and get up to investigate. I meander over and lean in the doorway, watching my employees drink soda and eat cake. Right, it's Ronald Jones' fiftieth birthday. As usual, I wasn't invited. The nerve, not inviting the boss to a party held at his family's dealership in his family's break room.

They knew I wouldn't come. It's why they never bother.

Kory looks up. "Uh, hi, Hawk." She holds out a piece of cake. "Would you like some?"

I shake my head. "Keep it down. Some people are trying to work around here."

"Yeah? And which people would that be?"

It's a dig directed at me. She of all people knows I do diddly squat around here. But she's never called me out on it until now.

Some of the workers snicker quietly. Then they huddle around the cake, and someone takes a selfie.

"That's one for the wall," someone says.

I return to my office, slowly this time. Why is it that part of me wanted to stay? Eat cake. Drink soda. Be in the picture. Laugh at the boss.

When I turn the corner, I stop. Pappy is sitting at my desk looking at my monitor. Damn it, I don't think I closed the file I was editing. I trot over and hit the power button.

He looks up, grinning. "Doing some light reading on your break?"

I can't tell if he's being sarcastic or not. He doesn't surrender the chair to me. *My* chair. He leans back in it like he owns the place—which he does. So being the dutiful grandson, I take the chair opposite the desk. "To what do I owe the pleasure?"

I *am* being sarcastic.

"Heard there was some excitement at your house last night."

Suddenly, my heart races. Visions of Addy stroking my dick and me licking her clit rush through my head. How could he know? Is he here to punish me for defiling the nanny?

Then it dawns on me. "You mean the fire department being called. It wasn't a big deal. Addison was in the elevator when it lost—"

"I know all the details, grandson. Did you forget who you're talking to?"

I try not to roll my eyes, or he might actually take off his belt and whip me. "Right."

"Poor girl must be traumatized. I'll bet she was all kinds of scared, maybe even out of her mind after what she went through in her accident."

I don't tell him he's spot on. That she was panicking, and I had to talk her down. That hearing the helplessness in her voice broke me. That I've never run so fast to get where I was going.

"You should give her a few days off."

"She's fine. She doesn't need it."

"And you would know this how?"

"She just doesn't is all."

"You still afraid of being alone with the tot?"

"I'm not afraid. There's just no point."

"Grandson, there *is* a point. What do you think this whole exercise is about?"

"You wanting to control everything."

His shoulders bounce as he chuckles. "Well, yes, I suppose there is that. I was hoping to see you come around before this. But I'm a patient man. There are still forty-six weeks left."

I do the math in my head, something I've gotten very good at over these past weeks. Forty-six more weeks equals over seventeen million dollars. Forty-six more weeks until I get my life back. My freedom. Control over my trust fund.

For a fleeting second, Addy's face appears in my mind reminding me of what I *won't* have. I quickly push it aside. There is a small compartment in my brain where I keep her. I let her invade the other parts from time to time. Like when I write. Or when she's sitting naked on her bed. Or when she infuriates me. But I always put her back in the box. I can't afford to have her throw my game.

"I have something for you." Pappy leans down and comes up with a flat package. He sets it on the desk.

I don't open it. I know what his motivation is, and this will not be anything good. More tickets for a vacation perhaps, this time without Addy. The thought makes my stomach turn.

"Go on now," he urges, sliding it closer to me.

I lift the lid, move the tissue paper aside and see a framed photo of Rivington. I immediately close the box. "Great, thanks."

He takes the box from me, pulls out the frame, and stands it on the corner of my desk. "I think it looks fine right here, don't you?"

"Sure. Whatever."

"Okay then." He stands. "I look forward to seeing it right there when I visit again."

He's so fucking passive aggressive it makes me want to shove a fist through the drywall. He knows I won't dare move it after that proclamation. *I* know I won't move it.

He nods to my computer monitor. "Guess you'll want to get back to your reading then."

Apparently, Kory isn't the only one who knows I don't do shit around here.

He leaves and I stare at the photo realizing it's not so much having a picture on the desk that bothers me. It's who's in the picture. I'd much rather it be Addy. I close my eyes and conjure up her smiling face, knowing I'm taking her out of the box in my head far more than I should.

"Isn't she adorable!"

My eyes fly open. Kate is leaning on my desk handling the photo. I take it back and set it down.

"I still can't believe you have a daughter." She closes my door, comes around the back of the desk, stands behind me and runs her hands down my chest from above. "What is it about single dads that make them so darn sexy?"

I stop the progress of her hands. "Was there something you needed?"

"You could say that." She breaks a hand free and leans over to put it on my cock. "Looks like you need it too. You're already hard."

"That's what happens when you barge in on me when I'm thinking about someone else."

She hesitates for a moment then proceeds to rub me through my pants. "But *I'm* the one who's here."

Her breasts cradle the back of my head. I contemplate going through with it. Kate is the much more logical option here. She's safe. Attractive. Convenient. Not off-limits. And she won't hate me ten and a half months from now.

But why, then, have I gone completely flaccid?

I remove her hand and roll my chair away. "I have to get back to work."

She straightens and studies me. "What gives? Do you not find me attractive anymore?"

"I don't have time for this." I motion to the door. "Do you mind?"

"Hawk…"

"Kate, read the writing on the wall. I don't want you here. I don't want you on my desk. I don't want you shoving your hands in my pants. I don't want you. Jesus, take a damn hint, why don't you?"

Tears well in her eyes. "I thought—"

"You thought wrong."

She shuffles out the door and I try to figure out if I feel guilty about it or not.

Later, on my way out of the office, Kory hands me a file folder.

"What's this?" I ask.

"Potential candidates for service manager."

My brows go up.

"Kate walked out an hour ago."

"She say why?" I ask as if I don't know I'm the asshole who's responsible.

"Do you really want me to answer that?"

I push the folder back to her. "Hire whoever you want. I don't give a shit."

Sitting in my Porsche in the parking lot I have a hunch that Kate is not the first person to quit because of me, and she probably won't be the last. So I shouldn't let it bother me. But something niggles in the back of my mind, eating away at me on the drive home.

When I step inside my house, however, every thought in my head dissipates when I see Addy out in the hot tub. The water bubbles up over her breasts making me wonder if she's naked. The closer I get to the back door, the harder my cock becomes. Despite my efforts not to, I've thought about her all day. Editing my book, I found myself adding more details to the way Adelaide looks at Jenson. More specifics about how they are together. More emotions and feelings when she touches him.

There is nothing I want more than Addy in the hot tub. I stop at the door and watch. She's sipping wine, listening to music. Her head leans back against the unforgiving concrete side, and I have the urge to slip in behind her and cushion it. I want to strip down, get in, lift her onto the side and stick my tongue in her like I did last night. Only this time, I'd get to see her come, not just hear her. The thought of watching her fall apart with my fingers inside her, the rosy hue of the sunset behind her, is almost enough to make me jizz right here.

I open the door. She opens her eyes, staring daggers into mine. Is she mad at me? Then I remember I don't care, because mad Addy is even hotter.

She turns off the music. "You're overstepping," she says with a sneer that makes my cock dance.

"What am I overstepping?"

"The boundaries of our relationship."

I take a seat on the chaise, right next to her prosthetic. "I wasn't aware we had one."

I realize that makes me sound like a prick, but it's hard to make a leopard change his spots.

She regards me with a stony stillness. "Our *working* relationship."

Something that feels a bit like disappointment races through me when she says that. I push the feeling aside, because, Christ, I don't want a relationship. I'm the last guy on Earth who should be in one.

"You still haven't told me why."

"You paid off my hospital bill."

"Oh, that. It's no big deal."

"It is to me, Hawk. I explicitly told you not to buy me a new prosthetic."

"I didn't buy you a new prosthetic."

"Ugh!" She hits the water, splashing some onto my shoes. "You are so infuriating."

"So I've been told." I stand and remove my shoes.

"What are you doing?"

"What does it look like?" I say, unbuckling my belt.

Her eyes follow the motion of my hands as I unzip my fly. My pants fall to my ankles, and I toe them off. When I unbutton my shirt and remove it, she can undoubtedly see my burgeoning erection. I take off my skivvies and stand naked before her, wondering if this is the first time she's seen a man's penis. She said she went to third base with Anthony Silverman, but we were talking about her body, not his. And damn it if I don't want to be the only man she's ever touched.

Damp hair tumbles around her flushed face. "You are not getting in here with me."

"Oh but I am."

"Then I'm getting out."

I take her prosthetic and move it further away. It's unfair of me to do, but nobody ever accused me of playing nice.

"Hawk, you're such an asshole."

She pushes herself out and sits on the edge, ready to bolt on one leg. And after last night, I know she can do it.

I quickly hop in the spa and pull her back down. "You can't run away from me."

"I think you're confusing me with some of your other conquests."

"You're not a conquest, Addy. You're different. And you could try to run but it would be useless. I'd find you."

Her head falls back and her eyes close. "Why do you keep doing this?"

"Doing what?"

"Being an asshole one minute and a romantic the next."

I laugh. "You think I'm romantic? Now that's something I've never been accused of. What would make you say that?"

"Oh, I don't know, the breakfasts, the looks, the... *sweetheart*." She swallows as if she was scared to say the word.

"You got me on that last one. That was quite uncharacteristic of me."

"So you've never...?"

I lean closer and my lips hover above hers. "No, I've never. Not before last night."

A small smile cracks her face.

"What?"

"With your reputation, I never thought I'd be your first *anything*."

The triumphant look in her eyes is even better than the pouty one from a minute ago. She has no idea that she has so many more of my firsts. I feel the box in my head opening. Hell, it's shredding to pieces.

We stare at each other, inches apart, both hesitating, both challenging. She's not going to break, although I can see in her eyes

247

how much she wants me. She wants to stay mad but can't. I'm trying to wait until she gives in. My dick throbs in the heat of the swirling water.

When I can't take it anymore—because I need this woman more than I need my next disbursement—my lips come crashing down on hers.

# Chapter Twenty-eight

*Addison*

"I'm still mad at you," I say when I have to break away to catch my breath.

"Good." His heated stare burns into me. "I like you mad at me."

"You're twisted. I—"

His tongue on my neck stops my words. All thoughts are on him. And his nakedness. As pissed off as I was, the moment he stripped down, I was stunned. I've never seen a fully naked man before. Not in real life anyway. And after seeing him, I'm willing to bet seeing anyone else would be a colossal let down. His arms and thighs are thick, a testament to how much time he spends in his home gym. His chest taut and rippled into an eight-pack of male godliness. And his penis—my insides shudder—it's male perfection if I ever saw it. Long, thick, and hard. And velvety soft if I remember correctly from last night. This time, I vow to be the one responsible for his orgasm.

He pulls me against him and swaps our positions so he's on the seat and I'm straddling him, the tip of his penis tickling the inside of my thigh. His kisses blaze a path to my breasts as he unties the string of my top. When his tongue finds my nipple, I moan into him. I also say a prayer—*please don't let Rivi wake up until this is over.*

*This.*

How far will it go today? Will he make love to me? He said we were going to take it one step at a time. But we've already done the other steps. Unless maybe he wants me to do to him what he did to me. I draw in a shaky breath, because *now* I'm nervous. It's one thing to touch his penis. Another entirely to put it in my mouth. What if I don't do it properly? What if I bite him? What if I choke?

"Addy?"

He quits toying with my breasts and looks up at me.

"Huh?"

"You went completely still. Everything okay?"

"Yes. I was just thinking about, uh, stuff."

"Relax, sweetheart. This doesn't have to go anywhere you don't want it to."

I nod, wanting this to go everywhere but anxious about it all the same.

He unties the strings of my bottoms, pulls them out from between us, and they float away. We're totally naked with nothing between us. And I realize how much it excites me. How much I want to finish what we didn't last night. How I want to feel him sink into me. How I want to look at his face when he comes.

A finger dips inside me. A moan escapes me and my back arches as I bear down on it, needing more.

"Do you know how fucking sexy you are?"

His words embolden me. And I reply, "Tell me."

"I want to do things to you I shouldn't. I want to touch you everywhere. With my fingers. My tongue. My cock." A finger moves to a place no man has gone. He touches the pucker of my ass. "Even here."

I stiffen. But even the thought of that is sexy and has my head spinning. Oh the things I want him to do to me.

"But not just yet," he says with a disarming grin. "Not today."

I try to decide if I'm disappointed or relieved.

He moves me off his lap and hoists me onto the side of the hot tub. Spreading my legs, he gazes at me down there as if he's a starving man at a Christmas buffet. "I've been thinking about this all day."

*He has?*

"The way you taste. How it felt when you came on my fingers. I knew I'd be doing this again."

My legs fall open easier than I should let them. I'm unabashedly on display for him. The sun is setting but he can still see me clearly. At this point, however, I don't care. I want his tongue on me. I need it there.

I lean back onto my arms and watch him tongue me. He sticks it inside me, moving it in and out before he circles my clit with it. He flattens his tongue against it. Then flicks it. Then lightly grazes it with his teeth. I almost see stars. His name slides off my tongue in a prayer.

"I need you to come, and I need it now." He thrusts a finger inside me. Then another. Then he toys with the opening to my ass, something that feels so naughty it pushes me into oblivion, and I not only say his name, I scream it.

When I stop convulsing, I mutter, "Oh my gosh. I'm sorry. Your neighbors."

"Screw the neighbors. Do *that*. Do that every goddamn time."

I look down into the water but can't see his penis because of the bubbles. "Did you, uh—"

He laughs. "Not this time. But I want to."

I hold up a hand. "Should I..."

He nods to his pants. "I have a condom."

I swallow, both terrified and excited at the very same time. "Are you sure you want to do this before I'm on the pill?"

"No. But if you let me, I'm going to anyway. Addy, I couldn't stop now if a bulldozer came crashing through the fence."

Serenity's face flashes through my mind. Do I really want to do this—risk everything? And just like she said would happen, my heart and my head are at a standoff. But it's my eyes that make the decision. Seeing him look at me the way he is—the way no man ever has. He's gorgeous. He's everything I shouldn't want and more. So, like Ren, I decide to throw caution to the wind.

I bite my lip and smile. "Get the condom."

Reaching over me, he pulls his pants in with us. His phone falls into the water. He grabs it and throws it on the concrete, not seeming to care if it's broken or not. He gets a condom out then tosses his wallet next to the phone. Next, he positions his legs between mine, kneeling before me, half in the water as his pants dance in the bubbles behind him.

Watching him put on the condom is sexier than I thought it would be. I can't help myself when I reach out and touch him. The condom is lubricated and my hand glides easily along his shaft. His eyes close, his jaw goes slack, and he breathes heavily. It's an amazing sense of power seeing his reaction. In a way, he even seems vulnerable. It makes me wonder if I'm the putty in his hands or if he's the putty in mine.

He slows my hand. "If you keep doing that, this will be over. But if that's what you want, it's okay."

"That's not what I want."

The fire in his eyes ignites even more. He scoots closer and puts the tip against me. "You sure?"

"Hawk, I'm sure. I want this."

He braces his arms on either side of me and slowly slides in. I gasp at the stretch, and he stills. I grab his shoulders and pull, letting him know it's okay. He inches in. "Tell me if you want to stop."

"I don't."

He pulls back and pushes in, slowly, then faster, gauging my reaction.

"Hawk, I'm fine. It feels good."

I don't tell him I have two vibrators that have been where he is. That if it's my cherry he's worried about popping, it's long ago been popped. But all the same, he's thicker than expected. And so much sexier than a vibrating piece of rubber.

"It feels more than good," he says. "It's fucking perfect." He sweeps my damp hair aside, grips the side of my neck and pulls me in for a kiss.

He's claiming me. My lips, my virginity. My very heart and soul.

Once I'm used to him, my hips move, meeting his every thrust. He groans into my mouth. I put a hand between us and push his chest away. "I want to see you."

Our eyes lock as he pumps into me. I can see what's about to happen as his glaze over. He thrusts a few more times, then his face contorts as if he's in pain, then total elation spreads across it as he stills inside me, gripping my hips like his life depends on it.

His head slumps. "Holy shit."

I tap a finger on my lips then ask, "Holy shit good or holy shit bad?"

"Definitely holy shit good." He holds the top of the condom as he withdraws. I wince. "You okay?"

"I'm good."

"I was hoping you'd have another."

"Hawk, I think losing my virginity is a feat in itself. Let's leave multiple orgasms for another day."

He smirks. "Challenge accepted."

He ties off the condom and tosses it aside. Then he stands, hoists me out of the water in his arms, and carries me to the chaise where he put my prosthesis. He hands me my towel, but he doesn't have one for himself.

I hold it out. "You need to dry off, too."

He thumbs inside. "I'll get another one."

When I wrap myself up, I notice his knees are red and angry and have cuts and scrapes all over. "You're hurt."

He looks down and shrugs. "I never even noticed. And believe me, I'd endure more than just banged up knees to do that again. You have no idea how beautiful you are, do you?"

I pull the towel tightly around me and glance at my prosthetic.

"You don't have to do that around me—be shy about your leg—it doesn't matter to me. So get over yourself if you think it does."

Suddenly he stiffens. I turn and look in the direction of his gaze. His brother, Hunter, is standing in the doorway.

Hawk, in all his nakedness, moves to shield me even though my back is to the door and I'm covered by a towel. "Get back in the fucking house!" he shouts.

Hunter looks at me and shakes his head. "I'll wait in the kitchen."

"Looks like you might have some explaining to do," I say.

"I don't need to explain myself to anyone."

"I'm not sure your brothers will see it that way. Just maybe put clothes on first."

He looks down as if it just occurred to him that he's still naked. He pushes a chunk of wet hair out of my eyes. "You okay?"

"I'm fine. Go. Put out fires. And maybe tell him to keep his mouth shut if you value your life. The last thing we need is *my* brothers knowing about this."

"No shit."

He fishes my bikini out of the spa and hands it to me. Then he collects his own wet things and walks to the door. He turns before he goes through. And he smiles.

How I love that man's smile.

And I realize that, no, this is most definitely not just a crush. But I'm not sure there is enough bubble wrap in the world to protect my heart.

Samantha Christy

# Chapter Twenty-nine

*Hawk*

"Fucking knock next time," I say, hitting Hunter on the back of the head as I pass him in the kitchen on my way to the laundry room.

"Dude, we never knock," he calls out after me. "You waltz into my apartment all the time. And we were supposed to watch the game here."

Shit. I completely forgot. "Well, things have changed. Knock now."

I dump my wet clothes on the laundry room floor and pull a fresh set from the dryer.

"What are you doing, brother?" Hunter asks skeptically when I appear in the kitchen doorway.

He goes silent when Addy comes in the room and mixes a bottle of formula. She's back in her bikini with the towel wrapped around her. She shakes the bottle, turns, and thumbs to the stairs. "So I'm just gonna feed Rivi in her room."

"You don't have to do that," I say.

"I think I do. See you later, Hunter."

He barely even looks at her. "Addison."

Neither of us says a word as she goes up the stairs, around the corner and into Riv's bedroom—which we know for sure since she makes a big deal out of shutting the door loudly and greeting the baby before turning off the monitor.

The security system beeps as my other brother walks right into my home. Hudson appears in the kitchen doorway, sees us and raises a brow. "Did I miss something?"

"That's the understatement of the decade," Hunter says. "If you'd been on time, you'd have seen what I did, which was Hawk boning Addison Calloway in his hot tub."

Hudson's jaw drops.

My head whips around, fuming at the notion that he saw Addy lose her virginity in the spa. "You were *watching* us?"

"Not exactly. But I saw her sitting on the lounger—naked. And with your clothes strewn about by the hot tub, I put two and two together."

I feel a sliver of relief knowing he only caught a glimpse of her back since she was facing away from the house. I don't want my brother seeing her naked. I don't want *anyone* seeing her naked. My jaw twitches at the thought. I'm in full-on protector mode and it's uncharted territory.

Hudson shakes his head over and over, disappointment oozing from his pores. "What in the ever-loving fuck are you doing?"

"It's really none of your business." I stride to the refrigerator, pull out three beers and hand each of them one.

"How long has this been going on?"

"Not that I have to explain anything to you, but this was the first time."

"Good." Hunter breathes a sigh of relief. "So you can fire her and move the hell on."

"I'm not firing her."

"Well you can't very well live in the same house as someone you had a one-nighter with. Way too messy."

I pick up my beer and head outside, averting my eyes from the hot tub, because I know all I'll see is her. I'm not sure I'll ever be able to look at it again without seeing her face when I put my dick inside her for the first time. The way she looked at me made me feel—I search for the right word—*significant*. And I know it's something I want to experience again. Yet somehow I'm pretty sure she's the only woman who could ever make me feel that way.

I turn on the TV, change the channel to the Nighthawks game, flip on the fireplace, and settle onto the couch.

Hunter and Hudson stare at me from the back door.

"This *was* just a one-and-done," Hudson says, cocking his head. "Wasn't it?"

I drink my beer. "If you're not going to watch the game, you're free to get the hell out."

"Jesus Christ," Hunter says, striding forward. "You can't be serious. You know you only want her because it's a big fuck you to her brothers."

"I don't know what the hell I want except maybe to watch this goddamn game."

"You can't date a Calloway," Hudson says.

"I'm not dating anyone."

"Well, whatever you call it, stop doing it."

I slam my bottle onto the table causing it to foam up and spill over. "Listen up, this conversation is over. Either watch the game or leave."

The French doors open and Addy comes out carrying Riv. Her hair is still damp, but she's fully dressed now in lounge pants and a sweatshirt. She deposits Riv in my lap and offers me a daring smirk. "You guys don't mind if I watch the game with you, do you? I just need to get a drink."

I'm speechless for two reasons. One, she wants to hang out with me and my brothers. And two, she's going to watch a baseball game. Before I can complain about holding the baby, she's back in the house. But strangely enough, I find I don't *want* to complain.

"You seem more comfortable with the kid now," Hunter says. "In fact, if I didn't know any better, I'd say the three of you seem almost like a family."

"Fuck off. That's not what we are."

"Are you sure about that?"

Addy comes back with a baby seat in one hand and a glass in the other. A bottle of wine is tucked under her arm. She looks at the three of us as we stare at her.

"Don't get up," she says sardonically. "I got this."

I sneer at my brothers. "Help her, you jagoffs."

They do as I say. Hunter takes the baby seat and Hudson grabs the bottle of wine.

She sits on the same couch I'm on, but not too close, leaving a respectable amount of distance between us. Which is good. If she came over and tried to hold my hand my brothers would blow a gasket.

For a second though, I want her to do exactly that. A vision runs through my head of us sitting out here sipping wine and holding hands. It's like looking at a friggin' Norman Rockwell painting. It's so normal. So ordinary. And so goddamn unlike me. So why then is it suddenly so appealing?

I banish the thought from my head and lean over, handing her the baby. She puts Riv in her seat up on the large coffee table in front of us and unscrews the bottle of wine. I'm amused. I have a good wine collection, but she doesn't touch it. She buys her own ten-dollar-a-bottle screw caps.

"You watch baseball?" Hudson asks.

"I had to see what the fuss was all about over Rivi's namesake." She turns to me. "You were right. He is really good. And it looks like they may be headed to the playoffs. I hope they win, I put twenty dollars on this game."

Hunter about spits out his beer. Hudson laughs. I ask, "You bet on sports?"

"I bet on Marco Rivington."

"How did you even know how to do it?"

"Tag showed me how. He has a bookie."

Tag. Her brother. A Calloway. And I'm back to wondering just how much shit I got myself into by sleeping with her. We have to keep this under wraps. Because her brothers would tar and feather me and hang me by the balls from Lloyd McQuaid's statue on the circle if they knew about this. And then they would kill me when it all goes bad.

I turn to my brothers. "Anything you see or hear tonight is to stay between us. Got it?"

Hunter chuckles. "Don't want to start World War Three, huh?"

"Just keep it to yourself."

The third baseman for the Nighthawks makes an error and the Phillies score a run. I jump out of my seat. "You stupid fucker. My grandma could've made that play. You're going to single-handedly throw this game you idiot. Shit!"

"Hawk, look." Addy is gawking at Riv, who's smiling up at me. "You made her smile again."

I cock my head and stare at the tiny human. "She's twisted."

Addy laughs. "Tell me about it. I got her to laugh earlier today, you know."

"Oh yeah? How?"

"By cursing."

My brow lifts and a smile cracks my face. "I would have liked to have seen it." I lean down. "You cursing."

Hunter clears his throat reminding us we have company. "So what did you bet?" he asks Addy.

"I made two bets, actually. Ten dollars on him getting a home run and another ten on him getting three hits."

"Do you know the odds?"

She shakes her head. "Plus something or other. I don't really understand all the jargon."

"I could teach you," Hunter says.

"Hell no!" Hudson and I shout at the same time.

Riv smiles again. Addy giggles. "Oh, you're going to have your hands full when this one gets older."

I take a long pull from my beer. Because I won't. My hands won't be full of anything forty-six weeks from now. Of Rivington. Of her. My life will go back to being exactly what it was before. I just never realized what that life was until now.

*Empty.*

During a commercial, Addy tries to make Riv smile by *not* shouting expletives. She doesn't even care how ridiculous she looks making all the funny faces.

This girl. She likes sports. She likes baking. She likes *me*. She's fucking perfect and she doesn't even know it.

# Chapter Thirty

*Addison*

"Oh my gosh. Finally." I lean down and give a smiling Rivi another Eskimo kiss. I whisk her into my arms and carry her downstairs. "Hawk! She finally smiled without cuss words."

He comes out of his office, chuckling. "Should we call the press?"

"Very funny." I set Rivi down in her baby seat. "Watch." I touch the tip of my nose to hers and rub it from side to side, tickling both her nose and mine. She smiles. "She's so darn cute. You try it."

"I'm not sticking my nose in her face."

"Hawk, come on."

"No."

My hands land on my hips as I scold him with my posture.

He rolls his eyes, grumbles, then leans over and does it. She smiles. "There. Are you happy now?"

"Very."

"If you tell anyone I did that, I'll deny it."

I hold up my phone. "Too late. I got it on video."

His face is full of surprise. "Do not send that to anyone."

"Let's see. I think your mother would love this. Holland for sure. Oh, and Hunter and Hudson." I pretend to tap around and text it.

"You little traitor."

I run away with my phone.

"Give it." He chases me around the room.

I bank right and my leg falls off, causing me to tumble to the floor while my phone flies in the other direction.

"You okay?" He gets on his knees.

"Damn leg."

"Maybe that wouldn't happen if you'd let me buy you a new one."

"You've done quite enough without asking permission."

He retrieves my phone and shows me the cracked screen. "At least let me buy you a new one of these."

"You absolutely will not." I take it from him. "This I can afford."

"You do realize I earn enough interest on my trust fund in about thirty seconds to pay for your phone."

My eyes go wide. "Really?"

"Maybe. I don't know. But the point is, it's nothing to me."

"That's why. You throw around money like there's a never-ending stream of it. I work hard for my money, and it makes me feel good when I'm able to buy myself nice things. When nice things don't come easily, you appreciate them a whole lot more."

He straddles me, his masculine mouth twitching into a wry grin. *"You're* a nice thing."

My heart does a little dance. Ever since the first time we had sex two weeks ago, he's occasionally said romantic things. Not often, because he's Hawk McQuaid. But when he does, they go straight to my soul.

Since that night in the hot tub, we haven't talked about what this means. We've been together almost every night in one way or another. Some nights he comes to my room. Others, he takes me on the couch. We had a repeat of the hot tub two nights ago, and this morning, during Rivi's nap, he cornered me in the gym after my workout. The man is insatiable. And apparently, so am I.

"Are you saying you appreciate me?"

"I don't know." His fingers close around my wrists as he presses my hands to the floor next to my head. "Did you really send the video?"

"I wouldn't do that. I was only teasing."

He leans over and his hot breath flows over my ear. "Then I appreciate you." He grinds his groin into me. "In all ways."

The doorbell rings. He doesn't move.

I peek around him. "Aren't you going to get that?"

He kisses my throat. "They'll leave."

It rings again and I hear a high-pitched, "Hawk!"

"It sounds like your sister." I shimmy out from under him.

"*Half*-sister."

"There you go with semantics again. Well, if you aren't getting the door. I am."

"Go. I'm not letting Dani in with a raging boner tenting my pants."

I look down and giggle, delighted it doesn't take much to turn him on. "Coming!" I yell and snap my prosthesis into place.

Heather and Dani are waiting at the door with a gift bag. "Addison," Heather says. "So nice to see you."

Dani runs around me. "Where's my cute little niece?"

"Great room." I nod to the pretty pink bag Heather is holding. "What's the occasion?"

"Dani wanted to bring a present over to celebrate Rivington's two-month birthday."

"Aw. That's sweet. Can I get you some tea or a soda?"

"Despite how my son treats you, you aren't a servant. I know where the drinks are."

I wonder what she would think about how her son treats me in bed. On the couch. In the spa. Then again, Heather went from being married to a McQuaid to being married to a Calloway. Somehow I get the idea she may be the only one who would like it.

A half hour later, Hawk finally makes an appearance. Dani runs over and hugs him. "I didn't know you were here."

He hugs her back, albeit somewhat reluctantly. He puts up a good front, but I've seen him with her when no one else was around and he didn't know I was watching. I know he's fond of her. They even have a secret handshake.

Deep down, I hope it's the same with Rivi, that he secretly loves her even though he pretends he doesn't. That she's wrapping her little fingers around his heart when she smiles at him. That he's starting to think of himself as a real dad.

"I *do* live here," he says.

"I know, but you're never around."

He's around a lot more than he used to be, I think to myself. *A lot more.*

"Dani and your mom brought Rivi a present." I pick up the adorable outfits and hold them up. "They're for her two-month birthday. Isn't that nice?"

"If you like tiny clothes with fruit all over them."

Heather walks over and plants a kiss on Hawk's cheek. I love that about her. She's not willing to accept that Hawk still holds a grudge. And if I had to guess, she'll spend the rest of her life trying to repair their relationship. "We should go. Come on, Dani. Let's go run some more errands."

I take Rivi from Dani and walk them to the door. "Bye, Dani. Bye Aunt Heather."

Hawk is looking at me funny when I join him again. "Sometimes I forget my mom is your aunt."

"Only by marriage."

"Still. Do you think it's weird that we're related and having sex?"

"I don't know. I mean we're not that closely related. Did you know *first* cousins are allowed to marry in about half the states?"

He pulls back, looking terrified.

"Don't worry, soldier. It's not like I Googled it or anything. Mia did back when she thought she was in love with her third cousin Wyatt."

His entire demeanor changes. Playful Hawk from earlier is gone and reluctant, stoic Hawk has taken his place. "I... think I'm going into the office today."

He grabs his keys.

I follow him to the garage. "Hey. Are we okay?"

"*We?*"

"Yeah, you know, you, me, this. Whatever we're doing."

"Sure. I'll catch you later."

I go to the kitchen, put Rivi down and slump into a chair wondering if I just ruined everything with my stupid comment. The last few weeks have been perfect. The sex has been incredible. Better even than how I imagined it would be. And every morning he makes me eggs.

Will he make them tomorrow? Will he come to me tonight? I'm being ridiculous. I should be able to make jokes around him without it causing such a reaction. Maybe it serves me right, getting into a relationship with a guy who doesn't do relationships.

But I know I won't do anything about it. Because being with him is better than the alternative. Even if there's no real future. Even if I'll get hurt. Even if I'll never find another guy like him.

I put Rivi down for a nap. Then I go into his office, open his laptop, and read.

## Chapter Thirty-one

*Hawk*

I've been avoiding her for days. Coming home late. Sneaking out early. Making excuses to stay away from the house. And she hasn't said a word about it. It's as if she knows what she said was like poison on my tongue: marriage. She couldn't really have thought that two weeks of sleeping together has us on that road.

Hunter turns off the TV when the game ends. "You didn't really come here to watch the game, did you? It's almost ten o'clock and you're showing zero signs of leaving. You haven't come over in weeks. You're avoiding her."

I lean back, cross an ankle over my knee, and stare into my bottle of beer.

"Oh shit," he says. "You're falling for her. Hawk, what the hell? You can't fall for Addison Calloway."

"I'm not."

He belts out a sardonic laugh. "Oh, but I believe you have. It appears, however, that you don't want to."

"Like you said. It's Addison."

"Looks like you have two choices then."

I drum the pads of my fingers on his leather couch. "Do tell."

"You could fire her."

I shake my head. "I can't fire her."

"Can't or won't?"

"Is there a difference?"

"Is the sun hot?" He laughs. "Well then it looks like you've got yourself a girlfriend."

My spine stiffens. "Girlfriend? No."

"Brother, I'm fairly certain she isn't a friends-with-benefits kind of girl. And since that's the only kind you want, it seems you're up shit creek and not even your trust fund can buy you a paddle." He thumbs to his bedroom. "I'm gonna turn in. You can crash here if you want, but sooner or later you'll have to suck it up, face the music, pay the piper, take your—"

"Yeah, yeah, yeah. I get it." I stand. "I'm outta here."

"Going home?"

"I don't know where I'm going."

Having only had two beers, I'm not violating our agreement when I get into the Porsche. I don't head home, however. I head to the only place this side of town you can grab a beer at this hour on a Wednesday."

"Just when I thought this day was going to end well," Cooper says when he sees me at the bar.

"Shut up and pour me a shot." I nod to the locked cabinet and throw a hundred-dollar bill on the counter.

"We're closing in twenty minutes," he says, sliding the small glass my way.

"Sign says eleven."

"We close early when no one is here."

"*I'm* here."

"Like I said, we're closing early. If there's something else you want, tell me now before I start mopping up."

"The bottle."

"You want me to leave the bottle?" He looks at it. It's at least twenty percent full. "You know how much we paid for that?"

I throw two more hundreds on the counter.

"Better add your keys to that pile or it's a no go."

I do what he says, even though it pains me to my core to follow an order given to me by a Calloway. But I'm not about to tell him I wouldn't drive anyway because I made a promise to his little sister. "Happy now, buttmunch?"

"Nothing about serving you makes me happy, McQuaid." He tucks my keys into his pocket and walks away.

I try to focus on the television, but there's nothing to watch. Just the evening news. So I watch Cooper pile chairs onto tables and mop the floor, the whole time holding back the comments on the tip of my tongue about him doing menial labor.

Then Serenity comes out from the back. She doesn't see me at the bar. All her attention is on Cooper. When she wraps her arms around him from behind, he drops the mop and holds her hands against him, looking like he just won the lottery. Or had an orgasm, I can't tell which. His face is full of some indescribable emotion. One I'm not familiar with. Or wasn't until recently.

I open the bottle and pour myself another shot.

He turns her around in his arms and starts dancing with her even though there's no music. They gaze at each other. Whisper to each other. Laugh with one another.

Something inside me shifts. All the oxygen is sucked out of my lungs like the wind has been knocked out of me. I'm fucking jealous. I'm jealous of a Calloway and his lady. I'm jealous because I want to be over there dancing with Addy like we're the only ones in the room. Whispering to her. Laughing with her. Doing *every* goddamn thing with her.

It physically hurts that I'm not. There's a sharp ache working its way through my body. A debilitating and unrelenting pain gnawing away at my gut. Could Hunter be right? Have I fallen for her? I close my eyes and picture my life without her. It's a soul-crushing feeling, like I've been torn open and left with a colossal void.

My eyes snap open.

*I'm in fucking love with Addison Calloway.*

I slam back another shot then head for the door, knowing I shouldn't go home, but will. Knowing I'll die if I don't see her. Knowing she's not the only one who's going to get hurt when this all blows up in my face. But being the selfish guy that I am, I don't care. Not right now anyway. All I care about is getting to her. Kissing her. Touching her. As much as I can for as long as she'll let me.

~ ~ ~

She startles when my arms go around her. It's dim in her room, but not dark. The nightlight is on.

When she faces me, she's not wearing the expression I expected. She's disappointed. "You smell like tequila. Did you drive?"

"I left my car at Donovan's."

"You *walked* here?"

I nod, wanting to tell her what I thought about the entire way. That I want her. That I can no longer picture my life without her. How she lights up every room she walks into and how her smile melts me to the core. How her beauty slays me and her strength inspires me. I want to tell her all of it and more. But I don't know how. I'm not brave like Jensen. I'm a coward whose only merit lies at the First National Bank.

"Why are you here?" she asks sleepily. "Booty call?"

I crawl in next to her. "No."

"Then what?"

"I'm not sure exactly."

She scoots away. "What's wrong with you, Hawk? You ignore me for days then climb into my bed like you haven't been. I'm not just going to lay around and be available for sex whenever you want it."

I sit on the edge of the bed. I don't know how to do this shit. Feelings. Emotions. It's like learning a new language. One I have entirely no basis for and zero foundation on which to build it.

"Answer the question. Why were you ignoring me?"

Instinctively, I try to protect myself. "You need to stop acting like we're a family."

"I've never acted like that. You're delusional if you think I'm any different than the day I walked in here eight weeks ago." She shoves a finger into my back. "You're the one with the problem. I know why you're doing this. I made a joke. A joke, Hawk. Funny, haha. And your tiny little brain took it somewhere it had no business going. But thank you for clarifying what I knew all along, that you're a jerk who has no intention of—"

I spin around and pin her to the bed. "Will you shut up, Addy? I fucking want you. I can't stop thinking about you."

Surprise crosses her face. And maybe elation. "I can't stop thinking about you either. And whether you want to believe it or not, *you're* the one who's changed."

"Only around you."

"You're not the man you were a few months ago."

"Because of you."

"Even so, I don't have any delusions about what this is. I know you're not the kind of guy who stays. You don't do relationships. And I've resigned myself to being okay with that."

"Even so, I want this."

She sighs. "Well, you have it."

"What if I want more?"

"More?" Her brows dip. "Then why do you have to make things so complicated? One minute you say you want me and the next you're a man on an island."

"Maybe because I have no idea what I'm doing."

Her face softens. "Hawk, I know what kind of man you are."

"You don't. No one does."

"You don't wear your feelings on your sleeve. Some might say you don't even have feelings." She puts her hand over my heart. "But I know better. I *see* you."

I roll off her, lie down, and trace the outline of her face. She thinks she knows me. She doesn't. Hell, *I* don't even know me. And no matter how much I want to get naked with her right now, I vow not to. Not tonight. Not after she thought I only came here for a hookup.

I cradle her. "This is going to be complicated."

She wiggles her ass into my groin. "Well from this position, yes."

I laugh. "Not that. Us."

"Oh, that. To say the least."

"What if I want to take you to dinner or something?"

She stretches her neck, turning to see me. Her smile is luminous. "You want to take me to dinner?"

I shrug. "It was a hypothetical. But maybe."

"Hypothetically, I guess we'd get a sitter and go into the city."

"A sitter who would keep their mouth shut? In this town? Unlikely."

"I know one."

"Who?"

"Sophie."

"Are you crazy?"

"I've sworn her to secrecy."

"About what?"

"Us."

I stiffen. "She knows about us?"

"I had to talk to someone. And it couldn't be anyone in my family. Or yours."

"So you decided confiding in the woman who works for Tag's best friend was the way to go?"

"She's a nanny. There's a code. Or…something."

"Fine. Hire her. I'll pay whatever it takes to keep her quiet. But if I end up in the hospital because she blabs, that's on you."

She turns around and faces me. "Hawk, you need to consider the fact that people might find out. Even if we stopped this right now, there are still people who know."

"Sophie and my brothers. And if you say Sophie won't talk, we're good. I *know* there's a bro code."

"There might be a few others," she says tentatively.

"Who?"

She shrugs innocently. "Holland."

"My *sister* knows?" I rub a hand across my jaw. "She's the biggest gossip in town."

"It's not a big deal. All she knows is that I have a thing for you. That's the extent of it. She has no idea we're, you know. And she's my best friend. She won't say anything."

"Famous last words."

She's quiet for a second then sucks her bottom lip into her mouth and chews on it. Damn, that can't be good.

"Addison, who else knows?"

"Serenity," she says softly, refusing to look at me.

I dart up and run a hand across my jaw. "Cooper's girlfriend? Are you kidding me? I might as well drive myself to the goddamn hospital. Do we know when the butchery is going to start?"

She sits up to face me. "Relax. She's known for weeks. If anything was going to happen, it would have already. She was very sympathetic to my situation."

"What situation is that?"

"Wanting someone I shouldn't."

"Good God." I pinch the bridge of my nose.

Her shoulders droop and she looks down at the bed. "I guess you're thinking I'm more trouble than I'm worth right about now."

I take her hand. "Then you definitely don't know me as well as you think you do."

"Fine. What were you thinking?"

"How quickly I can book a ticket to Yemen."

She laughs. I capture her mouth with mine and kiss her softly. Then I lie her back down and spoon her.

"Go to sleep," I say.

"You don't want to—"

"Oh, I do. Every damn minute of every damn day I do. But we're not going to. Not tonight. Tonight we're just doing this."

She relaxes into me. I hold her until she falls asleep. Then I get up and leave, glancing at the doorway across the hall, thinking how Addy has no idea just how complicated things really are.

# Chapter Thirty-two

*Addison*

We didn't say the words so I can't be sure. But if his behavior over the past few days is any indication, I think Hawk McQuaid just might be my boyfriend.

He holds my hand when we're watching TV. Plants kisses on my head when he leaves the room. Opens doors for me. Looks at me with those amazing smoldering eyes. And the way he makes love to me, even that has changed. I may be the only person in the world to ever see his tender side. And it's made me feel like I'm something I've never been. Special.

Everything is perfect. Well, almost everything.

I finish changing Rivi and take her downstairs. As usual, Hawk is in the kitchen making a breakfast he doesn't even eat. I wish he would connect with Rivi the way he's connected with me. He tolerates her. He does what he's contractually obligated to do, sometimes a little more in an effort to help me out. But he doesn't *see* her. Not in the way he sees me. To him, she's a chore that needs doing. An afterthought.

In an effort not to rock our otherwise amazing boat, I never bring it up. I have researched it, however. And based on my findings, it's not unusual for fathers to bond with babies long after mothers do. They don't tend to have as much skin-to-skin contact, interaction, and play time as moms.

*Moms.*

For the thousandth time, I remind myself I'm *not* one of them.

Clearing my head of that disappointment, I focus on Hawk. I love watching him make breakfast. It's become one of the highlights of my day. The way he floats around the kitchen whisking and stirring and toasting. Only now, when he puts my breakfast on the table in front of me, he leans in for a kiss. One I happily give him.

He claims he doesn't want us acting like a family. But this—right here—is exactly what families do. I keep that little piece of knowledge to myself.

As usual, he sits at the table with me, drinking his coffee.

"Are you going into the office today?" I ask, taking in his sweats and T-shirt.

"Thought I'd work from home."

"How exactly does one work from home and sell cars?"

"I don't sell the cars, Addy. I manage the people who do." He gazes out the window. "Or something along those lines."

"You hate being in the car business, don't you?"

He chuckles. "What gave it away? My complete lack of enthusiasm? My inability to spend more than a few hours at the office? The absence of a single ounce of desire to run the family empire?"

"Then why do you do it?"

"I'm thirty years old. I've spent my entire adult life learning the business."

"But if you hate it, why not leave?"

He shrugs. "I've thought about it. I'm just not sure what else I would do. I haven't been trained for anything else."

"Who says you need training? Just do something that interests you. Aren't you passionate about anything?"

I'm giving him an opening here. Will he take it?

He leans over and kisses my neck. "As it so happens, yes."

I giggle when his scruff tickles me. "Come on, there has to be something. A hobby you can turn into a profession perhaps?"

"You want me to become a professional sports better like Hunter?"

"Obviously not."

"Then what did you have in mind?"

*Writing, you idiot,* my head is screaming. But then it dawns on me that maybe he thinks his writing isn't any good. Based on his first three attempts, I'd whole-heartedly agree. But Adelaide's book is different. It speaks to me. He should publish it. It would be a success. I know it would.

"I don't know. What are your hobbies?"

"Well, there's you." More neck kisses. "You're my favorite hobby." He runs a hand up my thigh, which is still tender from the delectable beating it took from his prickly jaw last night. "And let's see… basketball. And money. I suppose that's it."

"Money?" I scrunch my face up. "How can money be a hobby?"

"I'd say it's a lot like you." He smiles a sinfully wicked grin and whispers in my ear, "I like to look at it. Touch it. *Smell* it."

My insides flutter. Then Rivi makes a noise, and he pulls away.

As he stands and refills his coffee, I lean over the baby seat and shimmy my nose against Rivi's until she smiles. Seeing her smile is one of the other highlights of my day. When I look up,

Hawk is leaning against the counter, tapping the fingers of one hand against the granite, pensively staring. At me. At *us*. Like he wants to say something. *Reveal* something perhaps.

"What?" I ask, self-consciously.

His head shakes. "Nothing." He thumbs to the hall. "I'm just gonna…"

"Okay, yeah." I pick up Rivi. "Well, we're just gonna…"

I stand here trying not to drown in the sea of awkwardness.

He walks away without another word.

"What the heck was that?" I ask Rivi.

She doesn't answer.

~ ~ ~

"I have something to tell you," I say to Holland as we stroll down the winding sidewalk of the park.

"I have something to tell you too."

We stop walking and look at each other. The tone of our voices indicates we're both about to hear something we may not want to hear.

"You first," she says.

"No way. You go."

She leans down and tucks the blanket around Rivi. "Why do I have to go first?"

"Because I want to know if what you're going to tell me is as bad as what I'm going to tell you."

Suddenly, I'm terrified. Is she going to tell me she saw Hawk with another woman? Did Hunter or Hudson blab and now she's going to present me with evidence that will make me want to quit my job and dump her brother? He wouldn't be with another woman, would he? We haven't exactly said we're exclusive. But he wants more. That implies exclusivity. *Doesn't it?*

Holland's hand lands on my shoulder. "Nobody died, Addy. And it's not something bad, per se. Just something you might not be pleased with."

I let out a breath. "Okay, well, same. Now are you going to tell me, or do I have to drag it out of you?"

"I got a job."

"Hol, that's great. Why is that something I wouldn't be pleased with?"

"It's in the city."

"Really? Well that's even better. Is it in fashion? Please tell me it is. And if you get a designer discount you *have* to share it with me."

"It is with a designer. Bellasandré."

My jaw drops. "You're going to work for Katarina Bellasandré?"

Excitement blossoms in her eyes. "I know. It's huge. And I'm pretty sure Pappy pulled some strings to make it happen. No way would they have hired me on my grades."

"Who cares what got your foot in the door. It's what you do once you're through it that matters."

"I'm so nervous. What if she hates me?"

I pull her in for a hug. "She won't. Everyone loves you. But I'm still confused. Why did you think I'd be upset?"

"Because I'm moving there."

"You're moving?" I ask, trying to keep the disappointment out of my voice. "Why? It's less than an hour on the train."

"The job requires me to be available practically all the time. I'll get some days off, and I'll come home on those, but otherwise, I can't be an hour away. Fashion is not a nine-to-five job. And I've been told Katarina is very demanding. Think *The Devil Wears Prada.*"

"Oh, wow. Nothing like getting thrown in the deep end." I grab her hand and hold it tight. "You're going to do great. I have faith in you. And if she hates you, just buy her out."

She laughs. "Sadly, her empire is worth far more than my trust fund."

"Just think, ten or twenty years from now there might be another girl excited because she just got offered a job working for the famous designer Holland McQuaid."

"I appreciate your confidence in me, but McQuaid does not sound like a fashion brand. I'd have to change my name, or maybe marry a guy with a really cool one."

"Or you could just go with your initials."

"HAM?" She belts out a sarcastic chuckle. "P.E.T.A. would be after me for sure."

"How about H&M? That sounds very chic and professional."

"Too bad that name is already taken. Okay, now it's your turn to spill."

I blow out a long breath and gesture to a nearby bench where we sit. "My news is not going to be as exciting. At least not for you."

"Come on, sister. Hit me with it."

"I think..." I look off in the distance, not wanting to see her reaction. "I think your brother might be my boyfriend."

When she doesn't say anything, I turn. She's shaking her head. "Oh, Addy," she says sympathetically. "Hawk has never been anyone's boyfriend. What makes you think he's changed?"

"When we were in bed the other night—"

"You *slept* with him?" she hisses, pinching her brow.

"Yes, Holland, I've slept with him. Your brother took my virginity three weeks ago and we've done it more than a dozen times since."

"And you think that makes you his girlfriend? Addy, he's using you. You're young and pretty and decidedly convenient. Of course he's sleeping with you. I'm going to kill him."

"He's not using me. And you aren't going to kill him. In fact, you can't tell him I told you. He doesn't want anyone to know."

"Sounds about right."

"He doesn't want people to know because it could get back to my brothers and neither of us wants that drama. You know as well as anyone how tenuous it already is between our families."

"And you believed him when he said that's the reason?"

"Yes."

"He's going to hurt you, Addy. That's what he does. He's incapable of love."

"I think you're wrong. He said he wants more. I gave him a pass, Hol. I told him I knew he didn't do relationships. But instead of letting it be what it was, he told me he wanted more."

"Hawk McQuaid—*my brother*—said he wanted more?"

"Believe me, I'm as surprised as you are. But look at Tag. His reputation was even worse than Hawk's. People can change."

Her arm comes around my shoulder. "For your sake, I hope you're right. Because I may not be around to pick up the pieces."

I hope I'm right, too. But I don't tell her that. I don't tell her that deep down I wonder if he's capable of love. Capable of loving me. Capable of loving Rivi. Because I know that no matter how much I love him, I could never be with a man who would turn his back on his child.

I stand. "We should celebrate your new job. Let's go out Friday. We'll invite Mia, Allie, Sophie, heck, we'll invite everybody."

"I don't know." She cocks her head. "Do you think your *boyfriend* would mind?"

My heart skips a beat hearing her say it. Hawk McQuaid is my boyfriend. A smile splits my face in two.

# Chapter Thirty-three

*Hawk*

"Hey."

I look up from my laptop. Addy is in the doorway. And she's swaying.

"I'd ask you how the party was, but by the looks of it, I'd say it was a lot of fun. How'd you get home?"

"Your mom. I wish you could have been there. Hunter and Hudson came."

"After the other night, it would have been too awkward with my brothers there. Not to mention it was at Donovan's, which means Cooper and Serenity would have been watching our every move."

"They all asked where you were."

"What did you tell them?"

"That I'm not your keeper and you don't keep me apprised of your social calendar."

I raise a brow. "Look at you being a good little liar."

"You're rubbing off on me way too much."

"I'd love to rub off on you right now. Do you know how goddamn sexy you look in that short skirt?"

She twirls for me. "I did dress up for the occasion."

"Come here." I close the laptop and pat the desk.

"In *here?*"

"Do you know how many times I've fantasized about taking you on this desk?"

Her eyes bounce from me to the expansive mahogany surface. My cock likes it when she bites her lower lip. Then she looks behind her. "I should go pay Cindy."

"I forgot she was here."

"Probably because she stays upstairs. I think she's afraid of you."

"That's ridiculous."

"With your reputation, not so much."

I stand, get out my wallet and hand her a hundred.

Her eyes go wide. "Being generous?"

"Get rid of her and come back down. I'll show you how generous I can be. Don't change clothes."

She smiles and turns.

I call her back. "Wait."

She sticks her head back in the doorway.

"Are you wet?"

"No. It wasn't raining."

"Addy." I stare her down "Are. You. Wet?"

Her face turns an amazing shade of red. She swallows. "I guess you'll see shortly."

I can hardly contain my excitement. I clear off my desk, get naked, and stroke myself a few times for good measure. I'd better be careful, though, we haven't slept together all week and my balls are as blue as a dead man's fingernails—despite all my 'lone rangering.'

She's been on her period. Which means she'll be starting the pill soon. Good thing since we fuck like bunnies.

The front door closes. The sitter is gone. I lean back in my chair and wait. I wait for five minutes. Then ten. She finally appears. "Are you trying to torture me?" I ask.

The surprise on her face at finding me naked and fully, spectacularly erect, is priceless.

"I wanted to brush my teeth and... stuff."

"Stuff?"

She shrugs. "I hadn't shaved in days."

"Sweetheart, your legs could look like a woolly mammoth and I wouldn't care."

Her chest rises and falls.

"You like it when I call you that, don't you?" I wink. "Sweetheart. Not woolly mammoth."

She giggles and walks toward me.

I hold up a palm. "Stop. Take off your clothes." She hesitates so I point to my dick. "It's only fair."

Our eyes lock as her fingers unbutton her blouse. When she's finished, it falls to the floor leaving her standing in a black lacy bra, red skirt, and knee-high white socks that make her look like a sexy college co-ed.

Reaching behind her, she unzips the skirt, which then joins her shirt in a rumpled pile.

"More," I command.

A hand comes up between her breasts and unclasps her bra. Her milky-white tear-drop mounds appear when she pushes it aside.

"Last thing," I say, eyes honed in on her panties. "You can leave the socks on."

I love that she seems both embarrassed and empowered at the same time. Her eyes don't stray from mine, even as her cheeks flame red. Her thumbs hook over the top of the lace, and she slowly works the scrap of fabric down her legs and to the floor.

"Pick them up and hand them to me."

She raises a snarky brow. "A souvenir?" She gets them and walks—no, struts—over to me, dropping them onto my hard-as-steel cock before leaning against the desk.

I bring them to my nose and inhale deeply before pointing to the top of the desk in front of me. "Sit and spread your legs."

She doesn't hesitate. She likes this game. Maybe even as much as I do. Her pussy is pink and glistening under the bright lights in my office. *Fuuuuuck me.* My cock is so engorged it may split right down the middle.

I roll my chair forward and dip my head. "I've wanted to do this all week," I say, then flick her clit.

She moans and leans back, supporting herself on her elbows. But she watches me. She always likes to watch. We have more in common than I originally thought.

I'm racing the clock in my head, trying to beat the last time I made her come. She's ultra-sensitive, super responsive, and so goddamn sexy. When I slide my fingers inside her, she pushes herself onto them. "Hawk," she mewls. She's close. This won't take long at all. My dick is throbbing so hard it hurts. I've half a mind to put it in her right now, but I used the last of the condoms from my desk last week. But I need a release. Goddamn it I need it now.

With my spare hand, I fist myself, pumping me and tonguing her to the same rhythm. I come at the same moment she does, both of us shouting; her my name and me a string of swear words.

"Shit woman. See what you made me do?"

She sits up and looks at my jizz sprayed all over my desk drawers. Her lower lip juts out in an exaggerated pout. "Oh, that's too bad. I was thinking I might try something new tonight." While looking at my increasingly flaccid cock, her tongue strokes her lips with a soft, sensual lick.

I try to figure out if she's joking. The heated expression on her face tells me she's not.

If she only knew how often I've thought of her mouth on me. I can't say how many times I've choked the chicken to that fantasy. "Seriously?"

She nods with a heavy-lidded stare.

"You sure?"

"I think I'm ready. I've watched videos."

I laugh out loud. "You watched porn?"

"I wanted to make sure I'd get it right."

I squeeze her thighs. "The next time you want to watch one, we're doing it together."

"You want to watch dirty movies with me?" she asks, her bright eyes alive with mischief.

"Oh, hell yes." If I hadn't just gotten off, I'd be hard as a rock right now. I stand and pick her up in my arms. "Give me twenty minutes and I'll be good to go. Let's take this party to bed." I start down the hall toward my room.

"*Your* bed?"

"As long as we're doing other firsts tonight, why not?" I deposit her on the bed, thankful Suzanne was here today to clean. "In fact, I think you should sleep here."

"Here? As in with you? All night?"

"I like having you close to me."

Her palm goes to my forehead. "Are you feeling okay?"

"Never better."

"If I knew a blow job would earn me the royal treatment, I'd have promised one weeks ago."

Laughter thunders out of me and it dawns on me that she's the only woman who's ever made me laugh.

"Wait." She points down the hall. "My phone. I left it upstairs."

"Believe me. You won't be needing it."

I deposit her on my bed and eye her leg. "Would you be more comfortable if we took this off?"

Her brows arch. "We?"

"Tell me how to do it."

She hesitates.

I sweep her hair aside and say into her ear, "Addy, I've been up close and personal with every inch of your body. No need to be embarrassed *now*."

"Fine." She scoots up and sits against my pillows as I peel down her knee-high socks.

"Press the button by the foot. That releases the suction."

I do it and her prosthesis slips right off. I touch her stump over the sock, surprised that she doesn't pull away. She's trusting me with her most vulnerable fears. It makes me feel ten feet tall.

The sock comes off easily but the silicone liner, not so much.

"You have to roll it down from the top onto itself," she says.

Once I have it off and she's bare, now completely naked, I reach out and run a finger along her scar. She flinches and then relaxes.

"You're the only one to ever touch Eileen. Aside from medical professionals."

I look up. "I want to be the only one to touch you *everywhere*."

A smile curves her lips. "If people only knew you were a romantic."

"Shhh. Don't tell." I place a kiss on her stump. "Is your scar sensitive?"

Her hand lands on my chest. "Is yours?"

"Yeah. I thought about getting a tattoo over it once but it might hurt too much."

"Hawk McQuaid is scared of a little old tattoo needle? Come on, I'll get one if you do."

Surprised, I lace her fingers with mine. "You want a tattoo? That's hot, Addy." I sit straight up. "Can I pick it?"

She thinks on it. "If I can pick yours."

My body shakes with laughter. "I'm not getting a tattoo that says *Mother*."

"And I'm not getting a tattoo that says *Hawk*."

"Agreed. No names. What else is off limits?"

"Curse words. Blood. Skulls."

"I see you've given this some thought. Wait, are we really doing this?"

She shrugs. "It might be fun."

"But we get final say, right? Like we get to see the design before it's actually embedded into our skin."

"Worried I might pick something too girlie?"

"You have to admit, mine will be a lot more visible than yours. I'm the only one who will see yours."

Her gaze falls to my chest. Possessively, she puts a hand on it, pushes me down so I'm lying on the bed, and climbs over me. "Is it bad that I want to be the only one who sees yours too?"

I stare up into her eyes wanting to grant her that wish. Wanting to give her… everything.

She leans over and shimmies on top of me, her hair tickling my face as her soft-as-sin curves beg to be touched. "Has it been twenty minutes yet?" she asks, lifting a sultry brow.

I remember what she plans to do to me, and my dick stirs under her weight. She smiles deviously, slides down my body, lowers her head, and makes my every fantasy come true.

# Chapter Thirty-four

*Addison*

Pain slices through me like the serrated edges of a jagged knife. It's excruciating. I can't move and the crumpled front end of the car is closing in on me. Fighting to free myself just brings more agony. I'm alone. And I'm trapped. Trapped like Chaz. Maybe dying like him.

I reach the strap of my purse on the passenger seat floor and pull it toward me, spilling the contents until my phone appears. I call 911. My head is fuzzy as I give the man on the other end the details, leaving out the part about how much I drank. Mostly because I don't even know. After Chaz's funeral, I raided my parents' bar taking everything I could carry. I'm in so much trouble.

He tells me to stay on the phone. But it hurts to hold it. I place it on what's left of the console. I'm lightheaded and nauseous. My whole left side hurts. I reach down to try and free my leg but come up with a handful of blood. I scream. The man tells me help is coming.

I can't keep my eyes open. The car is spinning. Or I am. A feeling of impending doom washes over me. Is this it? Am I dying? My poor parents. They will lose two children in a week. How could I have been so stupid?

*Everything starts to fade. I see lights. Bright lights. And the pain, it's almost gone. Good. I was getting tired of the pain. I close my eyes. When I open them, I look down. My leg hurts. But I don't understand why because it's not there. My leg is missing.*

*I scream.*

"Addy! Addison, wake up."

Arms come around me. It takes a second to remember where I am. Hawk's house. Hawk's *bed*. I catch my breath and sink into him.

"You okay?" he asks, rubbing my arm.

"Bad dream."

"No shit. You were flopping around and then you started screaming."

"Sorry I woke you."

"You didn't."

Light from the hallway filters in. I study his face wondering if he was doing more writing. "You weren't in bed?"

Anxiety takes hold. Maybe he had second thoughts about sleeping with me.

"I've been here. But I wasn't sleeping."

"What were you doing?"

"Watching you."

I peek at the time. "For two hours?"

He shrugs. "Just taking it all in. You know, in case…"

"In case what?"

"In case I fuck this up."

"You think you will?"

"I fuck up everything else in my life."

"Don't sell yourself short, Hawk. Deep down, you're a good man. You just need a chance to show it."

"So, the dream?"

It's not lost on me that he changes the subject whenever I give him a compliment. And despite his strong, cocky exterior, it occurs to me that maybe he doesn't think very much of himself.

"I saw the lights again."

He looks uncomfortable. It's not the first time I've noticed it when talking about the lights. He had the same reaction at the cottage.

"Hawk?" I touch his chest and run a finger across his scar. "Did you have a near death experience when this happened?"

"No. Why?"

"Because you look strange every time I talk about mine."

"Do I?"

"Is there something you need to talk about, from your surgery or anything?"

"Nope."

The way the stilted word comes out of his mouth tells me he most definitely does need to get something off his chest. He's holding something in. Something he needs to get out. I weave a hand behind him and stroke the nape of his neck. "Talk to me. You said you wanted more. Well, part of having more is sharing our feelings with each other."

He looks conflicted. His eyes close and his head sinks into the pillow. "Even if what I tell you might have you getting out of bed and walking out of this room and maybe my life?"

My insides churn. "All the more reason to tell me. We can't keep secrets from each other if we want to have a relationship."

"Is that what we're doing? Having a relationship?"

"Let's see. You bring me dinner every night. Make my breakfast every morning. You make me laugh even without trying. And you say the most random romantic things. Things that endear you to me more than you know. And then there's the sex. So, yeah, I'd say we're in a relationship. Face it, McQuaid, you have a girlfriend. Whether you admit it or not, that's what I am."

"Girlfriend."

It's like he's testing out the word. And surprisingly, he doesn't seem to hate it.

"Yes. And as my boyfriend, you should feel free to be open and honest about whatever is weighing on you. I promise not to judge you. Unless you're sleeping with someone else." I put my finger to his chest. "Now, if that's the case, I'll unzip your scar, reach in and squeeze your heart until it's empty. Because if you cheated on me, that's exactly how I'd feel. Empty."

He pulls me close. "I'm not cheating on you."

"Good. Then we can deal with anything else."

"You promise not to leave if I tell you?"

"I promise."

"I have a confession to make." He doesn't look into my eyes. Whatever he's going to say, he's ashamed. "I don't think you had a near death experience."

"How could you possibly know that?"

"Because I was there."

"What do you mean you were there?"

"The lights you saw. I'm pretty sure they were my headlights."

"Your headlights?" I move away and sit up, pulling the covers over me. "Hawk, did you run me off the road?"

"God, no," he blurts out convincingly. "I came upon your car afterward. Only I didn't know it was you. Not until the next day when the whole town was talking about it." He rubs his eyes as if trying to rid them of a vision. "I know I should have stopped. But I didn't. I thought about it for a hot second but then kept going when I saw flashing lights in the distance. I didn't want to get involved. And I sure as shit didn't want people thinking I was responsible in any way. It was a dick move. And I'm sorry."

I swallow. "The ambulance was coming?"

He nods.

"So then there's nothing you could have done."

"That's what I told myself. But, Addy, what if I'd gotten out of my car and helped you? What if those two minutes were the difference between you losing your leg and not? What if my completely selfish move altered the rest of your life?"

His words are laced with guilt and full of anger toward himself.

Realization dawns. "Is that why you paid off my bills? Oh my gosh, is that why you're with me? Because you feel guilty?"

He tugs me back when I scoot to the edge of the bed. "No. No way. I paid off your bills because I can. Because it was nothing to me but a huge burden for you. And I'm with you because you're beautiful. And sexy. And you make me laugh when no other woman ever has."

"No other woman? Really?"

He lays me down next to him and pulls me close. "Really."

"There's nothing you could have done. My leg was shredded. It was hanging on by a thread. Not to mention I was trapped. They needed the jaws to get me out."

"You must have been terrified. I'm an idiot. And a horrible excuse for a man."

"That's not true. You're a good man, Hawk."

"Name one good thing about me."

"You took in a kid you didn't want. And even though you were coerced, a part of you must have done it because it's the right thing to do. That's very honorable."

His eyes close and a hand runs through his hair. "You don't know what you're talking about. I'm not a good man. And I'm as far away from honorable as you can get."

"You would have stopped," I say. "If you hadn't seen the ambulance coming, you would have stopped. I know you would have."

"I wish I would have been there for you."

I cup his jaw. "You're here now."

"Yes. I am. And I'm not going anywhere."

"Promise?"

He kisses my forehead. "Promise."

"Well then, since I don't want to be the hypocrite in this relationship, I have a confession too."

He chuckles. "You're secretly addicted to porn?"

I want to laugh but can't. I'm afraid of how he's going to react to what I tell him. "Just please remember how understanding I was a minute ago."

"What's going on, Addy?"

I close my eyes. "I know about your books. I've been sneaking into your office and reading them."

His entire body tenses. He's silent. I suspect he's at war with himself, deciding just how mad he's going to be, but knowing he can't really be because of what he just shared with me.

"You *read* them?"

I panic and just start spewing everything from the beginning. "I'm sorry. I was looking for a pen a few months ago. The drawer was locked but then one day it wasn't, and I shouldn't have gone back in but I was curious, and a bit worried that you were—ironically—watching porn all day. So I searched for a password to your laptop and found the manuscripts. And then I guessed the password. You really should come up with something more secure.

And I found the draft and couldn't stop reading. I'm so ashamed. But I'm also honored. Because Adelaide is me and Jenson is you and I love the way they are together. And I love the way you look at me when you're writing. And I love that maybe I've been your inspiration. Because, Hawk, you have a gift. This book, it's amazing. It's a love story. In a way it's our love story. And I know we haven't said the words and after hearing this you'll probably fire me for such a violation of privacy, but—"

"Addy, shut up."

I try and catch my breath, feeling hot tears roll off my face.

He runs a thumb under my eye. "You… think my writing is good?"

Relief floods through me. He's not going to kick me out. He's not even mad.

"Not the first three. Those were bad. Like, you should burn them, bad. But this one. It's incredible. Hawk, you're not a car salesman. You're an author."

He leans back, amused. "I think you're a little biased."

"I'm not. I read a lot and your book has me engrossed. It had me breaking into your office just to get more. You have to publish it."

"You're crazy."

"Just think about it. I researched it. It's easy enough to format it and upload it for sale as an ebook. All you need is a cover. You can even get paperbacks made. Can you imagine, your book on a shelf next to John Grisham?" I cock my head. "Or maybe Nicholas Sparks, because, Hawk, you didn't write a spy thriller. You wrote a romance novel."

"I did not."

"You did. It's got elements of a thriller, and lots of suspense, but babe, it's a romance through and through."

He cocks a brow. "Did you just call me babe?"

My cheeks flame. "I, uh—"

His lips collide with mine. He kisses me until we're both blue in the face. But he doesn't take it further. He knows I'm raw from the two times we did it earlier. And that was *after* the blow job, which if I do say so myself, might have been some of my best work.

He snuggles next to me. "Addy?"

"Yeah?"

"As long as we're making confessions, there's something else I need to tell you."

I prop my head up. "There's more?"

He looks conflicted. Almost nauseous. Man, this must be a doozy.

"I…" He scrubs a hand across his jaw. "I'd feel empty too. Without you."

Why do I get the nagging feeling that's not what he was going to say? Was he going to say he loves me? Surely he was. What else would make him look like he was about to throw up?

But the declaration he gave was almost as good. And for the first time in forever, I'm at complete ease knowing I'm with a man who feels the same way about me that I feel about him.

In the distance, I hear a faint cry. I sit up. "Rivi. We should have brought a monitor in here. She's hungry."

He pulls me back down. "I've got this one."

"You sure?"

"You've missed enough sleep already. Close your eyes. I'll fix a bottle and feed her in her room."

He pulls on sweatpants, not bothering with skivvies. I smile as my eyes close, knowing I'm going to wake up in his bed later. And maybe every day after that.

# Chapter Thirty-five

*Hawk*

I can't stop thinking about what Addy said as I make a bottle. She thinks my book is good. Surely she's blowing smoke up my ass. But the thing is—I think it's good too. Yeah my first three were shit, but this one is different. There was purpose behind my writing. *She* is all over the pages.

Taking the back stairs, I round the corner into Riv's room, set the bottle down and pick her up. "You probably need a change first, eh?" I set her on the table and spill my guts to the tiny human who has no clue what I'm talking about. "Addy thinks I have what it takes to be an actual writer. It's ludicrous. She said I'm a good man. That I would have stopped if I hadn't seen the ambulance. But I'm not so sure. Everything I've done in my life I've done for one person. Me."

I gather her up, sit in the chair in the corner, and feed her. "I want to be the man she thinks I am. I want to be better. But a better man wouldn't have made that deal with Pappy. A better man wouldn't have agreed to one year with you only to give you up at the end of it. A better man would value people over money." I watch her slowly suck down the formula. "Why am I telling you this?"

Addy is down in my bed sleeping. *My bed*—a place no other woman has been for longer than the ten or twenty minutes it took to get my rocks off. And she's probably sleeping soundly after our talk. She thinks we're solid. She thinks we've shared all our secrets. She has no idea how wrong she is. She's way too good for me even though she doesn't believe it.

Addy is the angel to my devil. The light to my darkness. She's changed me. She's... she's everything I never knew I wanted. And I can't lose her.

I lean my head against the cushion. "I'm a goddamn idiot, aren't I, Riv? Can you hurry this along? I need to talk to her."

Minutes later, I'm heading down the main stairs to my bedroom. But Addy isn't there, and neither is her prosthetic. I peek into the bathroom. "Addy?"

Did she change her mind about wanting to sleep in here?

On my way to find her—because I *will* find her and carry her right back to my bed—I notice the light on in my office. Her clothes are gone. I pick up the pace, take the front stairs two at a time and go to Addy's room. The door is open. I flip on the light. She's not here either. I walk through to her bathroom. Nothing.

She's not in Riv's room either. I head down the back stairs, stopping halfway down when I notice the kitchen is illuminated by the open refrigerator. Okay, she got up for a midnight snack. Then my entire body tenses when I hear Rivington make baby noises through the monitor. I stride over, pick up the monitor next to the table and stare at it. Then I eye the unopened bottle of water next to the fridge as anxiety climbs my spine like rungs on a ladder. A ladder leading straight to hell. *Fuck.* She heard me. "Addy!" I run to my room, get my phone, and tap out a text.

**Me: Addy, you have to let me explain.**

I race through every room in the house, even the ones I already checked. I look out back. She's nowhere. I even look in the garage. Both cars are still here. Wherever she went, she went on foot—at three o'clock in the morning.

Maybe she's just clearing her head.

That's just wishful thinking, though. If she heard everything, I know for a fact she's gone.

I should go after her. But I can't take Riv. I could call someone. Holland maybe. But she'd ask questions I'm not prepared to answer. I'm stuck here for now. I shuffle to the bar, grab a glass and a bottle, and park myself on the couch.

~ ~ ~

Cries awaken me. The events of last night hit me square in the face. Shit. It's seven-thirty. I fell asleep. And Riv is crying. Rivington never wakes me. Addy always gets to her before her cries get too loud.

Dragging myself upstairs, I stand in Addy's doorway, staring at her empty room. I sit on her bed and put my head in my hands knowing I royally fucked up. She hasn't read any of the six texts I sent so I call her. My heart sinks when I hear the familiar vibrating noise of a phone and follow it to her dresser. She never goes anywhere without her phone. She wanted to get away from me so badly she left it. Jesus, she must hate me.

Riv's cries become more demanding. I cross the hall, change her, and take her downstairs for a bottle. While she eats, I stare out over the backyard, my eyes falling on the hot tub. The place I took Addy's virginity. The place she trusted me more than I've ever been trusted.

What am I going to do? How can I talk to her if she doesn't have a phone? Where would she go?

The answer to the third question seems obvious. She'd either go back to her parents' house or to my sister's.

I watch the clock, cursing it as the minutes tick by at a snail's pace. It's as if time has slowed down just to spite me. To torture me. It's a well-deserved punishment and I know it. As soon as it hits eight, I make a call.

Holland answers sleepily on the fourth ring. "Do you have any idea what time it is?"

"Sorry."

"What's up big bro?"

No way is Addison there. Holland is acting like her normal self. If she knew anything, she'd be chewing my ass out. "I just wanted to say congratulations again. I'm sorry I missed the party. I heard it was good."

"I know why you didn't come."

"No you don't."

"Addy's my best friend. She tells me everything."

*Apparently not this.* "Yeah? Well maybe you can keep your mouth shut about it, unlike everything else you blab."

"I wouldn't do anything to hurt her. And I may not agree with her choices, but I'm going to support her regardless."

"Thanks I guess."

"Mind if I go back to sleep now?"

"Later, kid."

"Kid? You do know I'm the same age as the woman you're shagging."

"Whatever. Bye."

What am I supposed to do now, show up at her parents' house? Why in the hell did she have to leave her phone?

Riv spits up all over me because I forgot to burp her. "Damn it!" I set her down in the corner of the couch and wipe it with my hand, but it just smears all over my chest. It's slimy and gross. I grab a blanket and clean it up as I try not to gag.

Then I hear a noise and freeze. Riv is laughing. *At me.* I can't help but crack a smile because no matter how much I've tried to deny it in the past, she's cute.

"Yeah, yeah, yeah. Laugh it up, kid. But now we both need a bath and I'm the last person who should be giving you one of those."

Her clothes are soaked. My chest is rancid. The blanket is ruined. Anyone else might know what to do in this situation, but I don't have a clue. What does Addy do with her when she needs to take a shower?

We go into my bathroom, and I look around. Can I just leave her on the rug? What if she crawls away? I glance at her. "Can you crawl? You can't even sit up so I doubt it. You'll be fine." I set her down and take my clothes off. She fusses. "I'll just be a minute," I say, turning on the shower. She squirms. Then more crying. "Damn it, how do people do this?" I glance from the shower to her. "Fuck it." I get down on the floor, take off her wet sleeper, remove her diaper and then stand up with her in my arms.

I catch a glance of us in the mirror. We're both naked. I momentarily wonder if that makes me a creepy pedo or something. Then I conclude I don't care because I just figured out a way to kill two birds with one stone and that makes me a fucking genius.

I hold her tight as I check the temperature of the water. She becomes slippery when she gets wet, and the thought of dropping her scares the crap out of me. "A little cooperation would be nice," I say. "I'll make you a deal, you stop squirming and I'll put you in that vibrating thing you seem to like." I carefully run water over her head, and she calms. Addy told me she loves baths. Maybe she likes showers too.

It's almost impossible to shower with one hand, and especially to wash my chest when I'm trying like hell not to lose my grip on her, but I do my best.

Turning off the water, I pat myself on the back for managing such a difficult task. I throw a towel over the bathmat and put Riv on it while I dry off, the whole time thinking about what a complete shit I am having underappreciated Addy for everything she was able to accomplish without even making it seem like an accomplishment. Then I hear a horrible noise, and no, it's not her laughing again. It's her taking a shit. All over my extra thick, hundred percent premium Turkish cotton towel.

"Fuck, Riv. Are you kidding me?"

She smiles. I swear she knows what she just did. Maybe it's her way of giving me the middle finger.

I turn the shower back on, pick her up, and hold her at arm's length while I run the water over her backside. Then I do something I never thought I'd do—I wash a baby's ass with my bare hand. Once we're both sufficiently clean, I step around the shit-covered bath towel on the floor knowing it's going to a landfill. I grab a second three-hundred-dollar towel, wrap it around both of us and drip my way upstairs to put a diaper on her before it happens again.

It's another hour before I can even think about last night again. How does Addy make taking care of Rivington look so easy?

When she's finally napping in her vibrating seat, I stare at my phone, wondering who I can call. Hunter and Hudson would be useless. I can't think up an excuse to call Addy's parents. No way in hell will I call her brothers. I only have one choice.

I tap Holland's name.

"Two calls in one day. To what do I owe the occasion?"

She still doesn't know.

"Do you happen to know where Addy is?"

Laughter dances through the phone. "You mean your nanny? And also, your girlfriend? No, I don't. The question is, why don't *you*?"

*Girlfriend.* The word is an arrow to my heart. Because I don't think she is anymore. And the hole left inside me is gaping.

"Hawk? What did you do?"

"Nothing."

"Bullshit. You never call me twice in one day. And as far as I know, you don't get up early either. What's going on? What happened last night? Did you dump her? Hawk, I swear if you hurt her I will disown you."

"I didn't dump her. But she's mad at me."

"Did you cheat on her?"

"Hell no. But I was keeping something from her. Nothing that had anything to do with her. It's not about her. It's more about me."

"That's cryptic. What was it?"

"I can't tell you. But you have to believe it's not about her or us. It's something I did before she was in the picture."

"Then why would she leave?"

Frustrated, I bite, "I don't have time for this, Hol. I need to find her."

"She's not answering your calls?"

"Her phone is here."

"She left without it? Hawk, I know you're not telling me something. She never goes anywhere without her phone."

"Just help me find her. But don't tell anyone. I need to talk to her first, okay? Make an excuse to show up at her parents' house, or wherever else you think she might go."

"Fine. But I know you did something. And understand, I'm not doing this for you. I'm doing it for her."

"Okay, great. Call me when you find her. Hey, do you know the name of the sitter Addy hired last night?"

"Yes."

"Mind telling me? Seems I'm in need of one."

"Suck it up and take care of Rivi yourself."

"Funny."

"I'm serious. Listen, you made your bed, Hawk. Time to lie in it."

The phone goes dead.

Immediately, I call Mom.

"Hawk, sweetie. How are you?"

"Can you come over and take care of Riv?"

"Sorry. No."

"Why not?"

"Holland texted me a second ago. She said you're having an issue with Addison. What happened?"

*That little traitor. She just promised she wouldn't say anything.*

"Nothing. A misunderstanding. Please?"

"While I appreciate you asking nicely, the answer is still no. Whatever you did, I'm not coming to the rescue this time. As a parent, you'll come to learn that a little tough love from time to time is needed."

"You're really not coming?"

"I love you, but no."

"Jesus." I scrub a hand across my jaw. "Fine. Bye."

For the first time in my life, I have a problem money can't solve.

I have absolutely no idea what to do.

Samantha Christy

# Chapter Thirty-six

*Addison*

I walk until my hip hurts too much to continue. Finally giving in, I sit on the nearest bench, freezing my ass off in my skirt and lightweight sweater. There's a store in front of me. I may not have my phone, but my credit card was zippered inside my skirt pocket. I should buy a coat and a pair of jeans. But for now, I'll just sit and watch the people of New York City until my hip stops throbbing.

I'm not sure why I ended up here. I guess I needed to go somewhere I could be invisible. Where people wouldn't ask what's wrong. Where I could just... *think*.

My head is flooded with questions. How could someone agree to such an arrangement? What kind of monster would make a kid bond with them and then give her up?

But that's the thing. They *haven't* bonded. It all makes sense now, why he rarely does things for her. How he's reluctant to make her smile. Entertain her. Or do much of anything. This whole time he's known what will happen. He's probably been counting down the days until he can be rid of her. While every day he's conning me into something else entirely.

Did he really believe I could be with a man who would kick his own child to the curb?

And Tucker McQuaid. What was he thinking? Did he really orchestrate a bribe using his great-granddaughter as a pawn? We all knew he'd strong-armed Hawk into taking Rivi, but like everyone else, I thought it was permanent. Did he think Hawk would come around? It's a hefty gamble to make with a child's life.

I gaze up and down the sidewalk, watching mothers pushing strollers and fathers walking their kids to school. All I see are families. Happy faces of parents and children. A couple walking hand-in-hand with their giggling toddler swinging between them.

What will Rivi look like at that age? Will she have parents who love her like they do?

Tears come to my eyes. It's only been hours, but I already miss her. And the truth is, I miss *him*. But I only miss the him I thought I knew before I found out his secret.

"Oh my god," a teenage boy says, gawking at my leg. "What happened to you?"

He's wearing baggy jeans that show half of his underwear, an oversized hoodie, and no shoes even though it's fifty degrees out and he can obviously afford them based on the brand name of the hoodie.

"Flesh eating bacteria," I say. I nod to his feet. "Got it by walking around barefoot on these very streets. Do you know what kind of shit is all over this sidewalk?"

His face turns white. He turns and walks—very carefully—in the other direction.

I'd laugh, but I can't. I'm not sure I'll ever laugh again.

Instead, I stand up despite my aching hip, go into the clothing store, and spend more than I should on a few necessities. Then I cross the street and get a room at the first hotel I see. I don't care how much I'm spending. I need to sleep before I fall down and really do pick up a disease on the street.

~ ~ ~

My grumbling stomach has me venturing out for dinner. Along the way, I see a man in a wheelchair. One of his pant legs is tucked underneath him—he's lost the lower part of his leg like I have—and he's holding a sign asking for money.

I flash my credit card. "I don't have any cash to give you, but I'd like to offer you a meal." I point to the diner down the street. "Care to join me?"

"Dinner with a beautiful lady? I can't remember the last time that happened. You've got yourself a date."

"Allow me." I step behind his older-than-dirt wheelchair and push him.

"Dinner and a ride. Why, miss, this day just keeps getting better."

I lean down. "Addy."

"George. George McNally."

I stop in front of the diner and offer my hand. "Nice to meet you George McNally. I'm Addison Calloway but call me Addy. Shall we?"

"Get the door and I'll roll on in."

The diner is small. There are only a few freestanding tables, all the others are step-up booths. George's wheelchair won't fit in those, and the tables are taken. A trio of teens just sat down at the last one. I walk over. "Hey, would you guys mind taking that booth instead?"

"We were here first," the girl says.

"I understand." I motion to George. "But he needs a table, not a booth."

One of her male companions looks behind me. "The guy's homeless. He'd probably dine and dash anyway."

"I'm buying the gentleman's meal. And you should be more empathetic."

"*He's* the one who's pathetic," the girl says. "Or maybe you are if he's the only date you can get."

"Is there a problem here?" a man asks.

"I was just asking if they wouldn't mind moving to a booth so this nice man and I might have a meal together."

The man points at the girl. "You three, out."

The trio stands and curses him before leaving.

"Oh gosh, I didn't mean for anyone to be kicked out."

"It was my pleasure. The girl didn't pay her tab the last time she was here. You probably saved me money. I'm Jensen, the manager."

"Did you say Jensen?"

"Yes. Why?"

I shake my head. "You just reminded me of someone." I turn. "Come on, George. Our table is ready."

Jensen leaves us with a couple of menus and we settle in. "You didn't have to do that," George says. "I'd have been fine with a takeaway sandwich."

"Everyone deserves to have a nice meal now and again. Now what'll it be?" I peruse the menu. "Meatloaf? Pasta? Ooooh, the sirloin sounds good. It comes with potatoes and mixed vegetables. I think I'll have that. Should we make it two?"

"Why are you being so nice to me, young lady?"

"People aren't nice to you?"

"No, they're not. They all act like those kids. You're practically a kid yourself, Addy. Why the interest in an old disabled man?"

I nod to the floor and pull up the cuff of my jeans, exposing the rod of my prosthetic.

He laughs. "Ah, two peas in a pod."

The funny thing is, he doesn't even ask what happened to my leg. And, ironically, he's the one person I'd tell the truth to.

A woman comes to take our order. George hands his menu to her. "Two steak dinners please," he says like he's ordered for a woman a hundred times before. "I'd like mine medium rare but best ask the lady how she'll take hers."

"Same for me. Something to drink, George? There's a decent house wine on the menu that would go fine with the steak. Although you'll have to drink alone. I forgot my ID."

The waitress leans down. "I got you covered, honey."

George smiles. "A hot meal and fine wine. What did I do to deserve this?"

The waitress winks at me and leaves.

George and I fall into easy conversation. Well, *he* falls into it, talking to me as if I'm the first person he's spoken to in a long while. And he doesn't hold back. He tells me all about his fall from grace. The embezzlement from his father-in-law's company where he worked. His divorce and subsequent estrangement from his son. When he got drunk and stepped off the curb, being struck by a truck leading to the loss of his leg.

He's saddest when he talks about his son. He hasn't tried to make contact in decades because he's embarrassed about what he did and his current situation.

I listen as I eat, becoming engrossed in the story he tells of the one terrible mistake he made that changed the course of his entire life.

Finishing up our meal, he says, "Addy, mind telling me what a nice girl, who's obviously not from around here, is doing taking an old man to dinner in the city?"

"Being hospitable?"

"Just how bad is this thing you're running from?"

"What makes you think I'm running from something?"

"You haven't told me a thing about yourself except your name. You're alone in the city. And I saw you sitting on the bench this morning and then going into the store to buy a coat and then the hotel across the street."

"So you were people watching too?"

"It's the best form of entertainment around. Listen, you don't know me. I don't know you. What could it hurt to unburden yourself?"

He's right. I do need to get this off my chest. I desperately do. So I tell him. I tell him everything over a second glass of wine.

"It's a shame," he says. Then he looks deep in thought. "The greedy bring ruin to their households, but the one who hates bribes will live."

"Are you quoting the Bible, George?"

"Indeed I am. Proverbs 15:27. I'm a man with nothing but time on my hands and a lot to repent."

I study him, knowing that with a shave and a fresh change of clothes, he would look like anyone's grandpa.

"I've got another one for you," he says. "Whoever loves money will never have enough money. Who—"

"Whoever loves luxury will not be content with abundance. Ecclesiastes 5:10." I wink.

He looks surprised.

I shrug. "I took a theology class last year in college."

"Ahh. Generous *and* smart. But Addy, it seems to me you're in quite a pickle. If you leave the man, you leave the child."

"But she's gone in a year anyway."

"Maybe, maybe not. You say he loves you?"

"I thought he did. But how can such a person love anyone?"

"His grandfather gave him an ultimatum. Now you give him one."

"Me? I don't have any money."

"You have something more precious than money."

"What's that?"

"*You.* Tell him if he wants you he has to keep the child."

"That would make me no better than him *and* his grandfather. And George, I don't want a man who has to be blackmailed into keeping his own baby."

"Can you think of any other way to continue caring for the baby you're obviously in love with?"

I fidget with my napkin. "There has to be another way. Maybe I could adopt her."

"I suppose you could. But you'd still be without the *man* you're obviously in love with."

My eyes close. "How can I be in love with him after what he's done?"

"Addy, as amputees, we face a choice every day of our lives. Fight or give up. I haven't known you long, but I can tell you're a fighter." He puts a hand on mine. "Good people make bad decisions. Believe me. I know. If I could take it all back, I would. Maybe you need to give *him* a chance to take it back."

The waitress brings our check and I hand her my card.

I roll George out the door and back to his spot. "George, it was so nice to meet you."

"Whoever is kind to the poor lends to the Lord, and He will reward them for what they have done."

I cock my head. "I can't place that one."

"Proverbs 19:17," he says.

"I'm not looking for any kind of reward."

"And that is precisely why you'll receive one. Now, go have yourself a lovely evening knowing you made this old man's entire year."

"I hope I'll see you again someday."

"You know where I'll be." He pulls his sign out from behind him, puts it in his lap, and smiles as I walk away.

Back in my hotel room, I think about George. How one mistake changed his entire life. Will Hawk regret giving her up one day? Will he lose everything over one bad decision like George did?

What George suggested isn't an option. Hawk doesn't even deserve an ultimatum. What he's doing is unthinkable. He's playing with a child's life. A life that literally hangs in the balance. *His* balance.

I'll file a petition to adopt her when the time comes. I'll kidnap her if I have to. Even if it means never seeing my family again. Seeing him again.

Tears fall. Because the thought of not seeing him, not being in his arms ever again—no matter how horrible he is—rips my heart out. And I ask myself for the hundredth time how I ended up falling for such a heartless villain.

# Chapter Thirty-seven

*Hawk*

Riv laughs again when I curse while changing her diaper. In my defense, it was the dirtiest diaper I've ever seen. Probably because she slept longer than usual. There are at least two shits in here.

"Just when I thought you were cute, you go and do this."

She looks up at me with wide blue eyes. Will they stay blue like mine? Addy once said babies' eyes can change color. "What?"

She stares.

"You're clean now. Don't look at me like that."

A hand roots around and grabs onto my finger.

I lean down and rub the tip of my nose across the tip of hers. She smiles.

"You tell anyone I did that and I'll deny it. Now, it's time to kick ass and take names. We're finding her today. Got it?"

The first call I make is to the obvious person: Holland.

"She still isn't back?" she says in lieu of hello.

"So she hasn't contacted you."

"No. Listen, I don't know what you did to her, but whatever it is, fix it."

"I can't fix it without talking to her."

"You'd better figure out how to find her because she's not anywhere in Calloway Creek. Believe me, I've looked." The fear for her friend and her obvious anger toward me are clear in the rising pitch and volume of her voice.

I sit heavily on the couch, knowing what I have to do, but wanting to do it about as much as I want a prostate exam from a fat, hairy, Russian dude. "Do you think you could get her brothers over here?"

"You... uh... *really?*"

"Hol, I have to find her."

"I agree, but why not go to her parents?"

"Johnathan and Libby? I'd rather face a firing squad than her folks."

"That's exactly who you might be facing if Tag, Jaxon, and Cooper get a hold of you."

"I know. But I have to. Can you arrange it?"

"I don't have to. You can."

"No way. They won't come. And I'm not telling them anything over the phone."

"You have Addy's phone, Hawk. Text them. Tell them you need them to come over right now. You know they'll do anything for her."

"Good idea. Thanks."

"Hawk?"

"What?"

"Can you tell me what time this shindig will happen? I figure you should have a witness."

"Yeah, sure."

Leaving Riv in her swing, I run upstairs to get Addy's phone. My enthusiasm is short lived, shut down by the password screen. I take it back to the great room and Google how many attempts I have. *Ten.* After ten failed attempts, the phone will reset to factory settings.

It's only a four-digit code. That makes this slightly easier. I think of possible dates she could have used. Her birthdate. The date of her accident. The date she lost her virginity. No, no, and no. I cock my head. It wouldn't be *my* birthdate, would it? Maybe it's an old code she set up years ago. One I could never guess. I haven't ever changed mine. And Addy could guess it in a second. Just like she guessed the laptop password.

Still, it surprises me how many dates I know about her. I'm not sure I've ever known a girl's birthday before, except for Holland and Dani. But none of them are correct. I'm running out of tries.

My eyes sweep left when Riv makes a noise.

Oh, shit. Of course. I type in 0802—Rivington's birthdate.

The home screen appears. My kid is her background.

I open her texts. She has a lot of unread ones. Even from Holland asking where she is, which is stupid because Holland knows I have her phone. I find a thread she has with all her brothers. What would she say? What would I say if I were her?

> **Me: Hey guys, I need you pronto. Something's up. Can you all meet me at Hawk's house in an hour?**

Within ninety seconds, they all reply.

> **Cooper: What's up?**

**Tag: Details?**

**Jaxon: Something wrong with Rivi?**

**Me: Just come over, okay? I'll explain when you get here.**

I turn off her phone so any replies they send won't be marked as delivered. They'll have to show up then. I text Hol from mine and tell her when to be here. Then I fix Riv a bottle and wait.

~ ~ ~

"What are you going to say?" Holland asks.

"I don't know."

"They're going to want to kill you."

"Yeah, I get it. Will you quit reminding me?"

"Maybe we should have Hunter and Hudson come over."

I exhale a pent-up breath. "The last thing we need is more drama. Besides, this is between me and them."

"Three against one? You're braver than I gave you credit for."

The doorbell rings. "Get that for me, will you?"

I make a strategic decision and pick up Riv. Then I sit on the couch. They're all dads. They won't take a swing at me with her in my lap. Not that I'm afraid of them, but I don't have time for a fight. Enough time has been lost already.

They talk amongst themselves as they come into the room. Tag glares at me and then looks around. "Where's Addison?"

"Can you sit?" I nod to the other couch.

Cooper crosses his arms over his midsection. "We'll stand."

"I'm not saying shit until you sit."

"Come on, guys," Hol says, taking the chair. "You can have a civilized conversation, can't you?"

The three look at each other and sit.

"Where the fuck is our sister?" Jaxon asks.

"I don't know where she is. That's why I asked you here."

Cooper takes out his phone. "Bullshit. She texted us."

I hold up Addy's phone. "*I* texted you."

Tag's face goes red. He sits on the edge of his seat. "What the hell are you pulling here?"

"Did you fire her?" Jaxon asks.

"No."

Cooper looks green. "Oh, shit. You fucked her, didn't you?" He stands. "I swear on all that's holy if you did anything to hurt her I will kick the living shit out of you, baby or no baby."

Holland hops up and stands in front of him. "It's not like that." She glares at me. "Is it, Hawk?"

"Sit back down and I'll tell you."

He sits reluctantly. "So you *didn't* sleep with her?"

I give Rivington to Holland and scrub a hand across my jaw. Damn, this is a position I never thought I'd be in.

"I… I did, but—"

The three of them get up so quickly, the couch gets pushed back. Tag has one foot on the coffee table and his brothers are circling it. Shit is about to get real.

"I love her!" I shout.

They stop in their tracks.

"Say *what?*" Tag says.

"Yeah," Holland yelps, jaw hanging wide open. "Say *what?*"

I move farther across the room and pace the wall. "You heard me."

"I'm fucking confused," Tag says. "Start from the beginning, McQuaid."

"Listen, I didn't mean for any of this to happen." I stare at Cooper. "You of all people should know you can't help who you fall for."

"This is not about me. Where the hell is she?"

"I told you I don't know."

Cooper and Jaxon yell. Tag puts a hand on their shoulders. "This could be good, guys. She left and he doesn't know where she is. It means she doesn't feel the same way." He turns to me. "Apparently our sister is too smart to fall for a dirt bag like you."

I look out the window and gaze at the hot tub. "You're wrong. She does feel the same way. Or she did."

"So you *did* do something to hurt her," Jaxon growls.

"I would never. But she overheard something unfortunate."

Cooper snorts. "Like you cheating on her?"

I give him a death stare. "Did I not just say I wouldn't hurt her? She overheard me talking to Rivington."

Tag paces the opposite wall. "Let me get this straight. She overheard you talking. *To a baby.* And that made her hightail it out of here without even taking her phone? What did she hear?"

I've thought about it all morning. And I know what I'm about to say could cost me everything. Every penny in my trust fund and the potential for more. But in all honesty, I think I stopped caring about that the minute Addy walked out. I'm willing to give it up to get her back. All of it. The problem is, I don't think even that would convince her.

"I made a bet with my grandfather."

Jaxon laughs. "We all know about your so-called bet, Hawk. But wouldn't you say it's more like a bribe? Or, what do you call it when you're forced to do something you despise?"

"Blackmail," Tag says.

"It was a bet," I say. "It's true that when Tucker heard I wanted nothing to do with Riv he threatened to take away my trust fund. But that's only the half of it. He... he, uh..." I can't believe I'm going to tell these three of all people. "He said he'd double the money if I kept her for a year. Even if I gave her up after."

"He *what?*" the other four adults in the room clamor.

"Why would Pappy make such a deal?" Hol asks. "That's ludicrous."

Cooper snorts air through his nose. "He thought you'd bond with her, and you'd end up keeping her."

I nod. "Yeah. Even though I told him it wouldn't happen."

Holland swats the back of my head. "You're an idiot. And so is Pappy."

"Yeah, I get that. We're idiots. But none of that matters right now. I need to find her. Explain things."

Tag laughs. "I'd love to see you explain your way out of this one. Wow. You were really going to raise a baby for a year and then dump her off on someone else. For money. Let's hand you the father of the year award right now."

"You can fuck off with your digs at me. Are you going to help me find her or what? You know her best. Where would she go? Who would she crash with?"

"Crash?" Tag strides forward. "Just how long has she been gone?"

My shoulders slump. "She left late Friday night."

"It's fucking Sunday. You didn't think to call us before now?"

"I was hoping she'd come back on her own."

Cooper holds out a hand. "Give me her phone. She's our problem now. She obviously doesn't want anything to do with you, as she shouldn't."

325

"I'm *going* to talk to her."

"Not if we have anything to do with it."

Holland steps forward. "Guys, can we all work together? Everyone in this room loves Addy, including this little girl who probably needs her more than anyone. Can you put your differences aside? Just for now?"

"For argument's sake," Jaxon says. "What did you have in mind?"

I scrub a hand across my whiskers. "I don't want to worry your parents."

"Agreed," Tag says. "Not yet."

"I thought we could split up and cover more ground. Drive around. Go to hotels. Show up at her friends' houses. Things like that."

"I'll go to Sophie, Mia, and Allie's places," Hol says. "Again."

"I'll hit Mom and Dad's," Jaxon says. "Just in case she's hiding out there and asked them not to tell."

Cooper pulls his keys out. "I'll check the parks and hiking trails."

"What about you, Tag?" Holland asks. "Maybe you and Hawk should ride together and drive around looking for her."

Tag and I glare at each other. "No," we both say at the same time.

He grinds his teeth. "I'll go myself."

"We're wasting time," I say. "Let's go."

I grab my keys and head for the door.

"Wait," Hol says, putting Riv in her car seat. "You should take her."

"I can't deal with her right now."

"Addy told me Rivi loves car rides. And, Hawk, if you're the one who finds her, this kid may be the only thing that will get her to talk to you."

She's right. "Fine. Whatever." I race to the kitchen and grab the diaper bag. "Can we go now?"

Tag corners me on the way out and sticks a finger to my chest. "Let's be clear. If anything happens to my sister, you're a dead man."

I brush away his hand. "If anything happens to her, rest assured, my life will already be over."

He looks at me oddly for a second then leaves.

With Riv secured in the back of the Caddy, I pull out of my driveway. Cooper, Jaxon and Holland have left already. Tag is waiting in his Range Rover by the curb. Is he going to follow me?

I don't even know where to go. And it makes me realize how much I have left to learn about Addison. I just hope I get the chance to learn it. All of it.

I rack my brain and page through every conversation we've had, searching for clues as to where she could be. She played soccer in high school. She loves to bake. She went to CCU. What was it she was going to school for? Chiropractor? Physical trainer? Psychologist?

Physical therapist. Yeah, that's it. What if she decides to go off somewhere and earn her PhD? The thought of her leaving town causes my chest to tighten and for a moment I can't breathe.

I stop at a traffic light. *Think!* Where would she go?

A horn blares behind me. I look in the rearview. Tag is back there. I pinch my lips and punch the gas. Brakes squeal. I glance to the side just in time to see something huge barreling toward me. There's no time to react. It's metal on metal and the sound is horrifying. The Caddy is being pushed sideways as it shakes violently. The nose of a truck is against my window and I'm helpless as I await my fate. Is this truck going to crush me? Will I flip over? Be pushed into a telephone pole?

Oh, Jesus. *Riv*.

We stop suddenly, having been jammed against something, and my head jerks sharply and hits the window frame. Music blares even though I didn't have the radio on. I reach to turn it off, but the knob doesn't respond.

"Riv!" I push aside the deflated air bag and turn to the back, unable to see her since she faces toward the rear. "Rivi!"

Someone appears next to me. It's Tag. He's lying on the front of the truck, sticking his head through the broken window. "Hawk!"

I try to undo my seatbelt, but the release is jammed between me and the console. It's inaccessible. "I can't get out of the belt. Can you get to her?"

"You're pinned against a building. The other side is inaccessible, and the truck is blocking these doors."

I reach up and touch my throbbing head, then I see blood on my fingers. "Move the fucking truck then."

"This truck isn't going anywhere."

I pull on the belt more. "Riv! Why isn't she crying? Tag, is she dead?"

"I can't get to her. Can you pop the back?"

I push the release on the liftgate. It doesn't open. "Nothing works!" I yell over the music. "Why the hell isn't she crying?"

"I hear sirens. Help is coming."

"I have to get to her. Tag, the belt is stuck. You have to help me!"

Tag looks at me strangely, maybe because of the hysteria in my voice. He disappears for a minute. I yell for Riv again and try to hear her over the music. She should be crying. I crane my head as far as it will go but can't see anything except a deflated air bag over the top of her head.

"Goddamnit!" I struggle with the belt more, trying to work myself underneath it. Nothing's working. I slam my head against the headrest.

A song plays on the radio. It's Addy's favorite. She plays it over and over when Riv is fussing. She'll hold Riv and dance around with her until she calms. I can close my eyes and see the two of them. But when I open them and see the grill of the truck twelve inches from my face, I know I may have just lost everything.

I can't fucking breathe.

"Here." Tag shoves something in my face. "Use it to cut the belt."

I open the pocketknife and slash through the shoulder belt and then the lap one. I throw the knife onto the passenger seat and dive into the back, bruising my hips, knees and shoulders on the way. "Riv!"

Moving aside the airbag, I see her. She's awake. She's tugging on the pacifier attached to her shirt and waving it around like she doesn't have a goddamn care in the world. I run my hands over her legs, her arms, her head. "You okay?"

She looks at me, giving nothing away. What if she hit her head? Could she have brain damage?

I lean over, put my face close, and brush our noses together as Taylor Swift blares through the speakers.

Riv smiles.

And I breathe.

~ ~ ~

"I can walk," I say to EMS.

"You have a head injury, Mr. McQuaid. And your daughter needs to be evaluated at the hospital. Though upon our initial exam, she seems fully alert and responsive." He gestures to the ambulance.

"I'm not riding on the gurney." I look down at Rivington. "And I'm not leaving her."

Tag walks with us to the back of the ambulance.

"How much trouble do you think I'm in?" I ask him.

His brows dip. "You mean with Addy?"

I look back at the trainwreck of cars. "With this. I ran the red light."

His head shakes. "This wasn't your fault. The truck ran the red. Your light was green. It's why I honked at you."

I reach out and hold Riv's hand in mine. "That's good to know. I'm not sure I could live with myself if I was responsible for anything happening to her."

"If I didn't know any better, I'd say you were acting just like a father."

"I am a father. I'm *her* father."

His brows meet his hairline as he looks at me in surprise.

"I told you about the arrangement with my grandfather. I never said I hadn't changed my mind about it."

"Really? Since when?"

I climb into the back of the ambulance and sit next to Rivington's car seat. "I suspect three weeks ago. But I may not have actually realized it until today."

A paramedic goes to shut the door, but Tag stands in the way. "Out of curiosity, how long have you and Addy been…?"

"About three weeks," I say as he gets pushed aside and the doors close. "Find her!" I shout.

~ ~ ~

Mom and Pappy stand at the end of the hospital bed, staring in disbelief. I told them everything.

"Keep the money," I tell Pappy as I sit up. "All of it. I just need to get out of here and find Addy."

Holland comes through the curtain pushing a stroller. Once again, I sigh with relief. The doctor said Riv is perfectly fine. I made sure they ran every test available just to make sure.

"I know where she is," my sister says.

I sit straight. "You do? She told you?"

"No. But she called me. She thought her family might be worried. She said she needed time away to figure things out."

"If she didn't tell you, how do you know where she is?"

"Because of the caller ID." She hands me her phone with the caller history pulled up.

"She's at The Blakely in New York City?"

She takes her phone back. "Apparently."

I swing my legs over the side of the bed. "I'm leaving."

"You can't leave," Mom says. "The doctor said they wanted to keep you overnight for observation."

"It's a bump on the head. They're only trying to cover their asses. I'm fine."

I half expect Pappy to put his foot down and stop me, but he stays quiet, observing from the corner as he occasionally pays attention to his phone.

Holland stands in the doorway when I go to leave.

I get in her face. "Move or I'll move you."

"Let the boy go," Pappy says.

Mom looks up from Riv. "Tucker, don't encourage him."

"The boy is in love, Heather. It's a goddamn miracle."

Holland and Mom share glances. Then Holland moves aside. "No driving until we're sure you're okay." She puts a hand on the stroller. "I'll watch Rivi."

"She's coming with me."

I can count on one hand the number of times I've seen my grandfather smile when he hasn't been around Rose Gianogi. *This* is one of those times. He pats me on the back. "You can catch a train into the city. I'll give you a ride."

Thirty minutes later, after signing myself out of the hospital against medical advice, we're pulling up to the train station.

I get the stroller from the trunk and attach Riv's car seat on it then stick my head through the window. "Thanks, Pap. For everything."

"Two miracles in one day."

"Two?"

"You fell in love. And you said thank you."

I laugh. Then I look at my daughter, relieved beyond belief that she came through the accident without a scratch on her. "Three actually."

"Three it is. And, Hawk?"

"Hmm?"

"The trust fund is yours. I've relinquished control."

My eyes widen so much they almost pop out of my head. "You have?"

"It's being transferred to you as we speak."

"But I was in breach of our agreement. I should get nothing."

"It was never about the agreement, grandson. It was about you growing into the man I'd hoped you could be."

I gaze at Riv. "Well, thank you. That's very generous." I hesitate before walking away. "One more thing," I say, knowing he might change his mind about the trust fund after this, but it's something I have to do. "Pappy, I quit."

"You quit?"

"My job. I quit. There are other opportunities I'd like to explore."

"It's about damn time." He chuckles. "I've never told you this, Hawk, but you're a terrible car salesman. Now go get your girl."

As I feed Rivington on the train, I gaze into her small, perfect face and wonder if I should change her name. It was a joke. A way to get under Addy's skin. But I realize how much the name has grown on me. Especially when Addy says it. "Rivi," I say aloud, liking it more and more.

My phone beeps with a banking notification. All of my accounts are set to alert me of any changes. I used to go in daily and add up my money. I haven't done that in weeks.

I open the notification. It says there is a deposit pending in my trust account. My heart stops when I see the amount. Pappy did it. Not only did he give me control of the trust fund, he gave me the extra money even though I was in complete violation of the agreement by telling a half-dozen people.

I should be elated, but instead, I'm overcome by sadness. Because even though I'm now wealthier than I ever dreamed, the money means nothing if Addy isn't there to spend it with me.

After sending a text to my financial advisor, I sit back and look out the window, watching the city grow closer.

Samantha Christy

# Chapter Thirty-eight

*Addison*

I roll George back to his spot after lunch. Never in my wildest dreams did I expect a seventy-year-old homeless man to become a friend. We've had some interesting conversations over our last few meals. He's kind. Spirited. But most of all, regretful.

Over a bowl of clam chowder, he tried to convince me to give Hawk a second chance, an opportunity to show me what kind of man he can be. And although I told him there was a fat chance in hell because that's one leopard who would never change his spots, there's some irony in the fact that I urged him to contact his ex and his son to right all his wrongs.

I get what George was saying. But there's one huge difference. He's actually sorry for what he did to tear apart his family. Money—why must *everything* come down to it? It really is the root of all evil.

On the short walk to the hotel I'm behind a woman pushing a stroller. A stuffed dog gets dropped onto the sidewalk. I pick it up and rush ahead. "Excuse me." I tuck the toy next to the baby. "I believe this is yours."

"You're a lifesaver," the woman says. "It's her favorite. She won't sleep without it."

My bottom lip quivers when I look at the baby. She's older than Rivi but has that same cherub look. A similar tuft of brown hair. And striking blue eyes. "She's adorable. You're very fortunate."

"Thanks. She's my first. Sometimes I still can't believe how much I love her. Like, I didn't know I had the capacity. Do you have children?"

I swallow, my heart screaming *Yes!* as my head shakes from side to side with the truth.

The woman thanks me again and scurries away, clearly uncomfortable by the waterworks running down my face.

Entering the hotel, there is another stroller parked at the desk. It seems there are strollers everywhere. On every street corner, and in every store. I'm sure there are strollers all over Calloway Creek. I've just never been so aware of them before. And every time I look at one I feel I'm being punished. For what, I'm not sure.

"Sir, I don't know how many different ways I can tell you I'm not at liberty to give out such information."

"Throw me a bone here. Just give me a floor number. I'll do the rest."

My heart lurches at the familiar voice. I give a second glance to the stroller realizing it's not just another stroller. It's *Rivi's* stroller.

Is this a coincidence? No one knows I'm here. I'm at war with myself. It's been less than forty-eight hours, but I miss her. I miss her so much. And although I know I shouldn't, I miss him. That's why it takes everything I have to walk away. I lower my head and walk quietly to the elevator.

"Addy!"

*Don't turn around. Keep walking.*

"Addison!"

I search for the stairs but have no clue where they are.

He comes up behind me. I'm not facing him, but I know he's there. I can sense him. I can *feel* him.

"Miss," the lady from the counter says. "Do I need to call security?"

I can't look at him. I stare at Rivi wondering if she knew I was gone. Wondering if her heart has been torn out the way mine has. Wondering why she's even here. "I, uh… no, it's fine."

She turns to walk away but Hawk taps her on the shoulder and hands her something.

"Sir, I can't take your money. I could get fired for taking a bribe."

"But it's not a bribe. You didn't tell me where she was."

"So then why would you give it to me?"

"I overheard you on the phone when I walked in."

Her face pales. "I'm sorry. That was very unprofessional. I shouldn't have taken a personal call at work."

"Take it." He tucks the money into her jacket pocket. "As a thank you."

"I didn't do anything."

"You did. You protected Addison. Consider it a tip, you get tips don't you?"

"Sometimes."

"Well there you go."

"I don't know what to say. Do you know what this means for me?"

"It's my pleasure."

The woman leaves, looking back over her shoulder like she's not sure he's for real. When Hawk turns around to face me I notice a small bandage on his head. I want to ask him about it. Part of me hopes one of my brothers got a hold of him. But asking him would have him thinking I care. And even though I want to get in the elevator and not look back, curiosity over something else gets the better of me. "What did you overhear on the phone?"

"She was pleading with her landlord not to evict her and her six-year-old son over seven hundred dollars."

My eyes bug out. "You gave her seven hundred dollars?"

"A thousand actually."

My brows dip. "Why?"

"Were you not listening? She was going to be evicted."

I shake my head. None of this is getting us anywhere. "I have to go."

"Addy, talk to me."

"There's nothing to say."

"You're wrong. There's a lot to say."

"I heard enough the other night."

"You have to let me explain."

I press the call button on the elevator panel. "I don't *have* to do anything. I'm going upstairs. Go home, Hawk."

"I told everyone."

"Told everyone what?"

"What you overheard on the baby monitor."

Surprise has me pausing. But the fact that he told everyone doesn't change anything.

The elevator doors open. I step in and turn, arms crossed. "Goodbye."

He holds the door and follows me in, pulling the stroller behind him. "You're not getting away that easy."

I nod to the stroller. "Why did you even bring her? And shouldn't you be telling your mom or Holland or your new nanny, or whoever is waiting outside that you're stalking me to my room?"

"There's no one outside."

"You brought her alone. To the *city*."

"Yes."

"Why?" I realize I'm asking that question a lot. And although the urge to kick him to the curb is grand, my desire to have him answer the question wins out.

"If you'll let me in your room, I'll explain."

I cackle loudly. "You're crazy if you think I'm letting you in my room. I may be naïve in a lot of things, but I'm not about to fall prey to your nefarious charm again. We can go back down to the lobby."

"Addy." He glances at the stroller. "I've got Rivi with me, what do you think is going to happen?"

*Rivi?*

I look at her. I study her. I trace the outline of her precious face with my eyes. I know I'm going to give in if only for the chance to hold her in my arms again. Realization dawns. "You're using her to get to me."

"Yes."

"Oh my God. You're so cocky you won't even deny it."

"Like I said, hear me out. I'll explain everything."

We reach my floor, and I step off. "You have ten minutes." I walk ahead, open the door, and hold it for the stroller, still in complete shock that he brought her here without any help. What game is he playing?

Rivi gets agitated. He roots through the diaper bag, pulls out a pacifier, sticks it in her mouth, sits on the small couch next to the bed, and rocks her stroller back and forth with his foot. I watch it all like a scene in a movie, wondering why he's playing the part of the caring father.

He stares at me for a long moment, then gazes out the window. "I can't remember where or when I heard this quote, but someone once said *'some people are so poor, all they have is money.'*

"Oh, good. Like I need more people quoting the Bible."

He looks back at me. "That's a quote from the Bible?"

"I don't know. Maybe not. But I'm pretty sure it was a Christian philosopher."

"Whoever it was, he or she is right. Addy, I have all the money anyone could ever need, but it's nothing without you."

Tears clog my throat at the sentiment. Then I remind myself they're just words. Words that mean nothing without actions to back them. He'd probably say anything to get me to come back to help fulfill his yearlong *obligation.*

My stomach rolls at the thought of what he agreed to. The tears turn to unbridled anger. "Lies," I say, pacing the room. "All that comes out of your mouth are lies. I can't even look at you. What kind of person agrees to keep a child for a year for money? Do you realize the damage you're doing to her? Whether you think she is or not, and whether you want her to or not, she's bonding with you. And you're going to turn her world upside down and rip her heart out. All for money."

"Will you sit?"

"I don't want to sit."

"There's a lot you don't know."

"There's nothing you could tell me that would excuse what you did. What you're going to do."

"Maybe not, but would you please give me the chance to try?"

He nods to Rivi. "For her sake?"

"You're a user, Hawk. You use people. You used me to care for her until she would be out of your life, and you're using her to get what you want from me."

"She's just the catalyst, Addy. Believe me, I know I have my work cut out for me."

I glance at the time. "You have six minutes left."

He breathes deeply like he's about to reveal his deepest darkest secrets. *Is he?*

"There's more to the arrangement I made with Tucker."

I sit on the end of the bed, a dozen feet away from him, fold my hands in my lap and wait.

"Everyone knows that I kept her because he threatened to take away my trust fund. But what nobody knew was he bet me I couldn't keep her for a year without falling in love with her. And the stakes of the bet were that if I made it a whole year, he'd double the money, no matter the outcome. The caveat was, I couldn't tell anyone. If I did, I'd risk losing everything."

I digest his words. "I don't get it then, why would you tell everyone?"

"Have you not been listening? I told you the money means nothing to me without you."

I blink rapidly. "Hawk, did you lose all your money?"

"We'll get back to that. The important thing here is to tell you that you left too soon. The other night, what you overheard was only half of it. I was on my way downstairs to talk to you. I was going to tell you everything, Addy. And most importantly, I was going to tell you I changed my mind. I changed it before you heard me over the monitor. Before you left. If I'm being honest with myself, I'd changed it weeks ago. I should have told you earlier, but

I rationalized that since I was going to keep her, what you didn't know couldn't hurt you. And I didn't want to hurt you. I didn't want to do anything that would change how you looked at me. Because no one has ever looked at me the way you have. But then you had to go telling me what a good man you thought I was. That changed everything. I couldn't have you thinking that about me. It wasn't true. And I needed you to know the truth when I told you I lo—"

"Wait." I try to process the overwhelming stream of information. "Go back. You're keeping her?"

"Yes, I'm keeping her. What do you think it is I've been trying to tell you for the past ten minutes?"

I push off the bed and go over to Rivi, gazing down on her, wanting what he's saying to be true, but knowing I can't trust him. "Keeping her for me isn't a good enough reason. What if we were to break up?"

"I'm not keeping her for you, Addison. I'm keeping her for me."

"Hawk, you forget that I know you. And you don't do anything without an ulterior motive." The woman from downstairs flashes through my mind. He did *that* without one. I push away the thought as it tries to invalidate my point.

"Look at me," he implores. "Look into my eyes. If you know me like you think you do, you'll see I'm telling the truth."

His striking blue eyes become windows to his soul. They paint a picture I want to be a part of. A story I want to believe in. But I'm hesitant. And for good reason. "And if I walk away? What then?"

"If you walk away, I'll be devastated. And so will she. Last week when I accused you of acting like we're a family, that was me projecting my fears. I've been the way I am for so long, it's hard to think of myself any other way. The truth is, though, that I want us to be a family. I need it. I need *you*. Damn it, I even need *her*." He comes over and takes my hand. "But to be perfectly clear, if you walk away, I'll still be keeping Rivi. She's my daughter."

Warm threads weave around my heart, repairing the damage that had been done. "I want to believe you, but I have doubts. How can a person change that drastically in just a few weeks?"

"Sweetheart, I changed the day we got stuck in the elevator."

"Liar."

"Okay, maybe the day after." He flashes me a charming grin that is hard to ignore. It heats my insides and makes my head swim. "What do I have to do to prove it to you? Isn't giving up my trust fund proof enough?"

"Did you really give it up?"

"I offered to. Cross my heart. You can ask my grandfather."

"You mean the co-conspirator?"

"I told him he could keep it all, Addy." He pulls his phone out of his pocket. "If that doesn't convince you, read this." He opens a text from Vince Cannon and scrolls up.

"Who's Vince?"

"My financial planner. Here, take it. Read it."

I take his phone and read the last few texts.

> **Vince: It will take a hot minute to set this up. I'll put your attorney on it. But to be clear, you want $20M, as in MILLION, transferred as soon as it clears from Tucker's account to yours?**
>
> **Hawk: Yes, you read that correctly. Twenty million.**

**Vince: In the name of Rivington Genevieve McQuaid?**

**Hawk: Yes.**

**Vince: Do you want to make provisions for any future children in this trust?**

**Hawk: Okay, yeah. Why not?**

**Vince: You're absolutely sure?**

**Hawk: Do it Vince or I'll pay someone else $400 an hour to get it done.**

**Vince: Give me a few days and I'll be back in touch.**

I look up from the phone. "You set up a trust fund for her?"
"Not just for her."
I swallow, not prepared to go there as my head is already spinning.
"And unlike the one Tucker set up for me, this one will be irrevocable."
"But… what will *you* do for money?"
"Believe me, I'll be fine. The twenty million was the extra money from the bet. He gave it to me now even though it's only been a few months. I thought it only fitting that it go to Rivi since she's the reason I got it. I still have well over nineteen million in my own trust fund."

Rivi cries. Instinctively, I stand. But he beats me to her. He lifts her up and cradles her, swaying her back and forth just as she likes it. Could what he's saying be true?

"Say something, Addy."

"I can't. I'm speechless."

He looks down at her tenderly and then at me. "You didn't let me finish before. There's something else you don't know. I'm in love with you."

My entire body melts. My heart expands back to its regular size. My mind explodes with all the things I'd been dreaming about: Christmases, birthdays, family gatherings, picnics in the park. I feel like I'm about to get everything I ever wanted. My eyes sting. My throat thickens. My heart soars. I'm excited. I'm terrified. I'm grateful. But most of all, I'm in love—with both of them.

He steps forward, Rivi filling the space between us. "And you love me too."

Tears spill over and wet my cheeks. "And I love you too."

He sighs heavily, air streaming out of his lungs like he'd been holding it this whole time. He leans over the top of Rivi and kisses me. I wouldn't think two people could share a kiss with an infant between them. But somehow that makes it even better.

Hawk lies down on the bed and puts Rivi next to him. I lay on her other side. We both have a hand on her as we stare at each other. I chronicle this moment. I want to remember it for as long as I live. The look in his eyes. The determination on his face.

*His face*—I reach out and touch the bandage. "Which one of my brothers do I have to thank for this?"

"None of them. I totaled the Caddy."

I gasp. "When?"

"This morning. Got T-boned by a truck running a red light. At first I thought it was my fault, but Tag saw the whole thing."

"Tag? What was he doing there?"

"I needed help to find you. I texted your brothers from your phone and asked them to come to the house."

"You asked my brothers for help? And they didn't kill you?"

He laughs. "I may have used Rivi as a human shield. A fact I'm not very proud of."

"It may have been what saved your life. So is the car really totaled?"

"It is. The truck pushed us right into a building. We were trapped for fifteen minutes."

"We?" My pulse races as my eyes land on Rivi. "Oh my God, was she in the car with you?"

"Yes. But don't worry, she's fine."

I take her little hand in mine. "You're sure?"

He chuckles. "I'm sure. I made them run about ten thousand dollars' worth of unnecessary tests to prove it."

"That's money I'll never complain about you spending."

"Addy?"

"Mmm?"

He brushes hair off my forehead. "I'm going to spend money on you. Both of you. So you better get used to it. I've never had anyone I've wanted to spend money on before. So please bear with me. Don't reject everything I give you. You deserve everything I want to give you and more."

"I don't wa—"

Fingers press against my lips. "I know you don't want anything. I know you'd never ask for anything. But don't you understand? That's why I want to give you *everything*. Do you know how scared I was in the car today? I was trapped, not able to get out of the seatbelt. For a minute I couldn't get to her. And I couldn't breathe. Not because I was hurt, but because I couldn't bear the thought of losing her. I'd already lost you and if I lost her my life would have been over. And it only reinforced what I already knew; that I didn't want to live another day without you. Both of you."

His eyes glass over. Hawk McQuaid is crying.

I lace our fingers together. "I agree to your terms under one condition."

"Anything."

"That you keep writing. I won't pressure you to publish, but, Hawk, you're so very talented. Write for yourself. Write for us. Just write."

"Agreed. As long as you keep being my muse."

"I suppose I could do that."

He stares into my eyes. "You knew I was in love with you."

"I'm not sure I knew. I suspected. I hoped."

"Addison, falling in love with you wasn't even a choice. It was more like a predetermined fate. Something I had no control over."

"It was the same for me."

Rivi squirms.

"As much as I'd like to make good use of this hotel room, I'm out of formula, so we should head home." He raises a cocky brow. "But rest assured, we will be making good use of every surface in my house when I get you there."

"I like the sound of that."

He hops over Rivi and hovers above me. "Oh, I plan on you making lots of sounds tonight."

We kiss, sealing the deal. We kiss until Rivi's little hand thwaps him on the side of the head.

"Someone's jealous," I joke. "She wants you all to herself. Sadly, I can relate."

He smirks and gets off the bed.

I get up and secure Rivi in her stroller.

"You'll never guess what she did yesterday," he says on the way out.

"What?"

"She laughed. *At me.* She laughed at me."

"Oh, Rivi! You laughed?" We enter the elevator. Hawk grabs my hand like it's something he's done a thousand times. I sigh. "I wish I could have been there to see it."

He leans close. "You may have missed the first one, but I want you to be there for every other."

"I want that too. And, hey, about your offer to buy a prosthetic…"

He throws his hands up in the air. "Finally. You're going to let me buy it?"

We reach the bottom floor and cross the lobby. "I'll let you buy one, but not for me." When he looks confused, I nod to the door. "Come on. Before we go home, I want to introduce you to a new friend."

# Chapter Thirty-nine

*Hawk*

"We're really doing this?" she says as we enter the tattoo parlor?

"Before you chicken out, yes."

The tattoo artist, Nigel, greets us. He and I spoke on the phone last night. He hands us a couple of binders. "You can choose from these or I can custom design one for you."

We share a look. He already knows what I picked for her. I paid him a shitload to design it after sending him photos and measurements of her stump. Photos and measurements I took yesterday after she fell asleep following our marathon session that was hands down the best three hours of my life. After almost losing her, I let her know just how grateful I was to have her back. I let her know six times. And then she dozed off in my bed, the place I always want her to be.

Addy refuses the binder. "I already know which one he's getting."

I draw back. "You do?"

She pulls a slip of paper from her pocket and hands it to me. Nigel looks at it over my shoulder. "Ah, nice one," he says. "A lot of people use art like this over their scars."

She's drawn a picture of a zipper. At the top of the zipper is a padlock. I point. "What's this for?"

"Well, the zipper allows access to your heart." She blushes. "And the lock is because I'm the only one who will ever have access."

Nigel chuckles behind me. But I don't laugh. Because this woman has once again slayed me. With her words. Her beauty. Her mere presence. I pull her close. "You're damn right you will."

"So you approve?" she asks with a smile.

"I do." I turn to Nigel and nervously ask for my design. Then I hand it to her.

She glances at it then at me. "A bird?"

I nod to it.

She studies it and I see the moment she makes the connection. "You want me to tattoo a picture of a hawk on Eileen?" She snorts and shoves me playfully. "Way to get around the no name thing. I was sure you'd pick a flower or something delicate like that. Or a funny saying like my night shirt."

"Sweetheart, despite appearances, you are anything but delicate." I take the picture and run my finger across the wings. I had Nigel design it so the hawk has his wings open and spread high, so they will go up and over either side of her knee, with the body down her leg and the feet under her stump, toes configured into the faint line of her stitches. "The hawk represents everything you are, and exactly what I see in you. It has a powerful mind and body. It symbolizes independence, adaptability, and ambition. Seeing a hawk is thought to be an extremely positive omen as they are often perceived as messengers from spiritual realms bringing tidings of good fortune." I take her hand in mine. "And hawks mate for life. They parent together, always go back to the same nest, and protect their nest with vigor."

A grin appears. "They mate for life, huh?"

I hand the paper to Nigel. "She'll take it."

He puts both drawings next to the tattoo chair. "I'll be right back. You decide who's going first."

Arms come around me. "You're a romantic, Hawk McQuaid. Admit it."

"Only with you, sweetheart." I kiss her forehead. "Only with you."

An hour later, my tattoo is complete and it's her turn. She's scared. It's why I kept my mouth shut even though parts of mine hurt like a bitch. And hers is much bigger.

She squeezes my hand when the needle touches her. "Say something," she begs. "I can't think about what he's doing or I might throw up."

I cock my head to the side and watch the brave woman I love get a tattoo for me. About me. Of me.

I was going to wait until tonight to say anything. Until our first official date out of the house. In public. For everyone to see. But watching her here, now, it just spills out of me. "Move in with me, Addy."

Her adorable eyes scrunch. "I, uh, kind of already live there, Hawk."

"You live in my house. But I want it to be *our* house—*our* bedroom, *our* bed—that you go to sleep in every night and wake up in every morning."

"You want to live together. For real?"

"Everything about this is real. And believe me, if we'd been together longer than three weeks, and Nigel wasn't sticking needles in your leg, I'd be asking you another question right now."

Her eyes become misty. She nods. "Yes." A tear falls. "To moving in and any other question."

I lean over and kiss her. I kiss her with the certainty of a man who knows his worth doesn't lie in his bank account; his investments; his portfolio. She's one of my most valuable assets. The other one is currently being spoiled by her grandmother. "I love you," I mouth.

She mouths it back as Nigel works away like he doesn't know we're having one of the most pivotal moments of our lives.

I pull back and let her squeeze the ever-loving shit out of my hand for the next few hours. Then we sit back and admire her new ink. "I look damn good on you, sweetheart." I lift her hand and kiss it. "Oh, and one more thing… you're fired."

# Epilogue

## *Addison*

*Two years later...*

"Oh my God." I tug on Hawk's shirt as we're escorted to a table in the front. "That's her. That's Baylor Mitchell."

He laughs at my fangirl behavior. "I know. I met her last month."

"I would die. She's like the best romance author to have ever lived. Do you know how many books she's sold? I have every single one, all ninety-two of them."

"You aren't going to embarrass me when I introduce you, are you sweetheart? She's just a person."

"I make no guarantees."

"Right here please, Mr. and Mrs. McQuaid," the usher says.

*Mrs. McQuaid.* I still can't get used to being called that even though it's been a month. I gaze at my husband as he pulls out my chair. He still gives me butterflies in my stomach every time I look at him. And he still makes Rivi laugh every time he curses. Only now, the curse words are kid-friendly ones he made up like figjit, drumbug, flibberbit, and scagmagger. His brothers and mine have both taken on the same vocabulary when they fight around her. And they do still fight, only I get the idea it's more nostalgic than anything else. A sport, so to speak. A pastime even.

And poor Rivi is going to get quite the looks when she starts cursing.

"I can't believe this is finally happening," I whisper to him.

He looks nervously behind him. "I can't believe everyone is about to find out. You know I'm never going to hear the end of this from my brothers. And *your* brothers—I can't even imagine the shit I'm going to get from them."

I turn and see his brothers and their companions being escorted to the table behind us. Then I see my family being seated at theirs. My heart pounds with excitement. With anxiety. I want this to go well for him. He's poured his heart and soul into these books. He's finally found his passion—other than Rivi and me that is—and it seems to bring him more happiness than I could have imagined. But even with as much time as he dedicates to his writing, I know whatever happens in his life and his career, we'll always come first. If Rivi trots into his office for a hug, he drops everything. If I ask him to reach something on the top shelf, he comes without a gripe. He showers us with gifts even though we don't need them. It's his love we want, and because he shows it in so many non-material ways, I tolerate his monetary generosity. Because I can trust him now.

I smile when I see George McNally and his son enter through the rear and sit at a table in the back. He no longer has to be pushed. He walks in unassisted. He waves to me. He's become like a grandfather. Hawk even got him a job at one of Tucker's dealerships. He worked his way up from janitor to car salesman in less than six months.

    But nobody, not even Holland, knows why they were invited here. Hawk has kept his new pastime very close to the chest. He hasn't let me tell anyone. But he has allowed me to read his books as he writes them. And I've become quite the editor if I do say so myself. Hawk and I have spent many nights acting out scenes—intimate scenes mostly—just to see if what he writes is even doable.

    After a year of begging (and a whole lot of sex), I convinced him to submit a few of his manuscripts, albeit anonymously, to an agent in the city. It took a bit of cloak and dagger, along with some harmless white lies, to get the name of the agent Baylor Mitchell uses. But Baylor is related to Amber Thompson, who is Tag's best friend, so it wasn't too hard with the exception of keeping Hawk's name out of it. When details of conversations started leaking to a few people in Baylor's circle, everyone thought it was me—that *I* was the writer. And I let them think it to protect my husband's identity and what he thought would surely be his humiliation.

    Earlier this year, when I got a call from Baylor Mitchell's agent, I almost passed out right then and there. She offered me a deal on the spot. Said she'd been in touch with a half dozen publishers who were all fighting over the right to publish the series. She said I was sitting on a potential gold mine. The number she gave me for the advance rendered me speechless.

    It was never about the money for Hawk, however. It was about validation. As a person. As a member of society. As a father. It was about leaving a legacy his daughter could be proud of.

    So here we sit, eight months later, looking up at a podium surrounded by drapes of scarlet curtains that I know cover multiple stacks and displays of the initial printing of his first three books.

Not *those* first three books—those were incinerated long ago. These books follow Jensen and Adelaide through their hot affairs, their heartbreaks, and finally their happily ever after. And he's halfway through the next trilogy that's about their daughter, Remington (because Rivington hit too close to home, and he was completely unable to pen any love scenes).

"Are you nervous?" I ask Hawk.

"Fuck yeah, I'm nervous. My goddamn head is about to explode. What if they're a colossal flop? What if nobody takes it seriously because I'm a guy?"

"Babe, look at who's presenting you. Baylor Mitchell wouldn't have agreed if she didn't think you had something special here." I glance at the curtains. "I can't wait to see the covers. You realize I'm the first person you're going to sign a book for, right?"

He laughs nervously and kisses my cheek. "You may be the *only* one who asks for a signed copy."

I pull back. "What happened to my cocky, confident guy?"

"Well, let's see, he had the nervous shits for two hours, then crippling anxiety for another three. Then he turned to tequila just so he could put on a suit and come here."

"All of that is about to end. You'll see. I have complete faith in you. And, hey, if this doesn't work out we can buy an island and hide away for the rest of our lives, wearing scraps of clothing made out of things we hunt."

Our eyes lock. "Do you know how much I fucking love you?"

"As a matter of fact, yes."

People keep stopping by our table to ask if we know what's going on and why the invitation was so vague. But before the incessant questions cause Hawk even more anxiety, Baylor Mitchell goes behind the podium and takes the microphone.

"Welcome everyone. If you don't know who I am, my name is Baylor McBride. I write romance novels under my maiden name, Baylor Mitchell. You're probably wondering why you're here and why a romance novelist is speaking to you." She gestures to the curtains on either side of her. "You're about to find out." Without looking at Hawk, she says, "Someone in attendance here has been keeping a secret from all of you. Which is no small feat considering the team it has taken to bring this to fruition."

My mother looks at me. Amber Thomson too. Even Holland. They all believe I'm somehow behind this. And they can barely contain their excitement.

"Tonight," Baylor continues, "I have the absolute pleasure of unveiling what will surely be the next bestselling series. These heartfelt, awe-inspiring, impeccably written books will surely give me a run for the money, not to mention the likes of Nicholas Sparks and John Greene. It's rare for a male writer to achieve resounding success in the world of romance writing. But I believe that is exactly what's about to happen. In fact, I have inside information that there is already interest in adapting the books into screenplays. So without further ado"—she nods to a worker who raises the curtains—"I'd like to present Hawk McQuaid's debut trilogy: The Forbidden Series: Forbidden Fruit, Forbidden Heart, and Forbidden Love."

Gasps and murmurs are heard throughout the reception hall. I even think I hear a *'What the fuck',* which was probably spoken by Hunter or Hudson. Or maybe Tag.

Slowly, and after the surprise abates, applause starts rumbling.

"Hawk," Baylor says, moving aside. "I think it's time to take the stage and claim your extraordinary work."

He swallows nervously, kisses my cheek and heads up. Looking at his brothers, whose chins are still on the white linen tablecloths, he pulls notes from his breast pocket. "Thank you, Baylor. And thank you to my agent, Jenna Tyson, and Dunn's River Publishing for taking a chance on me. While all those people have been indispensable in making this happen, there's one person without whom none of this would be possible. Before her, my writing was shit. Pardon my French. There was always something missing. Turns out it was her." He looks into my eyes. "It's always been you, Addy. Even before I knew you."

Tears prickle my eyes.

He chuckles. "Sorry to get all sentimental up here, but it kind of goes with the job."

The audience laughs.

"Before I go any further, I'd like to make the announcement that I'll be donating all proceeds from these books to The Prosthetic Foundation to provide assistance to those who have suffered limb loss."

I'm stunned. I had absolutely no idea. My heart gets bigger than I ever thought it could get. It's bursting from my chest with love for this man.

"I'd like my new bride to join me up here and read the dedication." His eyes capture mine. "Addy?"

I inhale deeply. He knows I don't like to be the center of attention. But this is his big moment and I'm here to support him. I put on my best smile, smooth down my fancy dress, and confidently walk up the three steps aided by my reliable titanium leg he gave me as a wedding gift. Whispers go throughout the crowd, probably from people who didn't know about my leg.

He pulls a book from the display. "Sweetheart?"

I open the book, turn past the title page and scan the dedication. Emotion clogs my throat. No wonder he didn't want to read it. No way could he have gotten through this without crying.

And my sensitive, romantic, mercurial man would never cry in front of anyone but me.

I turn to catch him smiling the proudest smile. He winks and taps his knee. We both know what that means. Since the day we got our tattoos, every time he thinks I need strength, he taps his knee, reminding me of what's on mine.

I pause to gather myself, take a deep breath and read it:

> "To my wife. My greatest supporter. My salvation. Without you I'd just be a guy pretending to sell cars. With you, the possibilities are endless.
>
> And to my daughter without whom I'd have never met the woman of my dreams. She has no idea how she's made me a better man just by being her father.
>
> Also, to the greater power that had the three of us trapped in the elevator that day so long ago. That fifteen minutes was the pivotal cornerstone of my life.
>
> And finally, I'd like to dedicate this series to my future children, of which I hope there are many."

I barely get through the last part. Because I have a secret. For two years we haven't kept things from one another. But I didn't want to steal his thunder today. Today is about him. His accomplishments. His achievements. His journey. Tonight, however, he'll find out he's becoming a daddy for the second time. And Rivi is going to help me tell him.

Hawk sees me choking up. He takes my hand, letting me know we're in this together. That we're *always* in this together. I smile through my tears as he sweeps me into his arms amidst the applause. "Our story is just beginning, Addy. And you and I, we're going to fill all the pages. Every single day for the rest of our lives."

~ ~ ~

"So this surprise," Hawk says as we pull into the driveway a few hours later, "does it involve that little black lacy thing I love so much?"

I giggle. "Well, no. But I can throw that in as an added bonus."

He parks in the garage and turns to me. "Do you know how much I love you, wife?"

"I do."

He leans over the console and kisses me. "I'm the luckiest sonofabitch alive because you said those two words to me last month. And I have a surprise for you too. Come on."

I try not to laugh on our way in the house. Hawk looks like a kid on Christmas morning. He's bursting at the seams, and it makes me curious about his secret. No way could it be better than mine.

When we get inside, Rivi is running through the great room wearing nothing but a diaper. "Daddy!" She bolts over and throws herself at him.

He sweeps her into his arms and plants kisses all over her face. "Hey, cupcake, why are you naked?"

"Yes," I say, raising a brow at Cindy. "Why is she naked?"

Cindy was supposed to have put Rivi in the *Big Sister* shirt I bought right after I took the pregnancy test this morning.

Interestingly enough, Hawk also seems disappointed that Rivi is naked. He, too, is looking at Cindy sharply.

Cindy throws her arms up in frustration. "I'm sorry. I didn't know what to do. Addy, you gave me the shirt earlier and then Hawk left me a bag with instructions. It had a different shirt."

"Different?" Hawk asks curiously, his eyes bouncing between the sitter and me.

"Here," Cindy says, shoving shirts at me. "I'll let myself out, you can pay me later."

She races out the door, leaving both of us confused.

I sit and unfold the unfamiliar shirt. It reads: *I ♥ my Mommy.*

My jaw drops and I look up at Hawk. "How did you know? Did you find the test?"

"What test? Clearly I'm not the only one confused here." He puts Rivi down and she climbs up next to me.

I hold up the *Big Sister* shirt. "Rivi was supposed to be wearing this."

His eyes go wide, and he swallows. He falls to his knees, putting his palms against my stomach. "You're pregnant?"

Tears coat my lashes. "I found out this morning. I didn't want anything to take away from your big day."

"We're having a baby?" he asks in utter amazement.

I smile big. "We're having a baby."

His arms come around me, pulling me to him. We hug, and cry, and tremble with excitement. Rivi worms her way between us wanting to get in on the attention.

"You're going to be a big sister," he tells her.

She claps and squeals.

"Wait a second." I look down at the shirt he bought. "If you didn't know, what's with this?"

He wipes wetness off his face. "Rivi has something to ask you. Go ahead, cupcake."

When Rivi doesn't say anything, he whispers in her ear. Then she turns to me. "Addy be my mommy?"

My heart stops, then thunders with joy. My throat is so clogged with tears, I can't speak.

Hawk takes my hand. "Sweetheart, for two years you've been a mother to her. You've raised her and loved her right along with me. You're everything to her. To *us*. So I thought it was time we made it official. I want you to adopt her."

I close my eyes and absorb the words. Since the day Hawk fired me as her nanny, I've hoped he would ask me to be more than a stepmother to her. Because she is so much more than a stepdaughter. She's mine. And no matter how many children I give birth to, she'll always be my first baby.

"I would like nothing more," I say through big balls of tears.

"I'll file the paperwork tomorrow," he says. He touches my tummy again. "I want us to be an official family before this little one arrives."

I nod over and over, a blubbering mess.

He pulls me to him. "This is one of the best days of my life. And I owe it all to you."

I chuckle. "A little different from the last time you found out you were going to be a father."

"Sweetheart, I don't even know who that man is anymore."

"That man is who I fell in love with," I remind him. "And that man will be the person I love until the day I die."

Now *he's* the one blubbering.

"Babe?" I ask, needing to know what he's thinking.

He looks at me with those incredible eyes that are icy blue windows to his soul. "So this is what it's like."

"What *what's* like?"

He puts one arm around me and the other around our daughter. "Getting everything I ever wanted."

Samantha Christy

# Acknowledgements

No Small Bet is my 25th book. **Twenty-five!** Oh, my goodness, I never would have thought I could write so many books.

I so loved writing Hawk's character, especially how he turned from certifiable asshole into an honorable daddy and husband. And Addy, the tenacious virgin who is stronger with one leg than most people are with two—she's had my heart since I introduced her in Unlikely Date.

Without my incredible team of supporters, editors, and beta readers, I wouldn't be able to live this exciting existence and do what I do.

My wonderful beta readers: Joelle Yates, Shauna Salley, Laura Conley, and Ann Peters. I'm so grateful you all continue to give me critical and honest feedback.

Thank you to my copy editor, Michelle Fewer (who is great at pumping my ego), and my promo peeps at Greys Promotions.

I couldn't do any of this without the help of my wonderful assistant, Julie Collier, who pushes me to write better and stronger characters.

If you loved Hawk's story, you're in for a real treat with Hunter's book, No Easy Dare. Watch his billionaire grandfather, Tucker McQuaid, try to manipulate the second McQuaid brother into finding happiness.

# About the author

Samantha Christy's passion for writing started long before her first novel was published. Graduating from the University of Nebraska with a degree in Criminal Justice, she held the title of Computer Systems Analyst for The Supreme Court of Wisconsin and several major universities around the United States. Raised mainly in Indianapolis, she holds the Midwest and its homegrown values dear to her heart and upon the birth of her third child devoted herself to raising her family full time. While it took time to get from there to here, writing has remained her utmost passion and being a stay-at-home mom facilitated her ability to follow that dream. When she is not writing, she keeps busy cruising to every Caribbean island where ships sail. Samantha Christy currently resides in St. Augustine, Florida with her husband and four children.

You can reach Samantha Christy at any of these wonderful places:

Website:      www.samanthachristy.com

Facebook:   https://www.facebook.com/SamanthaChristyAuthor

Instagram:   @authorsamanthachristy

E-mail:        samanthachristy@comcast.net

Printed in Great Britain
by Amazon

36f36fe1-c57d-4445-bb9e-3a3398179e6cR01